Six Years and
A Quarter Way Through

Six Years and
A Quarter Way Through

CASSANDRE BRISSOT

RESOURCE *Publications* · Eugene, Oregon

SIX YEARS AND A QUARTER WAY THROUGH

Resource Publications
An Imprint of Wipf and Stock Publishers
199 W. 8th Ave., Suite 3
Eugene, OR 97401

www.wipfandstock.com

PAPERBACK ISBN: 978-1-5326-7212-5
HARDCOVER ISBN: 978-1-5326-7213-2
EBOOK ISBN: 978-1-5326-7214-9

Manufactured in the U.S.A.   APRIL 4, 2019

To all who are lost, to all who are on their road to redemption,
to all who have been redeemed.

"For though the righteous will fall seven times they rise again."

Contents

Preface

ONE OF THE MOST difficult things to do is hurry up to wait, literally and spiritually. I've always prided myself on being a quick study but what do you do when the lesson you're learning is patience? These past ten years of my life I've been learning the same lesson, the promise comes before the process. Seventeen years, enslavement, and a prison stay after his dream, Joseph received the blessings shown to him. All the hardships he endured were part of the plan to grow him in faith and in standing.

As someone who has borne the agony of waiting in the desert, I understand Leah's disparagement that leads her away from her faith down dark paths. The good news is even when you leave God he doesn't leave you. I penned this story about a young woman's loss of faith, loss of self, and journey to a real relationship with Christ.

Maybe you're like Leah and have made many mistake on the way to rock bottom, or perhaps you're like Brice, spiritually grounded and battle tested, or like Cashmere, having heard the name of Jesus without understanding the magnitude of that name. Whichever character you most identify with, they all have redemption in common. Redemption is real and given freely through the blood of Christ.

Acknowledgments

FIRST AND FOREMOST I give all praise, honor, and glory to the Father, the Son, and the Holy Spirit. Thank you for drawing me near to you and for never giving up on me. Thank you for your grace and mercies that are daily renewed, without which I would be forever lost, thank you for redeeming me and making my dreams come true. I always promised to testify about your goodness on a grand stage, thank you for taking heed of my earliest prayers in life and fulfilling them at the least expected time. I could say thank you every second for the remainder of my life and it would still not be enough. Eternally, infinitely, humbly I thank you Lord, for using me, the worst of sinners, to display your love.

"She is clothed with strength and dignity; she can laugh at the days to come. She speaks with wisdom, and faithful instruction is on her tongue. Many women do noble things, but you surpass them all." To the woman more beautiful than all seven colors of the rainbow and more valuable than precious stone—Mommy, Mother of all, you are a warrior of the highest caliber. Your faithfulness, generosity, obedience, sympathy, caring, wisdom, justice, and grace make you all that's good in this world. I could never thank you enough but I will try. Thank you, Mommy, a million times for your sacrifices, a million times for your earnest prayers, and a million times for accepting all children of Christ as your own. You are wonderful and deserving of every honor. May God continue to bless you and keep you along with your children and grandchildren, whom I also thank for sharing you with us.

To Devoue, thank you for the prayers. You made a joyful noise unto the Lord, the prayers went up and the blessings have come down. Thank you to those who were here at the start of this journey though have now gone unto rest. Thank you to all who are still in the trenches praying and worshipping. Thank you for accepting my family into yours. I thank each and every single one of you explicitly, your prayers helped. The ride you gave me helped, the kind words you said to me helped.

To Quelle Amour, you are a phenomenal woman. Even in the most difficult of circumstances, you kept your faith; in the process you taught us, who were looking on, how to do the same. You blessed us every single day and reassured us that tomorrow would be brighter. Your sacrifices have not gone unnoticed—in short, thank you for a mother's love.

To Ernst, thank you for being a good man. You are slow to anger and rich in laughs. You never say no and are always willing to help no matter the request. I didn't expect you but I'm happy it was you.

To my siblings, Emanuella, my biggest supporter in life, you swear I can do no wrong and I love you for it. If everyone had a you in their corner, the world would be a better place.

To Jude, my older brother, who oftentimes felt like my father. Thank you for giving me your umbrella and getting soaked in the rain even after you told me it was going to storm and I insisted on not bringing a jacket anyway.

To Anthony, my younger brother, thank you for sharing laughs, your musical expertise, and conversing with me about the G.O.A.T.

To Herbert, you were my brother long before 2010, thank you for my first and only pair of Jordans, I loved those sneakers.

To the Louis girls, Emmily and Perinne: my sunshine and my periwinkle. You two make life so much better.

To Imani, we've been friends for fifteen years now, thank you for your sound advice, lifting me up in prayer, and your quest to know Christ better, which inspired me to do the same.

Thank you to everyone at Wipf and Stock for accepting my manuscript and making my dreams come true.

Thank you to everyone that has touched my life and shaped me for the better.

Chapter 1

I USED TO THINK I was special, born to be extraordinary; I hungered for the spotlight, eager for renown. It seemed inevitable to me I'd get everything I wanted until I found myself plunged into an existence of ordinary, punctuated by moments of particularly excruciating mundanity. I read somewhere once that everyone has a doppelganger. If that's true maybe mine is everything I used to be, everything I wanted to be but never quite became.

"What happens to a dream deferred?" I don't need the sticky note it's written on to remember my favorite poem. I've kept it on my desk all this time as a reminder to not let my dreams die, although lately it's become more of a taunt. I can't bring myself to throw it away though, so it stares me in the face as the man on the other end of my headset tells me how annoying I am and never to call his business again. "Sir, how can I be annoying you when all I've done is bring you business? In fact, if it weren't for the company I work for hardly anyone would know about your restaurant. The last thirty days alone we've gotten you five hundred views, how many sandwiches does that translate to? Quite frankly, Nikko's Patisserie and Giovanni's Italian Home-Style Cooking have a longer history and better cooks, at least that's what the reviews say. In short, your time would be better served thanking me." I shouldn't have said that. "I'd like to speak with your manager." That should've caused me to reconsider my tone. It didn't though. "She can't speak to you right now because she's busy making an intelligent business owner money. Don't worry we won't try to do the same for you." Click. Twelve and a half minutes. At least my metrics for the day will be high. By the bits of conversation assaulting my ears I won't be the only one.

Across my cubicle, the nine other members of my team smile, laugh, and close deals while I realize I'm more than halfway through the month having closed exactly zero deals with a twenty-five-thousand-dollar goal. The familiar weight settles in my chest; without warning the sound of laughter is replaced by the rhythm of my heart, beating like the bass line of a house song; loud, powerful, constant. My eyes water, struggling to translate images into sharp pictures. In one swift motion I rip off my headset and make a run for the bathroom. I sit on the toilet, head between my knees, breathing deeply and slowly. "I hate my job . . . I need this job it pays well . . . But I cannot take another four-letter word from some random person . . . This is temporary . . . Two years is not temporary . . . I am college educated, confident, beautiful, and talented, I have options, more importantly, dreams . . . What are they again? . . . You are favored . . . God, please help me . . . I'm fine . . . I'm fine . . ." After several more breaths I'm calm enough to leave the stall. At the sink, I survey myself in the mirror, same caramel skin, same round face, and same honey eyes, still beautiful; that's the general consensus anyway. I pat my face with a tissue, absorbing the sweat that's pooled above my lip and in my hairline. As long as I look okay everything will be okay. My mom always says, "The world doesn't need to get a up close look at your struggles." Judging by the mirror, my struggles are still secret.

Back at my desk, a direct message from my manager calls the entire team into a meeting, probably another round of motivational clips. I hope it's Ray Lewis this time, I cannot take another *Wolf of Wall Street* occult gathering. I work in the ad sales department of a popular tech company where the motto is ABC- Always Be Closing.' Day one of our indoctrination into the Jordan Belfort School of sales we are taught if you're not making money you need to be on the phone talking about how you can. The job is bad enough, especially the cold calls. The worst part though are the almost hourly motivational breaks which are almost always a viral clip of someone, usually an athlete, rallying his downtrodden team back to victory. Those clips I can handle, it's the Leonardo DiCaprio slides shouting at me to make sales that I loathe. The meeting turns out to be a pleasant surprise. We're treated to ten personal minutes to unwind. We decided to play Heads Up, a guessing game in the company of charades. It's ironic that the most fun I've ever had at my job is while playing a game to relax from my job. On my way back to my desk, Dylan, the poster boy for the hiring requirements of the company, joins me. During my interview I was told by the interviewer they were looking to hire outgoing college graduates. On my first day of work I soon learned "outgoing college graduates" means young, attractive, effervescent, charming, and did I mention good looking. Dylan has this whole Zack Morris thing going on; he's cute and fun to be around but not exactly my type. We're friends despite how vocal he is about his unrequited feelings for me. I tell him not to take it personally, I'm not interested in anyone.

Chapter 2

AT FIVE THIRTY I'M racing out of the office to the train station. I don't have anywhere to be, I just hate my job, I can't stomach being there a minute more than I have to be. The platform is crowded with school kids, performers, and the normal rush hour bunch. Keeping my ear buds in without music allows me to completely eavesdrop on the two women standing beside me with them being none the wiser. "This is the first weekend of the summer, we have to kick it off right, this is the season to turn up." While I'm sure our "turn ups" are vastly different, she is right, it is the first weekend of the summer. I decide right there that this weekend, no this summer, will be one to remember. I exit the train station. If I'm going to be great this weekend I have to look the part. I pull out my phone and shoot a quick text, "Hey, not interested in what you have going on this weekend, cancel all your plans and swing by at ten, see you then."

I was a little trigger-happy with my credit card at the boutique, I'll probably regret it when I get my statement, but as of right now I couldn't be happier with my purchases. I settled on two dresses plus to-night's ensemble; a red ruffle off-the-shoulder jumpsuit paired with gold heels, cuff, and studs. My cinnamon-streaked hair is in loose waves down my back, complementing the gold accents of my outfit. The sales associate was right, I do look phenomenal in this. I have a tendency to be overly critical of myself; tonight though I can find no fault. At ten I get a text from Amanda, "I'm fifteen minutes away," which means thirty. Amanda's awesome, pretty, stylish, has a phenomenal sense of humor, not to mention successful, but she is not punctual, ever. She's one of my dearest friends though, so I've learned to accept her flagrant disregard of time.

I hoped to avoid my mom tonight, so of course I run into her as soon as I leave my room. Due to the reality of our economy college graduates are starting off our adult lives with more debt than our parents. Many of us can't afford to immediately get our own place. We're left with little option but to be rent savvy. For many of us that means moving back home. I didn't have to move back in with my mom because I never moved out. I couldn't finance an out-of-state college so I stayed local, attending the City University of New York. I've never left the nest, which at twenty-six feels like a prison. I love my mom, we have a good relationship, but lately more than ever I feel like I'm suffocating and need to get away. "You look beautiful, Leah, where are you going?" It was one of those compliments that hid a bevy of unsaid things, my mom's specialty. "Amanda and I are going to have dinner then take in the scene. I don't have a specific place in mind, I really just wanted a reason to get dressed and look good." My mother fixes me with the look that as an adult reduces me to a child. "Leah, there's nothing wrong with dressing up and feeling good but know that your life is not accidental, coincidental, or without purpose. You don't need clothes to give you identity or destination. I've always told you, your greatest gifts are your faith and optimism; don't let anything, even delayed success, take that away from you." Having said all she was going to say she walks away, leaving me deflated and in a pensive state. My mom's like that; everyone goes to her for advice because no matter the pretense she can always see right through you. She's sage and most times you appreciate it, but sometimes it just leaves you feeling bare. My phone whistles, pulling me out of my own mind; without sparing another thought to my mother's words I grab my keys and hurry outside.

"OMG, Leah, you stay ready." I can always count on a confidence boost from Amanda. If I were wearing a brown paper bag she would still find a way to make me feel like I was wearing haute couture. "Thanks boo, you look great too, all eyes on us tonight." "Better you than me, you know I'm shy." I look at her pointedly, Amanda's as shy as she is punctual, "I'll remind you of how shy you are tonight when you're holding court in the middle of the dance floor." Our laughter subsides as we settle into casual conversation. "I haven't seen you in too long, how are you, what's new?" I can see only part of her face. Her eyes remain on the road but I hear the smile in her voice as she catches me up on what has been happening with her. "I'm good, really good, great actually. Mark and I have been talking about rings, I think he'll propose soon. Then there's work which is work but I'm only two classes plus a few licensing exams away from becoming a registered nurse. I'm in a good place." I smile to myself recalling when I first noticed a shift happening in our friendship. We were all friends, Amanda, Mark, and I, we'd known each other for years. Then on a boat ride two years ago I watched them taking a selfie and saw that the three amigos would soon be two. Neither of them knew they'd be here twenty-four months later; I did though, they're perfect together. Mark's easygoing nature tempers Amanda's fire, they make sense. "I'm happy for you."

I am happy for Amanda, I really am, but I can't help but feel a pang of pain for myself. Everyone around me knows what they want and how to get it, everyone is achieving their goals, adjusting to adulthood while I flounder in it. I've lost track of what I want besides a check on the fifteenth and thirtieth of every month. I accepted a temporary sales job I hate two years ago because I'm too scared to keep failing. While things are coming into focus for everyone else my path has become murky. I've always been the person that had it together but now I'm barely keeping from falling apart. "Li Li are you okay, you've been quiet for a long time?" I force the corners of my mouth to lift into a smile, "Yeah, I'm fine, it was just kind of a long day you know." Amanda, always ready to shake off bad vibes, readily accepts this answer. "Yeah, I do know, which is why I planned on getting a whole eight hours of sleep tonight, but as I recall I was told to abandon all plans and rescue you." "Umm, pretty sure those aren't the words I used but okay. I really am excited about tonight though, it's going to be just like old times."

Amanda made a huge fuss over me but she is not to be reckoned with tonight in a glamorous white dress; without question we make an impressive pair. It's no surprise the bouncer lets us right through the line. "What are you drinking?" I'm not much of a drinker but occasionally I enjoy a glass of wine. "I think I'll have a glass of sparkling rosé." Amanda rolls her eyes so hard that their rolling back into place is nothing short of a miracle. "I'm going to need you to do better than that, Leah. If you insist on only having one drink at least make it interesting." I have no idea how to order sexy drinks, although I placate Amanda and try again. "Can I have a daiquiri?" The sour look her face takes on is even more offensive than her eye rolling. "You can have fruit punch anytime you want, Leah." Right about now I want a Bloody Mary, if only to pour it all over her white dress. "How about you spare us both and just order for me." While Amanda orders us each a cocoloso I pay closer attention to the other attendees. "I don't even know why you're bothering." I almost miss her comment watching a group of women clamoring around the VIP area. "What do you mean, bothering with what?" I tune back into Amanda very distractedly, my attention remains with the desperate women, wondering what man could invoke this kind of shameless behavior? "You're not interested in anyone so why even pretend to be?" Although she was wrong in thinking I had a man in my sights she was right about my lack of interest in dating. I honestly cannot remember the last time I was even attracted to someone. The bottom line is, dating just isn't a priority for me right now. "I'm not pretending to be anything as you so astutely pointed out. I am not interested in anyone and I suspect it will be some time before I am, I'm not ready to let anyone into my world." What I didn't say to her is, I'm embarrassed to let anyone into my world. Between my dead end job, living with my mom, my anxiety attacks, and no longer being able to even imagine a fruitful life, no man would ever want me unless he was in the same boat, and in which case I wouldn't want him. I need to get my life back on track before I even begin to think about sharing it with somebody. I reassure Amanda I'm not closed off to love, I'm focusing on me, without giving her extra details. I can't handle any baseless assurances tonight.

Amanda's in the middle of insisting I be open to love in unexpected places at unexpected times when it begins to happen again. My mouth's secreting spit quicker than I can swallow; somewhere in the sea of saliva is my tongue, dry as a piece of parchment. From a distance, disjointed notes wail while sweat settles in the small of my back. Amanda's on mute, her mouth moves without making a sound, I force down as much anxiety as I can and mumble a hurried excuse. I'm gone from our table before Amanda can respond. Walking as quickly as I can without running I make it to the bathroom and launch myself into a mercifully empty stall without caring about the girls touching up their makeup at the sink. Silently I tell myself to breathe, that this will not defeat me even if I am huddled in a public bathroom having a panic attack. Maybe I cry out, maybe she's just perceptive, I'm not sure, but a beautiful pair of gold metallic booties stops in front of my stall and asks if I'm okay. "Yes, I'm fine, whatever you do don't eat the tacos." The booties laugh then retreat toward the door. It's a while before I feel well enough to leave the stall. In the end it's my fear that Amanda will come looking for me that coaxes me out.

On my way back to my table from the bathroom I notice everything I didn't on my way there, specifically the guy all the women were trying to get to in the VIP section. It appears most if not all of the women begging to be let in earlier were let in, they surround him on every side but he's staring at me. Even at a distance I know for a fact it's me he's looking at, it's more disturbing than it is flattering. He doesn't turn away when he realizes I've caught him, he doesn't smile either, he just stares as if to say, "It's about time you noticed, how dare you keep me waiting." Not to be intimidated, I don't immediately break eye contact. I stare back a little longer before continuing to Amanda. Right before I'm out of his line of vision I'm stopped by a waitress, "Excuse me miss, do you see that guy over there in VIP? He asked me to ask you, how long do you intend on keeping him waiting?" This guy's a piece of work. If he wants my time he'll have to come ask for it himself. I'll turn him down but at least I'll respect him a little. I angle my body giving Mr. VIP a good look at me while I rebuff his lazy attempt at flirting. "You tell him I said anything worth having is worth waiting for." The waitress looks at me with pure incredulity, "You do know who he is right?" The question has entered my mind but the answer isn't nearly important enough for me to entertain this conversation. "Nope, I'm not really all that concerned either." I'm almost out of earshot when she yells, "That's Trenton." My curiosity gets the best of me. I ask, "Trenton who?" Having just successfully baited and hooked me the waitress looks rightfully smug, "Just Trenton. He's a reality show prodigy; think Andy Cohen meets Shonda Rhimes. He's behind every successful reality show on TV right now, most importantly he's rich, really rich. If I were you I wouldn't keep him waiting." I resist the urge to roll my eyes. It's not her fault I wasted thirty seconds of my life listening to Trenton's selling points, which is that he's rich. "Thanks for the bio but you're not me, I pass."

When I get back to the table Amanda wastes no time in asking about my exchange with the waitress. I'm happy to fill her in if only to distract her from asking about my abrupt departure. "He actually thought you'd be impressed by him sending a waitress to give you a message? I'm not, a real man would have approached you himself, not via surrogate, although, you must admit he's not bad on the eyes." I look back over to VIP; it's too far from us to make out any specifics about Trenton. "How can you tell, I can barely see him?" Amanda leans into me, directing my eyes with her commentary to see everything they didn't before. "Seated he's tall, standing he must be well over six feet, my guess about six three. Look at how his shoulders fill out his shirt, they're broad and strong, good for leaning on. And that jaw, finely chiseled underneath his perfectly lined beard, girl he's fine." I follow Amanda's description closely, allowing her to paint me a picture. I see it, he's attractive but he's also a cliché—a money-flaunting, multiple-women-having cliché. I turn back around and find Amanda grinning at me, "Leah, are you interested in him?" Frankly I don't know, he's piqued my curiosity. I'm not sure if that's good or bad. He didn't do himself any favors with his leering and courier flirting, however it doesn't hurt that he's rich, successful, handsome, and wants my attention. "No, I'm not interested in him." I reach for the easiest response; I meant what I said to Amanda earlier, I'm not looking for a relationship. "I don't believe you but we'll find out in a minute because he's on his way over right now."

"Don't look at him, look at me, how do I look?" Amanda smiles knowingly, "Why does it matter, I thought you weren't interested?" Before I can respond, Trenton reaches our table then walks around it until he's standing beside Amanda, across from me. He's staring at me again. This time we're not separated by ten feet of space, he's inches away. I no longer need Amanda's description, I understand why women clamor to be in his presence.

His eyes are the perfect shade of brown for his honey-golden skin. Usually brown eyes share a dull sameness, but Trenton's sparkle with mischievousness. He's beautiful, I can't even pretend otherwise. I catch a whiff of him as he leans across the table to talk to me and my head spins he smells so good. "I like how you do what you do." The rich, smooth texture of his voice travels over the music ensconcing me; fortunately his voice is the only thing smooth about his speech otherwise I might've been a goner. "What exactly is it that you like, is it my lack of interest in your insincere attempts at getting my attention?" He looks at me with this satisfied smile, which is worse than his stone-faced stare, as if I just told him I love him. I'm tempted, really tempted to find my drink a new home, his silk cranberry shirt. "You walk in here slow motion, wearing red, then sit at the table that would give you the perfect vantage point to see and be seen. You want to be noticed, not by Joe nobody but by someone worth your attention. I see you but you pretend that my attentions are unwanted. Now you have me standing at your table explaining why you should return my interest, so again, I like how you do what you do."

The moment crackles with electricity, words are unnecessary, he has read between my lines. There's nothing left to do but offer him a seat; he's won that round. "I'm Trenton by the way," his hand remains outstretched for seconds before Amanda realizes I have no intention of taking it and steps in. "I'm Amanda this is Leah." My only acknowledgment of this exchange is a slight nod in his direction. "Leah, you're not speaking now?" He's decided to answer my surliness with some brashness of his own. "I'm absolutely speaking, I just haven't decided yet whether I'm speaking to you." I avert my eyes, careful not to look into his for too long lest I turn into one of those women begging to be near him. "How about I speak for a while then." I ignore his pomposity, at this point I'm positive it's a birth defect, and listen. "I'm executive producing a new show. We're still in the casting phase, we're almost through but I have a spot for you." Back when I knew I'd be a famous actor I believed I'd be discovered in some random way, in some random place, a chance meeting maybe. Now when those dreams are nearly dead I meet Trenton in some lounge I came to on a whim. Is this divine or another man running game on a woman? I'm inclined to believe the latter. "Really, you're going to pull the 'I can make you famous' line? What makes you think I'm interested in being famous?" Without asking or caring who the drink in front of him belongs to he lifts it to his lips, it's an incredibly bold action akin to leaning across the table and kissing me. Of course his drinking from my glass unsettles me, he expects that. What he doesn't expect is my drinking from it afterward. I drain the remaining contents of the glass in one swallow; "You didn't answer my question." Trenton raises an eyebrow, considering me, "I know you want to be famous. If you didn't your response would have been some variation of, 'no.' Instead, you're trying to decipher my legitimacy, am I a lying man promising an attractive woman fame and fortune so she'll show me gratitude or is this an honest proposal?"

"What kind of show is it?" Trenton smiles his first smile. Like everything else about him physically, it's perfect; clearly my acquiescing pleases him. "It's the kind of show that will make you a brand. From there the sky's the limit." My head's spinning, I probably should've paced myself. I'm having trouble keeping up with Trenton, who's in the middle of telling me how he can make all my dreams come true. My head finds my hands, where it would have stayed if someone hadn't pulled my hands away and forced my head up. I'm met by Trenton's dazzling eyes. I find I'm trapped by his beautiful face, right here right now I'm liable to say yes to anything he asks of me. "You're tipsy . . . beautiful too, so are half the women in this room, including your friend. What sets you apart is while they all scramble for my attention, you have it." Gently he places a finger under my chin, tilting it slightly so I'm looking up at him and our lips are perfectly aligned. "I'm going to make you a star, then I'm going to make you mine, got it?"

Seconds maybe minutes have passed when Amanda clears her throat, bringing us, Trenton and me, both back to the present. I'd completely forgotten she was here, she's been so quiet; I'm grateful for her interruption though. Trenton's last declaration was equal parts sensual and menacing. Amanda clears her throat once again, getting Trenton, who'd hastily busied himself in his phone once we broke apart, to face her; if I didn't know any better I'd say he was hiding his embarrassment behind his phone. "I can't argue with you, Leah is special, however you still haven't told her what the premise of the show is." He slips his phone back into his pocket giving Amanda his full attention; I'm annoyed they're having this conversation about me, without me, right in front of me. However I don't make a fuss because I actually would like to know what the show is about. "It's a competition-based reality show." I'm not too out of it to realize he just said the words reality show, being part of something like that would be the last word in desperation for me; I'm not quite there yet. Anger comes on quickly, with it a sober mind; he thinks I'm some untalented, fifteen-minutes-of-fame-seeking, anything-goes wannabe. That he would suggest this "opportunity" to me is insulting. "So you're here spewing lies of gold for some reality show? This conversation is exactly what I expected it would be, unworthy of my time." Furious, I get up to leave. There's a few seconds of waiting for the world to right itself; once I feel steady on my feet I look to Amanda, "Let's go . . . Now." I storm off without looking back. I don't stop until I realize Amanda isn't behind me. By the time I retrace my steps she's exiting the lounge. The sight of her upsets me somehow, I know her delay was due to Trenton and that is unacceptable.

Wordlessly we walk to Amanda's car; multiple times she asks what's wrong, she can tell I'm up upset. I'm too angry to answer her so we ride in silence until Amanda refuses to continue on this way. "Leah, I'm your friend not your enemy, don't shut down on me because he was a disappointment." Just like that my anger with her dissipates she's right, it's not her I'm mad at, I'm mad at myself for entertaining that Charlatan. That doesn't stop me from asking Amanda if Trenton was the reason it took her so long to leave the lounge. "Yeah, he wanted me to get you to hear him out." I roll my eyes at that, I've already heard him out, there's nothing he can possibly say to change my feelings on the subject or about him. I catch Amanda giving me serious side eye, I know her well enough to know she has something to say; I hope she says it soon since she's driving and I don't want to crash. "I want to say something to you without the risk of you biting my head off." I nod my head urging her to continue, I just want her to speak her mind so she could go back to watching the road. "Before we were friends what made me want to be your friend was how full of life you were. You were a fearless conqueror, but lately your fire seems to have gone out. I have no opinion on whether or not you should do the show, what I will say is this, I've gone to enough of your performances to know what direction you want your life to take and this nine to five gig isn't it. I'm not blind, I do notice things, like the fact that you haven't been to an audition or even an acting class in a long time. You've become complacent and I don't know why but you need to stop it immediately. Don't become this person that won't jump because she's afraid of falling." Amanda's wrong, I haven't become complacent. I grew tired of moving without going anywhere so I stopped; I no longer dream, what's the point when you wake up to reality. Every morning that I get up to go into the office I lose a piece of me. At first, I reminded myself daily that the job is temporary because I'd be cast in a project soon, that didn't happen though. I've been called many things—beautiful, intelligent, talented, gifted—I don't believe them anymore. As anxiety settles over my chest, the first line of the poem drifts back to me, "What happens to a dream deferred?" It suffocates.

Choking on my anxiety, I lower the passenger-side window and rest my head against the car door; I gulp air like water. Amanda's saying something about how I'd better not throw up in her car, that I shouldn't have drank my cocoloso as a shot trying to prove something to "the jerk." I don't bother correcting her assumption that I'm drunk, after all that's better than the truth, a truth I don't wish to tell, particularly not after the reprimand she just gave me. I'm happy to ride the rest of the way home in silence, focusing on my breaths. I've had three panic attacks today, my anxiety is getting

worse and I learned I'm not fooling anyone with my attempts at concealing my struggles. If Amanda's noticed other people have noticed as well. When she pulls up in front of my house she asks, "Are we alright?" That's Amanda, always ready to let go of bad feelings, which suits me just fine. "You and I are always okay." "Great, so that means you'll be my plus one to this all white rooftop day party tomorrow?" I planned on going to church in the morning but I've missed a few services already, what's one more?

My bedroom in the basement of my mom's house is tiny, with one window overlooking the concrete paved backyard. Even on the brightest of days, the sun struggles to make its presence known. Once you get past the perpetual darkness, size, and peach walls I thought were a good idea at seventeen, it's not so bad. It is in dire need of a remodeling though I can hardly stand all the reminders of what I used to be, the things I used to want. Now I look around my room and all of these things, the crown and the pictures, they all seem like props from a story a good friend told me a long time ago. I know every detail but she lived it, not me. I've imagined a lot of scenarios for my life but I've never imagined a reality that even remotely resembles my current situation. Sadness, a feeling I've grown very accustomed to, creeps into my heart where it gets sent out through my bloodstream to every part of my body until I'm sobbing. I don't even know why. Tonight's events replay in my mind's eye. Trenton wasn't a disappointment, he was exactly who I expected him to be—egotistical, arrogant, and enigmatic. His beauty is alluring, deceptive too. I suspect if I never see him again it'll be too soon. Even so, when he said I was special I felt special again, until he started talking about making me a caricature for mass consumption. I don't know if I wanted Trenton to be different, if I wanted anything from him, I don't know why I'm thinking about him at all.

I wake up the next morning with no recollection of falling asleep. I go in search of breakfast and run into my mom all dressed up. "You look nice, heading to church?" We're told beauty fades but my mother's never did, it may have changed but it's never left. Sometimes, like right now, I see her and think a woman like you could have had more, more than a backbreaking, hand-scarring, thankless job. Is my mom happy or did she settle? I try not to think too hard about the answer; for one, if she did settle, that would somehow make my life all that much more dismal; also my mom can read me like an open book and I'd rather not have that conversation with her. My mom thanks me for the compliment and tells me she was just on her way to wake me to ask if I were going with her. I busy myself with the coffee maker while I tell her I can't because I have plans with Amanda. I feel guilty about the relief I feel to not go to church. I've been feeling disconnected from my faith and the last thing I want to do is fake it when God knows it's insincere.

As sinful as it may sound what I need is a hiatus from church. My mom is clearly disappointed but she's trying to respect me as an adult so she just says "maybe" then leaves.

I didn't have time to buy anything new for the white party. Luckily I had the perfect gown in my closet: a sleeveless, lace, empire waist number. I add gold and mint accents with my jewelry and heels. White eyeliner, gold lipstick, and a braided crown later I'm ready to go. The rooftop is amazing; the DJ's great, décor's chic, crowd's posh, an all-around great party. I've had a few offers to dance but I've turned them all down; to appease Amanda I agree to dance with the next guy who ask. Not two minutes later I get a tap on my shoulder. I turn and come face to face with Trenton. "You've got to be kidding me, what in the world are you doing here?" Trenton puts his hands up defensively warding off my attack, "Whoa calm down, I'm here, because it's my party." No way is this a coincidence, this has to be a set-up, but that would mean Amanda's in on it. My eyes find hers. I want to know why she would invite me to Trenton's party, but she looks as taken aback as I feel; there's no way she knew. "Last night while you were in the bathroom the waitress who brought our drinks told me about it, I had no idea it was his party." Trenton steps right in between Amanda and me, completely concealing her , with nowhere else to look my eyes go to his face. "I asked the waitress to tell Amanda about the party. I guessed rightly that she would be the more level-headed of the two of you." I don't understand why Trenton would go through all this trouble to get me to come to his party; I can't possibly be the only woman to have ever turned him down.

Trenton working this hard for my affections is flattering, there are no two ways about it. The man is gorgeous, especially in matching linen pants and shirt, but I don't want to be on a reality show, and as for the other stuff, I don't know about that either. "You got me here, now what?" I fold my arms across my chest. I'm apathetic but my ears work. "Now, you stop running away from me and listen. By the way, I don't believe you're not interested in me for one second." My stomach flutters, I want it to be nausea not that Trenton's right. He faces Amanda, asking if she would be willing to give us a moment alone to talk. I don't object, maybe this conversation takes a turn I want no witnesses to. Seconds later I see Amanda retreating in the direction of the bar. He waits until Amanda's well away from us before continuing, "I told you last night I think you'd be great for my show, you have something." I throw my hands up in exasperation, "This again, I said no already, last night. Persistence is usually virtuous; on you it's suspicious. I don't trust you at all, meaning not even a little. It's your disingenuousness; I doubt you've spoken ten sincere words to me. So again, what do you want and how is it you plan on using me as a means to your end?"

The energy between us is palpable, if we were cartoon characters there'd be heat lines radiating off us crashing into one another. He takes a step toward me; instinctively I take a step back without looking, nearly falling backward over a chair. Trenton grabs me before I fall, pulling me toward him, trapping me against his chest. I'm as rigid as a board in his vice grip, I can't move or push him away, I stand as still as possible while his spearmint fresh breath tickles my senses. "Do you remember the first time we met?" "It was less than twenty-four hours ago; much as I'd like to I have not forgotten yesterday." I pretend to be unaffected, calm even, but I'm bothered by the nearness of him. He's a player, I know this, but the way he's looking at me with such naked vulnerability makes me want to play his game. Somehow he pulls me closer into his embrace where I hold my breath, afraid of where I stand, letting go, and of being let go of.

"No, I asked about the first time we met, last night was the second." His breath tickles my skin distracting me, which must be why I think I hear him say we've met before. I don't know what to say so I say nothing and let him talk. "Six years ago, end of summer, you and I both attended the Premier Network intern party." Now I'm paying attention, because I was an intern for Premier Network six years ago. I did attend an end of summer party. But I don't remember Trenton being there. "I knew everyone in the office by face if not by name, I've never seen you before last night." No way I'd forget Trenton if we'd met before. "You worked in the downtown office, I was at the midtown location, our paths never crossed until the night of the party. I arrived late. I had tapes to finish logging before I could attend, you remember what it's like interning. The party was mostly through by the time I got there. I was pissed because most of my friends were gone. There was no one there I wanted to talk to. I was halfway to the door when I saw you, in the middle of a conversation with a group of interns, who I also hadn't seen before, speaking passionately and animatedly about your dreams. After a few minutes of watching you in open admiration, your eyes found mine. That was all the push I needed to talk to you. Almost to where you stood I was stopped and pulled into conversation by a friend. I excused myself as quickly as I could but it was too late, you were gone. I hadn't seen you since, until last night when you walked back into my life."

It's loud, not loud enough to prevent me from hearing or to cause me to mishear; I catch every single word Trenton says yet I can make no sense of it. I think hes saying he saw me once six years ago and hasn't forgotten me since. My brain feels the same way it does when I've read one line twenty times without understanding it even a tiny bit. This has to be another line, except everything he said about that night, excluding the parts about him, I can confirm. On my last day of interning at Premier Network, the program director instructed all the interns to create a list of goals with a timeline. At the party I was asked about my list. I rattled off goals without any reserve. I didn't care who was listening or how ambitious my objectives sounded to unbelieving ears, I knew in a few years my list of goals would be a list of accomplishments. It didn't matter to me that no one else knew the same. I remember every bit of that conversation, but I don't remember Trenton. He looks at me expectantly with wide eyes, their usual luster gone; clearly he wants an answer from me, a concession of belief, a recollected memory, or a return of feelings. Whatever it is he wants, I can't give.

Suddenly being in the circle of his arms feels oppressive. I place a hand on his chest assertively, without speaking I let him know I want to be let go. Sans protest he releases me, although he doesn't look happy to. "I'm not sure what you want me to say." "I don't want you to say anything, I want you to know I've wanted you everyday for the last six years. You think I'm a womanizer; maybe I have been to other women, not to you though. Believe me when I say my interest in you is genuine. I thought I'd never see you again. Now that you've walked back into my life I'm never letting you go. So stop being hostile toward me and let me . . . like you." In spite of myself I like Trenton. I still don't trust him, but frankly this conversation has gone a long way toward mending that. He's growing on me, a fact I'd rather keep from him for the time being.

"How do I know you didn't stalk my Facebook, discover a few specifics, and string a story together?" He shrugs off the suggestion that he stalked my social media for the purpose of creating some elaborate lie. "You're free to believe about me whatever it is you want to believe, just as I am free to believe whatever it is I want about you." When he recounted the first time he saw me it was with awe and wonder. Now that he's met me I question if he still feels the same. I don't ask, my ego's too fragile to handle an unfavorable response; he tells me anyway. "You're unhappy, why shouldn't you be? You're bigger than the small life you lead. You deserve to be loved and adored by millions of fans around the globe, not doing whatever it is you're doing. I can't make you a star, you were born being that. What I will do is put you in a position to be seen if you let me." It wasn't another romantic declaration, it wasn't flattery either. Trenton is rude and insensitive but intuitive too. I stare into his gleaming dark eyes uncertainly, he's not the first man to offer a woman the world. The difference is he's in a position to make good on that offer. More than anything else I want to be fulfilled, satisfied, and happy; to make art, live creatively, and be rewarded for it. I want to be somebody, a factor. I don't want to die with all of this inside of me. I don't want to exist, I want to live, and Trenton can help me do that.

Trenton squeezes behind me, moving toward the chair I almost tripped over. Taking a seat he pats his lap, motioning for me to sit. I decline with a distasteful look he chuckles at; I take the arm of the chair instead. "Now that you know I'm on your side will you hear me out?" I nod my head. I'm still not keen about doing a reality show, but six years of waiting deserves a few minutes of conversation. "The working title of the show is Star Quality. It'll follow seven housemates, all aspiring actors. The cast will participate in weekly challenges to be scored by a panel of judges, followed by elimination of one member until a winner is chosen. The winner will not only receive a cash prize, they will also receive an agent, and a principal role in an upcoming major motion picture." When I heard the words reality show I imagined the worst possible scenario. What Trenton's describing is more American Idol less Jersey Shore. I even like the name. All I'd have to do is what I already want to do in the first place. "So it'd just be performances, no humiliating, degrading antics?" "I mean personality is always a good thing, but no—you in?"

Part of me screams 'yes I'm in, but the more rational part of me asks if I can have a few days to think about it. "Yeah, but I need you to meet with the producers tomorrow morning for an informal casting session. They want to see what you look like on camera and get a feel for you." I don't like the sound of a casting session. I was of the understanding that the spot was mine if I wanted it. Now it sounds like I have to audition. "Question for the sake of clarity and full transparency, is the spot mine if I so choose or is it mine if I get past the casting directors?" Trenton angles his body in the chair slightly so our legs touch. I think about the article I read that said when two people like each other their bodies curve into one another, adjoining in uncommon places. I lean as far away from him as I can. "For transparency sake, as you put it, I am the executive producer. This is my concept my project, the only one I answer to is the network. Your casting session is a professional courtesy, but make no mistake, I'll do what I want. I don't need anyone's okay. Is that clear enough for you?" I think I just got a glimpse of the Trenton the world sees; authoritative, powerful, and demanding; by contrast he indulges me.

Speechless, I nod my head. What is there to say? "Great, I'll text you the details once you put your number in my phone." Trenton hands me his cell while failing at suppressing a smile. "If I were you I wouldn't smile too broadly, seeing as how it took you six years to get my number." "Didn't you tell the waitress last night to remind me that all things worth having are worth waiting for?" Rolling my eyes, I say, "Make sure our communication is for professional purposes only." "Sorry, I don't make promises I have no intention of keeping." I'm pretending to be annoyed, but I'm flattered and somewhat looking forward to talking to him without the distraction of his face. "By the way, I googled you. I found a few articles about your pageant wins, some images, performance pieces on YouTube, and a Facebook page. No Instagram or Twitter accounts though." All that information is out there in cyber space, accessible to anyone with internet, but I don't like how much Trenton or anyone can learn about me without actually getting to know me. I'm old school in that way, I want to put the work in to getting to know someone. "Do you stalk all the girls you like or am I an exception?" "Yeah, yeah, what's your Instagram handle?" I shift uncomfortably, feeling nervous to reveal I'm social media inept. "I'm not on Instagram, Twitter, or Snapchat."

"What, you're not on the gram?" Trenton looks at me with wide, un-believing eyes. I don't blame him, I'm a rare breed. "Nope, it's too invasive and narcissistic for me. I can't imagine snapping selfies every few minutes to update the world on my life." Pulling out my own phone, I mime taking selfie after selfie, duck lips, no duck lips, smize, coy, playful. "Ooh look at me, wait now look at me, fifteen minutes later look at me again, ugh I'd die." Trenton actually laughs aloud, "I like you like this, playful, relaxed." Unex-pectedly he rises, pulling me up with him, we stand facing one another, my hands automatically go around his neck as his find my waist. "You know, I could totally make a case against you for sexual harassment?" His chuckle is low and guttural, "Be quiet, let's take this picture for the gram." That's when I notice his left hand has left its place on my waist and is now pointing a camera at us, ducking my head I say, "I told you, I don't have Instagram."

"Yes but that's about to change." He switches his phone to the other hand trying to get a better view of my face; I turn my head the other way. "Uh no, it's not." "Yeah it will, because you want to be successful. The enter-tainment industry is not about talent, it's about personality. Do you come to the table with a following? What's your brand? I checked out your Facebook page—no offense, it's dull, painfully boring. No one wants their timeline flooded with preachy memes. You have what, three hundred friends, maybe fifty pictures, the most recent being two months old. You're beautiful, no doubt about that, but this whole Ayesha Curry save it for your man thing just isn't going to cut it. You need to be provocative, unapologetically sexy."

As my arms fall to the side so does the moment. I'd let my guard down only to receive a hurtful reminder that I shouldn't have. His words sting. I'm not preachy, and what's wrong with having a page I wouldn't be embarrassed for my family or employer to see. When did things shift, where class and sophistication became a precursor to becoming a spinster while promis-cuity and lack of integrity got you to the altar and the best opportunities? "Basically you're saying I need to become less selective, less private, and less sophisticated in favor of becoming vain, self absorbed, narcissistic, and over sexed?" Trenton puts my arms back around his neck. They fall back to my side as soon as he lets go of them, I'm liking him less and less by the second.

"Times have changed, I'm not saying for better or for worse, but society has evolved. Not only the way we dress but also the way we communicate, our beliefs, values. We're less inhibited, restricted by antiquated ideals of morality provided by a book that bares judgments but says 'judge not lest ye be judged.' You're free to live as you want and feel as you feel, so why would you chose to live in a box?" I understand his success, he has a silver tongue; a lesser woman would be questioning her whole belief system. "Your argument would be more compelling if you weren't simultaneously emancipating and relegating me to a life of hyper sexuality, some might call you a pimp. You talk about not being put in a box or being judged, but you judged me to be boring and stiff because I don't have my life and body on display. If I have to become this new idea of woman to be a serious contender in life much less your show then I can't do it." My chest heaves with righteous indignation while Trenton remains the picture of calm; I wonder if he heard a single word I said. I'm on the verge of asking when he takes both my hands in his. All this touching is diverting; I can't remember to be angry with or cautious of him. "Listen, it's not a big deal, you're an actor, just act a little less reserved and act more carefree." I try to pull my hands out of his grasp but his hold remains firm. "By the morning, the casting directors will have studied your social media accounts, they'll call me with objections to you on grounds that you bring them no audience. I'll tell them I want you." Trenton raises an eyebrow at me, suggesting he wants me in more ways than one. Feeling shy, I look away as he continues.

"They'll be obliged to meet with you, reluctant as they may be. However, you'll walk in, enchant them, because that's who you are, they'll love you but have the same notes I'm giving you now. The way I see it, you have three choices: you can go back to the life you and I both know you hate, you can do things the hard way, be antiestablishment and all that, or you can let me help you. By the way, I'm great at what I do."

"Smile!" Before "why" has left my mouth I'm blinded by a camera flash. When my vision is no longer spotted what I see is a picture of myself flush against Trenton, his mouth alarmingly close to my ear. My first thought is we look good together; my second thought is we look like we're together. I reach for Trenton's phone but he holds it out of reach. "Delete that now." He's holding me back with one arm as I frantically reach for his phone. Laughing he says, "No, I like it. You don't look angry with me for once. I think I'll post it on the gram." Frustrated, I swat his arm, "You'd better not." "How about I make you a deal—pose for a picture with me that I *will* post and tag you in on Instagram, once you set up your account tonight." Trenton's point about the power of social media in today's world is valid; no denying that, I just don't care to be like everyone else, doing things for follows. "Why are you so against it? You have to use the resources available to you—your social media presence is your resume. All of today's biggest stars are social media successes. I can't force you to do anything, but I thought you were ready to stop dreaming and start living." Instafamous social media users aren't called influencers for naught; the masses turn to them for entertainment, politics, fashion advice, etc. What kind of chance does a non-social media imprint having aspiring actress have against someone who comes with a ready-made fan base? No chance, the information is out there anyway. I might as well begin taking control of what version of myself the world receives.

"But even if I join every social media platform in existence this very instant, there's no way I can get the kind of numbers the casting directors want by morning unless I'm trending. The only way to trend is to be famous, do something radically outrageous, or be involved with someone famous." I cut Trenton off before he can begin whatever salacious thing he's on the verge of saying, "Before you even go there, none of those three options are viable, especially not the last one, and sorry to break it to you, you're not a celebrity." Trenton tilts his head to the side with pursed lips like he ate something that left a bad taste in his mouth. "Ahhh, stop playing, people know me out here, if you disagree ask my three million social media follow-ers. What I was going to say to you earlier before you cut me off is you don't necessarily have to be dating a celebrity, you can be introduced to the world by one." This is true. I've lost count of how many influencers started off as somebody's girlfriend, friend, stylist, and so on so forth. Maybe I can let Trenton introduce me to the world, plus a cyber nod from him is as efficient as buying follows. "My three million followers always want to get to know the people I post pictures with. If I think you're interesting enough to know outside of cyber space, my followers will think the same." Trenton knows the business, he knows how to get me where I want to be, and I'm going to have to trust him, even if his advice goes against my judgment. "Fine, take the stupid picture, and you'd better keep it professional. That means both hands where I can see them." I angle my body to the right, my good side—he gets in behind me but keeps a safe distance—giving the camera my sultriest stare until the camera flashes. As Trenton's stepping out from behind me he whispers, "Stop fighting it, we're meant to be." I roll my eyes on principle, but I'm blushing on the inside. I take a beat before facing him, just to make sure I'm not blushing on the outside too. When I turn around he's looking at something on his phone, which is super rude, but whatever, I'm not up to facing off with him again. I feel kind of awkward since not ten minutes ago my arms were comfortable around his neck. No matter, I'm all business now. "I'm going to head out now, text me the info for tomorrow, I'll let you know once I've plugged into the matrix. Bye Trenton." I take a step in the direction I last saw Amanda when I hear Trenton say my name. "Trent. Call me Trent."

Amanda isn't happy about heading out early, but after my loaded conversation with Trent, sticking around feels weird. While we are leaving the party I get that being-watched feeling. I cast one last look around the room and see him watching me from the DJ booth. Clear across the room I feel him reaching out to me like some kind of psychic mating call, it's a new, unpleasant feeling being this aware of someone.

Amanda and I keep up a steady flow of chatter on the drive home, but my mind never strays far from Trent. Inevitably the topic turns to him and we dissect almost every word of our conversation. "So does that mean you're going to do it?" Amanda asks cautiously, her voice carefully neutral. "I haven't decided yet, but I am going to meet with the producers tomorrow for an 'unofficial casting session.'" My phone vibrates in my purse. Before I see it I know the text is from Trent. It's the first picture he took of us, the one I didn't want him to take. I saw the picture fleetingly the first time, I still had stars in my eyes from the flash; now I look at it hungrily. A small smile plays on Trent's lips while he looks at me, radiant and glowing; we look happy, we look in love. I save the picture and his number, then refocus on Amanda; she asks if I'm okay. In truth, I hardly know.

"So, what are you going to do about Trenton?" I try to match Amanda's casual tone, "What do you mean?" "Nothing, just that you two are completely into each other." I wouldn't say I'm completely into him, more like somewhat into him, which is more than I'm willing to admit to Amanda at the moment. "I'm not sure that's the case. Trenton likes that I don't swoon over him, it's exciting to an egomaniac to be turned down, mostly I think he wants me for his show." I left the lounge last night believing him to be that shallow, desiring me simply because I did not desire him. Today I know him to be more complex, capable of nurturing feelings for someone he saw once, for years. "Is that why I saw him wrapped around you, because you don't like him and he wants to cast you in a project? Okay understood . . . while you're busy *disliking* him, remember to protect your heart." It doesn't add up, Amanda's constantly lecturing me about being open to love, now she's telling me to guard my heart. "You literally said the opposite a few hours ago. The only thing that's changed between now and then is there being a potential suitor, which leads me to believe you don't only want me to guard my heart, you want me to guard my heart against Trent."

That was the worst fight I've ever had with Amanda, we've never spoken like that to one another. I didn't mean it when I said she was jealous or when I said she's just upset she can no longer live vicariously through me. I was just blinded by rage; how could she say the real Leah had been replaced by a desperate, weak, sugarless version? Of everything she said, that hurt the most. Doesn't she think I know I've lost my edge, why rub my nose in it? It's ironic how you can start your day knowing something as fact, and by the time your day ends it's no longer true. I thought Amanda was a forever friend; looks like forever came early.

Later, when I'm half way to sleep, I get another text from Trenton. He followed up his first text with the details for tomorrow's meeting. I'm surprised to hear from him again so soon. "Did you forget about our deal?" Following my huge blowup with Amanda I completely forgot I was supposed to start my road to stardom with social media domination. I don't want Trent to think I'm going back on our agreement; I stall him with aimless chatter as I fill in my bio and add pictures. "You normally conduct business so late at night?" His response is instant, "If I feel inspired." It takes me a few minutes to respond. I'm going through my photo gallery looking for unused pictures to add to my page. "So I'm your muse?" I get butterflies every time the text notification sounds, but I'm much bolder when I'm not standing in front of him. "Ha . . . more like my project." "Says the man that's been pining after me for six years."

I regret it as soon as the words leave my mouth. I was only teasing, but it was also careless and insensitive. I weigh apologizing then decide against it, it might make things awkward if he took it for the joke it is. Half an hour passes with no reply from Trenton. I try to distract myself from his radio silence by completing my Instagram profile. Once it's complete I have an excuse to text again. "You can follow me @leahalbanese." Within seconds of sending off the text I get his reply, "We'll work on your handle, standby." I don't bother replying, what's the point when my concern at the minute is that I've upset him. "Check your IG." I have dozens of friend request and comments stemming from the picture with Trent I'm tagged in, he captioned it #wishuponthisrisingstar. I'm reading through the comments (mostly flattering a few hateful) when I get a text from Trenton, another picture from the night. I'm breathtaking, if I didn't know it's me I wouldn't know it's me. I'm looking in the general direction of the camera not directly at it though; the sun shines brightly behind me, setting my face, my hair ablaze in light. I could've been painted into the ethereal scene. I'm at a loss, when did he take this picture of me, how did he take this picture of me without my knowledge? "Did you take this?" "Your beauty was so arresting I couldn't resist." It's difficult to guard my heart against Trent when he's disarming me at every turn, how can I defend myself against the man of my dreams?

Chapter 3

THE NEXT MORNING I'M dressed and almost out the door when my phone alerts me to a new text message: "It's been nearly twelve hours since your last post . . . no new pics?" Following Trent's post last night, I received one hundred thirteen follow requests, not to mention a slew of direct messages from random guys. I haven't checked Instagram this morning; no doubt that number's doubled. I hate to admit it but Trent was spot on about him making my social media introduction, which is why my only response to his text is to take off the cardigan I'm wearing over my jeans and tee shirt, and snap a picture. It's cute but not sexy enough for the kind of follows I need: I get on my bed and lay on my stomach with crossed ankles, bent legs, and try again. Better, much better. I post the sultry pic with the caption #welcomemetothegram. My phone vibrates again. "Nice, next time lose the shirt." I don't dignify that with a response. I'm almost out the door again when inspiration strikes me. I should record my day's adventures. If all goes well every aspect of my life will be recorded for posterity anyway, why not start now?

"Good morning people, thanks for the follows and likes. I'm new to the whole social media thing but someone suggested, well told me, I needed to stop being so stiff and living in a box. So here I am living a little and telling all of you about it, let me know how I'm doing. By the way, you know the jerk that called me stiff, I gave him my number, blame it on the alcohol, anyways I'm off to conquer the world now xoxo muah." I play it back once before posting it: I do everything right, bat my lashes at the right moment, give the camera bashful sweet smiles, and a sexy pout at the end. I added the part about Trent on a whim. Every good story needs a little romance. I'm not sure what I want to come of that situation but now I've given my followers something to tune in to, a reason to keep coming back to my page. I'll triple my followers by end of day.

I get off the train hurriedly, itching to check my notifications; to my surprise I've more than doubled my follows since last night. The video's a hit. I got tons of comments, mostly flirty. There's one from Trent too @ icutrent, "So you into this guy?" I smile to myself, walking into the building for my casting feeling more confident than I have in a long time. The receptionist at REALTV tells me to be seated, Stephanie Piscano will be with me in a moment. Looking around the vibrant office I see irrefutable proof of Trent's contribution to current television, not including Star Quality, he has three shows in production right now. A slender woman about my height with cherry blonde hair approaches me extending a hand, "Hi Leah, I'm Stephanie, pleasure to meet you." Behind her wide smile I see her sizing me up, deciding if I'm what she wants for the project. I match her broad smile easily; no matter what she thinks about me, she can't stop me from being part of this show. "Likewise, I'm excited to meet you."

We walk down a long hallway to a room with a green screen, camera, stool, and table with three chairs, two of which are filled. Stephanie takes the empty seat between what I assume are two crew members. "Leah, to my left is Jeremy Tillman, my right Matthew Cadman." They each greet me with a smile I return. Taking the only seat available to me, the stool in front of the screen, I do as I'm asked by Stephanie: state my name, age, city, state, and occupation. "Leah Albanese, age twenty-six, resident of Brooklyn, New York, ad sales." "Leah," if I had to guess I'd say Stephanie is the one to impress, it's no coincidence she's led the conversation thus far, "tell me about yourself." Simple question right, except it's not that simple for me, the list of things I know about myself has dwindled significantly. Not wanting to appear as dumbfounded as I feel I take no more than a few seconds to collect my thoughts. "You want me to tell you how great I am? I think I can do that." I begin slowly working my way through the things I absolutely know about me. "I'm a first-generation American, youngest of two girls. Most people describe me as . . . tough, I am tough; I'm from Brooklyn, not gentrified Brooklyn either, real Brooklyn, where weakness makes you a target. I had to be strong growing up, vulnerability wasn't an option, not outwardly at least. The truth about me most people don't know is, I'm a hard-boiled egg, tough shell, mushy insides. I love the arts in all its variety, even corny musicals with unrealistic happy endings. I love all things fantastical; you know that rare place where your wildest dreams collide with reality. I believe in magic, not the Disney fairytale magic, the kind of magic that takes an ordinary girl from humble beginnings to extraordinary endings. Most importantly, although I probably shouldn't admit this, I was told I could be 'preachy,' I believe in God: obstinately, unwaveringly, fully, and without question. I believe in he who is greater than all of this," I indicate the room, the building, the expanse, everything. "*He* gives my life purpose." I can't tell if they agreed with me, liked me, or simply found me entertaining; either way they're ready to follow wherever I lead.

"How do you imagine an ordinary girl becoming extraordinary?" asks Stephanie. "I imagine she wasn't all that ordinary to begin with. Some people are meant to be viewers, others are meant to be viewed, she just needs the right circumstance to step into her true self." The energy in the small room has changed, I've won them over, I'm no longer the nobody Trenton insisted on them meeting with, I'm the girl with spunk, with "it." Matthew and Jeremy, who have been utterly silent until now, give me thoughtful, approving looks, and Stephanie actually allows her smile to reach her eyes.

"Tell us about your childhood, about growing up tough." I hate that Stephanie asks this question; the answer is too personal, too complex for what I thought would be shallow conversation. What made my childhood tough is that I had to grow up fast; there was little time for coddling, for being a child. I consider myself blessed to have the mother I do; the sacrifices she's made to provide for my sister and me, I will never fully know; but with that said, her struggle didn't escape our notice. Watching my mother day in and day out toiling to barely make it has been my greatest motivation. At as young as seven years old what I wanted was to be rich so my mom could quit her job. I spent my childhood running to adulthood to help my family; now at a quarter way through, my mom is still struggling and I still can do little more than pray for the day I can help.

I think about joking my way through the question, then Trent's advice returns to me: make them interested in you. I take a deep breath before I bare my soul. "The first thing I learned about my mom is, she loves singing, later I'd learn it was her dream to do it professionally. When I became old enough to have dreams and passions of my own, I wondered why my mom, who is widely regarded in our community for her vocal abilities, did backbreaking work every day. Eventually I'd learn immigrating from a third world country, in the eighties, with little English, left you very few career options. My mother usually sang old hymns and hopeful spirituals, although there were times when her songs ran dark. I remember this one time in particular, while in my room hearing a haunting tune, I followed the melody to the kitchen where my mom stood at the sink singing despondently. I watched my mom until overwhelmed by her sadness, walked over to her and wrapped my seven-year-old arms around her waist. I held on tight as she sang in French about sacrifice, about loss of self. When she'd sang the last note I asked why she was sad, untangling me from around her, she stooped down to look me in my eyes and said, 'I'm not sad, the woman in the song is.' Naively I asked, 'Why?' A stray tear trickled down her cheek, it's solitariness making it all the more impactful. 'Because sometimes dreams are just dreams.' That night and almost every day since, I've prayed to God that my dreams wouldn't just be dreams, to not one day find myself singing that ominous song."

Someone's saying my name softly yet insistently; I can't respond, I'm still in my kitchen holding onto my mom, listening to her song cry. Revisiting that day has rocked me to my core, but I need to pull it together because I'm no longer seven; I'm twenty-six, sitting on a stool in a room full of producers, with tears in my eyes, allowing my chance to make something of myself slip away. Anxiety presses down on my chest, squeezing my lungs; I'm resisting, I won't give in, that'd be like giving up, accepting the fate of the unknown woman as my own. Stephanie says my name again, this time I acknowledge her, "Why don't you take a moment." Gratefully, I nod, not trusting myself to speak. Before I leave the room I see Jeremy, Matthew, and Stephanie watching me in silent stupefaction. I might have just ruined my shot or perhaps I just solidified it, there'll be time to puzzle it out later, for now I need to get to the closest bathroom.

I turn down the nearest hall and come upon a restroom almost immediately. My head rests against the cool wall as I catch my breath and let the frigid air blowing out the vents combat the rising heat of my body. I pat my face dry with toilet paper while inwardly commanding my anxiety to release me from its grasp. I've grown used to a constant heaviness, not always pressing down on my chest, but not out of reach either. The feeling never leaves but it's receded enough for me to finish what I've started.

Jeremy, Matthew, and Stephanie are seated in almost the exact same way I left them, awaiting my return. "Leah, are you ready to continue?" I wave off Jeremy's concern as unnecessary. "Yeah, I'm great, you know actors, overly dramatic." Jeremy smirks at me, then asks, "Are you involved with anyone?" Not exactly the smoothest segue, although it beats talking about my childhood. I've given them more than enough substantive moments. I take a different approach on this question. "Why, are you offering?" Jeremy's spluttering and reddening at an alarming rate, so I go ahead and respond to save him the trouble, "To answer your question, no, I am happily single, there's no man making me into an insecure blubbering idiot every other day." I laugh at the indistinct chorus of agreement from the producers' table. "Tell us more about your love life," Matthew's taken over where Jeremy, yet to recover, has left off. Discussing my love life is awkward although not an unexpected subject of conversation. I guessed it would come up. Fortunately I have little to say on the matter, I have no love life unless you count Trent but that's . . . It is what it is. "There's disappointingly little to say, I'm unattached, been that way for some time." Resolutely taciturn on the topic, despite their best efforts, they're forced to turn the conversation elsewhere. I didn't expect their next inquisition to be in regards to my faith.

"Earlier you mentioned having enormous faith, do you identify as Christian?" On the surface it's a harmless question, but I have an inkling I won't like the reason Matthew's asking. "Absolutely, without question," I respond, waiting for him to get to the point of his inquiry. I don't imagine the gleam in his eyes when he hears my reply, I've walked into whatever trap he's laying. "You're very adamant about your Christianity, would you call yourself devout?" My immediate thought is yes, then I think about when it was I last attended church or even said a prayer. I'm on the defensive now, feeling the need to justify how I believe. True, I haven't been diligent in my relationship with the Lord as of late, but that doesn't make me any less of a believer. "Faith isn't something that can be measured by words like 'devout.' I don't make judgments about the level of faith of others, I certainly won't do it to mine." I school my features into a hard scowl, communicating the closure of the topic. Stephanie and Jeremy accept this without challenge; Matthew, on the other hand, continues to needle me, asking question after question. I remain stoic, refusing to give in to his probing.

When Matthew asks if I have traditional Christian beliefs, I finally realize where he's been going with this line of questioning the entire time. "I see what you're getting at. Unfortunately for you, I won't give the world another Christian to persecute. I have my beliefs and the courage of my convictions, neither of which are up for question or debate. I have nothing further to add, I trust you don't either." Matthew shakes his head no vigorously, denying any duplicitousness on his part. I know better though. He's been trying to rope me into saying something controversial or unpopular, essentially setting me up to be hated. As tolerant as this country claims to be, it isn't so of Christians, except if you're willing to change your, as Matthew puts it, "traditional Christian beliefs." I hate that I shared with him the information he's trying to pervert against me. They look at me placidly, they've taken no offense to my icy retort; I, to the contrary, am done talking. Without waiting to be formally dismissed, I walk to Stephanie, Jeremy, and Matthew's table, shake each of their hands, thank them for the opportunity, and walk out of the room, straight into him.

I close my eyes, sure they're playing a trick on me. "Are you alright?" The voice is strong, smooth, deep, and unquestionably Trenton's. I sneak a peak out of my right eye, Trenton's here all right, my mind couldn't have fashioned him, handsome as he is. He's a welcome sight in an identical outfit to mine; albeit a surprise, but nonetheless welcome. "What are you doing here?" By the sly grin on his face I know he planned this run-in and the his and hers outfits. "I thought I'd come see how things were going." He's being glib again, leaning against the wall arms crossed. I thought after his admission last night things would be . . . different. I lean against the wall opposite him, mirroring his posture; I can be just as nonchalant as he can, "It went." He lets his arms fall to his side, "I know, I watched the whole thing from the control room." He's expecting me to blow up but I keep my cool, I'm not thrilled he saw my casting session but I figured, as executive producer, he would at some point. "How do you think it went?" Instead of sounding unconcerned, like I intended, I come across as uncertain. "I think it went well for the most part. There were a few tense moments which gave you depth, it all looked good to me." I didn't get the sense Stephanie, Matthew, or Jeremy are sold on me; fortunately, Trent doesn't care.

The hallway isn't particularly wide. If we stand shoulder to shoulder we'll brush up against both walls. If we cared to we could touch, but neither of us wants to be the first to let our guard down. Blanket silence spreads across the space between us, the kind of silence used to cover unexpressed words. From this distance it's safe for me to look into his handsome face and acknowledge the part of me that's longing for him, the way he spent six years longing for me. There's so much I want to ask: Why was six years not enough to forget me? Did finally meeting me make the wait worth it? What do you want from me now? Without knowing when I decided to, I cross to Trent; straightaway he turns, facing me. "I'm not sure what's going on in that beautiful head of yours but know this, I want to see you win. You have misgivings about me, which I get, but I'm asking you to give me a chance to show you the real me." My head finds his shoulder, where it stays as minutes pass in uneasy stillness. His fingers drum an irregular beat on his legs. That's when I know he's nervous too. I'm afraid to say yes, he's afraid I'll say no, I can't articulate the hesitation I feel nor can I shake it, thus the quiet stretches on. I sense Trenton casting about for an icebreaker. I know when he finds one because I feel the deep breath he takes before introducing it. "By the way, I liked your post this morning. I think you should have extremely high hopes for that guy." It takes me a minute to recall what video he's talking about. When I do remember I half regret mentioning him. "You're the only one that does, did you read the comments?" My voice comes out muffled; I'm still hiding in the crook of his neck. "You're playing hard to get, that's cute." "I'm not playing hard to get, I am hard to get." The playful banter continues a while longer before I decide I should go. Trent walks me to the lobby, he waits until I'm almost out the door to tell me the spot's mine if I want it. I walk away without responding, I'm not sure I know how to.

I binge watch bad reality TV for the rest of the day, which does nothing to help me make up my mind about the show. My mind's racing a thousand miles per minute with thoughts ranging from where I am, where I want to be, what to do—and Trent, always Trent. Its bizarre how well he seems to know me, understand me, better than friends I've known for years can say they do. I wish I knew him as well as he knows me. I don't know much about him. With the help of Google I can change that.

Shaw, Trenton's last name is Shaw, I hadn't thought to ask him before. It didn't occur to me that I didn't know it until I needed to know it. I find him in my IG friends list, which is now up to three hundred fifty in two days, not bad. His bio includes a link to a recent article profiling him and what they call his "Midas touch." The reporter, clearly charmed by him, manages to include a few details about his personal life, but most of the information could be gleaned from his IMDB page. Several more articles later I've worked up a loose timeline of his rise to success, nothing substantive though. A thorough search of his social media platforms tells me he works a lot, has lots of celebrity friends, loves good food, and the company of beautiful women . . . often. I do learn he's originally from Jersey, he moved to New York eight years ago, I assume for work. I am shocked to learn of his brief modeling stint. Trent doesn't strike me as the type to enjoy that sort of thing. He was good though, had the whole sexy brooder thing down, definite potential. Trent's most recent post, about an hour ago, is a picture of a delicious-looking meal taken at my favorite soul food place in the city. Idly I wonder who's joined him for dinner.

A comment from a woman with a very scantily clad profile picture grabs my attention, "How could you eat without me." The comment doesn't automatically mean anything, it could just be a random flirty follower trying to get his attention, or it could mean he made dinner plans with this woman. I click on her profile picture but her page is set to private. I go back to Trent's page to look through his photos. Some of the posts literally have thousands of comments from women wanting to be with him. I think that's what I've really been looking for, proof he's the womanizer I believe him to be; not a man pining after a woman he saw once six years ago.

Feeling like an insane stalker, I discontinue my investigation, plus it's getting late, I have work in the morning. I've uncovered enough about Trenton to know a further search won't make me feel any better about him, in fact I'm sure it'll do the opposite. For now I'll put it all out of my head, get a good night's sleep, maybe I'll feel better about it in the morning. Before I can go to bed though I have to do one more thing. I'm not exactly dressed for a video, in pajama shorts, but why not, my legs look great; I do ditch my baggy shirt in favor of a tank top. This time I go live, "Hey guys, I just read something that impacted me that I want to share with you. 'I won't make the difference, I'll be the difference.'" I actually read that on Trent's Facebook page, he hasn't updated it in years but it's still active. It caused me to

question if I'll ever get to be a difference maker, regardless of what I may feel toward Trent, my future has to be my number one priority. "That's where my head is right now, being the difference. I want to ask you all a question that I genuinely want to hear the answer to; are you where you thought you'd be six years ago? I can't wait to read your comments; I'll see you all on the other side of night. Oh by the way, the jury has returned a verdict; no I shouldn't have high hopes for him. Anyways, wishing you better luck than me, talk to you soon."

Chapter 4

THE SHRILL SOUND OF my alarm brings reality, the whirlwind of the past few days is over, time to go back to the real world. First things first, I check Instagram, thirty new follows and twenty comments, most of which are about my shorts, excepting a few. @themacattack wrote, "Six years ago I was in school to be an accountant then I got involved with this rap game now I'm getting paid, check out my new mixtape." Plans change, if you're lucky it's for the better, if you're not you end up selling ad space. I feel the customary dread I associate with the start of the workweek as I approach my office. Thank goodness for the three-day weekend, four days left. The elevator's loud with excited chatter teeming from every corner, "I'm already at forty thousand for the month, two hundred percent to goal." Can I truly be the only person that hates this job? Did the other one hundred ninety-nine employees of this office wake up one morning knowing they wanted to sell ad space for thelist.com? If I do not get off this elevator right now I'm going to scream. The next time the doors open I jump out, I'd rather trek up the stairs a few flights than listen to another minute of sales talk.

The stairwell's empty, as I anticipated it would be. I take a seat on the steps while my heart races against itself, faster, faster. Gripping the edge of the stair, I force pain into my fingers, asking my body to acknowledge the discomfort there, to forget the anxiety choking off my air supply. My first day on the sales floor was the first time I ever felt like this. Successful as a trainee but struggling as a full-blown account executive, I'd already made eighty cold calls by midday without setting a single sales appointment. My next call was to an HVAC company in south Jersey, "Hey this is Leah, may I speak with Nick?" I used my cheeriest voice, the one we were taught causes people to be less inclined to hang up on you. "This is Nicky, I don't know any Leah?" At his tone, I lost the chirpiness in favor of assertiveness. "I'm calling from thelist.com which I'm sure you do know, your business has been getting a lot of traffic on our site. Let's talk about how we can turn that into even more revenue for your company." That he hadn't hung up by that point—most people hang up after I say I'm calling from thelist—led me to feel optimistic, which is why I was completely thrown by what happened next. "Listen here, you no-education-having lowlife, I'm an honest businessman. I don't need you harassing me, tying up my phone line when I can be taking real calls. If you call me again I'll sue you and your employer for harassment. Get a real job, you bum." Before he was through with his diatribe something bizarre happened to me. The discomfort I'd been feeling wrapped around my heart, expanded through my whole chest, and burrowed into my lungs. In a haze, I ran to the bathroom for refuge, just as I have every time since.

After it happened again I debated going to see a doctor. Ultimately I decided against it, afraid of what the diagnosis would be. I did mention it to my sister Antonia, who's completing her first year of medical residency, albeit indirectly. I told her about a girl at my office suffering from unusual physical symptoms. She told me without speaking to her, examining her, or getting a medical history she could only speculate, but her guess would be that she was suffering from panic attacks. I picked her brain about why a young woman in good health could be suffering from panic attacks. "I'm not a therapist and again I haven't examined this woman, but she's probably stressed out; tell her to calm down, relax, she'll be okay if she does." Two years later, after doing my best to "relax," I'm still having them, more often than before too; at least I've learned to deal with them, for the most part. Like now I kept the worst symptoms at bay, I'm even ready to face today's torture.

Dylan's sitting in my chair when I make it to my desk, "I missed you yesterday, I hate three-day weekends." With a not-so-gentle shove I shoo him out of my seat, "Let me guess, you hate sunshine and white sand beaches too?" Dylan's not the least bit offended by my dismissal of him, it's part of our routine; he flirts, I shoot him down, round and round we go. "I hate anything that prevents me from seeing you." "Great, I'll remember that, now go back to your desk. I need to start my day." I don't wait for his reply, I'm nowhere near my sales goal for the month. To avoid an uncomfortable meeting about why that is, I need to be busy when my manager gets in, which should be any second. "Who's the guy?" I shrug my shoulders as-suming he must be referring to a new hire but too stressed to give it much of my concern. I tell Dylan as much. "The guy you gave your number to is a new hire?" My fingers immediately stop typing. My Instagram's public, no request needed to follow me. Dylan must be one of the growing number doing so. "Are you following me?" It comes out as an accusation, I'm being ridiculous. I created my Instagram page to gain a following, I just never considered that following might include my coworkers. "Try not to make me sound like a stalker when you say that. You know how the app generates suggested friends, people new to Instagram, you popped up so I followed. Now back to the question at hand."

Doing my best to overcome my embarrassment I return to my monitor, although mortification has given me temporary amnesia; I've completely forgotten what I was working on. Dylan's hovering, waiting for an answer. I pretend to not recall the question, "What did you ask me?" He sighs exasperatedly, "Don't play like you don't remember?" Feigning such great concentration on the task at hand that I can't possibly look away I say, "No one you know." Dylan leans over my desk blocking my monitor and crossing all kinds of personal space boundaries. I push back on my chair, scooting out from behind my desk to put some breathing room between us. Dylan can be dogged at times. I put up with him though because he's the only person in this company I call friend; so instead of expressing how thoroughly annoyed I am about this interrogation and his tactics, I let him.

"Forget about him, go to lunch with me today." His smile is open, inviting, the way Trent's never is: Dylan's handsome, funny, and loyal, but when I look at him all I see is a pal. "I don't think that's a good idea." His disappointment shows on his face, "Why not?" I roll my seat forward wanting the conversation to be over. I hate hurting Dylan, I do it so often that I sometimes forget it does *hurt*. I won't throw salt in the wound by admitting I'm not attracted to him, I'll give him another honest answer. "Because we work together, you know what they say, don't s—" He cuts me off before I finish, "I won't be working here forever." Dylan's the best sales person on the floor, masterful in his abilities to get a sale even out of the most reticent business owner. He's so good at his job that I never imagined he didn't want to be doing it. "You hate it here too?" "I don't hate it but it's not the career path I want. I'm going into sports management. I needed something on my resume to demonstrate my ability to sell—ad space, people, it's all the same thing. I won't be here much longer, maybe then you'll take me up on my offer." Dylan isn't drinking thelist.com Kool-Aid either, but unlike me, he actually has a plan. All I have is a desire.

While we're still talking, a notification from my calendar pops up on my monitor reminding me of the weekly office-wide meeting, taking place in five minutes. I walk with Dylan, who is looking very pleased with himself, to the meeting area. Regional manager Ellie House takes the floor. In typical fashion we start the meeting with an inspirational video, without fail it's turning into a *Wolf of Wall Street* worship meeting. "See those little black boxes? They are called telephones. I'm gonna let you in on a little secret about these telephones. They're not gonna dial themselves! Okay? Without you they're just worthless hunks of plastic." I cannot sit through this again,

I know every word to this speech by now. My eyes wander, desperate to find someone else resisting. What I see is everyone's eyes glued to the screen in earnest attention, as if we hadn't been forced to watch this clip no less than one hundred times. When the clip is over the rest of the meeting continues to unfold in ordinary fashion; sell, sell, sell, don't take no for an answer, "Always Be Closing," yada, yada, yada. At the end of the meeting we stand to close out with the *Wolf of Wall Street* chest beat accompanied by the money chant. If I wasn't sure before, I know by the last chest thump, I quit. I don't want to be a telephone terrorist.

Immediately after the meeting I direct message my manager, Tiffany, asking if we can talk. "Sure . . . meet in five." The minutes drag but the designated time arrives. "It's a shame, you know, cause I always taught you guys to keep pushing, to never give up the phone until you get what you want. Because you all deserve it." Here I am telling her I'm quitting because I hate this job; her response, as usual, is to quote Jordan Belfort. "That's another thing, you may find this life altering but Jordan Belfort is not a hero. He is the personification of the twisted American dream and what we'll do to have it." She looks as if I'd slapped her in the face open palmed, all red and splotchy with anger. "You know your attitude has been suffering lately, if you want to quit, go ahead, it's your loss." I leave Tiffany still reeling from my assessment of her idol. I almost feel sorry. Not sorry enough to regret my decision or to miss her once I'm gone. I won't miss this place at all. I put the last bit of my personal effects in my purse. "Going home early?" On second thought, I will miss something.

I loathe this job, the building, the meetings; I abhor everything about it yet I know if I look at Dylan right now I'll cry. It's absurd that I'm actually saddened to leave behind this place I detest, and yet . . . It's the devil I know. What lies ahead is unknown, therefore infinitely more terrifying. "I'm out of here, Dylan, I'm done." He stops my assault on my purse's zipper with a firm hand atop mine, "Are you serious, were you f—?" I cut him off, upset he would think for a moment that this wasn't my choice. "I quit, I can't stomach this job anymore. If your first thought is I must have been fired that means my performance is beginning to reflect my dissatisfaction. Better I leave now while the choice is still mine." I close my eyes to relieve the pressure building behind my eyes. I open them when I hear Dylan say, "I only noticed because I was looking." His voice is soft, almost mournful, he's taking my leaving harder than I am. Through packing, there's no reason to delay any further. I lead Dylan to the elevator bank to say goodbye. "What are you going to do, do you have another job lined up?" I didn't contemplate what would happen next, I merely reacted, maybe too hastily. I can't afford to fret over it now, what's done is done. I am touched by how much Dylan cares, though. I hug him tight. "Don't worry about me, I'll be fine." He clutches to me long after I've let him go, "Don't be a stranger." The elevator door closes between us, closing the door on one chapter of my life and hopefully opening a window to a new one.

Chapter 5

THE SUN'S EXTENDED STAY during the warmer months has always made summer my favorite season of the year. I sit in Union Square Park letting the rays of the sun coax me into a better mood; warm, bright days have always made me feel hopeful and I've never needed to feel more hopeful than I do now. The park is full of people: playing music, dancing, sitting, being carefree. I've forgotten how that feels. I gaze up at the bright sky looking for what life will be like for me in five years, I can't picture it, I haven't been able to for months. What I do see is the past.

"Okay guys, listen up, you all are cordially invited to be my guest to the Oscars, five years from now. Don't make that face, I'm being serious; I have it all worked out. In a few months I'll be certified SAG, thank you, Central Casting. Next year I'll have secured an agent, responsible for getting me the best auditions, all while I continue to do print and commercial modeling. Year three I'll have a career-making episode arc on a groundbreaking dramedy, then have to relocate to Los Angeles on the heels of that success. I'll read a script that I fall in love with and know that I have to be part of, I'll be cast in the supporting role but give an emotional performance. My agent will call me with the news that I've been nominated by the academy for best supporting actress. I'll stun on the red carpet wearing a Giambattista Valli gown. And when they announce I've won, I will give a moving speech I can barely get through because as much as I said I would do it, I never really believed I could."

My eyes fly open the way they do when I wake from a bad dream, but that was no nightmare, it's a memory. I remember everything, including Trent staring at me across the room, as he does now, from across the park. Blindly my feet find the pavement, carrying me to him. When I'm within arm's reach I slow my pace. I feel as if I'm seeing him through different eyes; he's the lady-killer I met at the lounge a few nights ago, he's also the guy who's waited six years to meet me. Diffidently he opens his arms, inviting me in. The gesture reminds me so much of the younger, less confident him that I barrel into his chest. After an audible sigh he asks, "What's wrong?" "Why do you think something's wrong?" He pulls away slightly without letting go, "You mean besides the fact that you asked to see me?" I smirk but my brain is in turmoil, how can I explain to him what's bothering me is definitely knowing he was truthful about six years ago? What does it mean, is it fate, are we meant to be? I can barely think about these questions let alone answer them. I decide not to tell him what I remember just yet, it can wait, at this moment the focus has to be on the most pressing issue. "I quit my job today."

Antonia would usually be my first call after a day like this. I thought about going to her but this is out of her league. My purpose in meeting with Trent isn't for comfort it's to get his help. "That's great news," he says. "You've freed yourself to chase success, starting with the show; taping begins next week." His hands find my face. His expression, so earnest, entreats my attention. I'm hanging onto his every move, sure he's about to erase all my doubts concerning him. "This is your time to go after what you want." Yes, I think I will. "You've been a hamster on a wheel, a dog chasing it's own tail; with my guidance you'll achieve everything you ever wanted. Don't cower in a corner, playing small, afraid, because it's not the conventional way of doing things. Who cares that it wasn't part of your plan, 'His' plan, or whatever else you believe. I'm going to make you a star, you can put your faith in that."

I pull away from him, disturbed, some part of me asked to meet knowing this is what Trent would say. He offered me the world the very first time we spoke, of course he would again. Deep down that must be what I want, no matter how perturbed I am by his language, because I'm on the precipice of accepting. I take a seat on a nearby bench. I don't know that I want to be near Trent now, or ever again. There's something intrinsically wrong with what he said, but God help me, I'm teetering. All I need is a slight nudge over the ledge, "Is this how you behave when you're afraid?" Trent asks, still standing where I left him. "I have no idea what you're talking about, what am I afraid of?" He joins me on the bench, "I'm talking about your dreams, bottom line is I can make them come true; just say the word, your wish will be my command." I look to the sky for a sign I know I won't get, maybe I've already received it, and it's sitting right next to me. I eye Trent and hope to God I'm not about to make a mistake, "I'm in. Make me a star." His smile is slow and not altogether encouraging, "Consider it done."

We sit side by side, neither of us speaking, my mind too full of what I just agreed to. When the adrenaline from the moment fades I realize the persistent buzzing in my ears is actually a nagging thought. What's in it for Trent? What does he want? Since we met I've been in a perpetual state of confusion about him. Initially I thought he wanted something from me, now I still think he does, but maybe not for the reasons I imagined. Unable to come to a satisfactory conclusion in my mind I ask him.

Trent leans forward, places his elbows on his knees, and interlocks his fingers. He's uncomfortable, whatever he's about to tell me isn't easy for him to say. "Earlier when you texted me I was wrapping up an important meeting," he begins. After several minutes he continues, "I signed a production deal today . . . The first story I plan on producing is a about a guy who saw a girl, once, six years ago. He can't get her out of his head or his heart. He dates and tries to care for other women, but even though he's never actually met her he knows she's the one. He works hard to be successful, to make a name for himself, believing he would see her again, and when he did he would impress her with all he'd amassed. Every club, every restaurant, every meeting he searches; hoping to see her face, then one day he does."

"How does he know she's 'the one'?" I ask. "Because she made him . . . she made him believe in love at first sight." Technically, Trent didn't say he loves me, he said the guy in the story loves the elusive woman, but what if he does? Do I love him back? "What if she doesn't feel the same way?" His eyes, ringed with emotion, hold mine, "He'll make her, he's not willing to lose her." My stomach flutters nervously at the intensity in his stare and the implication of his words. That's the second time during the course of this conversation he's said something slightly, *off.* I like Trent very much, if my reluctance were solely a matter of how I feel it would be a much simpler business. What's troubling me is what I see underneath the chink in his armor.

"Sounds like a beautiful story, although I'm sure I've heard it before." It's a hurtful answer to a hypothetical declaration of love. Trent thinks so too, I read as much in the stiffening of his posture and the hard line around his mouth. All sweet sincerity have gone out of him, he's angry and it's my fault. What's worse, I don't know why I said what I did; whatever the reason may be, I brace myself for Trent's justifiably equally hurtful reaction. "You're trying to push me away because you're afraid you like me as much as I like you. What you don't realize yet is I won't be scared off." I expected a nasty exchange not a return of his bravado. "For your information I'm not afraid of anything, I'm from Brooklyn, walking out my door is scary, you are not." The corners of his mouth turn up before he starts laughing, suddenly all the tension of the previous moment is gone and I'm laughing too.

Trent's hand finds mine, immediately our fingers interlock, a small gesture of pronounced significance; people in love intertwine their fingers. "Have dinner with me tonight, there's someone I want you to meet," Trent says more than he asks. "Who do you want me to meet?" I don't really care who it is, I'm going, he doesn't need to know that though. "Does it matter? You're unemployed, you have nothing better to do." I jab him in his side with a stiff finger, "You jerk, you're lucky a girl's gotta eat. Make sure you bring the black card, I have a taste for lobster and the most expensive wine they carry." "What makes you think I have a black card?" "If you don't I've given you something to aspire to." He stands and holds out a hand, which I take, to help me up behind him, "I like that you keep me on my toes." I hold onto him longer than necessary, when the sparks are more than crackling between us I pull my hand away. "You're learning, flattery will get you every-where, pick me up tonight around seven. I'll text you the address."

At six forty-five I arrive at Amanda's wearing an ivory off-the-shoulder blouse, tucked into raw denim high-waist jeans, and blue suede pumps. "Why's Trent meeting you at my house?" Amanda asks. She's usually wel-coming and friendly, though tonight she barely acknowledges me before she goes on a tear. "Because I don't want him to know where I live." "Why not?" Amanda isn't keen about the idea of Trent and me, that much I know, but her attitude right now is borderline hostile. I bite my tongue, hoping to avoid a fight with her. "Besides not wanting to explain still living at home, things are moving at a weird pace. We met four days ago, we've seen each other every day since. We're not dating but something is clearly happening there. I need to slow things down, get a grip on our situationship." Amanda hasn't let me in past her front door yet; she blocks my path with crossed arms and a cold demeanor. "You talked about him on Instagram two days ago, plus you posted about him thirty minutes ago. You like him enough to tell the world but not enough to tell him where you live, seems backward to me."

Before heading to Amanda's I posted an update video, I promised my followers I would. "We're grabbing dinner tonight, not a date, possibly the first step toward one." I hadn't given it a second thought until Amanda's re-mark. "And," she holds her phone out to me, "what's up with this?" Amanda's pulled up my IG, my first thought is I must have been hacked, then I think who would want to hack me? Worriedly I give my page a thorough review, I find nothing I hadn't posted myself, plus I'm up to nine hundred twenty follows. I shrug, unsure of what Amanda wanted me to see. She gives me a once over, I'm thinking Amanda's finally going to drop the attitude and acknowledge my outfit, she doesn't. "What's up with you? You're not acting like yourself." Up until this point I've tried to ignore her boorishness, chalk-ing it up to a bad day. I realize now no matter how reasonable I am, Amanda will find a reason to fight with me because she wants to. Two can play that game; if it's a fight she wants a fight she'll get.

"Odd, I was just about to say the same about you. Not five days ago you gave me a lecture about not settling, not being afraid to take risk, being open to love. The moment I take your advice you have a problem with my behavior. Usually you're my loudest cheerleader: encouraging, fun, and loyal, but lately all you've been, where I'm concerned anyway, is contrary." The look of disbelief on her face is one I've never seen her wear before, "I'm contrary? That's rich coming from the social media nun turned Instafamous hungry whore."

If Amanda slapped me with all the strength in her body it would have hurt less. "All of this," I sweep my hand between us, "is about your disapproval of Trent. What baffles me is, you were the one pointing out how gorgeous he is. When you started dating Mark I championed your relationship, has it occurred to you maybe it's my turn, that Trent might be the one to love me, the way Mark loves you. He may not be the man for me, maybe he is, the point is I won't know until I give it a chance." I can tell she feels bad about calling me a whore, her eyes won't meet mine. I'm nearly gone when she says I should be careful of Trent. She's soft spoken, devoid of anger probably because now I'm the angry one; she can't attack me then play the victim. I face her ready for round two, this time I'm going for the TKO.

"You told me I'd become passive about my life, well I'm awake now thanks to Trent." Amanda looks at me with sad eyes that only serve to further upset me. "From now on I'm doing me, I'm going to do whatever I feel is best for me without unsolicited commentary. No one is entitled to an opinion on my life. I'm doing the show, I'm going to dinner with Trent tonight, and if I want to post a million sexy pictures I will. If you have an issue with that, that's your business, because I'll be handling mine."

I leave Amanda's with thoughts of Ubering it home when a Mercedes Benz coup pulls up. I'm still admiring the car when Trent gets out looking like a walking Paul Smith ad. He looks good in his casual cobalt suit, if there is such a thing as a casual suit. I feel plain next to him. He came dressed to impress. Trent dressed to impress me; he wants me to know he's all in. He smiles at me and I think, "because she made him believe in love at first sight." Without a word he walks to the passenger door, opens it and waits for me to get in. Keenly I watch him as he closes my door, walks back around to the driver's side, and gets in. I think he meant to greet me but when his glimmering eyes met mine the words die on his lips, his hands cup my face as he leans in then jumps back at the shrill ringing of my phone. Without looking I send the call to voicemail, the only person I want to speak to is sitting right next to me.

"So you thought you'd upstage me?" I ask jokingly. "Impossible, but I did think I should compliment you by looking my best." Best doesn't begin to explain how handsome he looks. I haven't taken my eyes off him yet; I like looking at him without him looking at me, I get to fully enjoy how handsome he is, although I'd prefer to not admit it to him. "Oh this is your best? How disappointing." He scoffs at that, Trent knows how attractive he is, he needs no validation. To prevent myself from doing something impulsive like complementing him I turn the conversation to our plans for the night. "Where're you taking me?" "Unsigned night at River Blu." His eyes momentarily flicker in my direction holding mine long enough to see my reaction, one of satisfaction. I love River Blu. "Sounds fun." We talk about their best dishes as I check their Facebook for tonight's lineup. All the posts about unsigned night have tagged Cashmere Sage, the Instafamous stripper. "Is this who you want me to meet?" His eyes quickly travel between my phone and the road. "Yeah, she came into town early to host unsigned night. She'll be sticking around afterward, Cashmere's your castmate."

It might be having had my career efforts so recently compared to the antics of the Cashmere Sages' of the world, or maybe it's because I don't share the same fascination for strippers prevalent in our society as everyone else—whatever the case, I want no association with her. "Cashmere Sage is not a cast member, is she?" I'm really hoping this is Trent's idea of a joke, if not . . . she hasn't even left the pole yet, how could he put me in this position? "Yeah she is, something wrong with that?" His tone is dry, defensive, challenging. "For starters, Cashmere's beloved for showing off her . . . assets not her talent, whatever it may be. If she's part of the show no one will take it or anyone connected with it seriously." I feel somehow betrayed by him. Trent's none too happy with me either, I can tell by the clenching of his jaw. "First, she hasn't been a stripper for a while, although I don't see why it matters either way. Second, I wouldn't be so quick to judge her, Cashmere has the same aspirations as you, she's just not afraid to commit to doing whatever it takes to achieve them. Criticize her methods if you like, but she's hosting, meanwhile you're attending. You could learn a thing or two from her."

"Whoa, sensitive much? Clearly she's a sore subject for you and there's nothing she can teach me that I'd be interested in learning." I'm trying and failing not to read too much into his defense of Cashmere. It's not only that he defended her, it's that he did it at my expense. I don't want to be part of a show she's involved with for noble reasons; I might have discovered a personal one too. "One million YouTube subscribers and Instagram follows, not to mention over a hundred thousand dollars in partnerships, says otherwise." Why invite me out to see another woman, which he probably dated at some point—I do use the word date very loosely—then make a point of telling me how much more successful she is than me? When Trent pulled up earlier I thought tonight would be one of those nights that twenty, thirty years later I'd remember with fondness. I'll remember it all right, as the worst first non-date ever.

Trent parks in front of the restaurant but doesn't make a move to get out. I reach for the door handle then hear it lock before I can open it. "You do realize I can unlock it right?" Those are the first words I've spoken to him since our disagreement. The last twenty minutes have passed in tension-filled silence. "Yes I do, but I was hoping you'd give me the opportunity to apologize." I keep my head straight forward, I won't give him the occasion to charm me with his eyes. "Apologize about what?" He reaches for my hand; I'm quicker than he is in moving out of his grasp. His outstretched hand hangs midair a little longer before he lets it fall. "About, how south this has gone. Things were supposed to go much differently." I consider letting it go then remember how he made a point to recognize Cashmere's success by pointing out my failure. He's not getting off the hook that easily, "I don't know what 'this' you're talking about. You wanted me to meet someone, I agreed without knowing who, huge mistake on my part; we're here now, let's get it over with, let the play date commence."

Out of the corner of my eye I see his hand move, followed by the un-mistakable door unlock sound, "Let's go then." He no longer sounds apologetic, he sounds frustrated. "You denigrated me, what right do *you* have to be offended?" Anger rolls off him in waves crashing into mine, both of us feeling righteous in our indignation. "I'm sorry the night has turned into this raging battle, but I'm not sorry for what I said. You have such strong opinions on what you won't do and on what others have done, not realizing the only thing that will get you is the self achievement of being 'moral' but unsuccessful. You better figure out what you want, how much you want it, and what you'd do to get it, because Cashmere did and she's on her way to the top." He gets out of the car, leaving me to come to him or go home, to claim success or anonymity.

I can't help the tears sliding down my cheeks, I'm furious with Trent for causing me to feel even more uncertain about myself, my life. I feel that way enough without his help. Trent confirmed what I'd begun to understand, there is no longer a place in this world for a person like me. I'm beautiful, intelligent, sophisticated, and talented, but being those things won't get me anywhere. If I want to win I have to be more like Cashmere: sultry, sexy, uninhibited, down for anything. I know what I have to do; I wipe my tears, dab a bit of powder on my face, and take one for the gram.

Chapter 6

I FOLLOW THE HOSTESS into the dining room, where I see Cashmere Sage popping out of a too tight leather dress with her chest hanging out. She's draped a hand around Trent's shoulder as she feeds him an appetizer. Trent catches sight of me when I'm almost upon them. I ignore him and extend a French-manicured hand to Cashmere. "Hi, I'm Leah. I see you and Trent started without me." I address her in a friendly, nonconfrontational tone. She responds as I thought she would, with bright orange-clawed fingernails. "You know Trenton, patience isn't one of his virtues." I eye her hand comfortably tucked in the crook of Trent's arm and feel a surge of possessiveness. "Actually I know the opposite to be true of him, as they say." Ignoring Cashmere, I look Trent in his eyes. "Anything worth having is worth waiting for." "I always thought that was just something ugly prudes say." She snarls at me, literally snarls; if I weren't infuriated I'd laugh. "I understand how waiting could be counterproductive for someone in your field of uh . . . expertise." Her face contorts with rage, "Excuse me?" "Yes, you are excused, it seems that you're wanted on stage. Don't worry about Trent, we'll manage."

Trent interjects, telling Cashmere the manager has indeed been attempting to get her attention. With a kiss on the cheek, a pointed look at me, and a sway of her purchased rear, she's gone. I take the seat across from him, processing all that's happened since I quit my job this morning, something I probably would not have done if he hadn't planted the thought in my head. I might have lost a friendship defending my interest in Trent, a pain all the more acute due to the ridicule I endured from him after defending *him*. To add insult to injury he humiliated me with Cashmere. What have I done, is the question heaviest on my mind, but he can't answer that, I ask him something he can.

"How involved were you with her?" When he clears his throat I know ahead of time I won't like his answer, "I didn't wait six years to meet her." Trent means it to be reassuring; it is in some ways, it also far from excuses

42

what just happened. "What is the point of tonight?" "The point was for you to make an ally ahead of taping, and for us to enjoy each other's company. That obviously didn't work out." I have a hard time accepting Trent being naïve enough to believe Cashmere and I could be allies even if things went exactly as planned; she's his ex, I'm his next . . . maybe. It doesn't add up. "I think you meant rival, you want me to have a rival, someone to spar with for the cameras. Tonight has been a colossal mistake, it's gone from bad to worse. I'm going to exit before anything else happens to sink my opinion of you even further."

I take my time collecting my purse hoping he'll say something to convince me not to go, knowing he won't. I know this because he's on his phone, completely ignoring my presence. When I can no longer delay I get up from the table. Trent stops me with a look I can't quite read, whatever it means it causes a well of hope to surge within me. If he asks me to stay, I will, "I won't stop you from walking out of here. I'm too tired of fighting with you to try to do that, if you feel you have to leave, go." I'm holding on by a fraying thread and he just gave me a punch to the gut; the only thing keeping me from a total breakdown is the desire not to do so publicly. How can Trent feel strongly enough for me to not allow six years to erode his longing but not enough to stop me from parting with him again? "I agree with you about the constant fighting, I don't have it in me to go back and forth with you for the next few hours in exchange for five minutes of unguarded truth either." I pause to catch my breath and realize my heartaches, the cost of tonight's debacles. He's as handsome as ever but all I feel at the moment is fatigued. "I'm drained. You are draining. I won't keep arguing with you, so do what you like with whomever you like, just keep me out of it."

Sitting in the Uber feeling distraught I give into self-pity: I lost my job, best friend, and Trent all within a few hours. The worst part is both Trent and I being too disenchanted with the other to try to salvage this thing between us, six years of anticipation culminated into one of the worst nights of my life. My phone chimes, alerting me of a new email from ishawtrenton@gmail.com. My heart leaps in my chest until I realize it's merely an electronic copy, to be signed, of my contract for Star Quality. I skim it over without understanding a thing other than my own hurt. For a second I thought he was sitting in that restaurant alone, feeling as wounded as I am, missing me, wanting to apologize; I see now the only thing Trent wants is a hit show. Amanda was right, my first instincts were right. Maybe if I act quickly I can undo the worst of the damage entertaining him has done. I'll call Tiffany in the morning and pledge allegiance to Jordan Belfort.

The lights are on in the kitchen, meaning my mom's awake and moving around. There's no way in without facing off with her, something I am not prepared to do. I've never been good at lying to her. If I give it a few minutes maybe I won't have to. However when the third stray cat wanders over I decide I've waited long enough. My mom's clearing the table when I walk in. I smile, mutter a hurried greeting, and continue walking past her, but she says my name in that authoritative voice she reserves for scolding; habit induces me to stop. She examines my face with her knowing eyes, "You've been crying." I don't bother denying it; she didn't ask a question, she made a statement. My mom doesn't need me to confirm what she already knows. "You've been walking around for months like a shell of my Leah. Sometimes I get glimpses of my daughter, but this person," she indicates my whole being from top to bottom with a flick of her hands, "is a stranger. She has no courage, no faith, no hope; I want to know where my girl has gone?"

Barely holding it together to begin with, my mom's rebuke gnaws at the little bit of composure I have left. "I'm not equipped to have this conversation right now, I'm going to bed, okay." "No, it's not okay, you are my business until one of us leaves this earth; until then I will not sit and watch you fade away." I lose every ounce of self-possession I was struggling to maintain. "Okay you want to know what's wrong? Everything, literally everything, and nothing, because that's exactly what I have. I am twenty-six years old and I have nothing. My life is a joke; me believing I was different, special, set apart was the punch line. All my friends are successful, starting families, getting married, and I come home to my mom every night." I'm somehow managing to talk through the panic bubbling up within me, it's important I say the truth out loud at least once.

"I went to sleep one night with all the potential in the world and woke up as the woman in your song." My mom's face is a mask of confusion; she doesn't know what I'm talking about. That she could forget the song that shaped my life floors me, I have to make her remember. "Je me réveille des rêves d'ete dans le mort d'hiver. I'm dreaming of summer in the dead of winter. Do you remember all those cold weather advisories issued this past winter; warning temperatures were too frigid to survive in for extended periods of time? It was too cold outside to breathe. That's me every day, I can't breath. Every minute, every second, I fight a losing battle for air. I claw at the hands suffocating me until I finally comprehend the battle is futile; the hands crushing my windpipe belong to life. I've given up and welcome the rest of defeat."

It's a figurative and literal truth. I can't breath; every breath is harder fought for than the last. I fight through it knowing I won't be okay until I get it all out. "By the way, in a bout of irrationalism I quit my job and committed to a reality show because some guy I like talked me into it. Except we got into a huge fight. Now I've lost him, the show, and Amanda, who by the way also feels I've lost touch with myself. My life is disappointing to say the absolute least." My behavior's manic even to myself; I have no control of the frenzied energy fueling me. I've handled my anger and sadness so carefully for such a long time, not allowing either emotion sovereignty. I've swallowed down every hurt, every disappointment, and every tear until this very moment. I can't fight them anymore, they've overpowered their thoughtfully constructed boxes pushing to the surface. "What did I do wrong, huh, what? They say go to school, do this do that, if you do all these things you'll be successful, but I'm not, and now I'm out of options." I slump against the wall separating the kitchen from the living room, my chest heaving up and down. I'm lightheaded and scarcely able to stand; if not for the wall I'd be on the floor. I ward off my mother's concern, her attempts to come nearer to me, with an outstretched hand I can barely keep up. I don't want to be helped, I want to rage against my mom, Amanda, Trent, life, myself.

"Leah, Leah, tell me what's wrong." The panic in my mom's voice reignites my fury. "Don't you get it? I'm tired of faking it, faking being alive. Daily I go through my routine: one foot in front of the other, speak when appropriate, smile and nod, meanwhile I'm aching on the inside. I have about this much left in me." I hold my index finger and thumb an inch apart. "I'm going to use it to crawl into bed." My vision darkens at the edges; the fight has gone out of me, leaving me as weak as I truly am. My knees buckle, I fall to the ground hard, hyperventilating. Worn out, I let my eyes close, giving in to the mounting pain in my chest.

I thought your life was supposed to flash before your eyes before you died, a montage of the moments that shaped your existence. Mine is stuck; I see one moment only, my mom bringing a paper bag to my mouth while repeating something I keep missing. After a while I decide it must be the present, I guess I'm not dying after all. I'm still on the floor, head cushioned in my mom's lap, the word she's saying is "breathe." The bag worked, I'm not suffocating anymore; I do feel spent though. I don't know if I fainted or if fatigue floored me, but here we are, mother and daughter, lying on the kitchen floor in the aftermath of truth.

I wait for the questions I'm sure will come. They never do, the only thing my mom says is "we should go to bed." For some reason the thought of sleeping paralyzes me with fear, I'm afraid I won't wake up. I don't want to die alone . . . Minutes later I crawl into my mom's bed, something I haven't done since the age of twelve. She's not snoring; she's awake although she says nothing. I'm settled beneath her comforter when she finally does. "Let us not become weary in doing good, for at the proper time we will reap a harvest if we do not give up." After years of Bible study I instantly recognize the scripture as Galatians 6 verse 9. I don't have the strength to acknowledge

I've heard her, all I can do is let her voice soothe me. "I have always been so proud of your drive, but even prouder of who you are, your character. Don't resign yourself to defeat, your season is coming, but remember this: 'What does it cost a man to gain the world but lose his soul?'"

Chapter 7

THE NEXT FEW DAYS pass somberly in a haze of TV and social media. Friday afternoon I oblige my followers with a picture, armed with the remote and a bag of spicy Doritos, I smile for the camera. I'm surprised to see a reaction from Trent; we haven't spoken since the infamous night, unless email counts. He emails me daily, never anything personal, always business. I've yet to sign the contract and the first day of filming approaches. I've had time to calm down, to think about things forward and backward. What I've come up with is, I miss him. Stupid, I know but I can't help it, which is why I'm agonizing over if and how to respond to his reaction. Before I come to a decision Trent direct messages me, "Have you received any of my many emails?" I wait eleven minutes before answering, ten would be too obvious. "'Hey Leah, how are you?' would have been nice before jumping right into business." Trent's response is immediate, "Maybe I would've led with that if I thought it would be well received." He responds to himself before I can, "Hi Leah, how are you?" "Why do you care better yet what do you want?" His response comes in the form of emojis I don't know how to read. "I am not ashamed to admit I have no idea how to interpret that." It's not like there's such a thing as Hooked on Phonics Emojicon Edition, I'm going to need Trent to translate. "How about we have a real conversation; face to face. Would you be willing to meet me somewhere?" Desire defeats my resolve, I agree to meet, unbeknownst to him, at the pier near my home in half an hour.

It takes me ten minutes to walk there, I use that time to organize my thoughts: what I want to say, what I want from him. I'm so lost in my own mind that I don't see Trent until I'm standing behind him. He's sitting on a wood bench facing the water, mind clearly far away; he doesn't notice me. Trent's the most casual I've ever seen him in blue jeans and a long-sleeved white tee shirt. He's also the most unkempt and tense I've seen him. Even with one arm coolly draped across the back of the bench I see the stress in his posture. Inquisitively, I lean over his shoulder to get a peak at his phone; the thing he's been studying since I've arrived is a picture of me.

Trent turns and sees me, quickly he puts his phone away—little good it does, I've already seen the picture. He definitely has an eye for photography, the photo is brilliant. I'm a study of illumination, as the sun beams on me and off me from every angle, like tin I reflect light. It was taken the day we met up in Union Square Park. I remember feeling like Trent had been watching me for a while before I saw him, now I know he was. He's done it again, that thing he does that makes me question my harshest judgments of him. Trent's given me a glimpse of his truest self, reducing me to speechlessness. "I've been through a lot," he begins. "I've experienced some of the worst things that can happen to a person, because of that, I don't fear much. But I do fear not having you in my life." He stands, putting the full weight of his presence behind his words. "Since that night at the lounge I've been terrified of you getting away. It's hard to know if I should come on stronger or back off. We might part ways today never to speak again. If you decide you want nothing further to do with me I doubt I can change your mind, but at least with this," he indicates his phone, "I'd have something to hold onto."

Everything I planned to say is forgotten at the revelation of his anguish. He's hurt, as hurt as I am, more so even. His eyes have lost their luster, his smile their twinkle, he isn't being charming or guarded; Trent's being his most raw self. If I'm heartbroken, Trent is shattered. I feel the overwhelming desire to comfort him; I extend my hand, without knowing if it'll be a friendly or intimate gesture. He brings my palm to his lips deciding for me. My hand, still firmly in his, travels to his heart where it stays, hoping to mend the injury I've caused. He sighs heavily, exorcising the tension in his body. Nothing is resolved, but I'm blissful standing here with him forgetting the strain of the last few days.

We spend the next hour at the pier, sometimes talking, sometimes simply enjoying the knowledge the other is there. Whereas I've turned my gaze to the flowing water, Trent's eyes have yet to leave my face. "You're so creepy; if you weren't ridiculously handsome I'd call it harassment." I face him to find he's smiling; he's egotistical enough to bypass the insult and cling to the compliment. "I am exceptionally good looking, there have been many nights that I lay awake thinking of my sexiness. If I could share my pretty with those less gifted, well, I wouldn't, but I would allow them to gaze upon my beauty at length." Playful is not a quality I'd usually attribute to Trent, however there is no mistaking the playfulness in his voice now; oddly enthused I play along. "Fair sir, I do not know how you live daily afflicted, as you are with endless pools of adonis gifted to you." I put my hand to my forehead in dramatic fashion and swoon. "Oh gods be good, if you were to

but look upon my plain face with your fairness from henceforth to forev-
ermore I shall be yours." He pulls my hand away from my forehead with
two fingers gently placed beneath my chin, guiding my face to his, all traces
of puckishness gone. "I was thinking of beauty, but not mine, I was thinking you're even more beautiful now than you were six years ago. I wouldn't
mind waking up to you everyday."

My heart sinks into my stomach, is he making a statement or asking
a question? If it's a statement I can get away with not answering. If it's a
question I have to respond, but how? I have feelings for him, I want to be
part of his life; beyond that much, I don't know. Why did he have to ruin
the moment? I wanted so much to stay in our lighthearted bubble, maybe
I can redirect the conversation, recreate the mood. "You say that now but
it wouldn't exactly be this face you'd be waking up to." The vein in his jaw
twitches before he looks away annoyed, I pretend not to notice and chatter
on about skincare. "My girl beautymefab has changed my life. I found her
channel a year ago, now I don't understand how I survived without her. She
taught me about the ten-step routine; I know, it's a lot of steps, but can you
say miracle worker." My mouth is moving a mile a minute as I drone on and
on, but I think my plan is working. He looks mystified; I might've lost him
at beautymefab. I continue on for another five minutes about oils, toners,
masks, and essences before he stops me.

"Don't do that." I don't get the chance to ask what it is he doesn't want
me to do; Trent brings his index finger to my lips, shushing my unasked
question. "You're deflecting, hoping I'll feel embarrassed and abandon
the conversation. I won't. I'm too confident to feel self-conscious. I'm not
ashamed of what I've felt for you everyday for the last six years, but I know
you're not ready yet to have a real conversation about what that means." He
cups my face with gentle hands I lean into, "You are the most . . ." A small
smile plays on his perfect lips as he searches for the right word, "ironic person I know. What you fear most is also what you most desire. Love makes
you nervous: what you feel for me scares you, what I feel for you downright
terrifies you. Regardless of how many times you pretend not to hear what we
both know I said, it won't change a thing in my heart."

I am afraid of being with him, letting myself feel what I do. When he
touches me my heart races and I fear he'll let go. When we fight I'm petrified
we've spoken our last words to each other. And when I look at him, like I
am right now, I'm terrified he's already stolen my heart. But there's more to
it, so often I want nothing more than to surrender to him, but an unnamed
doubt seizes me. My defenses are weakening though, the only weapons I
have left against Trent are anger and humor. "You're completely off base, I'm
not afraid of love. I'll have you know the only reason I'm still on the market

is that I'm waiting on the man able to afford at *least* a four-carat ring, until then I'll remain happily single." He laughs out loud, "Four carats, I'll keep that in mind." As the laughter dies the mood shifts. "There's something I need to say."

"I owe you an apology." The absolute last words I expected Trent to utter. I thought at best we'd move forward pretending nothing ever happened, I never imagined Trent being thoughtful enough to admit to and apologize for his mistakes. "When I invited you to dinner I didn't intend on things turning out how they did. I waited six years to intentionally be in the same place at the same time with you, it was supposed to be perfect." He looks at me sheepishly, men like Trent don't usually say things like that aloud, sentimentality doesn't exactly fit their image. On a lesser man I might find his mawkishness unappealing, on Trent it has the opposite effect. I find it makes him slightly more real, more attainable. "Maybe I wanted it too badly," he continues, "which explains why Murphy's Law was in full effect." I nod my head in agreement. I envisioned Trent and me having an enchanted evening, not the catastrophe that ensued. Come to think of it that whole day from start to finish was disastrous. A wiser woman might call that a sign.

"Cashmere and I," he begins hesitantly, "we had a short-lived, completely casual fling ages ago." I shift in my seat uncomfortably at the mention of her. I figured out on my own they were previously involved , that doesn't lessen the sting from having it confirmed. I'm seated as closely to him as I was moments ago, but a distance has settled between us. Probably sensing it as well Trent hurries to explain, "I didn't think she would react to you the way she did, although in hindsight I should've foreseen her cattiness; I would have if I weren't blinded by my agenda. I thought meeting her would help you see there is no one linear way of achieving success. Cashmere didn't take the conventional route but she's made a name for herself. I'm serious about helping you accomplish your goals, but I want you to know what that can sometimes look like. There are multiple paths to the same destination. If the directions you're following leads to road blocks try another course."

I leave Trent seated on the bench while I walk to the edge of the dock, watching the water ebb and flow. There's logic in his argument, though the frame of thinking is unprincipled; the ends do not always justify the means. Bronze, muscled arms embrace me from behind, bodies perfectly in sync; it would be easy to ignore the part of me that is uncomfortable with his reasoning, but the better part of me knows I shouldn't. I resist the pull of amorous bliss long enough to voice the fault in his rational, "When you input a destination in your GPS it calculates multiple routes, however it prioritizes the best one." He sighs into my neck, sending pinpricks up my spine. "Which," he begins, then stops to trace the curve of my neck up to my ear, "is always," he continues, "the fastest route, which is what I'm offering." I still disagree with him. Sometimes the quickest route means paying an expensive toll, but I let the argument die. I don't want to have another heated exchange with him, I'd prefer to enjoy being in his arms.

Settled against his chest, basking in the sun, I suddenly feel sentimental. Being wistful and less defensive than usual, I ask Trent to tell me something, anything. It doesn't matter to me what he choses to share, I just want to feel close to him, like I truly know him. "We wrapped preproduction today, the only thing left is the issue of your contract, you haven't sent it back yet." Filming begins in two days, Trent's right to discuss business, although when I asked him to tell me something I had more romantic ideas in mind. Initially I didn't return my contract because I was upset with him; ultimately, my frustration exposed my reservations. I'm having difficulty committing to the project because it would signify consciously dismissing the principles that have guided me for twenty-six years. "L," Trent says, before turning me in his arms so we face one another; he's wearing the kind of indulgent smile given to defiant children. "We've talked about this already, you're doing it." If I don't, I'll have to get another sales job. I can think of very few things I want less; I guess I am desperate enough to do reality television. "Stop begging, I'm in," I say superiorly. "I'd better get preferential treatment too." I'm kidding . . . for the most part. I wouldn't want favoritism because I'm involved with the boss. Trent's so pleased he twirls me around; I pretend not to enjoy it, I think my smile gives me away.

"Tell me something," Trent says, parroting my earlier request. "What would you like me to tell you?" Gently, he pulls me down with him, taking a seat on the dock. Once we're comfortably seated, me swaddled in his arms and legs, he says, "Your story. Tell me your story." I smile to myself, realizing we're having "the talk." Every new couple has it, it's the conversation where you spend hours getting to know one another, discussing everything from first loves, first kisses, first heartbreaks, families, childhoods, dreams, etc. It's usually the turning point in a relationship from casual to serious. "There's not much to tell, my story's typical: Girl wants to be a star, girl tries to be a star, girl does not become a star, insert name here, add water, then stir," I say jokingly, despite how bitter the words taste in my mouth. "Nah, I think there's more to it than that, you just don't want to tell me."

There's nothing to tell, I didn't have one traumatic experience that altered my course. If anything it was many small things constantly knocking me down that have led me here. Wanting something doesn't mean you'll get it, it doesn't matter how much you beg, plead, or reason, there's no guarantee of receiving the thing you most desire. In the silence that follows my anxious reflections, I hear Trent's heart beating in his chest, reverberating through my back. It's almost as if it beats for us both. That foolish thought brings words I've shared with no one tumbling out of my mouth.

"Everything changed about two and a half years ago. The previous year had been one of the very best of my life; I was riding a high. After years on the pageant circuit I won the state title and placed in nationals. I was honored, interviewed, and profiled. I made guest appearances, attended charity events and balls, but the best perk of all was the countless opportunities. However, a few months after my reign ended, things slowed, I was fine with it at first; it gave me more time to focus my energies on auditioning. That changed though after going to casting after casting without booking a thing. The general consensus was, I had some talent but that I should focus more on my strengths; marketability. Don't misunderstand me; I have no qualms with being 'marketable,' the problem is the acknowledgment of that always came with a suggestion of improvement and disregard of the sum of what I have to offer. It was emotionally exhausting. I wanted to be part of something great, but no one would give me a chance to do anything meaningful. I began questioning myself, maybe I wasn't as talented as I thought.

"I began a six-week intensive at an acting school I'd attended off and on for years, to refocus and refine my technique. A few weeks into the program I was hand selected to participate in a showcase for notable casting directors. I worked hard, without a doubt I was prepared. My performance was without ornamental embellishment, just me, but what I lacked in presentation I more than made up for in delivery. After doing what I believe to be some of my best work, Julian, the casting agent, asked if I was currently being represented? Encouraged by the question—surely he wouldn't ask unless he was interested in being my representation—I answered, 'No, not presently.' After a quick notation on the sheet in front of him, he continued, 'Good, how comfortable are you with nudity?' 'Not particularly, I would prefer to keep my clothes on in my scenes.' I hadn't expected the question. My answer would have been the same if I knew it were coming, but maybe I could have delivered it differently.

"The apathy in his voice betrayed his dissatisfaction with my answers to his subsequent questions; whatever interest he had in me was quickly fading. I was losing his attention and the opportunity. Clambering for purchase I said, 'I know I have to put in my dues, I accept that, though I hope to establish myself as a serious actor, taking on roles of consequence.' Julian put down his pen and leaned forward in his chair, 'Let's you and I speak plainly, which is after all what this showcase is about, honest feedback. Looking at your headshot, at you, I see a beautiful girl. During your sides I saw a beautiful girl, but what else is there to you? When I sit in the casting chair I spend the duration of a person's performance asking myself, what does this person offer that no one else does? Why should you be singled out over all the other beautiful girls? I found nothing remarkable about your performance or anything unique to you. Your sides were okay, but they were just okay. What you do *have* is sex appeal, and everybody knows sex sells. Many women who've come before you have done well for themselves with much less, work that angle, you'll do alright for yourself.'

"Within minutes Julian was able to expose and validate all the insecurities I'd ever secretly harbored. I'd told myself I was special, he said I was not. I told myself I was set apart, he told me I was not; in fact, according to Julian I was more of the same. I wanted to shout at him that he was wrong, that I was talented but I couldn't find my voice. Numbly I left, though not before hearing him say, presumably to himself, 'Everyone wants to be a star although not everyone is willing to do what stars have to.' I left that room forever changed. I continued on with the showcase; there were three more agents to see, only out of obligation. I stood in those rooms, said the lines, catching only snatches of the feedback, certain words reappeared 'marketable,' 'potential,' but always followed by a no.

"Without a shred of confidence left, I finally stopped putting myself through the anguish of constant rejection. Julian was right, why should I be singled out above all the others? I accepted where I was in life, that I may never get much further, and got a regular run-of-the-mill job. Sometimes I think it's not so bad, at least I have a steady paycheck, other times, especially when a business owner is telling me off, I feel hollow. It pains me to admit how devoid of expectations I am. I used to refuse anything less than the whole cake, now I'd settle for the crumbs . . . Meeting you, seeing myself through your rose-colored glasses, has been the best thing that's happened to me in a long time. For the first time in ages I have something to hope about, I don't know how things will turn out as far as the show, or us, but it's been nice having those parts of me reawakened."

Trent allowed me to speak uninterrupted, the only indication he was paying attention were the small circles his thumbs made on the backs of my hand as I unburdened myself. Abruptly it occurs to me that I'm no better than Julian. I've killed Trent's dream. He has waited six years to meet me. Finally he does and I tell him the person he thought I was doesn't exist anymore, if she ever did. Without warning, I lose touch with my surroundings. With little explanation I disentangle myself from him, hope he doesn't follow, and run to the other end of the dock. Thankfully he stays put, giving me the space I need to pull myself together. I force myself to breath through the anxiety, reliving the day that broke my spirit has wrecked my composure. I'm careful to keep my back to Trent while staying in his line of vision. Gradually I regain my self-possession and walk back.

"Sorry for running out on you," I say when I'm within reach of him. "I was feeling a bit emotional, I needed a few minutes alone to collect myself." To stymie the onslaught of questions I feel he's on the verge of asking, I hold out my hand, palm up, in a gesture indicating stop. "I would really appreciate it if we didn't dwell on what I told you. It was hard enough to recount, minus having a play by play analysis." Without looking away from me, Trent quickly gets to his feet, eyes ablaze. When the silence has stretched long enough for me to question whether he intends on saying anything at all, he does.

"I'll respect your wishes and not bring it up ever again, but before I do I need to say one thing. You're not the girl that stole my heart six years ago." I've known for some time I'm not the woman he romanticized me to be in his mind, it's best he knew it too, before either of us becomes too attached to the other. Not wanting to see the deathblow come down, I focus my eyes on a spot just above Trent's head. "That girl," he begins while stepping back into my line of vision, "was pretty, idealistic, and a bit naive. I couldn't have cared for her half as much as I care for you. You're a different person than you were then: mature, grounded, evolved, and breathtakingly beautiful. I don't care who said what, you are talented. I've witnessed it. I saw you go into a casting room and captivate all the producers, spinning an ordinary question into a tear-jerking story about a sad woman in a song. You are beguiling, and despite your best efforts cannot be reduced to playing background to life. The woman that you are right now, in this moment, is a sight to behold and I promise she will be seen."

My throat aches with the weight of choking back emotion. I haven't thought of myself as anything half so complimentary in a long time. Head buried in Trent's chest I lose the fight against my tears, I sob, letting him assure me. It's been too long since someone has believed in me. "You're not so bad at jerking tears out of people yourself," I mumble into his shirt. He plants a kiss on my forehead, "Anytime you cry because of me, it'll be tears of joy."

Chapter 8

I EYE TRENT'S VEHICLE of choice today with open admiration. I don't know much about cars, however I do know this Audi coupe is everything. "Is this yours?" I ask, indicating the car. Trent nods, obviously pleased with my approbation. "I know it's in poor taste to ask, but how much *are* you worth?" I didn't give it a second thought when the waitress at the lounge told me he's rich, now I find myself quite curious. He opens the passenger door for me before responding, "I'll let you know." It's not so much that I care how much money Trent has, I care that I know very little about him, and most of what I've been able to discern I learned through social media.

Once he's in the car, I ask if his wealth is familial. The look of idiocy he aims in my direction is enough to disabuse me of that idea. "I'm good at what I do, I also make smart investments," he says with curt inflection. I gather family and finances are two subjects he'd rather steer clear of. I get it, I'd rather not speak about my family or my abysmal financial status, but Trent hasn't shared any private details about himself with me yet. Everything with him is always about business, the present, or me, why should I open up if he won't? "Note to self, don't ask personal questions," I stage whisper. I want my displeasure known.

Crossly I watch him input a familiar address into the car's navigational system. It's not until we head in the direction of the highway that I realize why it's familiar. "You're going the wrong way," I say unconcernedly. "My house is in the opposite direction." Trent's scarcely able to keep the pleased smile off his face, no doubt he believes my directing a comment to him means he's won the latest battle between us; little does he know. "No I'm not, look, the GPS says I'm on course." "You are on course, to Amanda's house, *my* house however is a few minutes away." His surprise is gratifying, funny too. "Wow, I thought that was just something girls did in bad romantic comedies, I'm disappointed in you." He's pretending to be more hurt than he is, trying to guilt trip his way back into my good graces. "Enough of the histrionics, I don't feel bad about it. Actually, you can use a little misleading from a female, deflate that ego of yours." "It's not an ego if you really are awesome," he says as we merge onto the highway. It's too late to turn around, we'll have to continue until the next exit. "Can I ask," he begins in a neutral tone, "why you lied to me, especially about something so small?"

I've become accustomed to Trent's bluster; whenever he does or says anything devoid of it, I'm helpless against his sincerity. I hate Trent thinking I'm a liar or worse that I lied to him. "I never said I lived there, you made that assumption all on your own. I asked you to meet me at that address, and I only did that because . . ." I break off, feeling diffident about the truth. "Because what?" I consider ignoring the question or deflecting until a brief moment of eye contact causes my heart to swell with the weight of my feelings for him. "Because," I repeat, "this thing happening with us frightens me. I don't know what to call it, how to handle it. You infuriate me in ways previously unknown yet here I am: wanting to throttle and kiss you at the same time. In between fights our . . . 'thing' is moving at warp speed, I don't know how to slow it down, much as I want to. Keeping my address secret a while longer is one of the few ways I've conceived of to exercise control over our . . . thing, which feels determined not to be reigned in."

"You love me, don't you?" The puff of exasperated air I let out turns into a chuckle, from there full-on laughter. Trent's laughing too. When I think that's it, we've gotten it all out, one of us starts up again, bringing the other right along. I don't even know what I'm laughing about, Trent was joking, but I find there's always truth in jest. The idea of being in love with him isn't funny at all, especially since I'm halfway there already. I guess I'm laughing because he's dangerously close to the truth. Trent keeps his left hand on the steering wheel as he reaches for me with his right. He could have easily taken it, like he's done before; this time though he gives me the option to put my hand in his. *Will you chose me* is what he's asking. Lacing my fingers through his, forearms wrapping around each other's like vines growing from the same root I say, *I already have.* His eyes find mine in the rearview mirror, "Our 'thing' as you call it, *is* happening, stop fighting it, let us be." Not wanting Trent to see me blush I direct my attention out the window, that's when I realize we've gone much further than we should have. "We're still going the wrong way," I say. "To your house, yeah, that's not where we're headed though." I don't bother asking where he's taking me, he clearly intends it to be a surprise. "Relax, we'll be there soon."

I quickly ascertain wherever we're headed is in Williamsburg, though I'm not sure where Trent could want to take me in the hipster capital of the world, then I see it. "How'd you know? I love Mad about Books." I'm so impressed with Trent for knowing about one of Brooklyn's hidden treasures and my favorite bookstore I almost miss his subdued expression, almost. "That's not where we're going is it?" He shakes his head no, "The place I'm taking you is close by though, and I think you'll like it just as much."

In spite of Trent's enthusiasm I'm feeling a little apprehensive. Last time he took me somewhere the evening ended in disaster. "We'd better not be on our way to another 'meet and greet,' I would hate to have to kill you so soon after we've made up." His shoulders shake with silent amusement, "You have the tendency to be a bit hostile, I like that about you." I slap him across the arm, testing the truthfulness of that statement. "I said I like you hostile, not violent. I promise it'll only be you and me." I relax, a tad, after Trent assures me I won't have to meet anyone, although I'm still not convinced I'll like the surprise.

He pulls up in front of a typical Williamsburg building: restored historical architecture, storefront facade, and bereft of the neighborhood's former inhabitants. We exit the car and head straight into the freshly renovated lobby of the, what I now know to be, apartment building. I look between the elevator bank, which is obviously a new edition, and the marble steps, wondering what we're doing here. My first thought is Trent's taking me to his place, but I dismiss that idea, it's too minor. Trent was excited about me seeing this place, there's something bigger at play. Thus far the epicenter of everything that's happened since I met him is the show, whatever this is it has something to do with that. A thought occurs to me, except it can't be right.

"I think I know where we are, but we can't be, are we allowed to be?" Trent presses the elevator call button. "I'm the creator and the executive producer of *Star Quality*; besides, I own this place, of course I can be here." Believing I misunderstood him, I ask, "What place do you own?" "This building, I bought it a few years back." The elevator arrives empty of occupants. He gets on, unaware I haven't followed. I'm still processing the fact that I'm standing in Trent's property located in one of the most desirable neighborhoods in New York City. He said he'd let me know how much he's worth; I'm beginning to understand exactly how much that it is. "L, you coming or do I have to go up without you?" He's resumed his cool kid act, underneath it he's thrilled I'm impressed. "No, I'm coming."

On the short ride up Trent begins telling me about his "smart investments," including this building. We get off on the third floor, which happens to also be the top floor, then exit through a door indicating roof access. We climb up a short flight of steps before going through another heavy door, this one being the last barrier between the roof and us. I grew up in Brooklyn but I haven't spent much time on rooftops, minus the fancy rooftop restaurants popular in the city. I imagine if I had hung out on more roofs they would all look something like this: cemented grey and barren. It's pretty plain, no fancy grills or Japanese shrubbery, but I like it up here; I can see the whole neighborhood, maybe my future too.

"Shortly after I sort of met you, six years ago, I successfully sold my first non-scripted series," Trent says. "With the success of that project I was able to purchase real estate, investment properties in burgeoning neighborhoods. This building was an old textile factory a long time ago before it was converted into an apartment complex. By the time I purchased it, it was just old and run down. I spent a ton on converting the apartments into luxurious lofts and a storefront. I almost bankrupted myself in the process but I did it, and it's proven to be a good move. "The storefront's leased to an exclusive art studio that I'll take you to once filming's wrapped, I think you'll appreciate their collection."

I'm in awe of all Trent's been able to accomplish. By the time he was my age he'd already bought this property, at only a few years older than me, he's achieved more than I could dream of. What I don't get is why he would want me, the only investments I've made are the free stocks given to every new employee of thelist.com. If I'm to have a fruitful relationship with a man that owns property, collects art, and has a different car for every day of the week, I need this show to be successful. "Come on," Trent says as he leads me back in the direction we came from. "I'll give you a tour."

"Wow, this place is amazing," I say as I take in the large swanky loft. It's a spacious duplex with floor-to-ceiling windows and dark stained hardwood floors. If I have to live in a random place for a few weeks, I'm more than okay with this being it. Dazzled by what I've seen of the place thus far, I cross the large, open-concept living room straight into the kitchen with high expectations. It does not disappoint, the kitchen is equipped with stainless steel, fingerprint resistant appliances, including a smart fridge. Presently its display is on default weather, date, and time.

Trent's watching closely for my reaction; it's important to him I like it, and I do. I rub a hand admiringly over the white marble that covers every one of the numerous counters, simple yet impactful, "With this much counter space and technology I might be amendable to cooking a meal. That's if we don't already have a catering company preparing spreads for us every day, do we?" "Your meals are taken care of," he says in a measured tone I know to mean, *there's something else I wish to say*. "This isn't the loft the cast will be living in, the cast house is below this one. The kitchen we're standing in is mine, I'll be living here full time for the duration of filming."

"I thought you said this is an investment property?" I'm too shocked by the many revelations to decipher how I feel about Trent and me technically living under the same roof in a matter of days. "This apartment has always been intended for my residence. It hasn't happened already because of convenience sake. With filming starting in a few days and my plans to convert the cast house into office space for my new production company immediately after wrapping, now feels like the time to finally do it." I can't believe I hadn't thought to ask him where he lives before we basically became roommates. At this point asking him would only be to satiate my curiosity, it has no bearings on what's happening right now; it's not even what I truly wish to ask. My mouth says, "Isn't it a conflict of interest or a faux pas living on the same premises as taping?" Meanwhile what I really want to say is *are you doing this because of me?*

"My living here is no different than having a production office on set, which there will be. And . . ." Trent hesitates for a moment before continuing, "I'm doing this for us. You're going to be spending the next six weeks practically locked in the house. It won't be easy for us to see each other. It's not like we can be affectionate on set, because no one can know about us for now, but if I'm living upstairs, filming doesn't have to get in the way of us to being together." I cherish the lengths he's going to, to be near me, moments like this I think I can love him forever. "You want us to use your loft for secret rendezvous?" I smile a little to let him know regardless of my sarcastic tone I approve of his idea. "Also a sanctuary from the cast house and a make out spot," Trent says. I purposely ignore his suggestively raised eyebrows he's all talk.

"While we're on the subject, why haven't you kissed me?" I school my face into a neutral expression. It's too late to backtrack, but I'm cringing on the inside. I can't believe I just asked him that. If I hadn't heard myself do it, I would refuse to believe I had. I'm thankful for the table between us, my last line of defense, although even from the other side of the island I feel the impact of his allure. The time display on the refrigerator shows three tension-filled minutes have passed with not a word from Trent. I waver a few times on the verge of saying forget I asked, but if I was bold enough to ask the question, I have to be bold enough to hear the answer. "I tried once," he drawls, "and regretted it afterward."

"Why is it exactly that you feel grateful to not have had the misfortune of kissing me?" I say more than a little wounded. Before I know what's happening Trent's left his side of the table, reaching mine in two strides; I face him, uncertain of what I should be doing. Hands circle my waist, pulling me flush to the body they belong to. Through ragged breaths Trent whispers, "You think I haven't thought about kissing you, being with you, every day of these past six years?" He holds me tighter, closer, bringing his lips to mine, where they brush without kissing; I gasp at his nearness, his invasiveness, the ache in my sides: It's painful in the circle of his arms but love hurts.

"When I picked you up from Amanda's I was nervous, I'm never nervous except when I'm around you. Your eyes were on me, making me lose all restraint, every conscious thought left my mind except one; if I didn't kiss you I'd die."

"Kissing you then would've been a mistake; I know what I want from you, I also know it can only happen if I let you come to me. So yeah, I'm grateful your phone interrupted us, because I wouldn't have been able to stop myself. It'll happen, I'm sure of it; when it does it'll be because you want me. Then I'll know you've decided and there'll be no turning back." The hair's breadth of space between us crackles with desire. Trent's waiting for me to make the move. I want to, though I won't. If we went there now it'd be a passion-fueled mistake. I muster all the willpower in my possession and gently push him away, "Come on, Casanova." He releases me, but not before placing a gentle kiss on my cheek.

I stand dazed, remembering the feel of his lips. When I come to, Trent's leaning over the balcony, telling me to join him upstairs. Obediently I climb the spiral wrought iron staircase and accompany him into the first room off the steps. It's a large yet plain bedroom, windows frame the north wall to it's right, an open door leading to the en suite. I step farther inside to exam the bathroom, it's larger than mine at home with a classic feel, the porcelain tub's a nice touch. "The cast house is laid out exactly like mine. Two and a half bath, five bedrooms, although only four will be used as cast rooms. The fifth one, which is on the ground floor, will serve as a production office. There are seven of you total, three girls, four guys, typical setup is two to a gender-specific room. Plot twist, one of the ladies will have their own. Who, is to be determined by audience votes compiled from social media. Each of you will make a short introductory video to be posted on your social media pages, the network's, and *Star Quality*'s. The person with the most votes wins the room."

"This show will be very interactive, that's why I've been pushing for you to grow a following," Trent says matter-of-factly. I don't know who the other female castmate is, but Cashmere has a huge social media footprint. I won't be able to beat her in anything dependent on follows. I spent much time deliberating over whether or not to do the show, without sparing a thought to winning or losing. Now that I understand the nuances of the competition I'm certain there's no way I can win. "You're overthinking it," Trent says, cutting through my internal strife. "There's nothing to worry about, just keep working on building an audience." I'm not sure if he's playing the role of executive producer, not wanting a last-minute cast member holdout, or supportive boyfriend. Neither characterization qualifies him to give honest, unbiased advice, but I appreciate his efforts at easing my mind so I play along. "I've built quite a fanbase in a short amount of time," I intone. "Yes, you have very loyal fans, now get some more."

The last room Trent shows me is the master. Unlike the other rooms in the house it's decorated: grey accent wall, large flat screen, and a black leather couch. I see subtle interior design touches in the tufted headboard and area rug. I like the various grey hues too, but it feels impersonal, so impersonal that the framed photo on the mantle genuinely surprises me. He doesn't attempt to stop me as I lift the frame, examining the woman in the picture. A tall, mahogany-skinned woman with corkscrew curls and chocolate eyes wearing a brown suede miniskirt, yellow sweater, and a small cross around her neck stares at a point past the camera. This woman is gorgeous. She's also Trent's mom.

"She's beautiful," I say while replacing the frame precisely as I found it. "Was. She was beautiful." I should have known her picture is the only personal touch in his loft. "My dad was a freelance photojournalist, sometimes portrait photographer, anyways he took that picture of my mom. It was his favorite. He said it captured her essence, the strength she carried inside her. He gave it to me before he died." I wrap my arms around Trent's muscular, over six-foot-tall body, hugging him fiercely to me. It's humbling to see a man so powerful cobbled by grief. If I could take his pain away I would. I stand static, giving him the stillness he needs to miss his parents in peace.

Chapter 9

THE DRIVE BACK TO my house is quiet. Trent's still in his feelings and I don't know him well enough to know what he needs. Once upon a time, I believed him to be calculating. I now see his demeanor for what it really is, meticulously controlled emotions. I texted him about an hour after he dropped me off to ask if he was feeling better, his response of "I'm fine" came immediately. He wasn't rude, though his intention was clear; he wasn't ready to talk.

I thought after letting our carefully constructed walls down we'd be inseparable. Maybe it was too much too soon, because I haven't seen or spoken to Trent, outside of a text inviting me to an industry party. I texted back "ok," thinking he'd offer to pick me up, he never did. With no job to go to, no friends to pass the time with, and an absentee Trent, I've had nothing to do except set social media abuzz. I've mastered the art of taking the risqué selfie. If it weren't for my ten thousand followers, at last count, I'd have gone crazy. I don't care how busy someone is, you're never too occupied to return a text unless you simply don't want to.

Yesterday I posted three potential looks for tonight's event, asking my followers to vote for their favorite. I'm surprised at how many actually voted on something as trivial as which outfit I should wear to a party. If only we could get the same turnout for elections. After a tally, the ivory T-strap dress emerges as the winner. It's simple, except for the slit running from the hem of the dress up my thigh. I've been getting appreciative looks from the moment I arrived at Shadowy Nights; I think that entitles my followers to a "thank you."

The club is proving its name to be accurate, finding light to go live is a task. Fortunately I find a pale shaft near the DJ booth, "I apologize for how dark it is in here but I want to thank you all for making sure I shine bright like a diamond in this darkened cavern. You have fabulous taste." I pan the camera up and down allowing for a full view of my ensemble. "I have to go now I'll check back in later." Before logging off a live comment catches my attention—@dontcha wrote, "Stop being so desperate it's not a good look." I ignore the dig, it's not the first I've received since my newfound popularity, and log off.

When I received Trent's invite to an industry party I pictured a moderately sized gathering, at a posh event space, with an exclusive guest list. I did not imagine I'd find myself at a crowded club advertising tonight as the official cast party for Real TV, hosted by the network's biggest star, Ileana Forester. Most objectionable of all is the twenty-dollar cover for general admission for anyone wanting to meet their idol. Which is how I now find myself cornered by this creep. Pointing to my ears, shaking my head no, and lifting my shoulders I mime, *I can't hear you, I also don't want to hear you.* He braces a hand on the wall behind me while crossing all kinds of personal space boundaries. "I've been admiring you since you walked in here," he intones. As uncomfortable as I am, I remain resolute in not squirming, it'll only encourage him. "I would hate for you to waste your time on me when there are plenty of beautiful available women here tonight. I however am not one of them—available, that is."

True, I haven't been able to get ahold of Trent since I arrived, despite calling and texting, but that doesn't make me accessible to this guy or any other. "Is directness your usual way or have I done something to offend you?" he asks. Losing patience, I respond with frankness, intending him to feel my disinterest and leave me alone. "You mean other than your general demeanor? No, you haven't done anything to offend me." He takes a few steps backward, when he's a healthy distance away he sticks out his hand as if to shake mine, while shouting over the music, "I'm sorry, Leah, my name is Lawrence Scott. It's a pleasure to meet you."

"How—how do you know my name?" I ask with rising alarm, at the same time as I'm trying to remember the self-defense moves I learned at my gym, in case he's a whacked-out stalker. "Oh, no. It's not what you think," he says with adamant denial. "I know you through your casting tape, I'm involved with *Star Quality*, and I follow you. On the gram I mean, not in real life. I assure you there's nothing sketch about me. I voted for the sequence miniskirt by the way, although seeing you now . . ." His eyes take me in from head to toe, "I must say this is a great look." Knowing Lawrence to be part of production doesn't make me feel any more inclined to talk to him, followers are supposed to be virtual numbers, not people capable of tailing me into my real life. The one silver lining of meeting him is his presence. As a member of the crew that means Trent must be here too. I look from side to side for him shamelessly, prompting Lawrence to ask if I'm searching for someone? Figuring it can't hurt to enlist his help, I answer truthfully, "Trenton Shaw. Do you know him, is he here?"

The look on his face says the last thing he wishes to discuss with me is another man, but he answers affirmatively. "He's up in VIP." Knowing he's close by sends me into a tailspin; I want to see him, to know why he's been ignoring me. "I think that's where I should be." Lawrence's laughter brings me up short, "Yeah you should, which is why I'll take you there now." He offers his arm in a gentlemanly manner of a bygone era, I put my hand in the crook of his elbow, allowing him to steer me through the crowd. "I was just thinking to myself that it's funny you asked about Trent. Last I saw him he had his hands full, if you know what I mean." I'm grateful for the dim lighting preventing my face from being an open book. "Yeah I think I do."

We step off the elevator and stop in front of a door protected by a bouncer. Lawrence tells him my name before he lets us both through. "Go right in, Ms. Albanese." I take a moment to look at him, wondering if he's a follower of mine also, if that's how he knows my last name. "You're on the list," says Lawrence to my unasked question. "I presumed you didn't know that when I saw you trying to maneuver around that crowded dance floor instead of joining all the other very important people."

VIP is a modest-sized room on the upper level of the club, with three solid walls and one glass one overlooking the less important clubgoers. It's crowded but not nearly as much as it was down in gen pop. The number of "industry insiders" temporarily puts all thoughts out my mind: familiar faces mingle, eat, and dance, including Trent. He's seen me now too. I can tell by the scowl on his face. I gather he's none too happy about my being ushered around by Lawrence. I, however, am just fine with my current situation. Trent hasn't called or sought any communication with me for two days. I come to this party he invited me to and find him literally wrapped in the embrace of another woman. Tightening my hold on Lawrence, I ask him to accompany me for the night. I don't bother looking back, without a question I've got Trent's attention.

I learn the meaning of networking with Lawrence as my instructor; between laughing and dancing he makes introductions: producers, industry executives, models, managers, agents—I meet them all. My cheeks burn from smiling but I keep on, mostly for Trent's benefit. At one point Lawrence joins him and his date in their antisocial corner while I busy myself in conversation elsewhere. When Lawrence returns, he points Trent out to me, "That's Trenton Shaw, weren't you looking for him earlier?" "I was, now I have you," I say, using my femininity against him. Lawrence smiles and introduces me to another business card–wheeling guest.

Concluding our conversation with Damon Johnson, a network executive, Lawrence says, "You did great tonight, I couldn't have lucked into a better date if I tried. I mean, you impressed Damon, that's huge, possible spinoff huge." I humbly wave his compliments away. I didn't intend on working the room, my aim was to show Trent I didn't care he's here with another woman. I didn't foresee successfully schmoozing a room full of execs or having a good time.

"Thank you for tonight," I say with sincerity. "Does that mean you'll let me see you again?" he asks. Lawrence is good company, he doesn't take himself too seriously and he's not bad on the eyes. He's shorter than Trent and broader shouldered, with thick curly hair on his head and a full beard. He has none of Trent's prettiness, to no deficit. He's handsome, he's just not Trent, who from what I could see is still preoccupied. He and his date are visible over Lawrence's shoulder. It would be easy to use Lawrence's fondness of me to make Trent jealous but I won't. I'm not into him, it'd be wrong to pretend otherwise. Lawrence reads my reluctance for what it is, "How about I give you my card. If you decide to use it great, if you don't then you can add it to your collection." I take it and put it in my purse, "I can do that." "I have to go now," he says. "Early morning obligations. Remember you can use the number on the card anytime you want."

Lawrence is barely gone a minute before I'm approached by Jeremy—of Jeremy, Stephanie, and Matthew, the interrogators from my casting. We spoke briefly earlier in the evening while he drained cocktails; he sought me out now to introduce me to Aiden, a cute, floppy-haired guy who will also be competing on *Star Quality*. After quick introductions Jeremy leaves us alone to get better acquainted. More out of something to say than genuine curiosity I ask if he knows whether there are more housemates here tonight. "Besides the two of us there's Beverly Boyd, she's over there." I follow his pointed chin across the room to the woman who's been pawing Trent all night.

The whole night I barely spared Trent a glance. Left alone though, I'm finding it more difficult to ignore his presence. He's still with Beverly: tall, willowy, honey blonde Beverly. Without Lawrence or Aiden, who's gone off to impress women with his pseudo celebrity status, it's best I leave too. I bypass the elevator for the stairs, I make it down one flight before I hear feet thundering behind me, "What do you want, Trent?" I ask without looking back to confirm it's him. He catches up with me, owing to the five-inch heels I can't run in. Taking hold of my arm he stops my path forward, "What were you doing with Lawrence?" he hisses at me. Pulling free from his grasp, I match his anger with fire of my own.

"I strongly suggest you check your tone. While you're at it you should reconsider asking anything about my actions. Last I checked *you* were avoiding *me*. Then you attend an event you know I will also be attending, because you invited me to it, with a woman who is my literal competition. Having done all that you have the gall to question someone's kindness to me? Are you really that unconscionable?" I suddenly feel very winded; I can't keep taking two steps forward to take one step back with him. "From here on out, we're going to keep things strictly professional, you're my producer, I'm your talent, that's it. We have no obligations to one another outside of that, date Beverly or whoever else you want, I can't care anymore."

I'm all but decided to push past him until I see his face. It's a mask of anguish. Beneath his opulent dress, gold silk shirt, burgundy velvet loafers, and picture perfect smile, he's miserable. "Beverly's my ex, we broke up weeks ago. She's here tonight because she was invited, just like you, and all the other cast members. Yes, I played a part in her being cast, but that was a favor for a friend, months before you came into the picture. Beverly has always been aggressive with her affections, tonight was no exception. I tried to get her to stop at first, but then I saw you with Lawrence . . ." I try to remember exactly what I observed their interactions to be, I recall her being very demonstrative, I can't remember him being the same. Even if Beverly can be explained away by happenstance and misunderstandings, what about everything else? "Say I believe you, that still doesn't explain why you've been avoiding me."

"I want you in my life, but I thought I could have that while still keeping parts of myself to myself; but I can't. You undo me. Once I asked my dad what it felt like to love my mom and lose her? He said to me, 'My heart, beats differently. Nothing feels the way it used to, everything's dull muted colors and tasteless food. It's like trying to capture an image with my camera, no matter what angle or lens I use I can't get rid of the glare.' If you could live in my heart, feel how it breaks every time you walk away or whenever you're not near, you would understand how afraid I am of you and why I panicked."

Warm hands enclose around mine, "There is nothing between Beverly and me. Even when there was, it wasn't much . . . I spent the whole night watching you laugh, smile, and charm the room. I felt like I did the first time I saw you: transfixed. Then you left like you did last time. I knew it would be six years until I saw you again, I couldn't handle that kind of heartache. Tell me what to do I'll do it, I will go up there right now and let everyone know it's you, it's always been you." I have to look away, the things he's saying, they scare and excite me, but Trent won't let me off the hook this time. "Look at me, Leah," he forces my eyes to meet his. What I see in them rocks me. "I'm too far past love to even have a name for it. I've carried you with me every day for six years, you're part of me, I won't walk around with a phantom limb any longer." With the hunger of a man that knows starvation he kisses me with complete abandon.

I've thought a lot about what this moment would be like in the last few weeks. Even when I wanted nothing to do with Trent, I imagined kissing him. I pictured kinetic energy borne of physical desire. I didn't envision this. There is no feverish touching or solicitous leading, though not because of an absence of passion. I feel how much he wants me but it isn't the predominant emotion, there's a beseeching in his kiss: "*Stay with me, be with me, love me, let me love you.*" He needs me to know, and I do. I'm too far gone to turn back, Trenton Shaw has forever changed my life.

"Trent, you better not be out here on your phone or I'll kill you." I've never heard Beverly speak but I'm sure the high-pitched voice that brings us back to reality is hers. The clack of shoes grows louder, nearer. I'm unsure of what to do; I have no time to decide before she's upon us and Trent laces his fingers through mine, his mind is set. "Beverly Boyd this is Leah Albanese, my girlfriend." cringe

I hope my face is more composed than hers; she's livid. After a moment of intense awkward silence I extend my hand to her, "Hi Beverly, it's a pleasure to meet you." She looks at my hand with rancid hatred then looks at Trent, "You and Lawrence sharing girls now?" Trent chuckles sarcastically at her comment, "I told you I was seeing someone." The look she gives me would bring Regina George, the queen mean girl herself, to her knees. "Was that before or after we showed up here tonight as a couple?" Her words are those of a betrayed lover, her mannerisms communicate otherwise. She may be surprised I'm the girlfriend in question but it's not new information. The pretense is for my benefit, Beverly's enjoying the showdown.

"Come on, let's get out of here," Trent says, urging me forward. I allow him to. I sense how fearful he is that Beverly's having an effect on me. I'm as sure of him now as I was prior to Beverly's outburst; she hasn't said anything Trent himself hadn't already told me. "Leah," she says haughtily, "you think you're special don't you, well you're not. Let me guess, Trent promised you a role in one of his shows, didn't he? Don't try to deny it, admit the truth and tell me which show?" In spite of her intended malice I answer without venom. I got the guy, the least I can do is not be ugly about it. "The same one as you." With a smile that doesn't quite reach her eyes she addresses Trent, "That was unexpected, but not beneath you." Her eyes remain on him though she aims her comments at me, "A word of advice, you're not the first, you won't be the last. Get what you can out of him and move on." Trent places an insistent hand on my back. He's done entertaining her. When we're nearly gone Beverly calls to me again, "I look forward to schooling you Leah, on lots of things."

Beverly didn't get to me in the ways she was hoping to, my feelings for Trent remain intact though I am curious about what I perceive to be a pattern of behavior. After several taciturn minutes Trent pulls the car over, "Are you upset with me?" I take his hand in mine, assuring him nothing's changed between us, even if I do have questions. "How'd you meet her, Beverly I mean?" He rubs his face vigorously, visibly frustrated, though he answers without prodding, "She was a bottle girl at a club I went to once; I don't remember which one. She was attractive and forward; we began seeing one another, very casually. To her I was a meal ticket, or at least a few fol- lows. You heard what Beverly said to you about getting what you can out of me, she certainly did. Beverly asked me to cast her in one of my projects, I had the power to make it happen and I enjoyed her at the time, so I figured why not. Which is how we ended up here having this conversation."

Trent making light of his involvement with Beverly reminds me of an account he gave me about another past relationship. "Beverly, Cashmere, me—do you have a fetish for wannabes or do you just like playing the hero?" He let's my hand go as if my touch burns him. Until this point he's been patient with me. Beverly too, but he's reached his limit. "I'm in the enter- tainment industry, every woman that says hello to me is aspiring to fame. I expect it, accept it even, but I pursued you, not the other way around." "So why do you treat me like you treat them?" I say with more anger than I intended. "You approached me with a sales pitch, why not with the truth?"

"I was scared," he says in a voice barely above a whisper yet fraught with emotion. "My only thought was I can't let you leave, I went with what I knew." I hear the truth in his voice, I felt it in his lips; what he had with Cashmere and with Beverly is what he had with them, our relationship is different. "I'm not upset anymore," I say with some abruptness. "Only promise I won't have to deal with this kind of stuff again. We're not sixteen, I will not have fights over the hot guy in school." He laughs, showing off his dimples. "That's funny because if Lawrence hadn't left when he did that's exactly how the night would of ended; in a fight." The smile on his face conflicts with the ice in his voice, he means every word. "I'd prefer not to see you get pummeled, it'd be rather embarrassing for us both." I get a genuine laugh out of him at that one.

"Can I see you tomorrow?" Trent ask when we're in front of my house. "I'm not sure, ask me again in the morning, hopefully I'll have finished packing by then. I'm going inside, get a head start on it. Thanks for the ride," I finish awkwardly, feeling apprehensive of what comes next. We shared a kiss, afterward Trent introduced me as his girlfriend, but I'm still me: in- timacy and commitment phobic. I usually don't jump in feet first. When it happened earlier I didn't know it was coming, there wasn't any time to be nervous. Now sufficiently forewarned, my stomach is in knots. Slowly, agonizingly slowly, Trent inches toward me. Lips touch, lightly at first, then firmer, this isn't the intimacy and expressiveness of the first kiss, this is passion and desire.

Trent pulls back, though the moment lingers in his hooded eyes and heavy breaths. "Being here with you like this, is a dream come true." We sit with locked hands, locked eyes, and locked hearts until I can't put off going inside any longer. "A car is scheduled to pick you up move-in day, but I was hoping you'd let me take you," Trent says in a measured tone. I think he's testing me, my answer will prove if I'm as committed to us as he is. Of course I am, the problem is Trent picking me up runs the risk of having to introduce him to my mom. There's no way she'll like him. Her disliking him, and she definitely will, won't change my decision to be with Trent; I respect her opinion and hate going against it, though there's no point in hiding him if I won't give him up. I guess that means I've made my decision.

Chapter 10

"What are you doing here?" Antonia doesn't live with my mom and I yet here she is, lying on my bed, using a pile of my clothes as a pillow. My sister is usually a welcome sight but since my mom found out about my panic attacks I've been dreading our next meeting. "Well hello to you too sister, I'm well how are you? Wait, I know the answer to that question. You've been having panic attacks and passing out on kitchen floors, so I'm going to go ahead and say you're not okay. But don't take my word for it, I'm only your sister, who also happens to be a doctor." Passive aggressiveness has always been Antonia's way. She thinks as long as her tone is conversational, regardless of how sarcastic, she's not being hostile. I would ignore her but I can't, she's in my space and now I'm starting to get upset too, "No preamble?" I ask while I shut the door. "Fine, we'll do it your way." I have a feeling this might get loud.

"No, I didn't tell you because I'm not obligated to share every detail of myself with you or anyone else. If that bothers you, I'm not sure what to say; but for sure, sorry won't be it." Avoiding open suitcases and scattered shoeboxes littered across the floor, Antonia makes her way to where I stand in the middle of the room. She looks at me and I at her for a long time before she asks, "What's wrong with you? I come here after a fourteen-hour shift, stay up nearly all night waiting for you, and you give me attitude?" I'm not happy about her staying up most of the night waiting for me. I also won't be guilt tripped for something that was her choice. "No one asked you to, that was your decision. An unnecessary one I might add, as you can see I'm fine."

"You are not fine, people who are fine do not have panic attacks." I haven't had one in over a week, I truly am okay. Antonia telling me I'm not is the only problem I currently have. "Mom told me you're unhappy about your life," she begins. "So what, your life hasn't gone as planned? Guess what, that's the case for most people. You're young, you'll land on your feet. Seriously Leah, get a grip." How can that be her response? What little contrition I may have felt evaporates. "I didn't call you seeking your opinion, professional or otherwise. I don't care what you think about what I'm going through; I care even less for your approach. It's easy for you to say get a grip when all the pieces are falling into place for you but for the many of us whose plans have gone awry, we can't just get a 'grip.'"

We've never argued like this, I'm afraid if we continue much longer one or the both of us might say something that can't be unsaid. Antonia looks at me with eyes almost identical to mine, with a disappointment in them I've never seen before. "For someone distraught over life you look pretty good, where are you coming from at this hour? Were you with that guy mom told me about?" My biggest pet peeve is my mom and sister discussing me behind my back. It drives me absolutely crazy. I'm on the verge of saying a few choice words to Antonia, the only way to refrain is to end the conversation. "I'm done talking to you, I need to pack, get out of my room." With her foot, Antonia kicks shut my suitcase then plops down on top of it. "Pack for what, where are you going?" She asks completely ignoring my request. "You're unemployed, you can't afford a vacation." It's not like her to be purposely hurtful. Where I'm showing restraint Antonia is not holding anything back.

"When did you become so tactless?" I ask as I walk around her, pulling random articles of clothing from the pile on my bed. "Actually what I would really like to know is what are you upset about, what did I do to you?" Antonia gets up from her seat, my suitcase, and pulls the shirt I'm holding from my hands. "Are you that self centered that you can't see how much you're hurting Mom?" This isn't about my mother, it's about me; I will not be emotionally blackmailed. "That's not fair and you know it, I haven't done anything to her," I scream. "Except worry her half to death with your self pity, I don't even know who you are anymore," Antonia yells back. Bringing our mother into this fight was a low blow and the push I needed to stop being civil. "Ditto big sister, I don't know who you are either." She expected to deliver unanswered blows, she didn't expect me to hit back. "To answer your earlier question, I will be gone for a few weeks not wallowing in my 'self pity.' You were right about me landing on my feet; I have, no thanks to you. It's a sad day when you realize the only person in your corner isn't your family."

Seeing her face empty of anger full of sadness, I almost take it all back. "I'm sorry, Leah, about how wrong this conversation went, I'm sorry you no longer know your family will always be on your side, I'm sorrier that you too will be sorry. I came here tonight to tell you, Leah Albanese, you are beautiful, intelligent, gifted, talented, favored, and unforgotten. One day you will be successful and fulfilled. But know your worth, know your strength, and own your struggle. It'll make you stronger and all the more worthwhile."

Silent tears slide down my face. Underneath Antonia's attitude is trepidation, she's scared for me and that's worrisome. First Amanda, then my mom, and now Antonia have confronted me. I can't ignore their concerns, but what's wrong with taking back control of my life? "What am I doing that has all of you so worked up?" I let Antonia lead me to my bed where we sit side-by-side, "Anything you do as a last resort is desperate. Most things you do because you have no other option are usually too risky to have considered in the first place. Sometimes it pays off, sometimes it doesn't, but it'll always cost you."

The weight that had been absent for a week returns to its usual spot. I surreptitiously rub the place as we become reacquainted. I had a plan. I was doing fine until all this talk about paying a price. "Explain further please," I say. I think I get what Antonia means, what I don't understand is how it relates to me. "Okay, take your job at thelist.com, that was an act of resignation. We were worried then too because you traded in your dreams for a jaded reality. You've always been the ultimate optimist, brimming with hope and full of faith; you made believers of us all. Do you remember what you said to Mom when she tried to get you to change your mind about your career choice? You said to her, 'You want to put a circle in a square peg, it won't work because it doesn't fit. I cannot be opposite my nature.' After that conversation she's never doubted you again. You're still that person, but more somber, more pragmatic, less hopeful; I can see it, Mom sees it, and it hurts. I believe in you and what you want, but why should not achieving it kill who you are? If I'd known that so much of your self-identity was wrapped up in achieving some arbitrary measure of success, I would never have encouraged you. You are who you are, and those things will make you a great actor. Being a successful actor will not make you great."

I choke back sobs from deep in my spirit. It's painful to see the worst of yourself through the eyes of someone who loves you. "I don't know myself anymore, I feel like a faded memory. I listen to you, Mom, Amanda, and Trent telling me to pursue my passion because I'm all these wonderful things. The truth is they're words that no longer resonate with me; I can't recall being optimistic, confident, beautiful, faithful or what those things even felt like. I don't feel talented, special, or favored; all I feel is despair at a wasted life. Sometimes I think, is it that you guys know me better than I know myself or are you all talking about someone who isn't real?"

Antonia looks at me with pity mirroring how I feel about myself. "Li, how about for now let us know and remember for you until you no longer need reminding, in the meantime guard your heart, trust your instincts, and have faith. Now enough of the heaviness, who's Trent?"

"Let me get this straight, this guy has been pining after you ever since he saw you at a party once six years ago?" I answer with a shy smile, sometimes it's still hard for even me to believe. "I didn't buy it at first, I didn't want to, then I remembered the party and him." Antonia looks at me with the same face she makes when she's reading a complex medical text, she's trying to decipher the things I feel but will not say. Before I make a conscious decision to, I'm spilling my guts to her about the uncertainties I shelter but try not to look at too closely. "Trent is intense, things between us are intense. Most of the time we're at odds. That might be because I won't allow myself to freely feel as I do or maybe it's because . . . I'm making a mistake." I said it, the thought that's nagged me from the moment I realized I have feelings for him. What if Trent is not the one, what if I'm deluding myself about him? "It's alright to take your time to work out how you feel and what you want; move slowly and trust your instincts, only make sure it's your instincts and not your usual resistance to love."

"I am not resistant to love." Everyone thinks because of my age and lack of dating history I'm anti love. That's not the case; to the contrary perhaps my ideas about love are too romantic, unreal even. "I've been waiting for my Godsend: beautiful without vanity, intelligent without arrogance, a leader without pretension, and financially stable with a portfolio." When I picture that man he doesn't have a face, I wonder if that's because he doesn't exist? "Your Godsend, I like that notion, the question is, is Trent that for you?" I shrug. "I don't know, what I do know is he has a hold over me, I scarcely know him but I want to give him all of me. I've watched you and Amanda fall in love and I've learned that love could be a quiet understated affair or it could be all-consuming, intoxicating, and addictive. What Trent and I have isn't run of the mill; already he's become intrinsic to my being, I have to let what he and I have play out, that's the only way forward.

We spend the rest of the night talking and trolling Trent's social media pages. Antonia concedes he is very good looking, "I see his appeal, Trent is a beautiful man." Eventually Antonia falls asleep while I stay up packing and thinking. The last thing she said was, she sees how much Trent has affected me but to be careful, "the deepest loves usually cause the deepest wounds."

The first thing I do when I wake is check my phone. There are three messages from Trent, all asking me to contact him when I get up. I call him, fearful something terrible has happened; the phone rings once before he answers, sounding alert and excited. "Do you sleep in every day?" There's a smile in his voice that puts one on my face. "You call eight thirty sleeping in?" I say, completely in love with this side of him. "Yes, when I wake up missing you and you're asleep." If I weren't sure before I know now, things between Trent and I have changed. We're no longer in a tug of war, we've surrendered to our feelings and officially entered the honeymoon phase.

"Nice play Romeo, what are you up to?" "Delegating, today is your last day of freedom for a while and I want it." Something about how he says "*I want it*" makes me shiver. "Isn't there a ton to do before we move in tomorrow?" I half say half yawn. I fell asleep right after Antonia left for work, that was only two hours ago. "Yes, but that's the beauty of being me, I can tell someone else to do it. If anything major comes up I'll be near. How about I pick you up around noon?" Noon's less than four hours away, that doesn't give me a lot of time to finish packing the rest of my things. "No isn't an option is it?" I would love to spend the day with Trent, I just don't know if I can get everything done before he gets here. "Nope, see you in a few hours, I'll be counting down the minutes." He hangs up before I can contest the plan.

Three hours later I'm packed and dressed, all that's left to do is say goodbye. "Hey Mom." I find her sitting in the living room. At my voice she looks up from the book on her lap. "Leah, where have you been? Feels like I haven't seen you in days." I take a seat on the couch opposite her. "It might actually be that long, I got in late last night, I had an event for the show." I see the disparagement in her eyes and the resolution not to verbally express it. "You've decided to do the reality show you mentioned?" It took all of a minute for my mom to make me second guess myself. It's possible I will never feel like an adult speaking to another adult, when it comes to her I will always be a child playing at adulthood. "Yeah, um, filming starts tomorrow but I'm heading out today. I'll only be gone for a few weeks and if I win or make it far it'll be great for my career. If I don't then at least I know I've given it all I have, then I can lay it to rest."

I squirm in my seat beneath her thoughtful eyes, she's not convinced, "Mom, it's a good thing. I wasn't sure about it initially but I've learned there are many paths to the same destination; no matter how it goes it'll be for my benefit." I repeat Trent's words, which I don't even fully agree with, to my mom. I feel so ashamed for doing so I can't meet her eyes. "When you were a child I could make decisions for you, protect you; you are an adult now and your life is your own responsibility. Go do what it is you feel you must and learn the truth. The sun rises in the east and sets in the west, the earth revolves around the sun, and there are only two paths but only one worth walking. Go, but come back. When you do, I will be happy to have you. I love you, daughter."

I asked my mom once why she never says "I love you" to Antonia and me. She said she does tell us, but only when we need to hear it most, that way it will always mean something to us when she does. In this moment it means, she's setting me free. "And Leah," I don't dare lift my eyes from my hands, where they are folded in my lap. "Yes, Mom." She walks around the coffee table and comes to a stop directly in front of me, forcing my eyes to hers, "Beware of wolves in sheep's clothing." She gives me a final piercing look before walking away.

Chapter 11

TRENT'S EARLY, SOMETHING I am immensely grateful for. Since my conversation with my mother, I've been sitting in a deafening silence. I practically run out the house when Trent tells me he's outside. While he's loading my bags in his trunk I see my mom watching us through the window blinds. Our eyes lock for a moment, in which I think about making formal introductions; then she closes the shades, sending a clear message. I shake off the sadness, fighting for acknowledgment in favor of embracing this fresh start and brand new opportunity.

"If it's okay with you, I want to hang out at my place," Trent says as we approach his building. The plan was to spend the night, but I can't say I'm not nervous. I hope when Trent says "hang out" that's all he means, I'm not ready for anything else. He parks in the garage I didn't know the building had. "The production crew will be in and out all day. Let's wait a minute, make sure the coast is clear before we go in." Trent and I have to keep our involvement secret. He believes there might be suspicions about his affairs with Beverly and Cashmere, though he's never confirmed them.

Trent goes in first, when the coast is clear he texts me to follow. I take my heels off to soundlessly climb the stairs, I don't want to get caught in the lobby waiting for the elevator. Inside Trent's apartment, free from the fear of discovery, we embrace in a way we haven't before: no one watching, no barriers between us, and nothing to stop us but our selves. "I have something for you," Trent says while holding onto me. "The last time a guy told me he had something for me, it turned into a really sexually awkward moment and I may have used my mace. Suffice it to say it wasn't a good situation." His whole body vibrates with laughter, "I promise you'll love everything I give you."

Anxious eyes meet mine as Trent puts a small velvet box in my hand. "Open it," is all he says about it. I study the box for a long time, I turn it side to side I even shake it before determining it is much too small and too light to house a four carat rock. Trent rolls his eyes, although I know him to be enjoying every moment. Inside, is a small rose gold cross on a matching necklace, beautiful and vaguely familiar? I drape the thin yet weighty chain across my fingers for a closer examination of its loveliness. Trent tells me to turn it over. Glittering beneath the sunlight streaming through the windows are the words, "I can do all things through him who strengthens me."

My faith has always been an integral part of me; I was raised by a woman after Christ's own heart, she tried to instill the same in me. As a child, going to church and worshipping God was compulsory for everyone living in my household. The older I got, the more it became a choice. Although it's been some time since I've made the choice to go to church or to even pray. I close my hand around the cross, feeling guilt, shame, and gratitude for this reminder of who I am. I'm not Catholic, I don't use rosary beads to pray, I was taught to carry the cross in my heart. But this cross, a gift from Trent, I will bear.

I hug him tightly, "I love it, thank you so much." It's a thoughtful gift, a reaffirming one as well, if he's not the one, I can't imagine who is. "Everything that is important to you is important to me," Trent says with emotion in his voice. "I respect your faith, maybe one day it can be mine too." I hadn't given thought to Trent's spiritual beliefs. Ideally I'd want to be with a man whose faith mirrors mine, though it clearly isn't a deal breaker. "The necklace—it was my mom's." That explains why I recognized it. She's wearing it in the picture of her I saw. "I was too young when she died to know what she believed. When I was younger especially, I'd imagine what kind of woman she was, a woman not unlike you." This changes things, it's too soon for me to accept a family heirloom, particularly one with quite this much sentimentality attached to it. If I weren't positive it'd break his heart I would give it back. As it is, I'll have to hold onto it.

Not until I've replaced the necklace back in its box do I identify the sadness and accusation in Trent's actions. As someone constantly having to justify their beliefs I've learned to spot the different kinds of skeptics. Trent is the classic "if God exists why do bad things happen to good people" nonbeliever. They're the most difficult to have discussions with about faith, tragedy will always be their measuring stick. Most people think that because God is perfect and almighty our lives should be too, we shouldn't experience fear, sadness, loss, suffering, injustice, or pain. We discredit the existence of God while simultaneously holding God accountable for the pain we've chosen for ourselves.

Hardships came into the world through the disobedience of man. Jesus in turn gave us redemption. But to a child who has just lost their parent, or anyone going through loss, it's hard for them to accept the mercifulness of

God. I won't say Trent's wrong to be hardened by grief, but he hasn't opened himself up to receiving the message: salvation, redemption, forgiveness, peace, and hope—those are the promises for the faithful. I surprise myself with how protective I still am about my convictions; I haven't so much as thanked God for a meal in months. My mom, Antonia, and Amanda were panicked over nothing, turns out I haven't changed as much as they feared.

We spend the afternoon on the couch watching old seasons of the *Real World*. I would've preferred to watch old movies, but Trent insisted, he said it would be a great last-minute cram session before the test. "Reality television is just like any other genre with the same key characters. The protagonist you root for because of their nobility of character—mind you it's reality TV, nobility of character is relative. Then there's your antagonist, basically the resident B—" I quickly cover his mouth, preventing him from completing his colorful description. "Language," I say, to which he shrugs good-naturedly. "Okay, a not so nice person, who rubs everyone in the house the wrong way. Then there are the B characters: the sexually liberated girl and the attractive guy with no personality; but the most interesting character is what I like to call the dark horse."

Trent pauses for dramatic effect before continuing, "The dark horse is the bad guy or girl with the heart of gold. Initially they're standoffish, lashing out at everyone. Eventually we find out they're seriously misunderstood, resulting in a one hundred eighty degree turnaround. Lastly we have the religious freak, judges everyone because they need to do a little more self-discovery themselves. They're usually hated and occasionally take on the role of the antagonist." One guess which character I'm going to be pigeonholed into. During my casting session the producers asked a lot of questions about my religious beliefs. Now I know why, I walked right into that portrayal. I don't want to be cast as a background player fulfilling a role; I want a real chance to win.

"I say this out of love"—never a good way to precede a statement; I won't like whatever Trent's about to say—"If I were you, I would be very careful not to become the on-screen dogmatist, no one likes a roommate who sits around disapproving of all the other roommates." I'm trying to figure out since when judgmental has become a characterization of mine. I don't care what anyone else does, I'm too busy trying to figure out my own stuff. I let it go for now, I'll double back to it later. "The biggest threat to the protagonist isn't the antagonist, it's the dark horse, who's usually a more interesting and well-rounded character. Now that you know the formula, how does it feel to have the answer key before the exam?"

The character breakdown was supposed to give me an edge, instead I feel concerned that my fate has already been decided. "You know every one of the cast members, you know what I'm up against; be honest, what do you think my chances are?" I hold my breath as Trent considers me without bias, "On talent alone you have a real shot but," he hesitates. "You can come across as stiff. If you want to win you'll have to loosen up. I know you're not a fan of Cashmere or Beverly, but don't make yourself the pejorative prude pitted against them. If you do you'll have given the producers the narrative, and the fans someone to hate."

"I'm not a fan of Cashmere or Beverly?" I ask incredulously, "How about they're not fans of mine, thanks to you." How can Trent ask me not to be in conflict with those girls when he is the reason they hate me. "You know what, that's neither here nor there at this point; I need you to promise me that you'll have my back. Please don't let them make a fool of me." I don't want preferential treatment, I want to be treated fairly, given the same chances to win as everybody else. "You have my word, I'll protect you as much as I can. Once you're in that house though, really it's up to you how things plays out." I can't ask anything more of him; once the competition begins it's all on me.

Filming hasn't even begun yet and I already feel my deepest misgivings about being part of this show coming to fruition. "This is exactly why I didn't want to do this." I yell in frustration. "I don't want to become a stereotype for mass consumption. Becoming someone I'm not just so I can be someone everyone likes." Distressed, I go to the window, hoping for a change of perspective. In front of the building stands a small group of crewmembers, two average-looking guys and a girl with green hair; they're smoking and speaking animatedly, probably talking about the unsuspecting cast. Trent's arms go around my waist and hold me to his chest. I'm grateful for the reassurance even if it doesn't change anything. "You have to stop worrying L, I promise it'll be okay. I don't know who'll win, but no matter what there's no losing for you."

I chose my favorite tee shirt and shorts for bed. In hindsight that might not have been the best choice of sleeping attire for tonight. The hem of my tee barely grazes my legs and my shorts were a hit on Instagram, that about says it all. I give myself a pep talk in the mirror while I tie my headscarf into a chic knot atop my head. On the other side of the door is Trent; I've never been more attracted to a man than I am to him. If I'm being completely honest I know the thoughts running through his mind, they're running through mine too. That doesn't change the fact that to do anything other than sleep would be a mistake.

Trent's sitting up in bed, MacBook in hand, when I walk back into his bedroom. I ignore the feel of his eyes on me as I cross to the empty side of the mattress and get in. With my back to him I say, "Goodnight," and pretend to go to sleep; as if I could, the air is too thick with desire to do that. There's a slight shift in the mattress before I hear a soft thud, probably the sound of the laptop being placed on the nightstand. Trent's ready for bed. He slides down further into the mattress, closer to me; I suck in air when his arm and his body curl around my form, hugging me snuggly to him.

I lay very still, very ridged, though his body has relaxed, coiled around mine. Uneven breathing of persons wanting to say something with the problem of not knowing how echo around the room. "Very few people know this about me," Trent says very softly, "I can read minds." His comment is so random and so ludicrous I momentarily forget to be tense. I turn and now we're face to face, it's more difficult to ignore the pheromones while looking into his glinting eyes. I feel intoxicated with his immediacy but I pretend otherwise.

"Are you telling me you secretly work for the psychic friends hotline?" I say in a low throaty voice that isn't mine. "Umm hmm, that's exactly what I'm saying," his breath, warm and sweet, only adds to the feeling of being inebriated. "I know what you're thinking right now." I play along if only to divert my thoughts away from his bare, perfectly sculpted chest. "Go ahead, tell me what I'm thinking about this very moment." Again I speak in a dialect that isn't mine, all flirty and sexy. I don't recognize this seductive woman who dallies against her mind's volition. I resolve to turn my thoughts to more innocent places.

"You were trying to not look at me or be near me; unfortunately for you, I'm trying to do the exact opposite. Let's see which one of us will get what we want." I gasp as Trent gathers me to him and kisses me. The moment stretches; the kiss grows deeper with no rush or reason to stop. Everything's fine until I recognize kissing won't be enough, that's when it hits me. I can't breathe.

I push Trent away, jump off the bed, and sprint into the bathroom all before he processes that I'm gone. First he calls my name. When I don't answer, hurried footsteps approach the bathroom, "L, are you alright?" The worry in his voice is audible over my mounting panic, I brace my hand on either side of the sink and force myself to answer him before he breaks the door down. "I'm okay, I'll be out in a minute." I don't listen for his response, I'm counting backward from one hundred. I'm not ready to disclose to Trent about my panic attacks; unfortunately not telling him is no longer an option.

By the time I reach one I'm still a little anxious but calmer than before. I wet a washcloth with cold water and dab it on my face to get rid of the flush on my cheeks. I don't want to look crazy when I tell Trent I might be. I open the bathroom door and walk straight into solid flesh. Trent looks me over, making sure I'm not physically hurt before demanding I tell him what's going on. "Don't try to tell me it's nothing because that wasn't nothing."

Gently, I nudge him out of the doorframe; I take a seat in the wingback chair near the fireplace. This conversation will be better had seated. Trent doesn't sit, he leans over the back of my chair. It takes some prodding but I tell him what I think he should know, the mildest version of the truth, with omission of my constant dread and the anxiety that never quite leaves me. I don't tell him those things for fear of what he will think of me. "L, there's nothing to be ashamed of, having a panic attack doesn't make you crazy and it won't make me stop wanting you." Having his support and understanding is an immense relief; however the impetus for tonight's episode wasn't the usual suspects.

"There's something I need to tell you, I haven't um . . . well the things is . . . it's not that I don't *want* to but . . ." I blow out a frustrated breath. "Do you need me to read your mind again?" Trent jokes. His hands go to my temples, where they make small circles, as he declares, "Your thoughts are coming into focus." With Trent on mind-reading duty I try explaining again, "This isn't my first rodeo. With that said, I haven't been to a rodeo in a long time, I don't plan on going back until my husband takes me." I look up at him, hoping he understood my lame metaphor. "Did you get any of that?" Eyes cast upward to the ceiling, Trent appears to be puzzling out my words, "Sort of, I understood everything outside of the rodeo references."

I groan in annoyance, why can't I say this the right way? Trent pulls me up off the chair despite my going limp, looking me squarely in the eye he tells me to try again, this time without the hard-to-follow analogies. "I made the decision a long time ago not to have that level of physical intimacy with anyone except my husband. I'm sorry for freaking out on you, but I guess my body reacted to what my mind was saying. If that's not okay with you I completely get it, you and I can be just friends, no hard feelings."

Slowly and deliberately Trent steps into the small gap between us with outstretched arms; he holds onto me in a way that communicates how much he never wishes to let me go. "Stop underestimating what I feel for you. I've waited six years—six. Do you think I can't handle waiting a little longer? In fact I foresee you having trouble waiting, I am irresistible, although it'll be fun to watch you try." He places a swift kiss on my forehead, which I return with a sweet kiss on the lips. Abstaining will be harder for him than he's letting on, but I love him for pretending otherwise. In truth, lying down tucked safely in Trent's arms, I think I can love him forever.

I wake up and without opening my eyes immediately know Trent's not beside me, we fell asleep entwined in each other, now my head rests on a pillow instead of his chest. I call out for him in case he's elsewhere in the loft but get no response. Crushing disappointment sets in, why would he leave without saying anything to me? I check my phone for a text from him but I have no new messages. I cast my eyes around the room for clues as to where he could have gone. A paper, folded in half on Trent's nightstand catches my eye. On the outside, written in beautiful cursive, is my name.

I woke up this morning happier than I've been in years; I had to convince myself I wasn't dreaming. I couldn't believe that the woman sleeping peacefully at my side had chosen me to love her. At six ten, the sun hit you in the most mesmerizing way, three horizontal rays of sunlight streaked across your body: lighting your right eye, your beautiful lips, and slender shoulders. The sun shone brightly, causing you to settle deeper into me. I kissed your eye and it fluttered opened for a brief moment. Your eyes are usually liquid amber but this morning it was a golden blaze twinkling like the brightest star of all. You closed it again, slipping back to sleep. My heart broke at that moment knowing that it would never be mine again because it was completely yours. I held you tight, captivated by your beauty and needing the reassurance of flesh and bone that you wouldn't fade away. I decided then that God must exist, because only he could have crafted you and gifted me you for safekeeping. I don't always know the right thing to say or have the perfect line on the tip of my tongue, but I heard something once that stuck with me for this exact moment. "I love you without knowing how, or when, or from where. I love you simply, without problems or pride: I love you in this way because I do not know any other way of loving but this, in which there is no I or you, so intimate that your hand upon my chest is my hand, so intimate that when I fall asleep your eyes close." I held you for as long as I could, letting go only at the last minute. I damned time and wished us more. When you wake I hope your first thought is of me and my every thought is of you.

My fingers trace his delicate script as I read the words I'm determined to commit to memory. Whatever doubts I may have held dissipate into nothingness, he is the man I will marry and love for the rest of my life, only that man could write this. Inspired by the beauty of his love I look through his drawer for pen and paper. This love won't go unanswered. *"I will love you outside of space and through the restraints of time. Today you are mine, to-morrow you are my forever, eternally you are my always."* I fold my response to him and place it on his nightstand where he can't miss it.

I'm happy and it has everything to do with Trent, I'm completely at ease even looking forward to moving into the cast house in a few hours. I'm feeling something else also, hopeful—I forgot what that felt like. Trent has given me hope; hope for us and hope for my career. In the course of a few weeks he's given me everything. My phone vibrates, bringing a new message from him. "Sorry I wasn't there when you got up, had to join the crew downstairs. I left you breakfast in the kitchen. I'll be back in time to coordinate your arrival. By the way I'm thinking of you." I waste no time in responding, I want him to know how moved I am by his letter. "I loved it, thank you." His response comes a minute later, "Breakfast?" I don't bother replying, we both know what I'm referring to.

After showering, I dress in a tan long sleeved midi dress. I accessorize with four necklaces, including Lena's cross, and I add bracelets to my wrist. My hair goes up in a high ponytail with a tight chignon. I add a red leather jacket to complete the look, then I'm done. There's nothing left to do except wait. Bored and alone, I take a more thorough look around Trent's place, starting with his office, easily the largest room in the loft. I head straight to his paper-littered desk and shuffle through them, not looking for anything in particular until something makes me stop.

The handwriting is Trent's, though the thoughts are scrambled. *"The six-year wait, he searches for her for years, finds her, wins her heart."* I remember Trent in Union square park telling me, "I signed a production deal today, the first thing I want to produce is a story about a guy that saw a girl once six years ago but can't get her out of his mind." He was serious about telling our story. The front door opens and closes while I'm still in his office. Trent didn't say I can't be in here, but I don't want him to think I've been snooping through his things. I replace the papers and quietly tiptoe into the closest room.

"L, I'm back, where are you?" I walk out of the guest room I ran into when I heard him come in, and lean over the bannister so we can see each other. Trent's as handsome as he was in my dreams last night, dressed down in a fancy hoodie, dark denim, and Chelsea boots. My heart constricts at the sight of him, then he's running to me, taking the stairs two at a time. When he's within reach I practically fly into his arms. In my ear he says, "I've been waiting all morning for this." We collide into one another heedless of everything else, including the growling of my stomach. Smiling, Trent says, "I bought lunch."

"This salad is delicious, I can't finish it though, I don't want a pouch before I go on camera." Trent's big hands mockingly pat my stomach, "I wasn't going to say anything but the dress is looking kind of tight around your midsection." I slap his hand away, "How sweet of you to let me know, count on me returning the favor one day." I ignore his pleas for mercy with a promise I will exact my revenge. "While we're on the subject, you should know I've decided not enter the competition for the private room."

I rush to explain before Trent starts asking questions. "I'm going to film my entry video for the contest, telling the fans they shouldn't vote for me but, for one of the other two ladies. I'll hate not having any privacy and sharing a room with Cashmere or Beverly, but it'll be worth it to appear humble and likeable. I've been thinking about the character breakdown, I don't want the producers defining me, I'll define myself." Trent nods his head approvingly, "That is the kind of thinking that will get you a win. Come on, let's work on your video. It has to go up at one, votes are tallied at six."

It takes me all of five minutes to get it done with Trent as my camera-man. "My peoples, my peoples, my peoples, how I've missed you all. It's been a whole two days since we've connected. I hope you've missed me as much as I've missed you. Gratefully I'm back and I come bearing tea. Real TV has been working on putting together a new reality competition called *Star Quality*; think *American Idol* meets *The Real World*, except it's an acting competition. Yours truly has been cast in the opportunity of a lifetime, but I need your help. That's right *I* need *your* help. There are three of us girls and only two rooms." I pause to let it all sink in.

"Now that we've all done the math, that means two of us will be shar-ing a room. The producers have decided the best way to chose would be by allowing the fans to do the dirty work. Each of us are responsible for creating a video like this one, to be posted through various social media platforms. The cast member with the most likes gets their own room. I'm so excited to be here that I've decided to not enter the contest for the private room but to send you, all of my loyal followers, over to realtv.com to meet the other ladies, hear their stories, and decide between the two of them. This will be the last time I post in a few weeks, but be sure to check out realtv.com for pictures and interviews with your girl. Follow me on Instagram, Twitter, and Facebook @lilialbaneses; until then see you when I see you."

I look to Trent for feedback. "That was great, you're a natural. You have sex appeal, charm, personality, and you're well spoken. How did I end up so lucky?" "Funny, I was thinking the same thing." We hug at length, knowing it to be the last time in too long. "I hate to let you go, but it's about that time," Trent says. With one last lingering kiss I grab my bags and leave to begin a new journey.

Chapter 12

ON MY WAY UP to the loft, after making it all the way down to the lobby without detection via the steps, the blue-haired producer I observed from Trent's window the day before detains me. She asks how I managed to bypass the crew set up outside waiting to capture our arrival. I repeat verbatim what Trent told me I should say if I were in this exact situation, "I was dropped off in the parking garage with no further instructions. I entered the first entry point I came across, it led to the gallery, which in turn led to the lobby. She bought my story but I didn't exactly make the best first impression, I know this because she made me exit the building then reenter with all my heavybags about twenty times before finally letting me up to the cast house.

The loft is the same layout as Trent's place, though it feels smaller filled with equipment and crew. I count three cameramen, but I'm sure there are cameras capturing our every move for perpetuity at all times. The two guys I saw with the blue-haired producer yesterday are here. I'm told not to acknowledge them while we are rolling. Past them, Cashmere sits cross-legged, crossed arms on the couch staring daggers at me. Blue-haired girl, Amy, approaches, "Leah, we need to get first meeting shots, for now it's only you and Cashmere, why don't you go over there and introduce yourself."

Cashmere and I are not friends but we are both here. I need this opportunity, if I have to play nice with her, I will. She's dressed in cutoffs, a low-cut tee that barely covers her double D's, and five-inch heels of course. She is attractive, but must she always dress like she just stepped off the pole? She stands to extend a hand to me, "Cashmere," her tone is polite if not exactly friendly. At least we're on the same page about how we are to handle this. "Leah," I answer. "Delighted to make your acquaintance."

We make small talk for the camera, asking the basics: where are you from, what were you doing before this, are you excited etc.? To her credit she is engaging and hides her dislike well. I begin to think we can get through this without incident. The arrival of another cast member gives us a

85

camera-free moment that Cashmere uses to say to me in a deadly soft tone. "Don't let this little act fool you, I hate you. If I were you I'd watch my back." She smiles at me sweetly then turns her attention, like everyone else, to the front door.

Cashmere and I both stand to greet Aiden. Like a man on a mission he walks directly to me, picks me up and spins me around. You would've thought we've known each other all our lives, not that we met once, in a dark club, for a few minutes. I return his hug, genuinely happy to see him and to no longer be alone with Cashmere. Normally overly cheery people put me off, but his smile tells me everything I need to know about him. He's a great guy: affable and outgoing. The producers love it; we're forced to reshoot our sincere greeting three more times.

Aiden introduces himself to Cashmere, he hugs her too, not as enthusiastically as he hugged me, still he does so with warmth. With the addition of Aiden we pass the minutes in easy conversation, mostly about him. He's originally from Venice Beach, California, and loves to have a good time. When we first met I was unable to appreciate much more than his brown curls; in the light of day I see everything I missed. Aiden's about five ten, lean without muscle, with a unique shade of grey eyes. He's fairly young, late twenties at most, small laugh lines frame his mouth, confirming what I already suspect; he laughs a lot. He's been here only a few minutes but already he's gotten at least a chuckle out of us all, crew included. I hope the rest of the roommates are as likeable as he is.

"So which of you beautiful ladies am I sharing a room with?" Aiden asks as he puts his arms around Cashmere and me. "The one of us that comes in the male variety," I say with a smile. "Ah, less exciting, but makes sense." Our conversation is cut short by the next arrival, this time two cast-mates arrive together.

The arrival of Corey and Zack is uneventful; it passes with no special note except the feeling that I've seen Zack before. Corey is professional-athlete tall with reddish blonde hair and blue eyes. Originally from North Carolina, he's recently relocated to Atlanta. Apparently he and Zack met at the airport waiting for their cars, realized they were both on the show, and decided to ride together. Zack is quiet as Corey relates the story, clearly he prefers to sit back and observe while Cory enjoys being the center of attention.

Corey could've jumped off an Abercrombie poster, he has that all-American look. Zack is equally attractive though in a very different way, he's about Aiden's height with delicate features and fine bones. His hair, shockingly jet black against his pale skin, is slightly longer in the front, shorter on the sides. He's thin, bordering gauntness, but it suits him. I'm studying his profile when it comes to me, "Oh my gosh, you're Ryder Grey."

Ryder Grey was my favorite character on a short-lived show a little over ten years ago, called *Lifeline*. It was a drama about a family dealing with the terminal diagnosis of their thirteen-year-old son, Ryder. The name didn't seem to mean anything to most of my castmates, which does nothing to appease Zack. He's looking at me with scary intensity. There's a question in everyone's eyes. I've said enough already, I won't say anything more. If everyone else is to be brought into the loop it will be Zack's doing.

"I began playing Ryder Grey when I was fourteen. After two seasons, the show was canceled. Afterward I did a number of guest appearances until taking time off to attend college like a normal person. Now here I am with all of you." No one says what we're all thinking, why would Zack need a show like this? Instead the silence drags on, worsened by the realization of our conversation being filmed. When the moment stretches into uneasiness, Aiden comes to the rescue. "Dude, your on-screen sister, Renee, was hot." A collective laugh, followed by a chorus of "Oh Aiden," breaks the tension-filled moment. We go back to talking, getting to know each other as we await the last of our roommates.

I was expecting Beverly. I've been expecting her since the moment I arrived. Instead in walks Brice Young, the last of our male roommates. He's Corey's height, ebony rich skin, and muscular with strong legs, which are on display in cargo shorts, Nike trainers, and a black tee shirt. It seems to me he's dressed as informally as he can possibly get away with on purpose. Brice is undeniably handsome, the most handsome man in the house. He is also the least assuming.

He greets the guys first with a formal handshake then us ladies. Cashmere nearly trips over herself walking around the coffee table to meet him, Brice catches her against his chest before she hits the floor. I watch as she casually grazes his chest with her fingernail while whispering something to him that makes him blush. He walks away from her laughing to himself about what she said. When it's my turn to meet Brice I'm smiling too, maybe Cashmere will be so enthralled by him she'll leave me and Trent alone. Brice greets me with a polite hug and magnificent smile. Unlike Aiden, whose smiles come as often as he breathes, I get the feeling Brice's are reserved for special occasions. If they weren't it couldn't be this spectacular.

It's an ordinary exchange but the producers ask that we do it again. After the second time, they seem satisfied and continue on. I didn't notice Trent come in. I see him now, watching me, looking none too pleased. I catch Cashmere smirking into her cup, so much for Brice keeping Trent and me off her mind. We settle back into our seats waiting for our last roommate,

Beverly. While the roommates talk I keep a wary eye on Trent lurking in the corner, being intimidating. Corey regales us with a story about flying out a window while Aiden tries to convince him he hallucinated the whole scenario. Cashmere says something completely inappropriate and a guy takes the bait, usually Corey or Aiden, sometimes Zack, never Brice though, which is unfortunate for her since he's the fish she's trying to catch.

"I'm here people, come greet me," Beverly walks in being more obnoxious than I remembered her to be. She's thrown everyone for a loop with her queen of the world act except for Cashmere, who saunters by all of our confused faces to in fact greet her. "Bev, doll it's great to see you." I watch them air kiss both cheeks, in disbelief, Cashmere is the last person I would expect to get along with Beverly, they both think they're the sun and everyone else orbits around them.

Unlike Cashmere, Beverly doesn't even pretend to not dislike me. I muster up as much sincerity as I can to welcome her to our new home. She returns my kindness with a dry "hello" that goes unnoticed by no one. Fortunately Stephanie cuts the moment short with a call to attention.

"Ladies, gentlemen, most of you know me already, for those of you who don't, I'm Stephanie, the show runner; these guys here are Jeremy and Matthew, the producers." Stephanie gestures to blue-haired girl and the guys I saw her talking to yesterday, "Amy, Rick, and Bryan are the production assistants. And this handsome devil hiding in the corner is Trenton Shaw. He's the guy that made all of this possible. Thank you, Trenton, for the check, I needed it." Laughter and cries of agreement go up around the room, led by Cashmere and Beverly. His only acknowledgment of the praise he's receiving is a curt nod; I know Trent well enough to know he's upset. He slinks back into his corner while Stephanie continues with the meeting. I'll find a way to get a moment with him later, for now Stephanie's speech has to be my priority.

With a tremendous effort I compartmentalize Trent and whatever is going on with him, and tune back in to hear Stephanie announce the host of the show, Iliana Forester. We clap as she walks out from a back room, ink-black hair flowing like a banner behind her. "The seven of you are here to fight for your dreams. You all want the same thing but only one of you will get it. You will be given assignments to be judged by a panel comprised of directors, producers, agents, and other industry executives. Starting week two, one person will be eliminated at the end of each weekly 'performance.' What is it exactly that you're competing for? The winner receives a talent agent, one hundred thousand dollars, and a role in an upcoming feature film. Now who's ready to get moved in?"

Indistinguishable cheers erupt from the cast; we're all ready to get settled in. When the cheers die down Stephanie takes over for Iliana. "Gentleman, you are free to break into pairs of your own liking; however, as you
know, the competition has already begun for the ladies; contending for the
single room. We received a total of fifty thousand views, the numbers have
been tallied, and we have a winner. Please direct your attention to the screen
to your right. At first nothing happens, then the television comes to life
playing my entry.

Instinctively I look to Trent, I want to celebrate with him if only with a
look. My eyes seek him in the corner of the kitchen he was occupying a few
moments ago; he's not there, he's gone. I try not to be too concerned about
Trent's absence, for all I know he's in the bathroom. If he doesn't come back
I'll go looking for him tonight when everyone's asleep. I don't watch as the
video plays in its entirety, instead I observe with satisfaction the looks of
resentment on the faces of Beverly and Cashmere. I'm as surprised as they
are, I didn't think I had enough followers to beat out a social media sensa-
tion. This win is huge; it means I might just be in the game.

"Congratulations Leah, you received the overwhelming majority of
votes on social media; however, since you did withdraw from the competition you've forfeited the prize." If I expected to win I wouldn't have withdrawn myself. Then again, maybe it was my withdrawal that caused me to
win. I do wish there was a way I could keep the room though, both ladies
have made it abundantly clear that whomever I room with, it will not be a
pleasant experience.

"Since Leah is no longer eligible for the prize, the room goes to the
runner up, Beverly." There is no applause; I guess no one appreciates winning by default. Beverly's mouth is a thin line of contorted anger. She didn't
expect losing to me for the second time, even if she did technically win. "I'm
so excited to be a part of this brand new exciting project and making all of
your dreams come true," Stephanie says, while looking us each in the eye.
"My advice to all of you is give it all you've got." Aiden cuts in with a chant
of "Go hard or go home." Corey follows suit while the rest of us look on in
amusement. Stephanie smiles tolerantly at the guys, then says, "Let's make
this a great season. Go get unpacked, the rest of the night is yours. We'll
convene tomorrow morning at ten."

Stephanie, Matthew, and Jeremy almost crash into Trent as he walks
back into the apartment. I overhear them inviting him to join them for dinner. He declines, citing work as the cause. He knows I'm watching as he has
multiple conversations with crewmembers, yet his eyes never meet mine.
Beverly and Cashmere, who know my involvement with him, linger behind
speaking in hushed tones, while the guys go off to claim their rooms. I'm

thinking I should do the same. Trent's ignoring me, there's no reason to stick around. I'll try once more to get his attention. If he disregards me again, that's it. Fortunately, he's over his tantrum and walking my way.

"Hey stranger," he answers me with a drawn and unreadable expression. A look I've never seen on his face before. "Good call on the video, it worked out well, you're off to a good start." I would thank him if he weren't radiating anger. Trent wants me to know he's upset with me. I get that much, what I don't know is why. I think back to the letter he wrote me this morning. No matter how upset he is, Trent loves me, and I don't want to fight with him.

I look at him through my lashes, in hopes my attempt at flirtation will soften him up. He tries to keep glowering at me but I break him. Through laughs he asks, "What am I going to do with you, I need you to tell me because I can't figure it out." From where they're standing, Beverly and Cashmere shout to Trent, "Do we all get one-on-ones with you or is that a special treat just for . . . challenge winners?" I would love to wipe the petty smirk off Beverly's face; she thinks she's clever with her kindergartener plan of holding what she knows about Trent and me over my head. He winks at me, relieving any doubts I may have about where his loyalties lie, before responding to them. "Hi ladies, I was planning on joining you as soon as Leah and I wrapped our conversation. However, there's no time like the present." I quietly slip away. As I walk up the steps I catch Trent's eye. In them is a promise to seek me out later.

I approach the first room off the stairs, the bedroom I'll be sharing with Cashmere, with trepidation. I didn't fully appreciate what I was doing by forfeiting the private room until this moment. In our room are two full-sized beds, two dressers, a floor lamp, and a chair. I pick the bed closest to the bathroom and the dresser nearest it. I decide to unpack only my tee shirts, jeans, loungewear, and undergarments; my dresses and really nice items I'll leave locked in my luggage stowed underneath my bed. As a former pageant girl I've seen the lengths women will go to sabotage each other, starting with personal effects. I like my clothes way too much to let them be torn, bleached, or stolen.

Halfway through my second suitcase I hear knocking at my door. I hasten to answer it, thinking it must be Trent. "Hi," he says with obvious question about the wisdom in coming to my room. "Hi," I repeat, looking at Brice in bewilderment. What is he doing at my door? I resist asking outright. Brice looks past me into my room, "Did Paris and Nicole not let you into their clique?" Laughingly I say, "Something like that, but I am impressed at how behind you are on pop cultural references." I'm rewarded with another smile, that's twice, maybe I was wrong, maybe Brice is just like Aiden.

"I admit I prefer ESPN to E news but I make it a point to befriend ladies that can keep me up-to-date on all the current celebrity gossip." While sharing another laugh I go ahead and invite Brice in. I still want to know why he came by, but I'm enjoying talking to him in the process. He enters reluctantly and stops near the door, I'm asking the reason for his visit when we're interrupted by Cashmere. "My, my, my, Leah, you do work quickly. Do you think your boyfriend will mind Brice being in your room?"

"Don't leave," she says to Brice reading his mind. "I was just dropping my things off, please don't stop on my account." She literally drops her bags on the floor in the middle of the room and leaves. Brice clears his throat uneasily, "I should go." I don't try to stop him. I watch as he walks down the hallway, still wondering what brought him to my room in the first place.

Still speculating at Brice's unexpected visit, and surprisingly missing the company, I continue to unpack. "Hey best friend," shouts Aiden from thedoorway, "we're all gathering downstairs to chill, you game?" I don't particularly feel like being around those hateful girls, but I don't want to make myself an outcast either. Aiden, sensing my wavering, charges at me,hoists me over his shoulders, and carries me downstairs kicking and screaming.

I demand to be put down several times, but since I'm laughing he doesn't take me seriously. In the living room I'm unceremoniously deposited onto the couch. I lie still catching my breath; when I sit up I turn to Aiden and say, "I have a very particular set of skills, skills I have acquired over a very long career, skills that make me a nightmare for people like you. I will look for you, I will find you, and I will kill you."

Laughter explodes around the room, Aiden and Corey, hands down the two most boisterous personalities, laugh the loudest. Zack, who must've came in during my speech, tries and fails to stifle a smile. Beverly and Cashmere come in from the front door together, "What are you guys howling about?" Zack tells them what's going on while I wonder where they were. "We were laughing at a game Leah just started, you want in?" I wasn't aware of any game, though I decide it's best I don't put Zack on the spot again after what happened earlier.

"Here's the deal, we'll break off into two teams: one team will say a famous movie line, the other will have three chances at guessing it. If you guess correctly you get a point, if not you select one member of your group to take a shot on the team's behalf. Any questions? If not, let's split up."

My team consists of Brice, Aiden, and myself. We lose the coin toss for who goes first. Zack's team huddle, deciding on the line Beverly ends up delivering: "I'm just one stomach flu away from my goal weight." Before either Aiden or I could think about it, Brice blurts out, "*The Devil Wears Prada*." We laugh at Brice knowing that, congratulate him, and let him choose the next line, "Just when I thought I was out they pull me back in." Pointing to Brice, Corey shouts, "*The Godfather*"; Zack provides, "part three." Cashmere takes a shot of Hennessey, even though her team correctly guessed the answer, then passes the bottle to Corey, who does the same.

We go into the last round tied up eleven apiece and it's my turn. "You had me at hello," Brice groans at my choice. It is a give away, no one seems to be able to answer though. Cashmere's unconscious, Corey's staring into the empty bottle, and it's possible Zack's asleep—he hasn't opened his eyes in two rounds. Beverley looks like she might know it but runs the risk of throwing up if she opens her mouth. "*Jerry McGuire.*" My heart responds to the voice I know so well. "Yes," I say, "but you're not on their team." Trent moves from the open door to the couches, "Cashmere's drunk, I'll take her spot."

His arrival rouses almost every one out of their stupor, except for Cashmere; at this point nothing can do that. "One last line for bragging rights," says Zack. If Trent's sticking around for one more line so am I. He sits down directly across from me, between Cashmere's sleeping form and Corey. "And lo, the beast looked upon the face of beauty, and beauty stayed his hand. And from that day forward he was as one dead." Tears I don't fully understand sting the back of my eyes, to him alone I respond, "Good things never last Mr. Shaw, *King Kong.*"

Trent rises from his seat, bringing the rest of the world back into focus. "Indeed, Ms. Albanese, on both counts, indeed." I watch with confusion, an ache in my chest, as he walks out the front door without looking back. Zack declares team Leah the winner for the second time today. To Beverley he says, "Watch out for this one." She grabs her discarded heels, gives me one more venomous look, then wobbles her way upstairs. Everyone except Cashmere, still asleep on the couch, does the same. I wait a couple of minutes before I tiptoe out the apartment; I have to talk to Trent.

I knock three times before he answers the door without inviting me in. His posture is angry and cold. I can hardly believe he's the same man, so stirred by his feelings for me he wrote them down. I don't know how to reach this version of him, "I see you finally remembered I exist," he says with malice. "What does that means? How could I ever forget you?" I step closer to him, wanting to close the emotional gap with physical closeness. He doesn't recoil from me, he doesn't welcome me either. "Looks like it from where I'm sitting and I have a panoramic view."

I look at him blankly not knowing how to respond. What am I supposed to say to that? Without warning Trent walks into his apartment, leaving the door wide open behind him. I assume he's left it open for me and follow him inside. He's in the kitchen rifling through the cabinets, that he could be searching for food in the middle of our fight breaks my calm. "What's your deal?" Trent slams the cabinet door shut, "You, you're my deal." He shouts. "It took only a few hours for you to forget about us, about me. I spend every other second of my day thinking about you and it's like I don't even exist to you anymore."

"What gives you the impression you don't matter to me as much as I matter to you?" I scream back. "Since we've met I've been taking my cues from you, I've trusted you with my deepest thoughts and my heart's desires, there is no greater intimacy or demonstration of how I feel than that." I see it happen, the anger leaving his body. "Trent," my voice is the softest it's ever been, "I need you to trust me, like I've trusted you." He bends his head low, placing a kiss on the cross that lies in the hollow of my neck then one on my lips. "I'm sorry, L."

The sunlight coming into my room is bright; it must still be early morning. I snuck back into the loft late last night. When I got in, Cashmere's bed was empty, as was the couch. I was too exhausted to give more than a fleeting thought to where she was. I don't know when she turned up but she's here now, sitting in bed, watching me. I try not to think about how long she's been surveying me while I slept soundly and unaware. "Good morning, sunshine, you got in late last night. One guess where you were." "You'd need more than the one, and you must have gotten in rather late yourself to know how late I was." Her lips curl in disgust. "Funny," she says, "if I were you I'd watch my back." Cashmere walks out, leaving me stupefied.

"My life has become a series of shouting matches and cliché confrontations," I mutter to myself aloud. "What'd you say?" Brice's tall frame fills the doorway; he happened to be walking by, overheard me speaking to myself, but thought I was talking to him. "Sorry, I wasn't speaking to you." Seeing I'm alone he says, "Sometimes, I speak to 'no one' too, he's a good listener." It's kind of him to lessen my embarrassment by admitting he talks to himself also. I may have a few enemies in this house but maybe I have a few friends too.

"Actually my 'no one' is a she." His dark brown eyes lighten with laughter, "Makes sense. We might have to introduce—" At that precise moment a brilliant shaft of sunlight fills my room so brightly I can't see, I squint against it while Brice looks into it reverently, the rest of his thought forgotten. I hop out of bed and draw the curtain, on cue Brice jolts back to the present. I don't know where he was a moment ago but it wasn't here with me. With a smile unlike the two he's given me before, he says, "I'm going to go have some coffee, you should think about having some too. I can tell you're not a morning person." I throw a pillow at him, which he deftly catches. "See, I knew you weren't." He's gone before the second pillow reaches him.

Intending to get a couple more minutes of sleep I flop back on my bed. Instantly turning on my side, my hand goes beneath my pillow, where it comes in contact with something foreign. My fingers close around the object, a key attached to a sticky note. Written in large print is, "Use it whenever you want, you're always welcome. BTW no cameras on the stairway up to my place." Trent can be impossible sometimes but mostly he's thoughtful and romantic. I'll try to remember that next time he upsets me; knowing him that'll happen sooner rather than later.

I put the key in the top drawer of my dresser for safekeeping; I've closed it before I register something's missing. Frantically I empty the drawer, the dresser, and my suitcases, but it's gone, my Bible is gone. I run down the steps screaming her name like a banshee, "Cashmere, where are you?" I find her in the kitchen with Corey; ignoring him I advance on her. She looks startled by my intensity though she tries to act tough, "What do you want?" What I want is to knock her out without being automatically eliminated; instead I slam my hand down on the island, "Where is it?" She jumps, startled by the noise. "Where's what, crazy?" I keep some distance between us, I don't want her to feel physically threatened, but I do want her to know I'm serious and I'm mad as I've ever been.

"You steal from me then call me names? Watch my back remember, this is how you want to play? Of all things, you steal my Bible." Cashmere jumps down from the island and walks toward me. I advise her not to come any closer for her own safety. "Your Bible? What do I need that for when I have all the scripture I need right here?" She lifts her tank revealing John chapter 3 verse 16 tattooed on her lower back. "You didn't take it because you need it, you took it to spite me." Corey, who I've yet to acknowledge, steps between Cashmere and me, "Whoa, we've been here talking the entire time. She didn't take anything." Of course he's defending her, he has a crush on her; in his simple mind that makes Cashmere incapable of guilt.

"Were you using your invisibility cloak in our room this morning when I woke up and found her staring at me, after which she proceeded to threaten me?" Corey clenches his fist and takes a step in my direction: Aiden and Brice, no doubt led to kitchen by the commotion, block his path. "Dude," Aiden places a hand on Corey's chest. "Calm down, alright bro?" He slaps Aiden's hand away, hard enough for anger to spark in Aiden's jovial face. Looking directly at me, Corey says, "Who cares, your Bible's gone, no one believes in that s—-." I erupt like a volcano before he completes his sentence. "I care, it's not for you to believe, that's why it was my Bible not yours or hers," I say pointing at Cashmere. "All she has to do is give it back." She yells over Corey's shoulder, "I don't have it. I didn't take it, I already told you, when would I have even had the chance?"

"This morning or last night, you had plenty of time." We stare each other down, separated by a wall of men. If they were to step aside I'd go straight for her, I'm angry enough to do damage. Behind me Zack clears his throat, I don't turn around, I won't break eye contact with Cashmere. "Just drop it, your things are missing and no one will admit to taking it. No amount of yelling, screaming, threatening, or violence will change that. You're only other option is to let it go. I suggest you do that immediately." Zack has a point, but it's easy to say "let it go" when it doesn't affect you. Also I hate his superior tone, all the words he's spoken to me thus far have been condescending. He doesn't care much for me, which is fine, but right now I have no desire to play nice.

I round on him poised to justify his dislike when a cackling laugh sounds from above us. Beverly leans over the banister wearing a white silk robe; once she sees she has our attention she says one word, "Funny." Brice predicts my reaction; before I take a step in her direction he puts a heavy hand on my shoulder, preventing me from running up the stairs after her. Unable to get any closer, I shout at her from where I stand, "I know what the two of you are doing and I'm not afraid of either of you. I've already beaten you twice and I'm going to keep on winning because I'm better than you, in every conceivable way. Keep messing with me and you'll wish someone would've warned you not to." I angle my body to look between both Cashmere and Beverly, "Now *you* watch out because I'm coming for you. Keep it. You need it more than I do."

I shake off Brice and head for the stairs. I'm half surprised he doesn't follow. I walk deliberately, keeping eye contact with Beverly. She doesn't move though she sees me coming, she stands her ground. Unlike Cashmere, she's unbothered by all that's happened, she relishes the drama. I keep my eyes trained on her until I'm in my room.

I scream into my pillow as I pace back and forth. I'm disappointed in myself for doing exactly what Trent told me not to, giving the producers their story; Bible-toting religious fanatic threatens feminist, accompanied by clips of me having to be restrained. I can't believe I let him talk me into this. "Knock, knock, can I come in?" Amy asks as she walks into my room anyway. She's not alone, she has a cameraman with her. They witnessed my blow up, only at the time I was too upset to care.

"Leah, are you okay, do you want to talk about it?" I take in Amy's small face and petite frame; her eyes are red and puffy like she hasn't slept in days. Even her blue hair looks dull and lank. Everything about her appearance is disarming, except I don't feel disarmed, I feel wary of her. Regrettably, "talking about it" is part of what I signed up for. "Yeah, I might as well," I say. Looks like I'll be first one in the house going into confessional.

The confessional turns out to be a small closet off the production room, which I estimate to be exactly where Trent's den is, in his apartment. I sit in front of a backdrop I'm assuming editing will alter, with a camera pointed at my face. "Tell me how you're feeling," Amy says. Between the confrontation and now, I've calmed down considerably, I'd like my property back, but I'm no longer angry, I say as much to her. "Okay talk to me about why you were so riled up before." It occurs to me that I was right to distrust Amy; she's dissatisfied with my calmness, she wants to capture me being belligerent and emotional. I won't give her the satisfaction. I'm inclined to be purposely boring, but that would be counterproductive. I elect to be straightforward without being explosive.

"Since the moment I met Cashmere and Beverly, they've been nasty to me. I can handle idle threats, however when you touch my property you've gone too far." She nods her head approvingly; apparently my response is inflammatory enough. "What is the source of the problem? You've known each other less than twenty four hours, what could've caused a showdown the likes of what we just witnessed." In truth I don't know. I've been assuming their problem with me is Trent, but we all have him in common, yet they get along just fine. So why do they hate me?

"A tyrant will always find a pretext for tyranny. They dislike me because they can, it's as simple as that." I shrug. "Where do you guys go from here?" We weren't friends before, we aren't friends now; nothing's changed except that they've made the first move. I was willing to stay on my side, let them stay on theirs, but that's not what they want. If a fight is what they crave, a fight is what they'll get. "When my things end up missing I take it very personally. I didn't want bad blood with Cashmere or Beverly, but lines have been crossed and teams have emerged. Let's be clear about this," I slide forward in my seat staring unblinkingly into the camera. "I'm no one's pushover, I'm not afraid of either of them or their guard dog, but they should be afraid of me. I'm going to win this and they're going to hate every moment of my shine #teamleah."

I storm out of the closet ripping off my mic pack as I go. My heart beats quickly and I'm short of breath. In the hallway I try to calm down. It's no use, all the stress of yesterday and this morning has gotten to me. A sharp pain ripples through my chest; I clutch my shirt, trying to get to the source, ease it somehow. Numbly I move down the hall, trusting my feet and memory to lead me to my room, quickly. I don't want to run into anyone or get caught on camera. I stop moving, slump against a wall, trusting it to hold me up, I'm going to faint.

I focus on breathing as my legs give out under me. I can't bring myself to care that I'm probably being recorded. Instead I sit there until I'm able to stand. I'm light headed but I get up without collapsing. Evidently I didn't make it more than a few feet past the interview room. No one has come this way, but that doesn't mean a person or camera didn't see me. I'll need to think of some way to explain this if need be, for now I have to get ready to meet Stephanie.

I make it back to my room. Cashmere's here too, touching up her makeup. She looks at me then quickly looks away. Silently I gather my toiletries, I'm feeling too weak for another round. I want to take a shower and get the day over with. "I didn't take your Bible," she manages to say without pausing the lining of her lips or diverting her eyes from her compact. "If it wasn't you, it was Beverly. You two are in this together." My tone is conversational, all the aggression from earlier is gone. "You sound jealous, are you sad the mean sluts aren't your friends?" She meant it to be a sarcastic quip but her voice betrays her. I almost feel bad, then I remember she threatened me. "You've been clear about where we stand from the inception, and I never called you a slut; that's your conscious speaking to you, not me."

Chapter 13

As I EXPECTED, I'm the last to arrive to the living room, where we're scheduled to meet with Stephanie. Luckily she hasn't arrived yet. Everyone mills around. Cashmere and Beverly sit together although they don't speak, Aiden's being loud and rambunctious, Corey laughs with Zack until he sees me and stops. Surprisingly, he waves; after the guys having to step between us earlier I didn't expect to ever speak to Corey again. "Leah, I saved you a seat," laughingly he pats his lap.

"As enticing as that sounds, I'm going to have to park it on the couch." I'm relieved to no longer be in conflict with him, that's one less person I have to be on guard against. Corey doesn't say the words but his actions tell me he's sorry. So am I. Brice takes the seat next to him, I watch without being able to hear what looks like a serious conversation. Eventually they fist bump and lapse into a more casual manner.

The front door opens, admitting Iliana. She comes in dressed for a night at the club in a body suit and sheer skirt. She looks nice but over dressed. I think my favorite thing about being rich and famous is getting to wear a ball gown to the grocery store and no one questioning the sense in it because that's what famous people do. Iliana addresses us with uncustomary seriousness. "As you all know, this is a competition, you're here to compete for your dreams. Only one person will win, the person who wants it the most." She pauses, letting the words sink in—which one of us most wants their dream? Me, I do, the farther away my dreams move from me the less I can breathe. If wanting it enough is all it takes to win, consider the competition over.

"Last night we discussed the weekly performance. In addition to that you will have weekly challenges. These challenges will help the judges make their decision on who stays and who goes. This week there will be no elimination, but there will be a performance and a challenge today, in a few minutes. But first, Stephanie would like to say a few words."

As it did the night before, the television screen turns on, streaming Stephanie live from what appears to be her office. "Good morning, guys, I hope you've all settled in well. I have some exciting news, we had our very first confession this morning." Everyone looks at each other, wondering who was the brave soul. I look around also, not wanting to give away it was me. "Remember you are all expected to do this at least once a day. Producers may seek you out, but you may also seek us out for a confessional. In addition I would like to remind you all that fighting is strictly prohibited. Depending on the severity of the transgression, your contract will be terminated, resulting in immediate elimination." I question if that's a general reminder or a specific one for me.

"If you are eliminated after a performance you are expected to head back to the house promptly to pack; you will be returned home in the manner you arrived. There is one phone for general use, located in the phone room at the end of the main hall. As you know, we are not paying any of you to be here; however, we are giving you a fifty-dollar-a-day food stipend. That stipend will be given to you once weekly, eight a.m. every Friday, for as long as you are here. Instructions for the following day will usually be conveyed sometime the night before. With that said, good luck to you all." The front door opens, admitting a man I don't believe to be crew. As he approaches, Iliana introduces him, "Without further ado, join me in welcoming Morgan Brockhart, your in-house acting coach. Morgan has worked with some of the best, now he wants to work with you."

Morgan Brockhart is an olive-skinned, hazel-eyed, middle-aged man with strong presence. In a plain black shirt, cuffed-hem dark denim, and dark porter boots he resembles a writer, a very pretentious writer. Morgan steps forward, claps his hands shortly calling us to attention. "Guys and gals, up, up, we have a lot of work to do, I have you for a short time and there's much work to be done. Clear the space so we can get started."

We move the furniture against the walls then stand in a circle in the middle of the living room; Morgan stands at the head of it, leading us through deep breathing exercises. "That's it, breathe in, nice and deep, and breathe out. Okay one more time, breathe in and breathe out." My lungs contract and expand with wonderful air, each breath glorious. "Now this time when you breathe out release all your pent-up energy, I want to hear you release your breath," Morgan breathes in and out audibly while shaking his hands and arms. "I want to see the toxic energy exiting your body." I thoroughly enjoy the breathing exercise, it's cathartic; I've gotten used to a constant uneasiness in my chest, after all this time. I forgot how it felt to be free of it, almost free of it.

"Okay now we're going to do another exercise. It's an oldie but a goodie, called Zip Zap. Real simple, one by one each of you will turn to your left, make eye contact with the person next to you, clasp your hands together, point with your index fingers, and 'zip.' We'll do this until the 'zip' returns to the first person, understood? Great let's go." He turns to his left, meets Zack's eyes, then says, "zip." Zack turns to Corey, "zip." We go on, stopping only once when Beverly gives a feeble "zip." "It's not 'zip,' its 'ZIP!'" Morgan's voice booms, "One more time!"

After going around the circle twice, Morgan stops us to introduce the word "zap," we substitute zip for zap. "Now we make things interesting," Morgan says in his carrying voice. "We're going to introduce 'boing' to redirect energy across the circle, whoever the energy is pointed at has to duck, then continue the energy going either way. If you don't duck in time you're out." Morgan sent the first "boing" to me, I see it coming and duck then "zap" Aiden to my right. We go around for a few minutes before the first casualty, Beverly, followed by Cashmere, in quick succession, then Corey, who looks happy about being out of the circle with the girls.

Momentarily distracted by Corey's awful pick up lines delivered to Cashmere, I almost miss a "boing." Luckily I duck in time and hit Zack, which he is not happy about. Great, something else to add to his growing list of why not to like me. The game comes down to Brice and me, back and forth we go; he was a formidable opponent in the large group, but I easily take him out for the win.

"Very good, people, very good. Now we move on to our challenge. I was, shall we say, inspired by your game last night." It's amazing how quickly you adapt to the cameras; I forgot they were present yesterday evening and that they're present now. "We're going to put a twist on what you started. Someone will say a line from a movie to start, the person responding must reply with another movie line. The only rule is it must make sense. You have ten seconds to answer, if not, you're out. If your reply doesn't fit, you're out. Last man standing wins the challenge, understood? Okay let's begin."

Aiden turns to Brice and says, "Hello, my name is Inigo Montoya. You killed my father, prepare to die." Brice is quick on his feet, his response is almost immediate. "I am your father." Morgan pauses the game to praise them on their quick wit and improvisational skills. In the best Heath Ledger impression I've heard, Corey makes eye contact with me and asks, "Why so serious?" I choke back a laugh before retorting, "I see dead people," this earns me a pat on the back from Morgan. "A talented group, I see, very talented." For my turn I address Aiden, "You don't understand, I coulda had class. I coulda been a contender. I coulda been somebody, instead of a bum."

Which is what I am." With a placid look, which doesn't quite suit him, Aiden says, "Frankly, my dear, I don't give a damn."

Morgan roars with laughter, a high-pitched, raucous noise, "Yes, yes, I love it." Aiden delivers his next line to Cashmere, who, to my surprise, responds fittingly. This is the first time Cashmere has shown any enthusiasm for anything we've done. Excitedly, she looks at me, "Roads, where we're going we don't need roads." I'm stumped, I didn't expect another turn so quickly. At the last second I come up with something perfect. "Fasten your seatbelts, ladies and gentleman, this is going to be a bumpy ride." Morgan takes my hands in his, wide-eyed and thrilled, he exclaims, "Yes, brilliant, this is what I love to see, spunk commitment. Bravo, bravo."

Morgan's a bit theatrical, to say the least, but his enthusiasm is infectious. We restart again, this time with Zack, who speaks to Beverly, "What we've go here is a failure to communicate." She splutters before saying, "As if." It's not the cleverest of comebacks, but it works. On and on we go until Aiden eliminates Cashmere. He then takes Corey out with a line from Macbeth; he's really good at this. For his next turn he fires at me, "Stella, hey Stella." I hold up one finger in a gesture meaning "one minute," then say, "I'll be back."

Barely containing his amusement at my last reply, Brice rounds on Zack, "The first rule of fight club is: you do not talk about fight club." I didn't see it coming, but stumped, Zack is eliminated by Brice. He joins the rest of his team from last night on the sidelines. Only Brice, Aiden, and I remain. "We're going to increase the difficulty," says Morgan with a hint of mischievousness. "By making it a conversation, keep the lines flowing, where one person leaves off the next must continue. Same rules of elimination apply." To Brice, Aiden says, "Toto, I've a feeling we're not in Kansas anymore." A brilliant change in inflection and a shrug of his shoulders gives Brice the perfect response of, "There's no place like home." Taking my cue from Brice, I say, "E.T. phone home." My voice raises an octave at the end of the word "home" to communicate it as a question. Gravely, Aiden utters, "May the force be with you." Neither Brice nor I are able to think of anything to say quickly enough, Aiden eliminates us both.

"You all did a fantastic job, so much so I'm confident you'll impress the judges. This week you will perform a two-minute monologue that somehow reflects you. This will be your introduction to the judges, show them who you are. Your monologue can come from a movie, play, book, or be an original of any genre. This is your chance to tell us a story about yourself, make it a good one. Spending this time with you today I feel that I've gotten to know you all, seen a glimpse of the strengths and talents you possess. You will all do well. I'll see you tomorrow at one . . . with your monologue in tow."

On his way out, Morgan quietly says to me, "Leah, a few people in particular stood out to me today, you are one of them. You've got chops, lovely, this is your calling." I've devoted a lot of time thinking about my dreams, I don't know that I've ever given thought to whether my dreams are also my calling. I once heard your calling described as your God-given purpose. I think most people never find theirs, I pray I'm living mine.

The boys lift and replace the living room furniture. Once everything is back in place we move to the kitchen as a group. Standing in front of the stove, Corey asks, "Who's up for lunch, I'm cooking?" "Can you actually cook or are you a master chef of take out," I ask while joining him. Red locks fall over his right eye making him look younger than usual, "I'm seriously a good cook, if this doesn't work out it's off to culinary school for me." Corey's lucky he has more than one dream. I don't have an "if I don't win"—try as I may to want other things, it's no use, I have only one dream.

"You're like an onion, my friend, you have layers." He snorts then puts us all to work as his sous chefs preparing a feast of spaghetti and tomato sauce. We break off into pairs, chopping, cutting, and the like. Corey suggests he and I work together; silently we dice tomatoes. "I wanted to apologize to you," he says without looking away from his task. I'm not upset with him anymore; even if I were, my anger would not be able to stand up to his remorsefulness. "Thank you for apologizing, I should've handled things better too." I cover his hand with mine, letting him know the fault isn't solely his. "I should've kept my head. In the future let's not ever attack each other again." We hug and go back to chopping and chattering.

Because Beverly's declaration that her extent of cooking is 'turning the coffee maker on,' she and Cashmere are given the most simple of tasks, boiling the water. They have plenty of time to chat up the guys and be generally annoying while the rest of us actually cook. "A man that can cook is muey caliante," Cashmere purrs. "In that case," says Zack, "I'll make the salad too." Smiling, Brice passes him the lettuce. "Typical, a beautiful girl tells a man she thinks something is sexy and they hop to it." Everyone looks at Beverly shocked, none of us imagined Beverly, who uses her beauty as a weapon, would find offense in that .

"You're saying that doing what the woman you're interested in asks of you is wrong?" Zack asks disbelievingly. "Men are so obtuse," I sigh. "Not all of us," Brice corrects. He's been so quiet I forgot he was here. "Women want us to do what they ask not because we think we'll get some sort of 'payment' but because we want to, because we care." Piggy backing off his point I elaborate, "It's the breakup scene in the breakup, 'I don't want you to do the dishes, I want you to want to do the dishes.'" Zack nods in comprehension and tries to explain it to Corey, who's woefully lost, while I come to a realization. Of everyone in the house Brice is the surprise—he's handsome, articulate, kind, confident, while also being humble, and he understands women. I don't know which character box he falls into but he's definitely a threat.

I look to Cashmere and Beverly knowing what I'll see before I do, they're looking at Brice like he's a meal. No way he makes it out of the competition without getting caught in one of their webs. My money's on Cashmere. She's staring at him hungrily, she wants him, no one will stop her, maybe not even him. I barely have this thought before Cashmere's charging at Brice, wrapping her arms around him, and kissing him full on as if the rest of us aren't here. He's too startled to kiss her back, that doesn't stop the guys from cheering on. Suddenly no longer hungry, I return to my room. Cashmere is a predator; she should be locked up for menacing and sexual harassment. Brice is a nice guy, he needs a nice girl. She is not that by any stretch of the imagination.

Tentatively my door creaks open. I don't bother sitting up, I have nothing to say to Cashmere. "Leah?" I'm up, off my bed, and in his arms in a matter of seconds. I don't know how or why, but Trent's standing in my room. "You have no idea how happy I am to see you." He laughs softly into my neck, "Things going that well?" he says sarcastically. When I don't respond, Trent asks what's wrong. I thought he saw the footage from earlier and knew I had a hard day. Part of me felt his title made him an omniscient presence in this house; nothing could happen on his show without him being the wiser. I don't really feel like reliving the details but I give him an abbreviated version. "I may have lost my cool this morning with Cashmere, Beverly, and Corey when I found that my Bible was stolen."

"I'm sorry it was a hard day for you, but we talked about this. Cashmere came in here with a big following, you want her fans to be your fans not your enemies. You've seen what the 'Beehive' can do and Beverly is Beverly. Like her or not, people will enjoy watching her." Right now I need him to hug me, not give me a lecture on strategy, can't he see that? "What do you mean by Beverly is Beverly, are you condoning her targeting me?" I step away from him, feeling betrayed, I need him to tell me he's on my side. "The truth of the matter is, Beverly is young, wild, and free. You, you're more inhibited. As a viewer, she'll be easier to relate to. If you want a chance at this, it wouldn't be wise to go up against her." That was the wrong answer; Trent completely missed the point about what led to the confrontation and why I'm now upset with him.

"I'm not sure when you stopped believing in me, but today I remembered how much I enjoy this, how good I am at it. As president of the Beverly Boyd fan club, you should know I'm going to beat her. Now I have work to do, please leave." There's this constant tug of war with Trent when it comes to me. From day one he's expressed his delight in who I am while also expressing the necessary changes he feels I need to make, which would make me someone completely different; I can't be both people. I hold the door open for him to leave; he does without a word of protest.

I sulk in my room, ignoring the loud amused voices coming from downstairs until my stomach starts to growl. "I like exotic women" is the first thing I hear when I walk into the kitchen. I move around fixing myself a plate of spaghetti unsuccessfully ignoring the conversation, the gang's seated around the island engaged in a colorful discussion. "Exotic, huh, which of us would you date if given the opportunity?" I intended on taking my meal back to my room but the dialogue has taken a very interesting turn. I squeeze between Aiden and Brice, who let me without hesitancy.

Cashmere pretends to examine her nails as we await Aiden's response, though I see how much the answer matters to her. Beverly, who asked the question, is so secure in his answer being her that she's the only one who doesn't laugh when he says, "Depends on which one of you will have me." Corey leans across the table to give Aiden a pound, "Nice save, bro, also very logical thinking, I approve." Zack shakes his head laughingly, "Aiden, you have no standards, any willing female is your type." I happen to be swallowing a mouthful of food at the same time Aiden replies, "Who can blame me? Is willing not your type or do you prefer to club your ladies over the head and tell them they want you?" My body doesn't know whether to laugh or swallow, I end up doing both and choking. Brice slaps me on the back multiple times before the food dislodges from my throat.

Crisis averted, we refocus on the question of Zack's type, though Corey has a few ideas of his own on the matter. "We know his type, right, Beverly." Okay, so there's something going on there, I completely missed it. "You can hardly hold that against him since I'm everyone's type." Typical Beverly, obnoxiously funny. "I've been rich and famous," Zack begins, "by the time I was twenty-one I'd 'dated' every type of woman. I've realized what I want most in a woman is for her to be non-spotlight seeking."

Judging by the awkward silence, I wasn't the only one who detected the raw edge to his voice. The conversation has gone from capricious to sedated, but just when I was sure there was no going back, Aiden comes to the rescue in the way that only he can. "Bro, even if she's a beast in the face?" Our laughter isn't equal to the quality of the joke, I think we're all relieved to be laughing again, Zack even more so. "Well no, I'd prefer her to be an attractive brunette. But once you've had a taste of the limelight you'll see what I mean."

Beverly barely notices his comment, which is telling; neither of them must be serious about the other. Beverly, blond and boisterous, could not be more opposite his perfect girl if she tried. Whatever they have is fleeting. Aiden, Corey, and Zack give faces to their perfect woman, courtesy of Hollywood, while Beverly tries to convince them that compared to her, every woman in life pales. Meanwhile Cashmere distractedly toys with a tangerine, deep in thought. I spare a moment in wonder of what she can be thinking when I notice Brice is as quiet as her and even more disconcerted.

"My perfect woman completes me temporally and spiritually. Her presence is restoring and reassuring," Brice says, bringing silence to every side conversation. "She's beautiful, beauty that inspires worship at her feet. It's amazing how she can be both gentle and tough, always knowing when to be which. She is resilient, tenacious, and courageous. Her fame wouldn't bother me because her words are both her power and her art; she knows what to say with it. She's not perfect, because I'm not, but together we're whole, she makes my lefts right and my downs ups. I don't want a hundred women, I just want her, forever and always."

For the second time today, Brice has left us speechless. He's tall and dignified, but he's also this self-aware, conscious, spiritually in tune guy. He's humble without weakness. The passion he spoke about his perfect woman with is enough to cause a woman to want to be her. Cashmere asks what we're all thinking, "Do you know her or do you just have a very active imagination?" Brice described her effortlessly a minute ago, though for some reason he hesitates now. "Yes and no, I'm not seeing anyone right now but I know what I want. What about you, are you seeing anyone?"

Batting her lashes she says, "Are you asking me out on a date?" She just can't help herself; if she's not being sex crazed she has no identity. Brice studies her for a long time, an uncomfortably long time, while the rest of us look on. I think about their kiss earlier and question my assessment of the kind of man he is. As I come to my own conclusions about him, he comes to his about Cashmere. "Has a man ever gotten to know you without the express purpose of sleeping with you?" The smile slips from her face. "Have you ever had someone value you; not your face but your spontaneity, your spunk, your shrewd business mind and tenacity?" With what appears to be a great effort She answers with her usual flippancy, "Honey, when you look as good as I do, all that other stuff is just a bonus."

I look at her for what feels like the first time; underneath the eyeliner she is a young woman with sorrowful eyes. Brice has known her as long as any of us. Somehow he saw beyond her vanity and her bark to the real Cashmere. He identified all her best character traits and forced her to acknowledge them too. Why wasn't I able to do the same? Cashmere's very forthcoming about her life story on her YouTube channel; I've even watched a few of her videos. She's spoken about living in group homes and what it was like fighting for survival; why didn't I remember that, was I too busy wallowing in self pity to see someone else's plight? Maybe I shouldn't have told Beverly to keep my Bible, I clearly need a refresher.

"What about you, Leah, what's your ideal man like?" I don't answer him at first, thinking it's just another way for Aiden to cut the tension. That he's flexing his muscles does nothing to convince me otherwise, not until he asks again. Beverly smirks at me with a devilish grin, eager for my response. I look to Cashmere, sure she'd be taunting me as well, but she's barely present, her mind clearly elsewhere. I think about this question from the viewer's point of view. They've gotten to know everyone except me. They know Beverly's cattiness, Cashmere's sensuality, Aiden's humor, Zack's seriousness, Corey's affability, and Brice's thoughtfulness, but what do they know about me? Nothing true, this is my opportunity to have a meaningful interaction, I have to take it.

I had this same conversation with my sister only a few days ago. It was hard talking to her about it, it's much harder with cameras and Beverly. I know what I want though for a split second I have a clear image of that person, which has never happened—my Godsend has never had a face—but the moment passes quickly and his features slip away.

"I'm a romantic, I believe in love at first sight, soul mates, and 'the one.' I don't believe all love happens instantly, your soul mate is always who you should be with, or that everyone finds their 'one.' You can meet someone your spirit already knows, already loves, yet that love is too toxic to prosper. Your 'one' is the best parts of you, not your ruin. Every love felt in this plane can be destructive if it doesn't have balance, respect, and boundaries. Everyone wants to be crazy in love, but some flames burn too hot to be tempered; remember, it was love that drove Romeo and Juliet to suicide, be careful to not find yourself ablaze."

Every pair of eyes in the room is glued to me, enraptured, hanging onto my every word. Whether or not they agree with me, I don't know. I feel like a professor at the end of a particularly thought-provoking lesson, all that's left to do is dismiss my class. "My ideal man will balance me and help me blossom into the woman I want to become. He will understand me, not only in the trivial things but my essence; what matters to me will matter to him. I don't know, maybe I'm all wrong about everything, only time will tell." Amy pulls Brice and Cashmere for interviews. The rest of us are reminded to go to the confessional. Since I already have, I skip it for now in favor of making a phone call. Before we split up we agree to meet back up in a few hours for a night out on the town.

The phone room is actually a closet fancied up with a coat of paint. In the middle of the small space are a red telephone, a glass end table, and a blue beanbag chair. Zack sits on the floor outside the room waiting. Inside, Beverly's on the phone. He lifts his head from his book long enough to identify my approaching form before returning back to his reading. We got off on the wrong foot, Zack and I; recognizing him as a child actor then announcing it to the group didn't win me any points with him. It was completely unintentional, though Zack has taken it as a deliberate slight.

To force him to acknowledge me, I ask if he too is waiting for the phone. "I need to call my manager," is all he says, though his tone suggests more. Zack may not like me but he dislikes being here more. Knowing we have that in common emboldens me to keep trying despite his coolness, "Can I ask you a question?" He doesn't look away from his book or recognize I spoke in anyway. When I'm positive trying to make nice is a lost cause, he will not be won over, Zack responds, "You want to know why I'm doing this. How'd I go from Ryder Grey to Zack Asher, reality TV aspirant?"

That is exactly what I want to know, though I would have asked more tactfully. He gives me a sidelong look, seemingly considering the advisability of answering my question. I read in his body when he decides to, he kind of deflates like a balloon. "Did you know our ratings weren't even poor? We were cancelled due to rebranding, apparently we didn't fit into the network's new direction, we weren't edgy enough." I lower myself to the ground opposite Zack, facing him, a small act of sympathy. "Cancellations are a real part of the business: bad reviews, low ratings, they are all part of the industry, but it chips at you. As an actor you know there are going to be extreme highs and equally extreme lows, but that kind of disappointment is in a category all its own."

Zack launches his book at the wall savagely. I try not to flinch. He isn't aiming for me, he's releasing frustration. It lands near me, though not close enough to have hit me. "I'm so sorry," he says, blanching at what he'd just done. I assure him I'm fine, that there's nothing to apologize for. Satisfied he didn't hurt me, he continues, "I don't even need to work, do you know that? My parents are smart, they invested my money well. I have more than I can spend, which makes life easier, but it doesn't stop me from feeling like I have something to prove."

As a child, wanting to be an actor is equivalent to wanting to be a princess, sure it *can* happen but it probably won't. When it doesn't, you comfort yourself with knowing that it was the musings of a child or it's such a game of chance that you are just one of the millions who didn't get that lucky break. But to beat the odds and live out a dream, then lose it never to regain it means it was you. You had the opportunity but you couldn't hang onto it. I don't think I could live with that. "My on-screen family all landed on their feet, two of them even won an Oscar, and me . . ." He lets the rest of the sentence hang in the air, unable or unwilling to complete it.

"A couple of months ago my manager told me about a reality competition for serious actors. Neither of us knew what to expect of it, but it's the best offer I've gotten in years. He also said something to the effect of it being an opportunity to circulate my name again, possibly reviving a comatose career. Thinking it may be my last chance to be in front of an audience, I agreed; I've resented the desperation that led to that decision every minute since." Returning to his usual demeanor, he declares finality to the discussion, "I hope that answers your question."

From the moment I recognized Zack, I have been conjecturing what circumstances would bring him to this place with beauty queens, Internet sensations, models, and former semi-professional athletes. Why would he, tested and proven actor, need this? I suppose because he's like me, like us all, sure of there being greatness inside us, desperate to showcase it to the world. I lean forward across the space between us, "This may not be the way you wanted it, but it might turn out to be the break you needed. You'll give another life-altering performance someday soon and the whole world will have no choice but to take notice." We pass the rest of the time waiting in comfortable conversation.

"Hey Mom, how are you?" I say to her voicemail, "I wanted to let you know I'm okay. There's nothing much to tell yet but everything's going well so far. Anyway, I'm going to go, I hope to speak to you soon. I'll call you again when I get the chance, say hello to Antonia for me." I hate feeling that my mom's upset with me, or worse, disappointed. I wish I could've made her understand how I was feeling and why I had to go, I was drowning, suffocating on shattered dreams and lost hope. Maybe if I win she'll understand, then things can go back to normal, the way we used to be.

I dial her one more time; when she doesn't answer I call Trent. I get his voicemail too. "Hey it's me, I don't want to fight anymore, let's kiss and make up. The producers are sponsoring a night out for us at some club called Venus, we're heading out around ten, if you're free maybe you can stop by, if you can't I'll talk to you soon."

Back in my room, Cashmere's rifling through her things, pulling out dress after dress. I clear my throat to get her attention before I can talk myself out of doing the right thing. "Come to accuse me of stealing something else?" she asks. I give myself a mental nudge past her attitude, "I want to apologize to you for my behavior earlier, I'm sorry." I still think she and Beverly are behind my missing Bible but I shouldn't have lost my temper. If I expected gratitude from her, or at the least civility, I was wrong, she looks at me with pure contempt, "I have no idea what he sees in you." She's been venomous to me since we've met; I assumed her spitefulness was because of my involvement with Trent, now I know it's more. If my relationship with him were as casual as the one she had with him or what he had with Beverly she wouldn't care. Cashmere hates me because Trent loves me.

"Brice asked whether I've ever had a man show nonsexual interest in me; no, I don't think I have, and Trent is worst of all. I met him through a friend at a party about a year ago. He's as pretty as I am, successful, and willing to help me with my career. He swept me off my feet, for the first time in my life I was in love. Weeks after we met, following a very long night, I was convinced we were on the same page. I was so sure that I told him how I felt. Do you know his response?" I shake my head no to the rhetorical question, "He said, 'Don't, I can't love you back.'

"I thought all he needed was time, I was prepared to give him that, but he was positive he could never love me. I cried, I screamed, I even smacked him. I blocked the door with my body, refusing to allow him to leave. I needed to know why not me. Over and over I asked if there was someone else. Fed up with me hitting him, he admitted to me he's loved the same girl for five years, that I deserve someone to love me the way he loves her. In that one sentence I got the most emotion out of him I ever had in three months.

"I stopped blocking his path then, I couldn't force him to feel for me what he won't. 'If I could be that person for you,' he said with sadness, 'I wouldn't, because that would mean I would have to stop loving her, something I could never do. My heart is too full of her to love anyone else.' That's when I punched him in the face." She smiles at the memory, "I expected him to be angry enough to hit me back, instead he looked at me like I was pitiful. I attacked him again with everything in me. I wanted him to hit me, that pain I can handle, but he didn't. Instead he held my arms at my side until I stopped trying to fight him.

"Calmer, I asked why he was spending his time with me if he was in love with someone else? I wish I hadn't asked that question, some things really are better left unsaid, but I did, and he was cruel to tell me the truth. 'She doesn't know I exist but I love her anyway.' It hurt so badly, so badly, of everything he said, that wounded me most of all. I screamed, 'How could you, how could you pass me up for someone who doesn't know you; I'm real and I'm here.'" Cashmere clutches her shirt, unaware she's doing it. The pain she felt then hadn't abated with time, she's as injured by it today as she was when it happened.

"After saying sorry he left, and we hadn't spoken again until the day before I met you. For months I tried calling, texting, dm, social media tags, but nothing. He didn't even call about *Star Quality*; Trent had Stephanie reach out to me. I wasn't interested in a reality show that wasn't solely my own, but I thought it was his way of getting back in my life, so I agreed. Even after I signed on to be part of the project he didn't contact me. Then out of the blue one day I get a text from him. He heard I was hosting an event, wanted to stop by, and would be bringing a 'friend' along. It was what I had been hoping for, so when he walked into the restaurant that night I was foolishly happy.

"He smiled at me when he saw me, I wanted him back. I thought he wanted me too. I didn't think anything of him being alone; I figured he changed his mind about bringing a friend because he wanted more time alone with me. Then you came in looking radiant and I saw the truth in his eyes. He looked at you like you were everything good in the world. I knew in my gut you were the girl. I found you on social media, lived on your pages for days, followed your posts. Without fail Trent reacted to them all, he has over three million followers, he only follows a few dozen back, all industry executives and celebrities, except you. You were her, you had to be. All these months I thought I had moved on but I hadn't." Cashmere looks at me with unshed tears in her eyes, "You broke my heart, Leah. So yes, I hate you, I will hate you for as long as he loves you."

I stand on the verge of tears for a woman who loved a man who did not love her back. I feel responsible for the agony she feels, but there's nothing I can do to make it right, no comfort I can offer her. I love Trent too, I haven't told him but I do. I'm sincerely saddened for her; however, he and I are together now. I've been adrift at sea with nothing except a steadily deflating life vest, slowly sinking under, which is its own special kind of torture—seeing your end but without a way to stop it. I'd given up, accepted the inevitable, when Trent came along in a lifeboat and pulled me in. He breathed new life into me; there is no separating us despite how much sympathy I may feel for Cashmere. We stand in the knowledge of what lies between us; with no way around it, I leave.

Emotionally fatigued from the day's events, tired from getting in late the night before, I lie down on the couch and quickly drift asleep. I dream I'm running on an old dirt road, in the kind of back woods I've only ever seen on television, from a mob led by Beverly. As hard as I push my legs, they're catching up to me. With the mob hard on my heels and nowhere to go, I start to panic. I come upon a fork in the road, the lane on the right leads to an old rundown house. The path to the left leads to a pretty colonial: white with a red door, and what feels like its own brightly shining sun. I want, even more than getting away from the mob, to claim that house as mine.

Instinctively my feet carry me to the right, on the road that leads to the broken-down house. I fight against my uncooperative body and turn back, opting to go left instead. The handsome house is equidistant from the fork and would undoubtedly be a much more pleasant place to hide. I stop running; nothing can get me here in this beautiful oasis of green grass and butterflies.

I follow the path, the house no more than twenty feet ahead, though after several minutes of walking I realizeI haven't closed the gap; it remains the same distance away. That's not all, the sun has gone from pleasantly warm to brutally hot and growing hotter by the minute. Sweat rolls down my arms, face, and legs while my mouth aches from thirst. The previously melodic chirping of birds is now a predatory cawing. I squint up and see vultures circling overhead waiting for me to keel over and die. At the rate I'm going that may be any second. I keep walking toward the house because what else can I do; suddenly I'm no longer miles away, I'm outside the white picket fence. I made it, I've arrived.

I enter through the gate, unto the walkway leading to the bright red front door. Thunder sounds above as big fat drops of water fall from the sky. Desperately thirsty, I lean back and open my mouth. A single raindrop lands on my tongue, it sizzles then burns like the spiciest hot sauce. My sweat and tears mingle inextricably on my face the rain has done nothing to cool the temperatures, if anything it's made the conditions worse. Long gone is the feeling of safety, something's definitely wrong, something's trying to get me. I have to get inside, it's my only hope. Running, my feet slips on the wet-pavement and I fall onto the lawn. The patch of previously fresh-cut green grass turns brown beneath me. I gasp, as the rest of the lawn simultaneously withers and dies too.

I look ahead to the house, only five feet away now, seeking refuge, but it too has changed. Where it was once beautiful it's now sinister. To my right, in the distance, past the clouds, the sun shines down welcomingly on the broken-down house, though it doesn't look so broken down anymore. It needs repair, but the potential is obvious. Why didn't I go there instead? A noise sounding like slamming doors pulls my attention back to my present danger; no amount of regretting my decision can change what I'm facing now. The slamming I heard are the shutters, now hanging off the windows, banging against the house. As I look on, the red door opens. I get to my feet, afraid to go forward, unable to go back. Through the door is an ominous darkness littered by what looks like flesh-rotted hands reaching toward me.

My feet are rooted to their spot I beg them to run while hands extend my way; they don't. A scream bubbles up inside me as skeletal fingers reach me. I sit up, eyes open, fearful I was dragged inside the house of horrors. Thankfully I'm on the couch where I feel asleep. I take deep, soothing breaths until I'm relatively calmer. I find that even in wakefulness I'm still afraid, very afraid. I haven't had a dream terrify me this much since I was a child. If my mom were here she would say it meant something. I have no idea what, for now I'll steer clear of colonials and traveling without water. I'm happy we're going out tonight, an evening of fun is exactly what I need.

The water is hot and blissful, by the time I step out the shower I feel reinvigorated. I dress in a floor-length, pale gold slip dress: loose in the right places, fitted everywhere else. I wear designer silver chain link sandals on my feet and an ornate choker around my neck. Perfectly coiled curls fall around my face for the right balance of pretty and sexy. I look at myself in the mirror, pleased. I took extra care in dressing because Trent might be meeting us tonight. I've learned an apology is always best given while looking fantastic.

"Stop right there," Amy halts me at the top of the stairs. "Doug, get up there now; Kevin, foot of the steps; Malcolm, you're on reactions." I squeeze against the wall as Doug runs past me camera in tow. As soon as the cameramen are in place, Amy cues me to continue down the steps. Quiet blankets the room as I make my descent. Inwardly I muse to myself that I know how Cinderella felt entering the ball.

Aiden meets me at the foot of the stairs with a gallantly proffered hand. "Telling you how amazing you look would do you no justice." His voice lacks its usual playfulness, expressing the depth of his sincerity. I'm struck with how much Aiden reminds me of Dylan, they're both mellow and mild tempered, it's easy to discard their feelings, so rarely on display. I'm honored and touched that Aiden would give me a real glimpse of himself. "Thank you, you don't look bad either."

"But not as good as you," Zack says, taking my hand from Aiden and bringing it to his lips; Aiden, always a good sport jokes that would still make him better looking than Zack. It's flattering having the guys, who are all handsome in their own right, clamber for the chance to compliment me. They've cleaned up well also: Zack clad in all black, Corey in jeans and a cardigan, and Aiden, who doesn't care about clothes and fashion, in dark denim paired with a white button-up.

Corey saddles up beside me while we await Beverly and Cashmere's arrival. "It's my turn to tell you how beautiful you look," he says. I'm fortunate to have always been told I'm attractive, nevertheless all this attention tonight is extremely flattering. "That's really sweet of you to say, you look good too." He blushes bright red, "Do you think so?" I wouldn't have pegged him as insecure, he seems very aware of his attractiveness. I don't like the idea of a self-conscious Corey. Determined he would believe me, I answer with emphasis, "Yeah I do, you look dapper in your cardigan." Restored to his normal cheer he says, "Go ahead, feel it then." I don't really want to but

I play along, the sweater is soft to the touch, I tell him so. "That's because it's boyfriend material." I laugh out loud, loudly enough to get the attention of the camera crew. I should've known better, no way is Corey insecure. "I don't know what we're going to do with you," I say to him. "You're worse than Aiden."

Still awaiting Beverly and Cashmere, the rest of us sit around the living room conversing. I notice Brice isn't here yet either. I ask Aiden, who he rooms with, where he is. Aiden points to the window in the far corner of the room where Brice has been sitting unnoticed. I'm enjoying myself joking with the guys, but more and more my thoughts drift to Brice's unusual behavior. I excuse myself with the intention of checking on him.

My heels click clack all the way over to Brice, yet his gaze remains fixedly outside. Reflected in the glass are unfocused eyes in a sorrowful face. "Everything okay?" I know he'll say yes, nonetheless I ask anyway. "Yeah, just thinking." I move from behind to beside him, troubled by his conduct. "Anything you want to talk about?" I ask while angling to see whatever it is that has his attention so completely. "No." With one word he communicates plenty, mainly that something's bothering him. I make sure the window seat is long enough to accommodate us both and that it's clean, then sit. I don't feel right about leaving Brice alone, if he wants to stay here I'll stay with him until we're ready to go.

Whatever Brice is looking at only he can see it. I shift my gaze from outside to him, not purposely but because my options are limited, him or the street. At the moment, he's the more interesting choice plus he cleans up nice. It takes me a second to recognize I'm not studying his profile anymore, Brice is looking at me head on, with an intensity that makes my insides squirm. I return his look through partly obscured vision; a curl hangs too closely to my right eye. I hold my breath as his fingers tenderly tuck my hair away from my face. "You always look beautiful, but right now, you're breathtaking." This more than any other compliment given to me tonight rattles me. I'm nervous.

Catcalls and whistles come from behind us, I jump out of my seat guiltily, fearful the guys were responding to Brice and me. Turns out the commotion is due to the arrival of Cashmere and Beverly in their habitual fashions: tight, extra tight, cleavage, stilettos. It wasn't much to look at, I was, however, grateful to walk away from Brice. Now that everyone's gathered, Amy informs us we'll be traveling in the house vehicle, which is outside waiting for us.

Chapter 14

AT THE CLUB WE'RE given the star treatment, including a table and free bottles in VIP. Aiden and Corey order shots all around; I decline, though I do accept a martini. The music is fantastic, I want very much to dance but with the cameras and our large party there isn't much room in our section. If I want to have a good time I'll have to do it with every one else on the dance floor. I start a domino effect, once I leave VIP, my roommates do also. I dance alone despite the countless offers to do otherwise. I left a message for Trent to meet me here, I know he'll come. When he shows I don't want him to see me dancing with a random guy.

I bump into Aiden and Corey on the dance floor, I overhear them promising several women to be on television. Minutes later I catch Zack doing the same thing. "Non spotlight seeking," I say to myself, echoing Zack's earlier remarks about his perfect girl. "I don't know about you, but I think her blowing kisses at the camera is very low key." I turn around and see Brice looking at Zack and his 'friend'; he sounds like himself again. Whatever weirdness passed between us earlier is gone, which is why I don't hesitate to say yes when he asks me to dance.

I'm having a great time with Brice, laughing and moving to the music, when I spot Trent looking none too pleased. I excuse myself, ignoring Brice's confused expression. I approach Trent prepared for a fight, he won't like that I was dancing with someone even if it was my castmate. The look on his face is placid, though the one he wore while I danced was thunderous. Up close, Trent's the picture of self-possession. I expect him to yell; instead he says, "You're going to make me have to hurt someone."

He pulls me behind him to a crowded, dimly lit corner of the room, where there are no cameras. Tucked safely out of sight we're free to be reunited. I run my hands over the lapel of his dark blazer and smile into his oncoming kiss. "I've been waiting for this all night." He quirks an eyebrow at me, "Were you? Didn't seem like it from where I was standing." So he is upset with me. The thing is, I'm not up for a fight now or later; there will be no further discussion about this. "Don't start," I say to him, "tonight I want to have fun, no drama." It's been a long day, all I want to do is unwind with my boyfriend.

"I have an idea," I shout over the music, "let's go to your place." His answering smile is broad, "Don't be a pervert. We can hang out while everyone's here." His hands slide down my back while pulling me closer, "Hang out or *hang out*?" Lightheartedly, I pull away, "You're so junior high school." His hands slide around my waist, pulling me back flush against him, "You look absolutely delicious. What is this, silk?" I nod, unable to speak around the catch in my throat. I'm not laughing anymore. "It feels great," he says breathlessly. "Meet me outside in ten minutes."

I don't want to leave without letting someone know. I think for a moment then decide on Zack, he'll receive the information without prying. Aiden would insist on escorting me back, Corey's too busy romancing a harem, and Brice . . . he's not an option. I easily spot Zack's ink black hair; he's chatting up the pretty brunette I heard him talking to earlier. I hate to interrupt, but desperate times. "Hey, so sorry about the intrusion. I wanted to let you know I'm going back to the loft, I have a headache." As expected, he asks if I want him to accompany me back. "No, please stay and enjoy yourself. I'll be more than fine. I only told you so you wouldn't worry at the end of the night." Equally as expected, he relents with little fight, "Okay, Leah, feel better, see you at home."

Trent and I make it back to the building in less than half an hour. It seems deserted, still I go in first; Trent is to follow fifteen minutes later. My first thought when I walk into his apartment, see the romantic lighting, and hear the soft music playing is: he anticipated me coming back here. He's presumptuous, nonetheless romantic. I'm sitting on the couch when he comes in, he stops at the front door, even feet away from him it's impossible to ignore how tantalizing he is. Everything about him, from the square of his jaw to the lean of his walk calls to me. I hate how untrustworthy I am around him, how much I want him, and that he knows it.

Wanting to alter the mood, I ask if he'd be okay with me changing the song, music always dictates the emotion. Trent holds his phone out to me, there are discrete speakers in almost every room in his loft but the music plays from an app. I walk from the couch to where he stands, conscious of his eyes lingering on the curves of my body; our hands touch for a split second when I take the phone, sending a jolt through my fingers. Ignoring it, I shuffle through his music library until I find something more suitable. Putting his phone down on an end table and slipping off my shoes, I say, "Fun fact about me, I'm a killer on the dance floor and tonight is your funeral."

Trent shrugs off his blazer, leaving it where it falls on the ground, his eyes gleaming with excitement. "L, I urge you to reconsider. I don't think you want any part of this loss I'm about to serve you." Rhythmic dance music fills the space. "Disclaimer alert, I like you very much but you're going down," I say to him as I feel the music out. "Now that I know you like me very much, I might have to take it easy on you," he drawls in that annoyingly charming Trent way. The beat drops and with it, my dance moves.

We go back and forth, song after song, until we're both tired and sweaty. "I have to admit you were a formidable opponent," I say to Trent as we catch our breath. I don't hear his response; one of my absolutely all-time favorite ballads comes through the speakers. I would have never thought Trent would know this song, let alone like it. His hands loop my waist, mine go around his neck, we move in slow circles around the floor. "I've always loved this song, I want to dance to it at my wedding." I feel his smile although I don't see his face, with mine pressed against his chest. Trent hates when I talk about my "future husband" as a mysteriously ambiguous figure. "Okay L, this will be the song for our first dance." I hide my answering smile, it's weird talking about marriage with Trent. It doesn't feel like a hypothetical scenario, it feels inevitable. We hold onto each other until car doors slam, bringing an end to our wonderful night.

I make it to the apartment with just enough time to lie on the couch and pretend I've been there the whole time. The door opens a minute later, accompanied by the sound of multiple footsteps, some of which are clearly unsteady. "Leah, Leah, Leah," Aiden slurs, "I missed you. I wanted a dance." He plops down on the couch beside me, followed by everyone except Cashmere, she goes straight up to our room. I sit up on my side blinking dreamily for effect, "I had a headache. Next time we go dancing you're my first partner, promise."

From Zack's lap Beverly says, "I hope you got what you needed to feel better," implications I'm lying heavy laden in every syllable she speaks. Casually, she continues on, "Did anyone beside me see our illustrious executive producer tonight? I glimpsed him then he disappeared." That explains Cashmere's going straight to bed. She and Beverly were together; if Beverly saw Trent and me, or at the least saw him and pieced the rest together, Cashmere did also. She's in love with Trent, it can't have been easy for her to see us together. I could feel sorry for her under different circumstances; at it stands my main concern is whether Beverly is about to tell all.

Corey, Zack, and Aiden either say no or ignore what they feel to be an irrelevant question. In the time it takes for Brice to respond, it occurs to me that he didn't pursue me after I ran off and left him in the middle of the dance floor with no explanation. We were laughing and having a great time before I up and left without a backward glance. Knowing Brice, he would've been worried about me. If all that's true, why didn't he follow me? Unless he did and saw I was fine. Our eyes meet before he says "no" in a tone too measured to be truthful.

I wake up in a cold sweat, heart slamming painfully in my chest. I dreamed of the house again. This time I was fully aware it held horrors but I could not resist the desire to walk through the gate; even knowing what it would become. Tonight's nightmare featured snakes, long poisonous snakes, slithering in the grass hissing at me. At first they held their positions, but when I tried to leave they darted at me, crawled up my legs and arms. I still feel the weight of them even now scuttling up my body, boneless yet heavy. They squeezed but not tightly enough to kill me; no, their job was to restrain, while the front door moved closer.

My fear in that spurious moment was the most real thing I had ever felt. I waited defenselessly as terror came for me, cursing myself for going back, I knew but I went anyway. Tears of anguish blurred my vision, an unlikely kindness; I didn't want to see what came next. I looked to the other house regretfully as a light came on in a downstairs window. I screamed though I made no sound. There was help in that house but the snakes kept me bound where I was. I silently screamed some more, somehow help heard me. At the shadowy figure who emerged from the house, I screamed louder. "I'm here. Help me." My throat burned but I continued until a chorus of hisses forced me to turn around. The front door was open, through it a hand reached for me out of the darkness, maggots crawled around the fleshless fingers. Help didn't make it on time. The hand had almost taken hold of me when I screamed myself awake at three a.m.

It's dark, though not as dark as it was in the nightmare house. Cashmere's soft snores, the only sound in the stillness of the room, are comforting; it means I'm not alone. Its recurrent pattern begins lulling me back to sleep, crippling fear washes over me; determined not to fall back asleep, I throw my covers back and get out of bed. Without turning on the light, I have to hold my hands out in front of me to find the door. The imagery of an outstretched hand, even my own, surrounded by darkness brings me back to the horror of my dreams.

I shove my fist in my mouth stifling a scream, the scream that could never make its way out of me in the dream. I still as Cashmere shifts in bed; the snoring resumes and with it my search for the door. I emerge into the hallway gratefully and pull the door closed behind me quietly. I see a soft glow coming from downstairs, without thought I follow it, craving the safety of light.

The light source is a single fragrant candle on the coffee table. When I went to bed the candle wasn't there and Corey's vomit was all over the place. Someone cleaned up, replacing the rancid scent of sickness with potpourri. "Leah?" I turn around, led by the direction of the voice. "I'm over here on the window." I see him, but indistinctly. After my dream I'm in no hurry to run into the unknown, I need confirmation it's him before I proceed. He leans into the scarce light coming in through the blinds from outside. It's him, it's Brice.

"Brice, what are you doing down here?" I walk to the window, the same one he was staring out of earlier tonight. I take the same seat I occupied earlier. "I could ask you the same question," he responds. "You don't look okay, you look sort of clammy." The last thing I was thinking about after waking up petrified was how I look. I'm sure Brice isn't trying to offend me, I'm also sure I do look clammy, but I didn't like that he thinks I do. Come to think of it, he doesn't look well himself. I'm offended enough to tell him so, "And you look haunted, so I guess we both look like hell."

He smiles at my cheekiness, "I actually am haunted, what's your excuse?" His tone is light, the words are heavy. "Maybe I'm haunted too," I say. That I'm awake, having this conversation, afraid to go back to sleep, means just that. Brice nods his head, "But that's most likely where the commonalities end." I lean my head against the window, tired; weakly I say, "Who gets exorcised first?" Mirroring my movements, Brice leans his head against the frame and smiles.

The light from the candle reaches our corner, illuminating his right side, revealing his faraway eyes, the hollows of his cheeks, the indent in his chin, and the square of his jaw. Much as he's haunted, he's handsome. I've been aware of it from the moment we met, but I've never studied the art of his face until now. Brice is unconcerned with his looks, always in plain dress, while Trent's first line of defense is his attractiveness. I mentally chide myself for comparing Trent with Brice; if I weren't so shaken up I might be uncomfortable with how aware of him I am.

Consequently I blurt out what's keeping me up, "I have nightmares." My admission startles him back to the present, away from his ghost. "Well one recurring nightmare," I amend, "it seems to be intensifying. I don't want to go to sleep and end up back there paralyzed with fear, where no one can see me, hear me, or help me." Brice holds my hand comfortingly, "Don't be afraid. 'For God has not given us a spirit of fear, but of power and of love and of a sound mind.'

"Second Timothy 1 verse 7. I had night terrors until I was thirteen. I would awake from nightmares crying and afraid. My mom would hold me, repeating that very same verse until I fell back asleep. Eventually I started saying it to myself, it became my prayer before bed, for a long time the nightmares went away until now." My heart aches for my mom, though it helps that Brice holds my hand, lending me his strength. His steadiness steadies me. "The nightmares don't bother me as much as the idea that they mean something."

"Pray, ask for clarity, trust, and believe." I'm astounded by his spiritual strength; I didn't know we shared a faith. That comforts me more than anything else. It's nice to be able to share that part of me with someone who understands it. "You remind me of my mom." He chuckles softly, "Is it the beard or the mustache?" I look at him dryly, "Don't talk about my mama, that's a guaranteed beatdown." He puts his hands up in surrender, "What I mean is, you have a wisdom I'm familiar with and that you can be maternal at times." We laugh, alternately chiding one another to keep our voices down.

"I was engaged." The pain behind those softly whispered words isn't lost on me. When I needed his strength he leant it. I want to do the same for him. The same way Brice took my hand in his, I take his in mine. I hold on tight, hoping he feels exactly how present I am. "Seriyah Anastasia Wright almost Young, was a beautiful, honey-skinned girl, with crazy curly hair. She had this one curl that no matter how many times she smoothed it off her forehead would always fall back into her eyes." I don't have to try to remember earlier tonight when Brice brushed back the curls off my face. With my hair styled this way I remind him of her, he was speaking to me but he was seeing her. My hair is still curly now but held back with a headband. I'm embarrassed of myself for thinking it meant anything more. He was being kind to me because I remind him of his ex-fiancée.

"I first noticed her sophomore year of high school. She didn't notice me back, which stood out to me, during that time in my life I didn't have to work for attention from women. I was a decent basketball player and popular, every girl noticed me except her. That's what attracted me to her, how self-aware she was; she never let everybody else's norms dictate hers. First day of junior year I saw her standing outside the school building with friends, looking beautiful, completely oblivious of me. I walked past her, stepped on her foot, and kept going. I knew she was too fiery to let it go. She'd find me to scream at me, I was looking forward to it.

"After third period she marched up to me, fire in her eyes as she pushed her way through my friends. I cut her off before she could let me have it, 'I've been waiting for you to find me all day.' She raised an eyebrow at me, 'So you did realize you stepped on my foot?' I didn't care that all my friends were laughing. I'd wanted to talk to her for a long time. Now that I had the chance I was going to. 'Of course I did, I meant to.' She squinted at me the way you'd squint at a word that you couldn't see clearly. Without responding, she started to walk away, leaving me devastated that I'd blown it. Then she looked back at me and said, 'Next time mean to be more direct.'

"The next day I saw her in the lunchroom. I didn't know what to say. I stepped on her foot again. This time she grabbed me before I got too far past her, 'Is this your idea of being more direct?' she asked me, with the curl falling into her eye again. So many times I'd watched her from a distance, wanting it to be my hands that tamed her curls. I don't know what made me bold enough to do it, but slowly I raised my hand and pushed it back while she watched me. 'I want you to be my girlfriend, do you think we can make that happen?' It was the first time I heard her laugh. I loved the sound so much I knew I wanted to make her do it again. We started spending time with each other that day, by the end of the next I knew I was in love with her.

"I received a full scholarship to play basketball for a school in the Big East. Seriyah was smart enough to be accepted too. Senior year of college, after our last regular season game, I proposed. It was a hard-fought game. Afterward, standing on the hardwood, looking at her cheering me on, I knew nothing would make me half as happy as loving her for the rest of my life. Without a ring, with just the promise to love her, I got down on one knee and she said yes."

The love he feels for her is palpable, it can't end well, otherwise we wouldn't be having this conversation, though I can't imagine how a love like that could fall apart.

"I lived in a house off campus with a few of my teammates, we were throwing a victory slash engagement party. I was on snack duty. Sariyah, being the incredibly selfless person she was, knew I was sore and offered to stop by the grocery store on her way to my house." His words falter as tears roll down his face onto our joined hands, my heart constricts as he visibly fights for control. Suddenly, I don't want to hear the rest of the story, but Brice composes himself enough to continue. "I was calling her for an hour before someone answered her phone, a first responder. They found her cell next to her; she was sending a text when she rear-ended an SUV. Her car spun out of control, bounced off the sides, and slammed head first into an oncoming car. She was dead by the time I got to the hospital."

I cradle his head in my lap as his cries turn into low, wounded howls. The candlelight burns down long before Brice is able to sit up. When he does, he looks at me the way he has all night, with soul-deep despair. His thumbs touch my cheek and come away wet, "You're crying." He wipes the rest of my tears away with a tenderness I suspect he reserved only for Seriyah. "I guess I am." It's hard to say who sought out whom, but by the light of the moon our hands find each other again. Keeping them linked, Brice closes his eyes and leans his head back, "I have nightmares too, I dream about the text that killed her. 'I miss you can't wait 2 spend the rest of my life with you omw to u now.' That was four years ago; time has passed, the agony has not."

I doubt there are any words in existence I can say that would ease his grief but I try. "I'm so sorry, Brice, if there were any way I could take your pain away I would. But Brice, this air you're breathing every second, the life you still have matters. Weeping may last for the night but rejoicing comes in the morning. One day it'll happen that thinking about Seriyah will bring you joy without pain, and when it does happen you shouldn't feel badly about it. You have to live, you owe her that."

He accepts my attempt at comfort with a squeeze of my hands. "Speaking of joy coming in the morning, the sun will be up soon. Maybe you should go back to bed." I'm not sleepy, I'm exhausted. I wouldn't mind a few hours of sound sleep if I could get them but I'm still afraid. Brice reads the fear in my hesitation, "Not ready to face your dreams yet?" I shake my head. "I have an idea, but you have to trust me, come here." I'm not exactly sure where he wants me to go, "Come where?" He sighs heavily, "To me, rest your back against me. You can sleep, I'll stand guard. If you seem to be in any distress I'll wake you up."

I do trust Brice. Without him having asked for my trust he has it. I settle against his chest only a little hesitantly. Maybe if his shirtfront wasn't soaked through with tears over his dead fiancée it'd be weird, but right now it's me giving him the privacy to grieve while I sleep. "Just for a little while. I want to be up before everyone starts moving around the house." Sleeping against Brice is like falling a sleeping on a plane, not a particularly comfortable position but you fall asleep quickly all the same. I'm pacified to sleep not by the rolling movements of a jet but by the sound of his voice murmuring to me, "For the Lord has not given you a spirit of timidity."

Brice wakes me about two hours later. He's the first thing I see when I open my eyes, his are ringed with fatigue, but no longer clouded with grief. I thought deep sleep wouldn't be possible for me with my fear so close to the surface, but he was able to carry me, which is no small feat, to the couch while I slept. I smile up at him from his lap; genuinely happy to see he is in better spirits. He returns my smile with a genuine one of his own, "I hate waking you, you seem so tired, but the crew will be here any minute. Why don't you go on up to bed, see if you can get some more rest."

I quickly sit up, affecting alertness I don't feel, "No, I'm not tired." I am still very much tired. That was the most soundly I've slept in two days. The problem is I'm not ready to try to do it again. "You are, you're also still afraid," Brice says knowingly. "Did you have another nightmare?" I didn't dream again thanks to his voice urging me not to be frightened. "No, I didn't have another nightmare because you were with me." As soon as the words are out of my mouth I regret them, it's a lot more difficult to be open and vulnerable in the light of day.

He doesn't hold my hand the way he would have last night. Brice too must feel the awkwardness of the situation. In its place he looks at me in a way that makes me feel bare. "I'm still here, if you need me call out and I'll come to you." In his eyes I see the ghost of the night before: the tears, the fears, the solace found in each other. The sound of the lobby door closing gets me up and on my way upstairs; in front of my bedroom door I look back, Brice is watching me. I want to say something to him, I don't know what; ultimately I give up on words and go inside.

Cashmere's still sound asleep when I crawl back in bed. Fear, knowledge, and confusion keep me awake. I'm fearful of falling asleep, overwhelmed by what I learned about Brice, and confused about last night. Dozens of thoughts scream in my head fighting for attention until I can stand it no longer. I have to let them out. I retrieve my luggage from beneath my bed. In the inside pocket I find my journal. I don't write about my day or use it in typical journal fashion, it's more like my record of ideas. Sometimes I hear or read something I don't want to forget, or I'm struck with a beautiful idea I have to write down. I packed it almost as an afterthought; I hadn't been able to write for months. Unexpectedly I found inspiration here in both Brice's pain and Trent's love.

Before last night I had never witnessed a pain deep enough to hobble a grown man. "I held you for as long as I could, letting go only at the last minute. I damned time and wished us more." I've read that line what feels like a hundred times, always seeing Trent and me as we were that morning—him holding me close and me asleep. Now I see heartbroken Brice weeping in my arms. Cashmere's snores have stopped, she must be awake, probably staring at me again. I keep at my task, disregarding her presence. Pen moves across paper, pouring out of me till there's nothing left to say. When it's complete, I put everything back in my luggage except for my journal. I've never shared my writing with anyone before, but I didn't write it for me, I wrote it for him.

Amy's on the other side of the door when I open it to leave my room. "Good morning, Amy, how was your night?" I try to sound as if the sight of her does not annoy me. "You're cheerful this morning, I take it you're feeling better." Amy looks to her left, to her right, then stage whispers, "I ran into Beverly last night, she told me you had to leave early. Between you and me, she said you were sneaking out to see a guy." Beverly gossiping about me is no surprise. That Amy is up here telling me pisses me off. I have never been a fan of Amy; it's a relief to be justified in my dislike of her.

It's moronic to be upset at a snake for being a snake, nonetheless Amy luxuriating in our discourse, trying to brew drama bothers me. She needs to know I have very little patience for pettiness. "That's ridiculous, teens sneak around. Grown women act at their leisure." I avoid giving her a direct answer. For reasons he hasn't explained, Trent is positive Cashmere and Beverly won't tell everyone about us. They haven't though, Beverly has toed the line. I look pointedly at Amy, wanting her to move out of my way; she doesn't. "That was one of the nicer things she said about you," Amy says in a complicit tone. "Her last confessional featured a guest appearance from Cashmere, very funny stuff, seven minutes dedicated to you."

Amy has proven herself to be an untrustworthy rabble-rouser; her intent in telling me all this is to incite me against them. I'm not pleased but I've also learned sometimes you have to give the people what they want, "Is that so?" I say, playing along. "You know what, Amy, I suddenly feel the need to confess." The immediate delight in her air is disgusting, though I pretend not to notice it for the sake of doing what I set out to before being cornered by her. "I'll find you in a few minutes," I say as I squeeze past her. "I need to do something first."

My room is the first off the staircase; there hasn't been an occasion until now for me to walk down the hallway. Approaching his room, I hear low urgent speaking. Believing it to be a bad time I turn back; then I hear my name. "For Lord, you have said, 'come to me all ye that are weary and burdened, I will give you rest. Take my yoke upon you and learn from me for I am gentle and humble at heart and you will find rest for your souls. For my yoke is easy and my burden is light.' Leah, finds her heart burdened and afflicted, but a sacrifice to you, O Lord, is a broken heart and contrite spirit. Lord, please receive my broken heart and renew her contrite spirit. Help us to not grow weary but bless us with endurance to run the good race. Where her sleep is troubled, please grant her rest. Help her to know herself in you, her strength, her talent, her gifts, and her beauty that the world will not dictate her identity to her. Help her, Lord, to not crave the position so much that she spurns your presence, for all things shall perish, but the word of the Lord shall stand true. I thank you, Lord, for your instruction through prayer, your guidance through faith, and receiving my request through love. I pray to you not in worthiness or merit but humbly in the name of Jesus Christ, my savior."

Eavesdropping is wrong, especially eavesdropping on prayer, but Brice was praying for me. He is doing for me what I haven't done for myself in weeks, asking God for things on my behalf I've never thought to ask. He is a wonderful man. One day when he's ready, he'll make a special woman very happy. The hardwood floor creaks beneath my feet, causing him to look out the crack in the door; I don't move quickly enough, Brice spots me.

He doesn't seem phased by my overhearing his private moment. I on the other hand feel like I've been caught with my hand in the cookie jar, sputtering and tripping all over my words. "I'm sorry, I didn't mean to. I heard you and then I heard my name, I'm sorry." At his amused look I stop trying to apologize, I'm not doing a good job and he isn't interested in it. Standing directly in the middle of the room as he is, sunlight streaming in, it's difficult not to notice his light or make mention of it. "You have this lit-from-within quality, do you know that?" His beautiful mahogany skin is too deep to rouge at adulation; it does, however, glow extra bright at my observation.

"I'm not mad at you, no need to flatter me. As a rule, if I'd be ashamed for people to know about it, I won't do it." I smile inwardly at his modesty while remembering the last person to speak those words to me. "My sister said something similar before I came here." "So now I echo your mom and your sister," he shrugs. "At least I'm getting closer to my own age, maybe next time I'll sound like your brother." Neither of us laughs, probably because the idea of Brice being my brother isn't funny. To emphasize that, I point out I don't have any brothers. He eyes me curiously, him inside his room, me outside, "You know it would it'd be easier to have this conversation if you came in."

I take a few tentative steps into the room he shares with Aiden; basketball shorts, tee shirts, and hats are stacked on a collapsible shelf in the corner of the room. I would take a seat except there is none, other than Aiden's empty unmade bed or Brice's, which is expertly made, minus the book on the pillow. Needing something to do I pick up the discarded book; *The Odyssey*. "You're reading Homer?"

Brice takes the few steps that separate us and neatly plucks the book out of my hand, "It's not the most contemporary stuff but it's great reading." Despite the gentleness he employed to take the book from me, I sense I've offended him. "I think you misunderstand me, I love *The Odyssey*, it's my favorite Greek tragedy. What you heard in my voice was surprise, you have a knack for doing that, everything about you is unexpected." The more I learn about Brice the more I appreciate who he is. It's unbelievable how many good things he is in the exactly right proportion: kind, compassionate, humble, modest, and thoughtful. If I didn't witness the brokenness that also lives inside of him, I would call him perfect.

"We just met. I figured you'll learn something new about me daily, if that surprises you, we may need to have a conversation on how these things work." I ignore his sass and allow him to lead me to a seat on the bed beside him. "Other than my Classics professor, I don't know another man who reads Homer for fun." He flips through the book without stopping on any particular page, when he reaches the end he flips through it again. "It is unusual to see a young man enjoying a story about intellectual prowess over physical, resisting temptation, and piety," Brice agrees. I take the book from him, remembering my experiences with it.

"When I first read it, I understood it only on the most basic level. I only sort of grasped his literal voyage as a battleground for his internal struggle. When I read it in college, I recognized the journey wasn't the one Odysseus took to get home, it was an expedition of self-discovery, Odysseus versus Odysseus. I read it again years later and that time it read like a diary." He looks at me with exaggerated confusion, "Wait, you're saying the story isn't about Odysseus's passage home?" I mirror his light and teasing tone with my own, "I'm saying we should meet for weekly book club, I like talking literature with you." Eyes alight he says, "I just like talking to you, period."

I like talking to him too, though I'm not sure I should. Also, why hasn't he said anything to me about Trent? I was positive he saw me but he hasn't mentioned it. Is it that he's too polite to bring it up or did he not see me? I look into his face, wishing I knew what to make of him. Choosing not to respond, I get to the reason I sought him out in the first place. I pull my journal from where I hid it underneath my shirt. For some irrational reason I didn't want Amy to see me with it. "This is for you, well one page, it's in the back." I thrust it into his hands. "You can return it to me later," I say, while walking out.

All of us except Brice are eating breakfast in the kitchen when Iliana unexpectedly comes in. After quick greetings, we are told going forward our lessons will be held at a location close by. Excited at the change of scenery we rush through the remainder of breakfast then pile into the van. We arrive at a small community theater, where Morgan is already waiting for us. "Yesterday you were instructed to choose a monologue, today we'll be working on them one-on-one, with me. Do not waste time; while you wait your turn be productive. Corey you're first up."

We fan out to rehearse, every person in their own corner muttering to themselves. For the first time I see how important it is to each of us to win, even Aiden, the consummate bohemian, is serious, his posture lacking its usual facileness; nobody is here to play around. If I want to win I need to be great.

Most people work from a printed copy of their monologues, I don't. There's no danger of me forgetting words that are written on my heart. I look around the room and see Brice a few feet from me in a hunched position murmuring to himself, which gives me an idea. I've been approaching my monologue from Trent's point of view, but maybe I need to be Brice.

Corey reappears, informing Beverly she's up next. After about half an hour she returns looking very sour about something. "Zack—Simon Cowell not—would like to see you." She sits, arms crossed, literally shaking with rage. Clearly unable to stand it any longer, she shouts to no one in particular, "Is Morgan, like, legit, or is he some has-been that never made it but thinks he can tell us how to do it?" Aiden laughs and says, "Just work on it, Bev," then goes back to his monologue.

When it's my turn with Morgan I enter through the stage doors not knowing what to expect. Morgan's welcoming smile promptly puts me at ease. "Lovely Leah, tell me what piece you've chosen." Apprehensively I begin, "I have always had trouble finding the right monologue for myself, but the original piece I'll be doing today was penned by a friend, it's truly a beautiful piece of art." Morgan was sitting perfectly erect but somehow sits straighter. "I'm intrigued, show me."

I lay down on the floor, stage center, locked in the embrace of a lover unseen to everyone but me. Blocking out both the cameraman and Morgan, I let myself feel again the grief that tore through Brice's body as he howled in anguish. "I woke up this morning happier than I've been in years." The words pour out of me as I remember Brice bent in pain last night. "I held you for as long as I could letting go only at the last minute," the tears come as fast as my words. Approaching the end, I sit up; place a tender kiss on the forehead of the lover who is never to return. I stand over the body, ready to leave but not before my final goodbye, "When you wake I hope your first thought is of me. My every thought is of you."

Morgan calls scene before I can, I'm afraid to look at him, scared he hated my performance. I lost control of my emotions during my mono- logue; forcing myself into Brice's state of being was more emotional than I thought it would be; I couldn't hold it together. Finally I face him; with an uncharacteristic seriousness, Morgan says, "Listen to me carefully, Leah; casting directors, producers, agents, the whole industry will try to put you in the pretty girl box. You won't be sought after for the 'ugly roles,' the roles that push boundaries and call for real talent. Don't let them do it to you. Take a bow, Leah, you're a star."

On the way back to the Loft, Zack suggests dinner. Since he offers to pay we all agree. I sit next to Aiden in the van, resting my head on his shoul- der. These past few years I stopped believing I could do it, I came into this partly to prove to myself I can't. Having Morgan reaffirm what I've always known in the depths of my being has me lightheaded with relief.

At dinner, no one talks about their monologues or their one-on-ones with Morgan, though it's on everyone's mind. Aiden and Corey are the life of the party as usual, doing their best to keep the mood light; Aiden regales us with a tale of the time campus security detained him for streaking. Of course we enjoy his story, he's a great storyteller, but it isn't as interesting as Brice is pretending it is.

I try several times to catch his eye; he won't look at me. I didn't think much of it that he didn't sit next to me on the car ride over, now I'm thinking he's avoiding me. We were fine earlier today after I gave him the poem I wrote for Seriyah. I can't imagine what's changed between then and now. The only thing I can think of is, maybe his one-on-one with Morgan didn't go well. Hopefully he'll feel like being more social later. I miss my friend.

The ride back home is just Cashmere, Beverly, and me; after dinner the guys announced their intentions to go to a bar, probably to pick up women. Turns out Cashmere and Beverly have plans of their own. They make a big production of getting dressed in the skimpiest dresses they own, all the time saying things like, "Some people are just boring, they don't know how to let loose." I hang out in the living room reading a magazine until they leave; as soon as they're gone, I retrieve the key Trent left me from my drawer then head up to his place.

I let myself in without knocking, wanting to surprise him. I walk around the loft shouting his name, but Trent isn't home. I'm trying not to get worked up over him being out, he's a busy man. I can't expect him to sit around at home all day waiting for me to visit, although it's nearly midnight, not exactly business hours. I'll wait up for him, he can't possibly be gone much longer.

I curl up on the couch in the living room watching a *Hey Arnold* marathon. Eventually I drift off to sleep. At first I dream I'm a tenant in Arnold's boarding house, he and I are hanging out with Stoop Kid watching the gang play baseball, then the dream changes. I'm being chased again; this time Helga leads the pack. The fork looms up ahead, but in the middle of it is my mom.

Although I know it's her, she looks much younger than I've ever seen her in real life. I run to her, seeking her protection. She holds her hand up, palm first, indicating for me to stop. Skidding to a halt I fall at her feet, groveling for help She looks at me covered in dust and tears, and speaks with a voice that is familiar and unfamiliar, "What is it that you run from, daughter?" I gesture behind me, expecting to see the mob that's no longer there. My momentary relief is dulled by my confusion at my mother's coolness.

"Mommy, they're chasing me, please don't let them get me," I cry. She bends and lifts me up off the floor as if I weigh little more than I did as a child. Her grip is strong and urgent though she does not speak or move with any haste. "I'm not here to talk about them, they can do you no harm, I'm here to talk about you." Baffled, I echo her words back to her, "Talk about me?" She smiles kindly at me, the first maternal thing she's done since she appeared in the middle of the road.

"Leah, what are you seeking that can only be found in that house?" I hate the beautiful house of horrors, why would she think I want anything in there? "No, Mom, I don't ever want to go back." I try to meet her eyes, I can't, they burn brighter than the sun. "Then why," she begins, "are you standing in the front yard?" As I'm swallowed by darkness I catch a last glimpse of my mom standing in front of the old house. Strong hands drag me inside while she says something I can't hear.

A single tear slides down her beautiful, stoic face, then I'm waking up in a cold sweat. I'm still on the couch; I'm still utterly alone. I'm afraid, I'm so afraid. Right now I'd rather share a room with Cashmere than stay in Trent's forlorn apartment. I scribble him a note before leaving, "I waited as long as I could, it's now 3:53 a.m. Maybe I'll see you tomorrow."

I enter the dark apartment as quietly as possible, tiptoeing across the floor, unsure if anyone is back yet. My foot is on the first step when he speaks up, "Leah?" Automatically I look to his favorite window, know-ing that's where Brice will be. "We've got to stop meeting like this," I joke. The air around him moves slightly, he might be laughing, I can't say for sure. "Randomly in the middle of the night?" Brice says, "I'm alright with it." I search his voice for a hint of laughter but find none. Only old ghosts could've brought him down here to sit in the dark at this time of night.

"Brice, are you okay?" I hear the breath leave his body. "For the most part, but I should really be asking you that question. You're the one sneaking in at four o'clock in the morning." I'm troubled by the accusation in his ques-tion, what does he think I was doing? "I wasn't sneaking, I was being quiet. I didn't want to wake anyone." I hear him leave his spot on the windowsill, I see him walking toward me, with the help of the light filtering in from the street. When he's close enough for the features of his face to come into focus he says, "Leah, where were you?" I hear in his voice the answer matters to him. After all we've confided to one another, it's a gross betrayal lying to Brice, but I don't see that I have any choice. "I had another dream, the worst yet, I needed to get away. The roof is a good place to do that." Mentioning the dream brings the terror flooding back. All at once Brice, the living room, and the loft are gone; I'm being dragged into a wall of darkness.

A small sob leaves my body as I succumb to panic. Hands attempt to take hold of me, I slap them and take a step backward. "Get away from me!" I whimper though I intended to scream. I take another hasty step, trip, and fall, hitting the ground hard. Pain explodes in my knee, with it comes perspective. My knee hurts because I tripped over an ottoman running from Brice, not an unknown horror.

"Leah, it's me, I need you to calm down, just breathe," he pleads. My lungs feel like they're made of mechanical parts—cogs and gears grinding against each other without oil. It hurts to breathe. Warm hands cup my face, "Leah, listen to me, breathe, do you hear me? Breathe." Though I can barely see him, I picture his warm steady eyes. I let them guide me back. I mimic the pattern of his breaths until my body remembers how to do so on its own.

When the anxiety passes, Brice helps me up and over to the couch then goes into the kitchen. With the lights on I see him more clearly now, I expected him to appear haunted as he did last night; he doesn't, though I can't name the expression he wears. He returns with a makeshift ice pack, which he puts on my knee. I've known Brice for a few days and already he's proven himself to be a good friend. After the way I freaked out I owe him an explanation for my behavior. "Do you want to know what happened?" I ask, bracing myself to tell him. "I know what happened, you had a panic attack. I recognize the symptoms."

Curiosity momentarily mutes the pain, "How are you able to, discern I was having a panic attack,?" Brice moves the compress off my knee gently prodding it with his hand, "How does that feel?" It's sore but nothing I can't handle. "Much better. Thank you for everything, but you haven't answered my question." He sighs, "Because after Seriyah, I had them too."

I'm not surprised. I imagine it's a normal reaction to what Brice has experienced. "I saw a therapist after the first time it happened. It was helpful in that it aided in identifying the reason I was having panic attacks, which always transpired whenever it hit me that she wasn't coming back. A weight would settle over my chest, then my lungs would stop working; I would fight for air that never came. When it was particularly bad my vision would blur. Whenever that happened my legs were next to go." I hung on his every word, his experience so similar to mine he could be describing what I've gone through.

"The first time I had a panic attack I was still living with my teammates; they called an ambulance. Doctors ran a series of tests before confirming my heart was in perfect condition, maybe the problem was my mind." Carefully, Brice lifts my banged-up leg, placing it on a pillow resting in his lap. "I knew I wasn't crazy, but sometimes, I wasn't sure. I went to Dr. James; she confirmed I wasn't insane, just overwhelmed with grief. Once I figured out the source, I've been able to control them." Done doing all he can for my knee, he shifts his attention to the greater issue. "So Leah, why?"

I don't know why, I tell him as much. "I think you do, you're just not aware of it yet." I used to think I was panicking about life, but the last few times I've lost it have disproved that theory. Maybe I'm cracking up. Deep in thought about the possibility of me losing my mind, Brice has to repeat himself twice before I hear him; when I finally do I'm unsure I heard him correctly. I think he asked why I didn't tell him about my boyfriend.

"Are you or are you not involved with Trenton Shaw?" There's no point in denying what he already knows. "Yes, I am." I was certain Brice saw me run off with Trent, perplexed as to why he hadn't brought it up yet. Now that he has I wish he hadn't. He nods his head without comment. After minutes of reticence, I feel compelled to explain. "I didn't say anything earlier because the optics aren't good. We don't want the other contestants thinking I have an unfair advantage." He doesn't look at me when he asks, "Don't you?"

I can't decipher if it's curiosity or something better disguised and much harder to identify in his tone. Maybe he thinks I've been gaming him and everyone else. It's not an unreasonable sentiment or question; that doesn't stop me from being offended he would think I would want to win that way. "Actually, no, I don't. I've been working as hard as you and everyone else; I deserve to be here. If you don't agree take it up with the producers." I swing my leg off of the pillow, getting shakily to my feet; the first step on my knee is awful. I push through it, limping to the stairs. I do stop to ask if this is the reason for the silent treatment earlier.

I probe him for the truth, wanting to know the depths of his anger, though I anticipate a denial or no answer at all. "I was working on the notes Morgan gave me while you were having your one-on-one with him. Beverly and Cashmere pulled their chairs to where I sat alone. I hadn't even acknowledged them before they said, "We don't want you wasting your time pining after her. She's already taken, one hint who, you know him." It wasn't hard to figure out they were talking about you or who your boyfriend is. You ran and left me on the dance floor at the club, and you two had that weird thing our first night. I figured he was interested in you since then, I just never thought you would be interested in him."

Why wouldn't I be interested in Trent? That Brice is inferring something unflattering about him upsets me, he doesn't know him, what can he possibly have against him? "Well, you thought wrong." I surprise myself with how coldly I respond to him when Brice has been nothing but kind to me, except when he insinuated I would use my relationship with Trent to sway the competition in my favor. "You should probably stay off your knee. If you're going upstairs, go, if you're staying down here you should sit."

Brice is so intrinsically good, I don't know that I could show that much concern for someone who just bit my head off. That's what's truly disconcerting me, not Brice thinking something's wrong with Trent but that I would be with someone dishonorable. I don't want to lose his good opinion of me. "I'm sorry," I say while easing myself down onto the steps. "Leah," Brice intones, getting up from the couch, walking in the direction of the stairs. "I didn't mean to hurt your feelings, I'd never want to do that, I'm so sorry I did." I scoot over, offering him the seat beside me.

I wince when he lifts my hurt leg, replacing it on his lap. "What did you mean when you said you never thought I'd be interested in Trent?" He rubs his tired eyes; he's exhausted yet avoiding sleep, just like me. "It doesn't matter what I meant, like you said, clearly I was wrong because you are." He's mostly joking though he evidently didn't appreciate that moment of the conversation. "Tell me, please," I whine. "Not likely, I won't speak a word against your *boyfriend* or my boss." I realize I'm fighting a losing battle after the way I reacted; if I were Brice I wouldn't clarify either.

"Fine, be that way, there was something else I wanted to ask you anyway." Brice closes his eyes and leans his head against the bannister, "Go ahead . . . ask me." I take a minute to remember it exactly as it was said before I ask him about it. Satisfied, I begin. "When we were all talking at the table a few days ago, right before Cashmere stuck her tongue down your throat, you said you wouldn't mind a girlfriend who was in the spotlight; as long as she knew what she wanted to say with it. What do *you* want to say with your limelight?"

Brice opens his eyes, caught off guard. "And you say I have a knack for surprising you." He laughs. "So let's not grow tired of doing what is good. At just the right time we will reap a harvest of blessings if we do not give up." Shivers reverberate through my body at his words. I don't know if it's the cold air from the cooling system or my spirit responding to the verse that nourished it most of my life.

"Galatians 6 verse 9 were my magic beans growing up, now I don't know. I really just don't know." Brice sits up alert, all traces of fatigue gone, "Why don't you know anymore?" Feeling unbearably sad, I lay my head on his shoulder. "Things were very black and white as a child; pray and believe without doubt. If you do that, you'll receive what you prayed for. I've prayed every day, multiple times a day, if that were true I wouldn't be on a reality show, I would've made it already. Thinking about it now, this fell into place when I hadn't prayed. It's easy to say be good, do good, and God will bless you, but when you've been those things and it hasn't gotten you anywhere you start to reevaluate."

I wouldn't be shocked if lightening struck me down. I hadn't said those things aloud to anyone before, I'm not sure I mean them, I hate that I can't say I don't. I hold my head up as Brice shifts in his seat to face me; in this pale shaft of light he looks otherworldly. "I hear everything you're saying, it's not completely without merit either, but it is without greater understanding. Let me ask you this, why do you serve God?" The word serve is used too lightly; I haven't as much as said "God bless you" after someone's sneeze in months. "Is it habit or is it because you understand God to be a genie?" I confronted Cashmere heatedly over my Bible being missing, now challenged about my spirituality I have no answer. Why would I fight Cashmere to defend an article of my faith but not defend my faith itself against Brice? The truth is terrible, having my Bible meant I still believed; without it I couldn't overlook the truth: my spiritual life is in grave peril.

Brice is an executioner exacting divine truth; his words a sword relentlessly cutting through bone straight to my soul. "A lot of people lose their faith because they never had any to begin with; things don't work out exactly as they hoped so that must mean God doesn't exist. That kind of facile thinking means there was never a true relationship with Christ, only a desire to be blessed. Jesus himself says that things will be difficult but take heart because he has been victorious over the world." I do want to be blessed and I am angry that I'm not; I just didn't know I was before this conversation.

I've suffered blow after blow, why shouldn't I be angry, am I not justified? I ask Brice, "Why does the Bible say you'll receive what you pray for by faith in Jesus's name?" I have asked in prayer, why have I not received. "It's true Jesus says that you will receive whatever it is you ask for if you pray to the Father in his name, but the context of it is this: God desires to have a relationship with us all, and through that relationship he will bless you so that you will be a blessing to others." My fingers go to the cross I wear on my neck, feeling ashamed to bear it on my body yet not in my heart.

Brice must've read my mind because his words echo my thoughts. "He loved you enough to die for you, why are you so quick to turn away from him?" I hastily wipe a stray tear from my eye. Brice touches the necklace I've worn every day since Trent gave it to me. "If you're only serving God for a quick blessing you'll always be disappointed. How can you believe in Christ only as a benevolent figure that exists to help you when you need something? He's not Santa Claus, he's Jesus Christ. You can't deceive him with half-felt prayers and selfish ambitions. Your relationship with God is like any other; you have to work at it. His inheritance is for those who seek him first with their whole soul, spirit, and minds, everything else will be achieved along the way."

Within me, my spirit stirs back to life. Of course I know everything he's saying to be true but how do I keep on living like this? "How am I to accept that this is all there is to my life, why are some people wealthy and fulfilled beyond measure while others have little? Is it wrong to want more for myself, is it wrong to have dreams, to fight for them at any cost?" Speaking is a challenge for me, overcome as I am with anger and shame. Brice lifts a hand to my cheek; it's so comforting I lean into it, eyes closed.

"You cannot have a testimony without a test, and faith cannot be forged without fire. Leah, you've been blessed even if it's hard for you to see it right now. God has trusted you with little, have you given him reason to trust you with more? Pray and ask to be a good steward over what you've been given, pray for endurance to run the good race. I promise God's not through with you yet."

I've been blind with self-pity, I couldn't see how ungrateful and unfaithful I've been. Talking to Brice, I realize how much I need to change, which should be discomforting but it's not, it makes me feel lighter, it means there's hope for me. Without overthinking it, I remove Brice's hand from my cheek and lace it with mine. "I'm going to close my eyes for a bit, what about you?" he asks. Outside of the two hours I got with him on guard duty last night, my sleep has been fitful. I'm exhausted and in dire need of rest, but I'm all too aware of what dangers wait for me in dreamland.

Reading my reluctance, Brice says, "You can lie next to me, like you did last night, I promise to protect you." It doesn't denote anything gauche, how safe I feel with him, friends comfort friends. Repeating that in my head I follow him to the couch, where he sits and I lie, stiffly. "Leah, relax," his laughter a soft melody in the quiet room. "We've been here before. I swear I won't bite." Feeling foolish for being awkward I settle into a more comfortable position with my head in his lap. "Obviously, don't be so uptight, Brice." His laughter is the last thing I hear before I fall asleep.

Chapter 15

"THAT'LL TEACH ME TO bet against Amy. I was sure Cashmere would be the first to get caught hooking up but whoa, were we wrong." My eyes flutter against the remnants of sleep and the beginning of wakefulness, when I do open them there's a camera on me. "What the—, get that camera out of my face right now." I throw my hands out, trying to knock it away. The cameraman simply pulls back and keeps right on filming. I try to get up but I'm trapped in place by an arm, Brice's arm. That's when the severity of the situation settles in. Brice and I were caught asleep together on the couch. While we know our friendship to be strictly platonic, no way anyone else will buy that. What if Trent finds out, how am I going to explain this to him?

With newfound urgency I heave Brice's arm off me and get up, my knee buckles as soon as I put my weight on it. I have to fling my arms out to steady myself. When I'm sure I can stand my ground I turn on the crew. "Not everything is for the camera," I yell. Doug, it's his camera I tried to knock away, says, "Well then you shouldn't have agreed to participate on a reality show, princess." I'm deciding if it would be worth it getting kicked off the show to smack him, when someone says, "Who do you think you're talking too?"

While the camera guys search for the speaker I instantly recognize Brice's voice and turn to him. He must have woken up during the commotion. "Say another disrespectful thing to her, just one more word, and you'll have to talk to me. I promise you that's not a conversation you want to have." Brice stands up, all six-plus feet of him, addressing Doug, who has mysteriously gone quiet. Everyone stares at him, including me. I've never seen him upset, it's a scary sight. Brice takes me by the elbow and leads me away, "Leah, let's go, they'll have their story at any cost, even if there's not a story there."

In the kitchen over hushed voices he says to me, "Look, I know you're freaking out but I saw this coming." In my alarm I almost miss what Brice said, "What do you mean you saw this coming, what is there to see?" He puts a hand on either of my shoulders drawing my eyes to his. "Think about it, Leah, why would Cashmere and Beverly feel it necessary to tell me about your relationship status unless they thought it would cause drama between us. They must think there's something between you and me, and if they believe it then the producers must believe it too, or believe they can sell it."

I get the sense Beverly does things like this for sport. Cashmere has more noble motives; she's in love with Trent, that's all the incentive she needs. Brice raises a valid point, though why single him out, why not tell the whole cast? They must genuinely believe something to be going on. I need to talk to Trent; I have to tell him before he finds out. "I'll be back in a while," I say to Brice, "I need to clear my head." I disregard him calling after me as I leave the kitchen, slightly limping.

The front door opens on my way out, admitting Cashmere and Beverly, stumbling in wearing last night's outfits, the worse for wear. I had no idea they were gone all night, I assumed they were home. "Oh, Leah," Cashmere slurs, sloppy drunk, "we were just talking about you. It's like that commercial, it's seven a.m., do you know where your boyfriend is?" It would be easy to dismiss her comment as drunken ravings, but a drunk man tells no tales. Plus she's right; I don't know where my boyfriend is; however, if they do, I expect his whereabouts won't be my problem much longer.

"Look, she's going to cry," Beverly says. "It's okay, Leah, he did it to us too. I told you, you weren't special." I'm tempted to ask them outright if they were with Trent, but the cameras are rolling. Instead I walk around them to the front door, still favoring my injured leg. I double back to grab my discarded heels, though I don't put them on inside. Beverly, Cashmere, Brice, and the crew are all watching my every move. I want out as quickly as possible.

I painfully make my way up to his apartment and let myself in without knocking; I still have his key on me. I let the door slam loudly behind me, I want him to know I'm here; I won't limp around his loft looking for him. Trent comes out of his bedroom and looks down over the bannister at me. Like the rest of us, he is for the most part in last night's outfit: slightly wrinkled black button-up over perfectly fitting black denim. He looks good, real good. I have to remind myself I'm angry with him. I miss him. If I hadn't caught him undressing from being out all night I would be in his arms right now, but I have and nothing else can matter.

The momentary light in his eyes at the sight of me is quickly replaced by remoteness. "What's up," is what he chooses to say to me. Granted, he doesn't know about my run-in with Cashmere and Beverly, but I spent hours alone in this apartment waiting for him and all I get is a "What's up?"

like I'm a casual acquaintance. Is he angry with me too? "Did you get my note?" I ask, broaching the subject thoughtfully. "No, I must've missed it." I left it on his nightstand, there's no way he missed it unless he wasn't home to see it. "How was your night?" I say, getting more to the point. "Fun," he answers shortly. Trent knows exactly where I'm going with these questions and he's challenging me to get there.

I don't bother asking, I reveal to him I know. "With Cashmere and Beverly, I'm sure you had all types of fun." He sucks in his breath through clenched teeth, "It's not what you think." Whatever he's upset about, Trent didn't bank on me knowing he spent the night with Beverly. "I'm not sure what I think, this is your chance to help determine that."

He walks down the steps slowly while I wait for an explanation. "I didn't plan on meeting them, I was at an industry party last night. They showed up and flirted their way in. They hung around all night but it was nothing." His version of events isn't unbelievable, but it doesn't make me feel any better. They've pitted themselves against me yet he keeps a friendly rapport with them. It's a constant betrayal, especially since their issue with me is him. There's been disharmony in our relationship since the show started filming. I thought it was the frustration of forcing distance between us, but possibly there's more to it.

"Maybe you're being honest about that much, there's no way for me to know; or perhaps you don't care as much as you'd have me think." If Trent was ice before he's all fire now. "Don't pretend this has anything to do with Cashmere and Beverly; you know no one exists for me other than you. This is about Brice." So that's his issue, why he's been cold since I arrived. I would've welcomed a conversation with him about Brice, in fact I want to talk to him about Brice, but he didn't give me the opportunity. Trent made up his mind and chose to deal with me accordingly.

I meet his ardor burn for burn. "I see you're not only partying with Cashmere and Beverly, you're getting your information from them too. Let me clarify things for you, there's nothing going on between Brice and me. We've both been having trouble sleeping and happened to have crossed paths one night. He's been kind to me and has asked nothing of me in return. You would've known this if you were where you were supposed to be last night." Trent's never looked at me the way does now; I wouldn't have imagined he could. "Why are you so naive, of course he wants something from you, and it's only a matter of time before you give it to him."

Disgusted, I back away from him, never taking my eyes off the sneer on his face. I get he's angry, but it's no excuse for what he said or his thinking I would give to Brice what I haven't given to him. My already sore body clenches in pain as I accidentally back into the door. Seeing I'm hurt, Trent tries to help me, but I shout at him not to touch me. There's regret and sadness in his voice too, I pretend not to hear it. Palms up, he approaches me like you would a wild animal you're trying to pacify. "L, you're hurt, let me help you."

I hate that he's somehow turned this around on me. I clamp my mouth shut, determined to say nothing more to him. I open the door, ready to leave, perhaps for good. "I won't be up to see you again," I say, before pulling the door closed behind me. A loud crash sounds on the other side of the door, I don't stop to investigate, I keep going until I'm outside.

Through that whole exchange he never once apologized, he felt justified because of what he thought I was doing. Love keeps no record of being wronged. Love never gives up, never loses faith, is always hopeful, and endures through every circumstance. He didn't have faith in me so he decided to pay me back, that's not love. I sought after *him* last night not Brice, but unlike Brice, he wasn't there for me. He was busy partying with the girls who have vowed to make my life miserable. I'm not sure if we broke up, I am sure I need space.

I don't know where I'm going but it isn't back to the apartment, at least not for a little while. I walk around the neighborhood until I end up on a bench in the Parks and Recreation preserve area directly across the street from my bedroom in the loft. I sit watching the people young and old walk to the train station, hurrying to school or work, everyone with purpose. Once upon a time my walk had purpose too; it's been aimless for a while now, although less so lately. I sit unraveling my thoughts, dreaming in my waking, standing at a fork in a road; I have a decision to make, except the choices are not yet clear to me. I still see my mom picking me up from where I fell before her, then my feet taking me where my mind knew I didn't want to be.

I hit the bench frustrated; I'm exhausted with being exhausted. I can't keep going the way I have, running on emotions, not knowing if I'm coming or going. I close my eyes, focusing on the beating of my heart, my body is responding to the disquietude of my mind. I feel its strain but I will myself to be still, to search my spirit. I hone in on the last two years of my life, where all this started. The picture that finally emerges is that I lost myself.

Without any forethought, just a great need, I begin to pray. "Dear Lord, the author of my faith, the redeemer of my spirit, and the hero of my soul. I come before you bowed down, broken, and in need of your grace. Please Lord Jesus Christ, come take your rightful place at the head of my life, be seated on your throne. I am not worthy but you have justified me by your blood. I am troubled and my spirit is weak but your grace is sufficient; in my weakness your strength is made perfect. Lord, lead me in your paths of righteousness for your name's sake, let not my will be done, Lord, but yours. Please bless me with discernment and clarity of mind that I may honor you with my life. Take this constant pain from me, please, Lord, and set me free to serve you. I trust in you, please help me to be trustworthy too. I pray to you humbly in the name of Jesus Christ, my savior." I keep my eyes closed even after I'm done, basking in peace for as long as possible. I'm still unsure which juncture I'm standing in, but I have faith it will reveal itself soon.

Back at the house, I have my first test of my newfound tranquility, as soon as I walk in. Aiden is getting his mic from Doug, who's smart enough not to make eye contact. Aiden smiles at me brightly, "Leah, where have you been?" I laugh because being around Aiden makes me want to, his cheerfulness is infectious even if only temporarily.

In our room, Cashmere's sound asleep. I divert my eyes away from her sleeping form and see someone has left something on my bed, my journal and a Bible. The Bible is worn with use but not mine. Scribbled in a corner, on the first page, is the name Brice Young. I pull out the piece of paper being used as a bookmark. It's blank though the page features a highlighted passage. "Don't copy the behaviors and customs of this world but let God transform you into a new person by changing the way you think. Then you will learn to know God's will for you, which is good and pleasing and perfect."

It couldn't have been easy for Brice to part with this. I hope he sticks around, I don't want to be here without him. Brice included another paper bookmark, this one in my journal. I flip to that page and find two words, "My favorite." I hadn't anticipated him reading everything in my journal, just what I wrote for him, though it feels nice to have my work appreciated, especially my favorite piece. It's also incomplete.

"I knew a lovely girl, with a lovely face, who lived in a lovely place. She was stripped of her lovely and left bare; does lovely still exist there? What is lovely if lovely won't see it too?"

Cleaned up, I go back downstairs, where the gang, minus Cashmere, who's still asleep in our bedroom, is huddled in the kitchen. Amy pounces on me as soon as she sees me. "Leah, you got a flower delivery. We were waiting on you to let them in." There's no time to process before I'm opening the door and receiving a dozen long stem red roses. I do it three times before it's to Amy's liking. The cameras stay with me while I read the card to myself; I successfully argue my way out of sharing the contents of it on camera.

"The first time you walked out of my life you made me want to be worthy of knowing you. When you walked out of my life this morning I realized I haven't become the worthwhile man you deserve. But time and experience has taught me that good things come to those who wait. Please meet me at your favorite bookstore, I'll be there until five. I don't care how long it takes to get you back, I will. I'll wait another six years if I have to."

I finish reading the card, fold it, and put it in my back pocket. Everyone's waiting for an explanation but there will be none. I keep my face expressionless. With the footage from this morning and now the flower delivery, the producers are on cloud nine, they could not have written a better storyline. If I pretend the flowers aren't a big deal maybe I'll escape the love triangle plot. Zack looks critically at my bouquet, "Leah, you know you're not getting off that easily. Do you have a boyfriend you forgot to mention?" My eyes move from Beverly, who's surprisingly quiet, to Brice, leaning against the counter staring at my roses.

After walking out on Trent I would have to say no, we are not together at the moment, though it seems like a technicality in light of his declaration to win me back. Not knowing how to or even wanting to, I elude giving a direct answer, "Wouldn't you like to know," I say. Aiden laughs, "Yes we would like to know, do you have a secret boyfriend?" Beverly appears to be choking on the truth; before she can spit it out I decide it's best to respond, "It's not a secret it's just new."

Corey, sage as always, says, "If I wanted my girlfriend to know I miss her or whatever other reason you send flowers, I wouldn't spend a fortune on roses that are going to die anyway. I'd just send her a text then sing her an original." Corey begins singing the most pitiful ballad known to man; Zack pats him on the back, "Stick to acting man, although you're only slightly better at that." Corey playfully smacks Zack, who responds in kind.

Everyone's attention shifts to Zack and Corey's horseplay, almost everyone. Beverly's keeping her eyes on me, but I expected that, she knows who sent the flowers. In her mind her plan failed, which means she'll be trying a new approach to break us up soon. Little does she know her scheming is no longer necessary. I haven't decided yet what to do about Trent; whatever it is I won't figure it out here surrounded by everyone. On my way out of the kitchen I notice how withdrawn and forlorn Brice looks, I poke him in the arm while everyone is focused on other things. I mouth to him, "What's wrong?" He shakes his head. Something's bothering him, but I don't want to bring more attention to us, so I leave it alone.

Amy pulls me into confessional while everyone else breaks off to rehearse; the first performance is tomorrow. The majority of my interview is about Brice and what's going on between us. I have to vehemently deny any romance multiple times and threaten walking out before Amy moves on. Little surprise she starts asking about "my mysterious boyfriend" next. I remain tight lipped, she's right up there with Beverly and Cashmere for people I would never talk about my relationship with. When she tells me I'm done, I exit the interview room at a run.

I bump into Brice outside waiting to go in. "Hey," I say, surprised to see him, but it makes sense Amy would want to interrogate him about me. "Hey yourself," he responds somewhat stiffly, apparently still bothered. Resolutely, I continue, there's something I need to say to him. "I'm happy I ran into you, I wanted to thank you, for everything." I reach for his hand, desiring him to feel the sincerity behind my words; surprisingly he lets me, I wasn't sure he would. "Brice, you've been a Godsend." I pause, startled by my own choice of words; not wanting to look too deeply at them, I rush to continue, "Thank you for your kindness and for the gift you left on my bed. It's among the best I've ever received," I say. "I don't know, those were some pretty flowers," he intones, voice rich with doubt? He doesn't wait for me to respond, Brice reaches past me and pulls open the door.

I walk away, not completely sure what happened. At first I think I'm imagining his voice, but when I hear footsteps behind me I turn back and see Brice jogging to catch up. His long strides quickly close the distance. Looking more like himself, he says, "Meet me tonight, same place, same time." Once again he walks away before I can respond. Brice is throwing me for a loop, he's incredibly hard to read, but I'll worry about that tonight; as for right now I have to determine if I'm going to keep Trent waiting or not.

Back in my room, Beverly and Cashmere are together, they snicker and stage whisper about how amazing last night was. They think they're hurting my feelings exposing a great secret, but I already know they were with Trent. I also know nothing happened. If something noteworthy did, they would've told me as soon as they walked in this morning. Because he was honest about what happened, because I love him, I've decided to meet him, at five thirty. The note said he'd wait for me until five, if he's still there that means we have a shot. If he's left then, we'll cross that bridge when we get to it. Whether we sink or swim will be because of us, not because of juvenile antics employed by his scorned exes.

It's five thirty-seven when I arrive at the bookstore. Two men and one woman stand on line for coffee; I spot a few stragglers perusing the shelves, none of them are Trent. He's too tall and too good looking to not notice, if he's here I'll see him. I walk up and down the aisles, each time I reach the end of a row my heart sinks; he didn't wait. I realize in that moment just how much I wanted him to be here.

On the verge of tears, I sit at a table, bowed head and numb. "Excuse me," the voice is unfortunately female. In front of me is a young waitress holding a cup of coffee. I don't mean to be rude, I just don't have the where-withal to be patient with her mixing up orders right now. "I didn't order any coffee," I mutter, dismissing her. Instead of leaving she sets the coffee down in front of me; brimming with excitement she says, "I know you didn't. That guy over there sent it to you." I follow the direction her index finger is pointing to the opposite side of the room, where Trent is leaning against a bookcase, watching me.

My heart soars at the sight of his beautiful cocky face. He's here, he waited The waitress clears her throat, recalling my attention, "He told me to asks you, how long do you plan on making him wait?" I laugh out loud, thinking back to the first time he sent a waitress to ask me the same question. I let him come to me then, I'll let him come to me now. "Tell him, anything worth having is worth waiting for." She beams at me. At her age, no more than seventeen years old, this is probably the most romantic thing that's ever happened to her. It's not happening to her though, it's happening to me. I lift my cup to him in acceptance of it and whatever else he's offering.

I take my time sipping my coffee. By the time I'm done, Trent is nowhere to be seen. I don't stress, I know he's still around. It's cute, his game, I'll play it for now. I go over to the stacks, scan the fantasy section. I figure when he's ready he'll find me. In the meantime there's no point in wasting a trip to the bookstore. I'm weighing the virtue of purchasing one of three possible books when the waitress reapproaches me. "Hi again, your Romeo asked me to give you this." She holds out a small piece of folded paper between her index and middle finger. "I never renege on a promise, I did say you could have whatever you like and I do mean whatever."

I smile at his swagger and return to shopping, which thanks to Trent just became a lot easier. The waitress, Sarah, hovers around me, delighted at the turn her day has taken. She's sweet, but there's no chance of me getting another note from Trent if she isn't around for him to give it to. I give her all the books I want, asking her to hold onto them at the register while I look around some more. She looks a little disappointed that her next task is to take my books to the register but still excited to be involved. "Let me know if you need anything else, even if it's that you need me to carry a message or something." I laugh louder than I should, feeling uncharacteristically giddy, "I'll keep that in mind, thank you."

At the register, while Sarah scans and bags my items, I muse over Trent's show of charm and wealth but also how much thought went into this. The choice to meet here is because I like this store, because I enjoy books; regardless of what's going on in our relationship he's been paying attention. Sarah makes small talk, asking everything from what genre of literature I most enjoy to how I found this place; she asks everything except what she really wants to know. Am I going to continue to make him wait? Truth is, I'd like to know the answer to that question myself. Trent reappears in time to sign the receipt and lead me out of the bookstore, into his car. Sarah looks sad to see us go, but happy that wherever we are going, we are going there together.

We drive without speaking, sneaking shy looks when we think the other isn't paying attention. "Aren't we going back to the loft?" I ask when I notice we miss our turn. "No, we're not going back just yet. I'm taking you someplace else, if that's okay with you?" He looks at me out of the rearview mirror; when our eyes meet he quickly looks away. "I don't think that place works for us," he finishes. I thought about asking what he meant, then I considered it: despite a nearness of proximity he feels miles away even now. He might be right about his loft not being a good place for us, or maybe it's just us.

"So where are you taking me?" For a brief moment there's a return of his usual hubris. "That I can't tell you, you're just going to have to trust me." My thoughts wander in the silence until, "Since You've Been Gone" starts blasting through the car stereo. I chuckle inwardly at the irony of the song selection while Trent hurries to changes the station. "Hey, I love that song, put it back." I put on a big production of singing loudly and off key, mostly for his benefit; he's reading into it way too much. "Your turn," I say. "Let's do this *Pitch Perfect* style. Did I tell you that's one of my favorite movies?" A smile teases the corner of his mouth, "That is a travesty, please share that with no one ever again."

We laugh straight through to the last bar of the song, when I try to showcase my nonexistent vocal talents, my voice cracks on the last "gone," bringing an end to my singing ambitions. Being more at ease than I was a few minutes ago, I say, "I wasn't trying to say anything, you've only been gone a few hours, that's not long enough to dedicate a breakup song to you." I meant to put Trent at ease, in its place I've caused him to be insular and guarded.

At length he says, "I'm not gone, you are. You haven't been with me for days, outside of our one date that started with me seeing you dancing with another guy." It doesn't bother me that Trent has concerns, what does annoy me is being blamed for our issues. "First, I invited you out, I knew you were coming, why would I do something I didn't want you to see? You're being jealous and possessive; I won't be controlled or guilted into a gilded cage. Second, your advice to me was to open myself up, I do just that and you accuse me of leaving you. Meanwhile you're the one staying out all night with two women you've dated, who coincidentally hate me." Singing and playing around like we were almost caused me to allow our chemistry to let our conflicts go unresolved, not for the first time. We have to figure things out; today one way or another we make a decision.

Trent parks the car in front of a particularly handsome brownstone in a residential neighborhood. He unfastens his seatbelt and reaches to the back seat, gathering my shopping bags, as well as some of his own things. Evidently we've arrived at where we're going. When Trent sees I'm not inclined to move an inch, he says, "We're here." Still annoyed with him, I reply testily, "I see that, but tell me where 'here' is exactly?" He smirks, the kind of smirk that makes me temporarily forget I'm upset. "This is where I wanted to take you. This," Trent points out the brownstone I was just admiring, "is my house."

I imagined dull, drab grey cement buildings when Trent told me he owned property, not a beautiful home in affluent Park Slope. Brownstones are selling at a premium, unquestionably it's a good investment, but it seems too personal, too cared for, to be an investment property. This is the kind of place you buy to raise a family, put down roots.

I let my fingers trail, admiring every inch of the stoop as I walk up the steps. "I bought it during the housing market crash. The sellers were desperate to get rid of it so I got a really good deal. It's four floors, eight bedrooms, and four and a half baths. It's been under the care of a property management company since the renovations were completed. My last tenants moved out six months ago, I brought a contractor in to do some upgrades, which were completed three weeks ago. The management company has called about it at least a dozen times in the last month, but I don't know, I'm thinking I might be ready to make it my home."

Bronze wrought iron double doors intricately fashioned with sunflowers open up to the marble floor of the foyer. A crystal chandelier hangs from the ceiling above me, marking the spot as the center of the room, where you can choose to enter left to the parlor, right to the study, or climb the grand staircase. Everything about this place is finely crafted, accentuated with painstaking detail, the designers—interior and architectural—were able to add modern touches while keeping the old world grandiose feel of the original construct.

"You're so blessed, this is what people work for their whole lives." Without seeing the rest of it, I love this house. I wouldn't do a thing to it, one day I hope to have something like this for myself. Trent nods, "I've been lucky, gotten a few good breaks." His tone is measured, his words are too even, and his demeanor too polite. "Who has a marble fireplace?" I ask while admiring his. "People with good taste and means." I shake my head, thinking to myself that stroking the ego works every single time. "Meanwhile we poor folk make do with huddling close on cold nights." He snorts, "Don't be dramatic, you're not poor."

"Really? My bank account hasn't gotten the memo." Trent looks at me like I'm brain dead; I guess poor jokes aren't funny to rich people. "You do know you have whatever I have right?" This is the part where I usually spurn his offers with a declaration of independence and self-sufficiency, but since I spent the last hour spending his money my usual response won't do. Also the concept of being able to buy whatever I like is starting to grow on me. "Can we have that in writing or something?" I say jokingly. "Funny you should say that." He let's the rest of the sentence go unsaid.

Actually there's nothing funny about Trent today, everything about him lacks his usual temperament. I decide to write the moment off as one of a long list of awkward things that have happened since we met up today and continue on with the tour, moving to the patio door. From the patio we go to the formal living area, just beyond there I stop in my tracks at the winding staircase connecting the ground and second floor.

I touch the bannister lightly; afraid it will retreat back into my mind at any minute. How many times have I dreamed about walking down a staircase identical to this one to my prince charming, waiting adoringly at the foot of the stairs? I'm dressed in a beautiful white ball gown with hand-worked crystals, lace barely there sleeves, and a ten-foot train. My hair's kept in place by freshwater pearl hairpins, and when I motion to put an escaped curl back in place I see the biggest diamond I've ever seen before adorning my ring finger. Holding my hand out in front me, I get a better look at my solitaire princess cut diamond ring.

"Do you like it?" "Godsend" is right below me, dressed in a black tux and white bow tie. It's the weirdest thing, I can see him but I can't see him. I know he's handsome, that he's smiling at me, but his features are indistinguishable. He extends his hand to me and says, "I've been waiting for you." Slowly his face begins to come into focus, "Leah, Leah, earth to Leah." I come out of my reverie disappointedly, all I needed was another thirty seconds and I would've been face to face with him. "Leah, are you okay? Were you having a panic attack?"

This is the first time he's mentioned it since I told him. I almost forgot he knew. I don't plan on ever talking to him about my panic attacks ever again, especially when I was simply daydreaming. "No, I'm not, I spaced out for a second admiring the staircase. I'm fine, come on, I want to see the rest of the house." Trent holds my hand, stopping me from climbing the stairs. "Wait, hold on, we need to talk." I thought we'd finish the tour before we got into the heavy stuff, but now works also.

I let him lead me back into the living room; he explains that he hadn't gotten a chance to get the power turned on yet, which is why we're seated across from one another Indian style in the dying light of the evening.

Trent's still visible, but only just. "I'm sorry for accusing you of cheating on me and for speaking to you in a way I would kill anyone else for, if they ever did. I'm sorry for everything that I did and said, but I'm most sorry for the look I saw in your eyes when you walked away from me knowing I caused it. I knew I hurt you and that hurt me. I never want to cause you pain again."

His apology is heartfelt. I'm almost decided to forgive him, but we haven't addressed how things got here. "Thank you for apologizing. I'm sorry too, that I haven't made you feel secure about where I stand. I want to move forward but I need to know how things escalated to where there was almost no turning back."

"I went to the loft hoping to see you, but it was empty. I walked back to the production office and found Stephanie and her team. She told me the cast was at a theater rehearsing. I was ready to leave when I noticed they were working on a storyboard: guess who was at the center of it." The shock of his implication must register on my face because he answers my unvoiced thoughts with a nod of his head. "Yeah, you." It wasn't difficult for me to guess why; Brice warned me they'd have their story. I guess they had it worked out before we did.

"Apparently Amy brought it to Stephanie's attention that something is developing between you and Brice. They were in there talking about how they could see it from the moment you two met, they actually said 'sparks flew,' which is why they shot it over a million times. I counted at least twenty time codes for romantic moments between the two of you, including from the night before. He watched you, held you, talked to you, all while you slept—the whole time, Leah, the whole time." Trent's voice, colored with hurt, anger, and disappointment, brings tears to my eyes. I wasn't trying to hurt him. We just so happened to meet up while running from our demons. "Leah, how could you let him care for you that way?" Trent is absolutely justified in his anger; I shared a moment of intimacy with another man. He doesn't know it wasn't romantic at all, if he did it would change his disposition.

"At one point he carried you to the couch and watched you sleep; he didn't touch you, he just watched. I watched you like that once, just as he did, with the same gradual dawning that I was in love with you. There was no audio but I watched him watching you, whispering to you as you slept in his arms. That more than anything else destroyed me. You're beautiful, I expect people to be attracted to you, what hurt was that it was more than a physical appeal. I felt it; we all felt exactly how much he cares for you. The whole office looked on in silent awe. Then Jeremy had the brilliant idea to start teasing your 'relationship' on True TV's social media pages #relation-shipgoals. I had to act like I was pleased, but how could I be, the world would aspire to this great love story that my girlfriend shares with another man."

Abruptly he gets to his feet and goes to the window, he braces his hands on either side, pressing his forehead into the glass. I want to console him but guilt holds me in place. "Leah, I'll only ask once, whatever you say I'll believe, but I need you to tell me right now once and for all; he's in love with you, that I know, what I don't know is, if you're in love with him too." I can bear his anguish, the result of a huge misunderstanding no longer. I'm not sure if Brice would be okay with what I'm about to do but it's the only way to save my relationship.

I tell Trent all about Seriyah, how heartbroken Brice is but that he didn't let that stop him from being kind to me. "Without audio I can see why they would assume it was romantic, but it was just two people in need of comfort." Trent keeps his attention trained outside the window while I remain seated on the floor. When I'm done I wait for him to come into understanding of everything I'd just shared. "I hear you, but I saw the way he looked at you, he's in love with you." Admittedly there was a moment when I was confused about Brice's feelings for me too, but it was only a moment.

"Yes, he looked at me lovingly because he was haunted by the memory of his fiancée. He may have been projecting, which I doubt, but even if he were it didn't mean a thing. I assure you that not only does he not have feelings for me, he knows about mine for you." At that last admission he turns to face me, his face lacking the worry in his voice. I did it, I reached him. "Oh yeah, and what would those be?" I roll my eyes, "They would be not the point of this conversation. The point is Brice knows we're involved, which I would like to point out didn't matter to him anyway, because he's still in love with his fiancée. Plus he's in Cashmere's field of vision, which brings me to my question, how does this tie into you being with Cashmere and Beverly all night?"

Looking less hurt and more ashamed, Trent retakes his seat on the floor across from me. "I wanted to make you jealous, I wanted for you to feel how I felt. I invited Beverly out with me, she invited Cashmere. Before you ask, absolutely nothing happened. They linked up with some guys and dirty danced for drinks all night." I take a minute to consider how to verbalize what I want to say. "What disturbs me most . . . what I'm having trouble wrapping my mind around, is why? Why not confront me, scream, get loud, and angry? Why try to hurt me? Why would you purposefully conspire against me with people who hate me, is it that you hate me too?"

I would be less upset if they randomly met up and spent the whole night together, but it was a preconceived betrayal, I don't know what to make of that. "How could you even think that, I love you so much it hurts, can't you see that?" I do see how much turmoil he's in; I wish that could make what he did better. "I've never had my heart all in with anyone before, this is all new to me, including how to handle adversity in the relationship. There's an ache in my chest only you can make go away, but you're with him, you're always with him." That's twice now in the course of this conversation that he's told me he loves me. I knew it though he's never said it. We should be enjoying the first "I love you," but right now I can't get past the part where he conspired against me. What I did was inadvertent, his was purposeful.

"Brice is my friend, he's been kind to me, he put his pain aside to comfort me when I needed it. He's not asked anything of me or crossed any lines. You yourself told me no one cares about the truth, it's perception that matters. Which was your excuse when Beverly attended the cast party as your date. So who cares about an unsupported storyline. Maybe it might even help me win, which is what this is all about anyway; me going for my dreams, not some housewives drama. I will not stop talking to him, you've done exactly what I have, with people who have less honorable intentions, but you punish me for it. It's not alright nor is it okay."

If we are to have a future, Trent needs to know his hurt doesn't justify his hurting me. With his head in his hands, he says, "I have no right to ask this of you, but I will anyway—forgive me, please. I was wrong. I don't deserve you, but you're the one person I want, living without you for me is not living at all."

I cross the small space between us with my hands cupping his face. The sun has gone down, in its place are the harsh streetlamps outside, but I don't need it to see him with my heart to know the truths that exist there. His eyelids flutter closed at my touch. With his face trapped between my hands I say, "I forgive you. Let's be together, love each other, but let's not hurt one another." He lets out the breath I didn't know he was holding, pulling me to him clumsily.

I recognize his relief, it's the same relief I feel when I take my first panic-free breath. "I've wanted to do that since this morning when you walked in with your eyes ablaze," Trent says while hugging me close. "Do you know my heart actually skipped a beat when I saw you? Here you are telling me off yet I wanted nothing more than to hold you." Even without light, I know him well enough to know his pulse is throbbing at the base of his neck, as it always does when we touch. The air goes from relief to charged as our caresses change from consoling to carnal. On baited breath, I wait as he places delicate kisses on my shoulder, causing me to shiver. He laughs into my neck, pleased at his handiwork.

I'm suddenly very aware of him, and nervous; I try to move away, but he senses my squeamishness and holds me more firmly to him. "I love you," he says again, this time I can enjoy the pleasure those three words bring. With an unexpected swiftness he reaches behind me and pulls me squarely into his lap. Feverish heat overcomes us, butterfly kisses becoming bites of passion. I gasp in surprise and pleasure, he responds by biting deeper and fiercer.

Trent is strong and sure of what he wants, gone is the gentleness he normally employs with me. He's hungry and desperate with desire. By the time he makes it to my lips I'm there with him, wanting everything he wants. He gets to his knees without putting me down; his strength is impressive and exciting. We lie near the one weak shaft of light, though it's bright enough for me to see his heart slamming in his chest, the desire in his eyes, and something else. Something that scares me. Trent wears the darkness of night, it sticks to him and he shines in it.

I have a moment of terrible, soul-deep terror; I scramble away from him directly into the light, the only protection I know from darkness. "L, what's wrong?" I pull my knees to my chest, whimpering in fear as he moves closer to me. I squeeze my eyes shut, praying to wake up. Peeking through my lashes I see he's moved into the light, there are no more shadows. Whatever I thought I saw before is gone. What is there is a handsome man hurt at my constant rejection of him.

"L, I'm sorry, I got carried away. When I'm with you I can't think straight, my body and my mind are at constant war. I know I have to let you come to me, sometimes that's easier said than done, but I would never force you . . . to do anything you don't want to do." It's not only embarrassing but also baffling; I have no idea why I keep sabotaging things with him. What's worse is he blames himself. "You didn't do anything wrong, it was me, my hang-ups, I'm sorry I ruined the moment." He disentangles my arms from around my legs, pulling me forward and gathering me against him. "You didn't ruin anything, there'll be plenty of time later, right now we can enjoy each other's company. Come on, let's go poke around upstairs, find some candles."

Searching for candles in the dark is no easy coup; we give up after about thirty seconds, deciding on a store run instead. We score candles, flashlights, and takeout before heading back. In the master bedroom we light and line candles all around the base of the floor. By candle light, the master suite is a large, shadowy space. I walk its length picking out details. The vaulted ceiling is an especially nice touch, so is the electric fireplace—less fancy than the brick one in the parlor, but definitely a better aesthetic fit for the room.

The en suite is a complete surprise, with his and hers sinks, clawfoot tub, and separate shower. "I feel like I'm in an episode of *House Hunters*,"

I shout to him from the shower. I'm trying to get a better look at the brass details. "I'm tempted to ask you if we can afford this place." Trent walks into the bathroom, the picture of domesticity holding two lit sandalwood scented candles. I think he smiles, it's hard to tell with his back to me, while he puts the candles down near the others.

I watch him with a smile on my face; at being in the most beautiful home I've ever seen with the man of my dreams. Just a month ago I was beyond miserable, suffering through panic attacks, selling ad space to small businesses, and hourly "inspirational meetings," now I have almost everything I want. "What are you smiling about," he asks. I wrap my arms around his neck, "You, I'm smiling at you." His arms go around my waist. "I take that to mean you like the house." Between kisses I tell him I don't like the house I love it, "because you're in it and I love you too." We're close enough for me to see his pupils dilate with delight, "I have waited six years to hear you say that." Standing in his bathroom, no electricity, deliriously happy, I'm sure I mean it.

"It's getting late, do you want me to take you back to the loft?" We're in a good place; I'm not ready to leave it. "No, I want to stay right here with you. Well maybe not exactly right here in the shower, you know what I mean." He chuckles, "I was hoping you'd say that. I'll be right back, I have pillows and blankets in the trunk." I slap his arm, "If you had the foresight to pack blankets why not pack candles? You could've saved us a lot of stress." Shrugging he says, "I'm a big picture person."

I drift off shortly after we settle into the warm down comforter. Between one minute and the next I'm sound asleep then I'm waking up in a cold sweat, clutching my chest. Beside me, Trent stirs without waking; gently I remove his arm from around me. I made it to the point in the dream where my mom is saying something to me I can't hear over my fright.

In tonight's dream the floor rolls underneath me, hands reach up from the ground grasping me around my ankles. I fall to the ground, being dragged under. I claw at the dirt, fighting for purchase, my nails are bloody from breaking off at the bed, but I keep fighting. A powerful arm snakes my waist, pinning me to the ground, then with a heave I can still feel in my body, pulls me down into the earth. It pulls me slowly, giving me enough time to see my doom. I keep my eyes on my mom as I swallow my first mouthful of dirt, wondering why she doesn't help me.

I get up as quietly as possible and tiptoe to the bathroom. The candles are burning low but thankfully still burning, I don't think I can handle complete darkness right now. I splash my face with cold water; without towels, I use the tee shirt Trent gave me to sleep in to wipe my hands. They're shaking, a reflection of my inward panic. I wish Brice were here, "Oh shoot, Brice!"

I cover my mouth quickly, I hadn't meant to speak aloud, especially not his name, he's still a sensitive subject between Trent and me. I can't believe I completely forgot about him, he never asks anything of me. The one time he does I completely flake on him. He's probably sitting on the windowsill right now, looking out as the moonlight illuminates his sad, handsome face while waiting to hear my approaching footsteps. I wonder how many times he's said my name tonight already, hoping a trivial noise was my arrival. My stomach twists in knots thinking of Brice whispering my name like an unanswered prayer in the dark. I'll have to apologize to him first thing in the morning. I should bring him a chocolate cupcake, he told me they're his favorite.

Now more bothered than before, I sit on the only available seat, the toilet. I wish I knew why I was having these nightmares, I wish I knew what my mom was saying to me, I wish Brice wasn't waiting for me right now, I wish I was with him. I sit for a long time before I return to bed. When I do, I cuddle up close to Trent, hoping he'll chase my bad dreams away. Every time I fall back asleep I'm back at the beautiful house of horrors.

Chapter 16

THE MORNING SUN IS brighter now than it was when I succumbed to sleep for the last time, around dawn. Before I open my eyes I know Trent's awake too and probably watching me. "Morning," he says. I face him, repeating his greeting back to him. He looks good, and in typical Trent fashion has fresh breath first thing in the a.m. "You obviously slept well last night." I mean it as a statement but with my lack of sleep and growing fatigue it sounds snide even to my own ears. Thankfully Trent doesn't seem to notice, he puts an arm around me and shifts me beneath him. "Of course I did, you were with me; you however, clearly did not." His tone is playful, edged with concern. "No, I slept fine." At the moment I'm more concerned with brushing my teeth than my nightmares, I just don't think our relationship can handle my morning breath.

"Why are you so cranky?" Trent says teasingly. "I am not, I'm trying to spare you my current oral situation." He holds my face in one hand, squeezing, trying to force my mouth open. I clench my jaw shut tightly, fighting against the pressure to open it; if a relationship is to work some things should remain a mystery. "Open up, let me see how bad it is." I shake my head no; letting go of my face he stops his efforts. "You're right, I thought I smelled some tartness coming from you earlier, it'd be best if you handled that a.s.a.p." I decide to make him pay for his reverse psychology; I blow the biggest hottest breath I can manage into his face. He doesn't wrinkle his nose, turn away, or make an obnoxious comment; surprisingly he kisses me.

"Smells sweet; in all seriousness, did you get any sleep? You look exhausted." There's no point in saying I did, as it's clear to him I hadn't. "I slept some but bad dreams kept me up most of the night while you were dead to the world. By the way, drool isn't sexy ever on anyone." After decrying my assertion that he drools or that he could ever not be sexy, he asks what my nightmares were about. Normally I'm open with Trent, but I don't want to talk about it. I want to forget until the next time I face sleeping. "You know your standard Wes Craven nightmare stuff." He rakes the air in front of me, with invisible claws, "Freddy's coming to get you." It's a solid Freddy Krueger impression. I scream while scrambling out of the blankets. My arms and legs flail wildly, accidentally kicking Trent in the shin. The pain doesn't keep him from laughing at me; I myself am caught between amusement and furiousness.

"You shouldn't play like that, I could've killed you. You know I'm from Brooklyn, we don't play those kinds of games." Through tears of laughter he says, "Oh yeah, how would you have killed me with your shrill screams?" I settle back into our pallet, maintaining a safe distance from him. "Keep talking tough guy, I might have to show you what Brooklyn's all about." He waves my threats away, "Yeah, yeah, yeah, if you say so. But are you sure you're okay, I've notice that you're a bit . . . jumpy." I am jumpy, I'm also incredibly tired, I'm also not well rested enough to have a conversation of this magnitude. I tell him I'm fine, just sleepy, an answer he readily accepts without further discussion.

Trent can be intense at times, a sense only heightened by the fierceness of his stare, like the one he's giving me now. "Why are you looking at me like that? It's making me uncomfortable and you look creepy." I thought I'd grown accustomed to it, but no, I'm still skittish under his gaze. "Come with me, I want to show you something." We climb a tucked away set of stairs leading to a converted attic. The skylights overhead admit unobstructed sunlight into the large space. I walk around the room, admiring its vibrancy and bold color pallet; sage with gold decals and soft white accents. I'm partial to loud walls in personal spaces and this room is absolutely meant to be a personal space.

Shelves cleverly designed to mimic the slanted shape of the attic line the focal wall. They're empty now, but this is meant to be a library or an oasis, my oasis I think. I glance from side to side, quickly finding what I seek; reading nooks, the perfect place to enjoy literary adventure, line the walls underneath every window. This is the female sanctuary I've always wanted, designed even. The decal on the walls strongly resembles the swatch I've been holding onto. This is by far my favorite room in Trent's house that he's owned for years but feels specifically tailored for me. It's unlikely but I have to ask.

When I face Trent he's watching me like he was before he showed me this. It's flustering having his eyes on me so intently. "Did you just have this . . . is this new?" At an arm's length away he says, "Construction on this room finished three days ago. It's yours, the first of two gifts I plan to give you today." I don't know if it's what he's saying or the way he's saying it, but my heart rate speeds up. "Leah, for much of my life I've felt like this room, pretty to look at but empty. The first time I saw you, six years ago, my life changed, I knew you were the one for me; I wouldn't rest until you knew it too. In these past weeks you've filled my life with more love than I've known since I was seventeen and orphaned. I can survive without you but it wouldn't be living, you make my life worthwhile. Fill my home; fill this room like you've filled my existence with you. I had this room built for you to show you that I know you, really know you, and know how to love you. I love you not with a fleeting love but the kind of love that took hold of me six years ago at first sight and hasn't loosened its grip since."

Trent gets down on one knee and from behind him produces what I know to be a ring box. "I told myself I'd wait but I can't wait any longer. Leah Albanese, you are unusual and sometimes flat out weird. You love Disney movies and you think Cinderella is a great study of human character. You put on this front of being tough, surly, and combative, but it's only because you have the biggest, most generous heart of anyone I know and you're terrified of having it broken. Your secret ambition is to give everyone a second chance because you believe everyone to be inherently good. You didn't know that I knew that about you, but that's what I'm trying to say. I know you, the good, the better, and the best parts of you. You've trusted me with so much already, now I'm asking you to trust me with the rest of your life. Do me the honor of being Mrs. Trenton Michael Shaw; L, will you marry me?"

My vision blurs with tears, I can't see the ring but I don't need to. I've doubted and questioned him every step of the way, but he's been all in since the beginning, no matter what. He knows me in ways that I thought I kept safely hidden away, I couldn't have dreamed this up any better. Just when I thought my life was virtually over Trent stepped in and resuscitated me. Of course I'll marry him, how could no ever even be an option.

His face is alight with joy, which does more than anything else to convince me I made the right decision; we're happily engaged. Our celebration is short lived though; at minutes to eight I have to get back to the loft; there are many things to be done before my performance later. "You'll be great tonight, and if things don't go as planned that's okay. I've been working on a script for you, if you have no qualms with favoritism . . . or you can simply enjoy being the wife of a very wealthy man. I want you to know that's completely an option." There's laughter in his voice, I'm sure he's joking although I would like to know about which parts explicitly. Most women would love to stay at home reaping the benefits of marrying well; I, however, fully intend on the continued pursuit of my dreams.

"I've never felt more confident about a piece than the one I'm performing tonight, which you should be there to witness, by the way. Morgan says I've got chops, real potential, so as you can see there is no reason for things to not 'go well.'" He wraps me up in his arms, obviously trying to distract me with affection. "Did Morgan say that? He's very well respected in the industry, if he says you're golden you're golden. I meant well, sorry if it didn't come across that way. Everything is going to be perfect no matter what, because we have each other, and I, Mrs. Shaw, am very well connected," he says. "Almost Mrs. Shaw, and tell me this 'husband,' will you be there tonight?" "With bells and whistles."

I was sure I'd get bombarded with questions the moment I got home, but I don't run into anyone when I get in. The only person I encounter is Cashmere, who ignores me when I stroll into our bedroom. She looks to be rehearsing, I assume with the first performance hours away everyone else is doing the same. I want to rehearse myself, but I'm having trouble focusing, my mind keeps wandering to earlier events.

Against Trent's objections, I convinced him to hold onto my ring until after taping. I couldn't stroll in here after being out all night wearing an envy-worthy rock on my finger. There'd be too many questions; right now first and foremost I need to keep my head in the game. I look at my empty hand achingly; I almost passed out with shock when I saw the six carat, pink, solitaire diamond. I love my ring almost as much as I love the giver.

Cashmere's saying, "Come in," before I, lost in thought, have even registered there's a knock at our door. Amy, always an unwelcome sight to me, steps inside. "Welcome back, Leah, we were just about to send a search party out for you." Tensions between us have been high ever since I changed my mind about using my confessional to bash Beverly and Cashmere. It was Brice who talked me out of playing into her storyline. I'm grateful to him for that, among a host of other things. "Unfortunately for you, I'm back in one piece and without a story to tell," I offer. "Very unfortunate indeed, we're having a meeting in five," she's gone before she's finished her sentence. Cashmere follows; pausing at the door, she says to me, "How's your boyfriend, Trenton, I mean, not Brice. I know how Brice is." She laughs at her own quip, "Good luck tonight, I promise you, you'll need it."

I'm not affected by Cashmere's insinuations about Brice and me, that's old news. Though I am more than a little perturbed by her last comment that she knows how Brice is. I hope it doesn't mean something's wrong with him and I'm responsible for it. I'm sorry to have stood him up, I'll tell him as much, but for the sake of my relationship I'll have to put some space between us.

I see Brice before I make it all the way downstairs; he's having a conversation with Aiden and laughing. He doesn't appear upset at all; in fact he looks great, well rested. With a wave and a chorus of "hey" in every direction I greet the guys then plop down on the couch beside him. Instantly, I know he's upset; he doesn't even blink, as I brush up against him, hard. Unwilling to let him ignore me I say, "Hi." Without looking at me Brice says, "Hi back at you . . . stranger." All his anger poured in one word, "Really, I'm a stranger now? I'm sorry about last night. I hadn't planned to spend the whole night out but I got . . . caught up." His eyes flicker briefly in my direction before looking away injured. "Yeah, you were clearly . . . 'caught up,'" he says, looking pointedly at a spot on my neck. "It's cool, I get it. Shaw kept you busy." Brice gets up, takes the seat between Cashmere and Corey on the opposite couch, and leaves me sitting alone.

I dash back upstairs to my bathroom, knowing what I'll see. I skipped the mirror this morning, but study my reflection now. It isn't my most polished look, particularly since it's yesterday's, but there's nothing off about my appearance except the huge hickey on my neck. I've always found them to be tacky, an invitation to make assumptions about a person. I wish I'd noticed it earlier, before I ran into Brice; it was adding insult to injury. I didn't expect his angry to be hurt; I don't know how to apologize without disregarding Trent's feelings, but I don't want to discount Brice's either. I cover my hickey with makeup, hoping no one else noticed, then head back to the meeting.

Stephanie walks in accompanied by Matt, Jeremy, and Trent; he's cleaned up since dropping me off. He's in a white button-up and ecru denim jeans; maybe he should wear a white tux for our wedding, it's definitely his color. I look away from him, trying to keep the smile off my face, then my eyes meet Brice's and I no longer have to try not to smile. I avert my attention to Stephanie, who's in the middle of instructions for today. "Tonight is a big night. You have your first performance at five; it will be held in the theater you've been using for rehearsals. Three judges will evaluate your performances. No one will be eliminated tonight; however, this performance as well as next week's will be taken into consideration with Morgan's notes for your first elimination. We'll be leaving here at three, don't be late. If no one has anything else to add that's it."

Brice is off the couch and up the stairs within seconds of our adjournment. Everyone else, Cashmere and Beverly being the exceptions, quickly follow. I know Trent to be only half listening to Amy, who he's talking to, by the smile playing around his mouth, the one he reserves for me. I hang out in the kitchen, busying myself with sandwich makings until he makes an excuse to be where I am. We stand across from each other at opposite ends of the island; anyone who cares to look could see the energy bouncing off us. "I'm happily surprised to see you again so soon," I say.

"Are you wearing your mic?" I fight the urge to respond sarcastically. "Of course not, if I were I would've contented myself with just looking at you. I hate to admit it, but you might be as pretty as me." He laughs aloud; quickly catching himself, he coughs to cover it. "You know what they say about insanely hot people dating unattractive people." Cutting him off I say, "Yeah I do, thank goodness you're rich, if not I'd have no use for you." He tries to look derisively at me, which lasts all of five seconds before he's back to hearts in his eyes. "I'm going to head out now. I have a meeting with the distribution company in an hour; by the way, start thinking about what you want in terms of an engagement party. As soon as you're done with all of this we're getting hitched."

I love his enthusiasm about marrying me, but my main priority is the competition. "Can we hire an event planner, please, and by we I do mean you." "Whatever you like, babe. I'll have my assistant make a list of the best planners in the city. I have to go now, it was good looking at you." I run a hand through my hair in vain, attempting to make myself more worthy of his compliment. It's so annoying how sleeping without a hair scarf will leave you with frizzy hair, even if it's not yours. "It was better looking at you." Leaning forward as much as he can, arms braced on the island, Trent says, "Doubt it." I blush at the memory of last night pre freak out, my flush deepens when he follows up with, "I can't wait for the honeymoon."

He walks around the island almost past me, at the last moment he half turns, "It's not being a pervert if it's mine," he says while licking his lips. "You don't own it, you just have unlimited leasing options," I remind him. "*After* you sign the contract, I might add." He laughs aloud again, drawing attention our way. I take a small step back, giving Trent permission to leave. "I love you," he says. The cameraman's walking toward me, mic in hand. "Yeah, well, same." Trent laughs all the way out the doors.

At two forty, all seven of us are in the van and ready to go. Nerves are on high and tempers are running short. Even Cashmere and Beverly are being cold to one another, no doubt due to everyone's mounting anxieties. We're held in the wardrobe closet while we wait our instructions. Normally I love being surrounded by pretty clothes but not tonight. The closet is too small to comfortably accommodate us all; add the pressure of having to perform and it's just downright uncomfortable.

After a while, Amy comes in to explain how things are going to happen tonight. We'll meet the judges and hear the prizes as a group. Afterward we'll return to the closet to wait our turns. We can watch each other's performances backstage if we chose, but we must be very quiet. Once Amy is gone I return to my few inches of privacy. The door opens again, admitting Zack, fresh from changing. He has ditched his low-slung jeans for breeches and hose in authentic Elizabethan fashion. I've never doubted that his monologue would be good, now I'm certain it will be great.

I was confident in my costume choice before seeing Zack, but maybe it doesn't do enough to further my performance. Dressed in a simple white sundress with my hair in beach waves, I was hoping the judges would see me as airy. Considering the looks he's eliciting from around the room I'm not the only one second-guessing my wardrobe. The calm and confidence I've had since my first one-on-one with Morgan is waning. Zack's commitment points out to me all the ways I'm underprepared. He's tackling something Shakespearean, something I wouldn't even attempt in my dreams. Anxiety settles in my chest like a bowling ball as I'm gripped with the thought that Morgan is wrong, I can't do this.

I hold on tight to the edge of my seat, trying to force myself to focus and breathe without making a scene. Brice, who I've hardly seen today, takes possession of both my hands and kneels in front of me. Conversationally, he says, "Leah, take a look at me." Gone is the anger from earlier, he's the Brice that's been unwaveringly good to me. "And the peace of God, which transcends all understanding, will guard your hearts and your minds in Christ Jesus." In low deep tones, he talks me through my almost panic attack. I ignore the rest of the room and Beverly's grin. I keep my focus on Brice and his voice.

Whatever anxiety I felt is gone, Brice helped me through it. There's just something so comforting about him, that's why loosing his friendship bothers me. "I thought you weren't speaking to me," are the first words I say when I'm recovered enough to speak "I never said I wasn't speaking to you. Granted I'm not exactly happy with you, but I would never sit back not helping you if you needed me and I could. I don't know what you're used to, but people who—" he breaks off abruptly; rubbing the back of his neck, he continues, "People who care about you don't behave that way." I'm still holding onto Brice's hands, I refuse to let them go, not until I've had my say. "Thank you for being my friend, one of my best. Sorry that I haven't been the same for you." It's difficult to gauge what he's thinking, he looks kind of sad, but his face always has a trace of sadness. Without responding he pulls his hand out of mine right as Amy walks in. "Alright people, show time."

The theater looks the way it normally does, like my high school auditorium, with the addition of a table draped in a red cloth and three empty chairs, positioned stage left. For the first time I wonder what kind of budget the show has, the benefit of a non-scripted project is the minimal production cost, but this is next-level thriftiness. We line up, women in the front, men behind us, facing the judgeless table. Iliana comes out on stage wearing a bit of a custom herself, a gold latex dress with hood. Her skin and lips shimmer with large specks of gold glitter. It isn't pretty exactly; it is, however, attention grabbing. Again I question my fashion choice for tonight. The cameras split their attention between Iliana, the judges' table, and us. Stephanie isn't in sight, though I know she's on the other end of the earpiece Amy's pushing deeper into her ear. Amy nods her head in affirmation, cues the cameras, signals the stage director, who calls for silence and counts us in.

"Welcome, Ladies and Gentleman, to your first performance on *Star Quality*, may it not be your last. You are competing for a cash prize, representation from one of the best agents in the business, and a featured role in a major motion picture. We know why we're here, now let's meet the people who will determine for how long. First we have Legacy Media executive Acer Price." We clap politely as a small, squat man emerges from off camera and takes his seat. "Next we have agent to the stars, Eloise Gunner." Eloise is a classic beauty: tall, lean, dark haired, and light eyed. She doesn't smile, her face wears a guarded expression; she'll be the one to impress. "Lastly but certainly not least we have screenwriter, director, producer, overall industry insider, Lawrence Scott."

Immediately I recognize the name; I met him at the cast party. He mentioned he was part of the show. I didn't bother asking in what way, now I know. He came on strongly at first, but by the time he left he proved to be a decent guy. Lawrence takes his seat without much fan faire. "Now you've met the judges, it's time they meet you. Break a leg."

I'm not sure how our performance order was determined, though it's been decided Aiden's up first. Corey and I stick around backstage for moral support. "Hi, my name is Aiden Hassan, I'm pretty much the resident beach bum of the house." The judges chuckle before Eloise takes control, "So tell us about the piece you'll be performing today." He pushes his hair back off his forehead, "I think my strong suit is laughter. I don't like negative emotions, drama, or any of that sh— stuff. I like to make people smile, which is what I hope I can get you all to do. Especially you," he points at Acer, who's been smiling from the moment Iliana introduced him. "You look like you haven't smiled in about three seconds." He's won the judges over with his affability, they're laughing with him, excited for his performance. "*The key to faking out the parents is the clammy hands.*"

I have to hand it to him, Aiden is amusing to watch. I've never been much of a *Ferris Bueller's Day Off* fan but I might have to give it another try. Waiting for the first of his critiques, Aiden stands with knotted hands behind his back. "Son, you've got real chutzpa, you were fantastic," says Acer. "Might have even given Mr. Broderick a run for his money." Aiden relaxes enough to unknot his hands. "Yes, Aiden you were funny," Eloise begins. "But my concern is that you haven't challenged yourself. You readily admitted to us, you don't like anything negative, which leads me to believe you'll only do what comes easily for you. True actors aren't afraid to push the envelope, challenge themselves." I knew Eloise would be hard to please, not impossible. It's our first performance, she doesn't know enough about him to make those assessments.

"Personally, I feel you've nailed comedy," Lawrence says, echoing my thoughts. "I would cast you in the role of comedic relief in a heartbeat. I think Eloise is right in that you'll have to show us more range through the course of the show, but there are a number of successful actors who've built careers at being funny; Eddie Murphy . . . Jonah Hill, just to name a few. You did a solid job." I decide to go ahead and like Lawrence, he's fair and honest.

I hug Aiden as soon as he walks off stage, "You were hysterical, I hope I do half as well as you did." He smiles good naturedly; like he said, he doesn't like negative emotions. He and Corey walk off set; I stick around for Cashmere's monologue. She saunters in wearing platform shoes, knee-high socks, and a plaid miniskirt. I hadn't connected it earlier, but as soon as I see her on set, I know what she's doing. She introduces herself to Acer and Eloise then stops at Lawrence.

"Wow, very nice to meet you, Lawrence." He is flattered and on the verge of responding when Eloise shuts down the exchange. "Cashmere, your time here will be better served wowing us all, seeing as how it is a group decision." Flushed with anger, maybe embarrassment, Cashmere apologizes for her behavior, then dives right in. "So, okay, like right now, for example, the Haitians need to come to America."

Cashmere isn't entirely convincing as Cher Horowitz, but she isn't horrible either. Acer praises her costume and "commitment to the role." Lawrence says, "Not bad, but be careful of your scene choice on auditions. Don't give casting directors a reason to typecast you. Do things that are unexpected of a beautiful woman such as yourself." Eloise, looking visibly unimpressed, addresses her next, "Cashmere, do you know what written work *Clueless* is an adaptation of?" Cashmere, having no answer, remains silent; I know and despite not being her biggest fan would give anything to be able to tell her, just to shut Eloise up.

She raises an eyebrow at her, "I see. It is a modern day retelling of Jane Austen's *Emma*. Much like Cher, Emma is a silly, aloof young woman, not unlike . . . well . . ." Eloise doesn't finish her statement, but she doesn't have to, the implications are clear. "I'd suggest you to chose a more mature female character next time and show us depth, because right now you're coming off as shallow as a pond." Cashmere waits to be formally dismissed before running off stage. Corey's up next, I want to stick around for him, but someone else needs me more.

I find her crying in a bathroom stall, her tears audible through the closed door. "Cashmere," I say, "it's Leah." She stops sobbing long enough

to shout at me to leave. "Cashmere, I know we aren't exactly friends but—"
She cuts me off angrily, "Exactly, we're not friends, so what do you want, to
gloat?" I take a seat on the floor outside her stall without concern for my
white dress, "Cashmere, I don't hate you. I don't even dislike you. I would
gladly be your friend, even after everything that's happened between us. I
won't apologize about Trent because I love him too, and he loves me back,
but that's no reason for us to be at odds.

"Eloise was harsh, spiteful, and wrong. She doesn't know how strong,
brave, and resilient you are." She snorts disbelieving, "And you do?" I force
myself not to react to her hurt. "Yes, I do. I'm subscribed to your YouTube
channel, it's amazing. I love your makeup tutorials, your Q & A's, but my favorite videos are your story times. You've been candid about your struggle.
No one has the right to diminish what you've overcome no matter how
many stars she represents." I can feel the weight of my words getting through
to her, "I'm just so sick of people assuming I'm dumb or some kind of sex-
crazed vixen. I want people to respect me, my dreams, and all I've done to
get here."

I've thought those very things about her but I was wrong. "The truth
is, we can't make people like us or respect us, but we can respect and love
ourselves. Someone wisely advised me not to let the world dictate my identity to me, so now I advise you the same." There's no sound from her side of
the wall until the bolt is being pulled back. She extends a hand to me that I
take, to help me up. "I don't know why you're being so nice to me, but thank
you, I get it now . . . why everyone loves you." I shrug, "Not everyone, I can
think of two people who aren't fans." We laugh, "One person, just one." In
a completely unforeseen move we hug. In amicable conversation, we head
back to the waiting room together.

The dressing room is empty except for Brice, who seems preoccupied
with his script. I ask about everyone else. "They're watching Corey's performance, at this point it might be Zack on stage, maybe even Beverly. I'm
on after her, I'm just doing a last-minute run-through." Cashmere squeaks
in shock, "I told Bev I'd watch her perform . . . come with?" I tell her to go
ahead without me, I'll be on soon, one last run-through before my turn
would be wise. Truthfully, I want a moment alone with Brice, I'm not sure
I'll get the chance again.

Once the clack of Cashmere's shoes against the floor is a distant sound
I turn to him. He's already looking at me; he probably waited for the same
sign to know the coast was clear to speak, "So you and Cashmere are bff
now?" "Possibly, I'm keeping my options open, though, if you want to come
and reclaim your position." With a smirk he says, "See, I was unaware I relin-
quished it, but thanks for letting me know, I'll keep your offer in mind . . . I

need you to do something for me." I'm so happy to have Brice as a friend again I'm ready to agree to the favor without even knowing what it is. "Don't watch me perform." I'm confused by his request, we're joking again, he can't possibly still be upset with me. Why would he not want me to see his performance? "I get nervous when I have a large audience," he says. "I can't confide in the others like I can you, please help me do my best by not being there."

"Thus conscious does make cowards of all"—Zack is already on when I arrive backstage, thankfully he has only just begun. I missed Corey's performance but I would have truly regretted not seeing Zack's rendition of Hamlet's "to be or not to be" soliloquy, which was, in a word, fantastic. By the time he says, "Be all my sins remembered," I am convinced there is no better actor in the world, let alone this competition. There is no applause while Zack awaits his critique.

Acer rises from his seat, leading the judges in a standing ovation of praise for Zack's performance. "Magnificent, spectacular, superb." Zack accepts his applause graciously with the poise of a seasoned actor. After such a great performance I'm not surprised that even Eloise is unable to find fault; she does, however, find issue with Zack. "Okay, you have talent but do you have likeability and earning potential? Will you drive fans to the box office in drones, or better yet, spark hash tags? I'm not sure you will. You'd be a phenomenal stage actor, but film I don't know; I'm not sold. Tonight's objective was to introduce yourselves to us, to choose a monologue that tells us something about you. I was impressed with your acting abilities, but I'm not sure you're a star. Next time choose something less rigid, with more personality; who knows, maybe you'll prove me wrong."

Zack remains outwardly composed, as if her opinion had little effect on him. I know how much Zack wants this, how much he needs it, but studying him now I think I understand Eloise's critique. As a viewer, I'd want a reaction from him; Eloise may not just be harsh for fun, she might actually have some valuable insight. "First, Zack, I want to say I loved you as Ryder Grey. I loved you more tonight as Hamlet. Unlike my colleague, I believe tonight to be about showcasing your strengths and I will not ridicule you for doing exactly that. I found no flaw in your performance, best performance of the night so far."

Eloise takes offense to Lawrence's comments and jumps in to champion her earlier statement, "I wasn't ridiculing him. I was giving him constructive criticism, unlike anyone else on this panel." Lawrence looks at her incredulously, "What do you know? You buy and sell personalities. Acer and I find talent, you destroy it for the highest price." Before it can get much more heated, Amy steps in, calling for a five. When we resume shooting it will be with Beverly.

"I'm Beverly Boyd, tonight I'll be performing an original piece." From the instant she lies on the floor, panic bubbles up in my chest. "I woke up this morning happier than I've been in years." It is completely impossible, yet Beverly is performing my monologue; the letter Trent wrote me that I made into my performance piece. Not only does she have the words, she's performing it just as I had for Morgan during our one-on-one's. I run off stage, brushing past Cashmere and Corey as the walls begin closing in on me. Outside the stage door I put a hand over my heart, feeling its pounding.

After Beverly, Brice goes on, then I'm up after him. I have fifteen, twenty minutes tops, to figure out a plan B, and "she stole my monologue" won't cut it. I rack my brain, but all I come up with is kill Beverly, which might make me feel better but will do nothing for my current situation. I can perform it too, but I think the same original monologue from the both of us would not go over well with the judges. I can fall back on my old audition monologue but it was never good enough.

I wish Trent was here but he's not; I haven't seen him yet, besides he can't fix this for me. I need to think, maybe I can wing it, but I'm too nervous to go out there unprepared. I need something that I know, that I can master in about ten minutes, that says something about me. I get an idea, I'm not sure whether it is brilliant or crazy but it's the best option I have. Without further agonizing I run into the waiting room, rifle through the costumes, and find what I need in no time. I discard my clothes, quickly dressing in the too-big suit. I put my hair in a low ponytail, careful to get every strand. I don't bother running through my lines, either I'll nail it or I won't, it's too late to guarantee the first. I shrug it off and make my way back to set.

Brice walks off stage with a restored calm, his performance must've gone well. He stops when he sees me, I shake my head "no," I'm in no mood for conversation. I'm angry, blood-boiling angry. If Beverly had the misfortune of running into me right now I don't know what I'd do. My only solace is hoping Eloise made her feel small. I'm not even nervous anymore, just burning mad. Called on set, I swagger on stage and stand in front of the judges.

"Please introduce yourself and your piece." I am glad for Eloise getting straight to the point. "Leah Albanese, I'll be performing Jordan Belfort's monologue from *Wolf of Wall Street*." Head trained on the ground, I place my hands behind my back, walking the length of the stage back and forth. I cross stage left behind the judges' desk, stopping between Eloise and Lawrence. I place a hand on both of their shoulders, bend down low, and say in stage whisper, "See those little black boxes?" I point at the telephones I can so clearly see in my mind, the ones I picked up every day for two years, desperately trying to sell ad space to a business owner, hoping to make my numbers and not get cursed out. "They are called *telephones*. I'm gonna let you in on a little secret about those *telephones*."

I walk out from behind their desk, still speaking to them, the cameras, and everyone else that's watching. "Okay, without you they're just worthless hunks of plastic." I spring up on the judges' table like a cat or deranged person, speaking passionately at the top of my lungs, "My warriors, who will hang up the phone . . ." I jump down, landing lightly on my feet, "Let me tell you something, there is no nobility in poverty." I repeat it louder this time, then a third time. Spinning around with my arms held high above my head and wide, I scream it a fourth time, "There is no nobility in poverty!" I continue on in this frenzied way, "You'll be ferocious! You'll be relentless! You'll be telephone terrorists!!!!" My chest rises and falls as I fiercely meet the eyes of all the judges. I straighten my suit jacket and make sure my hair is still in place. "Now," I say in normal tones, as if I weren't just screaming, "Let's go knock this out of the park."

The theater erupts in applause; whistling and screams of "encore" come from above me. Following the cheers to the balcony, I spot Morgan accompanied by Trent leading the applause. I had no idea he was here, I wonder if he was here the whole time, if he saw Beverly's performance? Acer recalls me to the moment, "Leah, you are frighteningly delightful. You had drama, passion, and command. You were my favorite performance of the night." I blush as Acer gushes over me. Lawrence, who typically commentates last, skips over Eloise, "I'm sorry, Zack, I might have spoken too soon. Leah, you were electrifying. From the moment you walked out on stage, you demanded attention. I shuffled back and forth between your headshot and the person performing in front of me, unable to believe you were one and the same. Truly I did not expect such a strong performance. I am speechless you are . . . wow." Lawrence's praise is a relief, I was afraid he'd harbor ill feelings toward me, but he is a consummate professional.

Eloise watches me with a closed expression. I'm sure of her impending criticism but I care very little. I just pulled that out of nowhere. I'm proud of myself. Nothing Eloise can say to me will take that away. "I don't often find myself speechless; when I do it is either very good or very bad. I cannot find one thing to criticize you on. You made my night. Leah Albanese, I look forward to seeing more of you, because you are a star." My face splits into a smile as I breathe out a sigh of relief; I cared more than I thought. I don't know how, but I just knocked everyone else out the water. I look up to the balcony, wanting to celebrate my victory with Trent; he's gone, I don't know where. I'm sent back to the waiting room along with the rest of the cast, the judges need to deliberate. Although no one will be sent home, they will do a formal ranking of tonight's performances.

I sit alone, not ready to speak to anyone yet. I'm happy it worked out for me, but it doesn't change things. How was Beverly able to steal my monologue? Did Cashmere somehow orchestrate this? Did Cashmere steal my letter and give it to Beverly? That's not likely, I keep that letter locked in my luggage; even if Cashmere was able to get into my luggage, how would Beverley know it was anything to me other than a love letter? A sinister idea begins forming in my head. I hope I'm wrong.

Iliana greets us as we retake our places on set, "Ladies and Gentleman, welcome to your first judging. As you know, there will be no elimination today; however, your performances will be ranked from best to worst. The last two names called comprise the bottom two. In normal circumstances, one of the two would be eliminated, but again, tonight everyone is safe. Your rankings will, however, carry weight toward next week's elimination. Without further delay we'll begin. When your name is called step forward, collect your headshot, then line up horizontally, stage left."

The judges standing in a straight line behind Iliana step forward. Holding the stack of photos out in front of her, Eloise begins, "The first name we will call is the person we feel had the best performance tonight; Leah, step forward please." I retrieve my photo excitedly, it feels amazing to be called first, to be validated. Zack is called next, followed by Brice. Zack was fantastic tonight. If Brice was called immediately after him he had to have been good, too. I hate that I didn't get to see his performance. Aiden is called, afterward Cashmere.

Corey and Beverly make up the bottom two; while I feel badly for Corey I smile broadly. Justice could only be more poetic if it were an elimination night. Corey looks nervous; although no one will be sent home tonight, the anxiety is written all over his face. Contrastingly, Beverly is the picture of calm. "Both of you find yourself in the bottom two for the same reason, your performances paled in comparison to your peers," Eloise says. "Neither of you chose monologues that highlighted your talents. Corey, your monologue was not ambitious enough, and Beverly, although the words and concept were intriguing, you failed to convey them. Maybe your talents are best suited for writing. The question is who did the best of the worst?" Eloise pauses, building suspense, "Corey, you're safe. If tonight were an elimination, Beverly, you'd be going home. My advice to you, Corey, enough with *The Hangover*, and you, Beverly, don't overreach."

Amy tells us we have to do our post-performance interviews before we can go. Her questions are mostly reactionary: how do I feel to have been ranked first, my opinions on the bottom two, etc. I do tell her based on the little I saw of Beverly's act, the judges were absolutely right in choosing her as the worst performance of the night. I leave Amy with a broad smile on her face and go in search of Trent. He hasn't reappeared since after my performance. I hope he's nearby.

I run into Morgan outside the theater, where he greets me with applause. "Morgan, you're making me blush." He removes from my face the hand I'm hiding behind. "What is most endearing about your modesty is its genuineness. I must ask, much as I enjoyed your performance, why did you not do the one we worked on?" Morgan is one of the few people who must've realized what happened out there tonight and maybe the best person to discuss it with.

"You and I both know I didn't change my piece voluntarily, somehow Beverly was able to learn what I was doing and beat me to the punch line." He nods his head expressively, "Yes, I did witness that unfortunate butchering of a fine work, but what was most disturbing to me was that she attempted to perform it exactly as you did, down to the inflections in your voice and nuances of your movements. She's much too unrefined to perfect details . . ." Morgan stops short, realizing something too unbelievable to say aloud; I'd gotten to that same conclusion an hour ago.

"It makes you wonder, doesn't it? No doubt she studied me, the question is how. The rehearsals were closed, minus the cameras; the only way she could've known is if she saw my film." I don't tell Morgan the rest of my theory; I don't accuse Amy of trying to instigate an epic confrontation. I don't know if Cashmere is involved. I hope not, but I can't definitively call it either way. What's most alarming is if I'm right, as I suspect I am, Beverly was just a pawn in all this. I have to talk to Trent about all this soon. "Leah, I know where you're going, and I agree with you, but be careful." He pats my arm softly before walking away, leaving me alone and unnerved.

"I don't know about you guys, but I'm too pumped to call it a night, let's go do something." Corey hasn't stopped talking since we got in the van; he's on a natural high from not being sent home. Being around him right now, it's hard not to feel the same. Predictably, Aiden, always willing to have a good time, is first onboard. "Dude, I'm down and I know exactly what we should do." We all agree to go to a karaoke bar; Aiden even makes a suggestion for which one we should go to.

"I have to warn you," I announce to everyone, "I'm the reigning karaoke queen." "Sorry, Leah," Cashmere replies. "I know we're friends now, but tonight you're going to be dethroned, because I am the karaoke empress," she says without the venom I've grown used to expecting from her. "Not likely, better men have tried and lost, but I accept your challenge." Cashmere and I, much to everyone's surprise, playfully banter about who is the real karaoke champion. No one mentions our newfound friendship, but Beverly does pull Cashmere into a hushed conversation, carried out in short, harsh tones.

Back at the house I freshen up and change my clothes before helping her find something to wear. "Question, do you own anything less . . . revealing? I mean, its karaoke not a meet and greet on the corner of Hollywood Boulevard." For the first time since I met her, Cashmere laughs genuinely; it isn't flirty or antagonizing, it is a moment of amusement. "How'd you have me dress, like I don't have anything worth flaunting?" She pushes her already large chest out in front of her; my sigh doesn't quite cover my smile. It's an indescribable joy not having to be a mute in my own room, having someone to laugh with.

Pulling out white skinny jeans completely ripped down the front and a graphic tee, I toss them to her. "I think I found something, pair that with your gold wedged sneakers, the watch you're wearing, and a couple of thin necklaces. I have dozens; you can borrow some of mine. And Cashmere, next time one ripped knee will suffice." We joke with one another but I chose my words carefully with this fresh friendship. I haven't figured out our boundaries yet, besides the obvious, and I'm not sure if I should trust her. "I'm going to slip this on, I'll be right back." She pokes her head out of the bathroom door, "Leah, remember, one good turn deserves another." I look at her dryly, "Friends don't force poor fashion decisions on their friends," I say, as I shoe her back into the bathroom. I'm still laughing when Beverly walks in without knocking, "We need to talk."

My mood improved significantly on the van ride back, there is no longer any urgency to my anger. I still haven't decided on what I'm going to do about Beverly, but my plan was to take my time to figure it out. That she's confronting me takes the decision away from me. I lead Beverly out of my room into the hallway, not wanting Cashmere to overhear our conversation. I don't want to believe Cashmere was involved, but if she was it was before we became friends. I'm more than willing to forgive Cashmere for her hypothetical involvement, no questions asked, but I have no desire to do the same for Beverly.

The door is barely closed behind me before she attacks. "You may have Cashmere, Trent, the judges, and everyone else fooled, but you're not fooling me." I listen to her with tightly crossed arms over my chest; I need the physical restraint to keep myself from completely losing it. "I want to pass along a friendly warning to you, keep your mouth shut about tonight. If you tell on me, I'll tell on you. It's enough to get you disqualified, I checked." As if reading my mind, she says, "Don't even think about denying it, I have proof, footage of you walking out hand in hand the night of the party. You don't want war with me, I have over a hundred thousand followers, I will drag you and tag you." Check and mate. Contrary to popular belief, all publicity is not good publicity. I've had a taste of social media backlash, seen celebrities get bullied off the Internet; I want no part of it. "Fine, I'll play by your rules for now, but I'll still win and all you'll have had is fifteen minutes." I open the door behind me. "Consider me warned," I say, "consider yourself warned too."

Chapter 17

JAM SESSION BOASTS A lower level, with fine dining, and on the upper level, several private karaoke rooms. Surprisingly there's a room large enough to accommodate our party. Aiden orders pickleback shots all around; whiskey and pickle juice is probably the single worst combination I've ever consumed, but when in Rome. After two rounds we're ready to battle it out. "Shall we split into teams?" I ask. Corey leaves Aiden's side and puts a lightly muscled arm around me, "I'm on Leah's team, she's a winner." "And that's why you're not," Beverly sneers, "you'll always be the friend of the winner with that attitude."

The sting of Beverly's words is felt around the room. She's usually pleasant to the guys. We're all too shocked about what she said to reprove her, "I'm on Leah's team," Cashmere says, shooting Beverly a disgusted look over her shoulder. "Because winners stick together." She sat between Brice and me on the ride over here also. I hadn't thought much about it, but perhaps our friendship comes at the price of theirs. Aiden volunteers himself and Zack to be on Beverly's team, more out of a need to be the peacemaker than a desire to work with her. Brice is the only one without a team, I would gladly take him but the choice is his to make. "I think I'll sit out the group round, you need a judge right?"

"First category," Brice calls to us, "friendship. Team Beverly you're up first." Both teams huddle over a song catalogue accompanied by cameras. I've gotten used to them always being around, but the production assistant recording us on his phone is new. "Hey, what's up with the phone?" Amy responds before he can, "We told you guys this show is interactive. We're going to stream live on social media, tag all of you, get more followers for the show. I'll remind you that everyone here signed a contract, meaning you've all agreed to this." I have no choice but to be okay with it, I did sign the contract consenting to basically everything. As much as I distrust Amy, she is right, I'll just have to deal with it. I shake off my discomfort and jump back into the discussion about song choices.

"We're ready to embarrass team Leah," Aiden says with a conspiratorial wink. He's Beverly's teammate but he doesn't share her intensity and he's a friend to us all. My team's suggestion comes from Corey, his good mood deteriorated. I hadn't seen Corey this angry since the morning he and I argued. It's upsetting how much Beverly got to him. He has stopped having fun and now has something to prove.

Zack stands front and center with mic in hand, in off-key tones he belts out, "Oh baby you, you've got what I need." He and Aiden switch off rapping the verses while Beverly basically prances around stage gyrating all over them both. Aiden returns her suggestive moves with some of his own, meanwhile Zack takes care of the singing, which is unfortunate because he is not musically inclined. Although I have to admit it's entertaining if not vocally sound.

When it's our turn my team starts with our backs to the room. Corey turns around when the beat drops, "Yo, I'll tell you what I want, what I really really want." Cashmere spins on her heels, "So tell me what you want, what you really really want." I turn last, "I'll tell you what I want, what I really want." Together we sing, "I wanna, I wanna, I wanna, I wanna, I wanna really, really, really, wanna, ziga, zig ha." Corey is not a dancer but insists on doing it anyway; he does a weird rhythmless two-step the whole song but his energy is catching and so is our performance. I finish with an air kick in homage to Mel B and the Spice Girls.

Brice takes a moment to decide who won that round while we catch our breaths. I honestly have no idea which way things are going to go; #teamLeah rocked but so did #teamBeverly. Having come to a decision, Brice says, "Both teams were good, it was a close call, but I'm going to have to give that round to the Spice Girls and Guy." My eyes immediately seek Beverly's; hers are currently engaged in rolling upwards. "Of course you chose her team, you're Leah's number one groupie." She's reached a new low tonight; Beverly's been manipulative to Brice but never outright nasty. I don't know if it's almost being eliminated or my friendship with Cashmere but she is being absolutely horrid.

In a most likely career-killing move, Roger, the new production assistant, volunteers to be our unbiased judge alongside Brice to prevent any further claims of unfairness. Our next category is "girl groups." My team is first since we went last the previous round. Cashmere is the star of our performance, as it happens she really does have a knack for karaoke. Without her "Left Eye" our version of "Waterfalls" would've bombed. She did such a good job I was sure we'd take round two as well; that is, until Beverly's team comes out swinging with "Push It." Aiden and Zack push it all up and down the room, they even push it in my face a few times. Doubtlessly #teambeverly took that round.

On a food and beverage break, I saddle up next to Brice. He's given up his customary tee shirt and jeans tonight, opting for slim raw denim and a fitted button-up. "Can I bribe the judge?" He thinks about it for a minute, "Might have to, I'm still kind of upset with you, the win is probably going to team Beverly otherwise." I give him the sternest look in my repertoire, "Don't even entertain crazy thoughts like that." We laugh before settling into silence. I break it, remembering something he said. "Am I forgiven?" Brice looks down at me through his lashes, "I'll let you know . . . You look good up there, comfortable."

My stomach flutters unexpectedly, I shift in my seat to get it together, hopefully it's not the hot wings. "You have to do a song with us, you can't play spectator all night." He takes a sip of the liquid in his glass, "I'll think about it." Brice is different tonight, he's cool, and while it has its appeal, it isn't him. He's always handsome, but he's usually less pretentious about it. He never acknowledges his effect on women but tonight he's flirtatious. Brice responds to the looks he's getting from random women and entertaining the comments from Cashmere. There's even something in the way he's speaking to me that's sexy and cool but utterly unlike him.

"What's this all about?" I wave my hand up and down, indicating him, from his attitude to attire. He looks great but not like himself, it's more of a Zack outfit or something Trent would wear. The revelation brings me up short, tonight Brice reminds me of Trent. He puts his drink down and looks at me through his lashes again, "I don't know what you mean. I'm being the same me I always am, maybe it's you that's different." I am different, I am engaged, but he's different too. He doesn't give me a chance to respond, he calls both teams back into competition.

"Now that all you divas are refreshed, our next category is: two rounds of love gone wrong." Before getting up to group huddle on song choices, I whisper in Brice's ear, "Do not conform to the ways of the world." I don't finish the rest of the verse or explain, he'll get it.

Food extinguishes the fire in #teamBeverly's bellies, overall their performance is bland. The one bright spot is Aiden; he's a charming Justin Timberlake singing the lead vocals for "Tearing Up My Heart." Other than that there are no special moments. #TeamLeah on the other hand is hoping to redeem ourselves from the last round. I instruct Roger to start the music while we begin outside the room. The music starts cuing Cashmere in. "Rah rah ah ah ah Gaga Oh la la," she sings while breaking into a syncopated dance routine keeping time with her words. Cashmere dances up to Brice and Roger, it's uncomfortably provocative but Brice handles it well.

Corey and I relegate ourselves to the background for the entirety of the song, Cashmere doesn't need us for this. Locking eyes with Brice, Cashmere sings, "Want your bad romance." It looks great but I don't like it, Brice is in a very fragile state, he can't be come onto like that. Cashmere wins that round almost entirely alone: sexy, dancing, and sexy dancing are all her areas of expertise. I mentally chide myself, remembering that I like her now.

Round four kicks off with more N'sync. Zack sings the first verse as best he can while Aiden handles the other two. Beverly does what she always does for every song. She constantly shies away from the mic; she relies on Zack and Aiden's talents. It seems to me Beverly is the one guilty of doing exactly what she accused Corey of. The difference being Corey is decent enough not to take credit for someone else's work. Their performance closes with Aiden singing, "The truth remains you're gone," and Brice excusing himself.

I saw the look on his face as he walked past me on his way out; it's the one I've grown accustomed to over the course of our acquaintance. It's the look he gets when he's overwhelmed with longing for Seriyah; no matter how much he aches for her, she's gone. I want to go after him, but maybe the best thing I can do for him is give him space. I'll have to do so soon anyway for Trent. We wait on Brice for about ten minutes before he comes back in looking restored . . . to me at least, I'm not sure anyway else noticed how affected he was earlier.

#TeamLeah takes our place with me singing lead. Admittedly I'm not the next great vocalist but I do all right. Singing "one time, one time . . . two times, two times," Corey and Cashmere are the Wyclef and Prodigy to my Lauren Hill as we croon "Killing Me Softly." I keep it cool, that is until the bridge, that's when I sing my heart out; I own the riffs. After that hands-down defeat, #teambeverly is all sung out. Cashmere, Corey, and I celebrate our victory with the quintessential victory song, "We Are the Champions." Brice and Aiden join in while Zack tries to coax Beverly into a better mood.

"Hey Bev, that's why you'll always be a loser, because we're better than you." Corey isn't typically spiteful, but Beverly was horrible to him earlier. Although no one begrudged him his brash moment it did make things tenser and more awkward than need be. Cashmere might've been feeling some residual fondness toward Beverly, because she shifts the moment from Beverly onto herself and me. "Leah, we make a good team and all, but we haven't decided who the karaoke queen is. I issue you a challenge, one round, any song of your choice, everyone votes on the winner. Do you accept?" I nod consent, "Without a doubt."

Aiden tosses a coin in the air and tells Cashmere to call it. "Heads," she shouts. When it lands he picks it up exactly how it fell and declares, "Tails. Leah, it's your choice, who's up first?" Cashmere is smart in her song choice; "Super Bass" is current and catchy. She has the audience simply because they like the song; add the fact that rap sung is her niche and you have all the makings of a good performance, really good actually. She wasn't quite Nicki but she is an entertainer. Cashmere didn't do her talent justice today with the judges, she undeniably has . . . something. Trent was spot-on in casting her.

To beat Cashmere I will have to outperform her, I'll have to get the crowd on my side. Cashmere finishes up to resounding applause, hands me the mic, then takes a seat on the couch next to Brice. I notice she's been very aware of him tonight. I also notice he doesn't seem to mind. I push whatever it is going on between them to the back of my mind and step up, determined to be crowned Ms. Karaoke.

The music starts and automatically I know it's the right choice as I watch recognition dawn on everyone's face. "Get into the groove, boy, you've got to prove your love to me, yeah." I swing my head and hips exaggeratedly from side to side in perfect Madonna imitation. Seeking and finding the most engaged person, I sing, "Get up on your feet, yeah." I pull Corey by the collar of his shirt onto the center of the floor with me. My hips never stop swaying, I never stop singing as I seek my next target. One by one I get everyone on his or her feet, "Only when I'm dancing can I feel this free."

Sandwiched between Corey and Aiden I sing into one camera then the next. The feeling in the room is amazing, everyone is dancing, even Beverly. Thankfully, Zack had gotten hold of her because I wasn't going to. Amy and Roger are dancing on the side; in fact, the only person who doesn't seem to be having a good time is Brice, who is still seated. I've purposely ignored him up until this point, but I can't anymore. I dance my way over to him, "I'm tired of dancing here all by myself. Tonight I want to dance with someone else." He laughs before letting me pull him up, it's amazing how many times you can listen to a song, love it and never gleam any meaning from it, then all of a sudden one day you hear it and finally hear the words.

"Step to the beat, boy, what will it be." I spend the rest of the song singing to and dancing with Brice; as long as the song lasts, so does our moment. The song ends, breaking the spell and bringing the realization that Trent will see this footage and I will have hurt him again. Before either Brice or I can say or do anything further, Cashmere jumps between us, "Leah, I bow to you." I hug her, happy to not have to look at Brice, "Let's call it a tie." Someone replays the song, this time we all sing together.

Two hours after getting home I'm tearfully padding to the telephone room. I need to talk to my mom. I've only tried calling her the one time since I've been here. I haven't spoken to her since the day I left home but right now I need her. The phone rings three times before she picks up; it's late but she sounds awake and alert. "Mom?" She lets out a heavy breath, "I thought it was you, Leah, are you alright?" Of course she thinks something's wrong, here I am calling her at four in the morning like a crazy person. I will myself to calm down before responding,

"Yes, I'm fine, the phone gets pretty tied up around here during the days with everyone making calls." My mom knows me well enough not to believe me, though she doesn't press me on it, the one time I wish she would. "Why are you up so late, did you just get in?" Translation, *are you living a life of debauchery now that you're out of my house?* "No, Mom, I got in a while ago. I'm up because I've been having trouble sleeping," I say, my tone tinged with annoyance; I don't want to bicker, I want to have a conversation, to be comforted. "I'm having nightmares again. Well *a* nightmare, just the one, over and over again." Through the phone I see the concerned look on her face before she ask, "What are you dreaming about?"

I tell my mom about the mob, the fork in the road, and the two houses: the one of horrors and the other; the house I thought was broken until I'm being drowned in darkness by the false beauty of the former. When it's too late, I see it was never ugly, it just needed repairs; I regretfully watch it become beautiful, kicking myself that I hadn't chosen that path instead. I tell her about her recent appearances and the dream that woke me tonight.

"You're waiting for me at the fork with tears streaming down your face, again you say something I can't hear; I leave you to return to the house of fear. Before tonight I'd never made it to the front door, I would be detained on the lawn by the agents of evil trying to deliver me to the obscure malevolence waiting beyond it. Tonight the lawn is empty of snakes and corpse hands, and the front door is closed. I could probably turn around and walk off the property. I don't, I watch in consternation as I knock on the door, it swings open, then I willingly walk into a black hole where arms I don't see drag me away."

I pause, hesitant to share with my mom the rest of the dream, it's more disturbing than the beginning; nevertheless I continue. "Someone I can't see rips my clothes off, without sexual intent. Somehow I know their objective is to make me metaphorically bare, to strip me of self. I try covering my body with my hands, though in complete darkness, I don't want to be naked. Suddenly a flash of lightening strikes, ripping a hole in the side of the house, someone, a man running at top speed, yells my name. I scream, 'I'm here,' he sees me, doubles his efforts, I wake up before he gets to me." His face, so clear before I woke up, escapes me the minute my eyes open.

My mom is quiet for a long time after I've stopped speaking. "Mom, are you there?" Her response comes in the form of the humming of an old hymn, one I haven't heard in years. "Close your eyes, Leah, open your spirit and let's pray." Twenty minutes later I hang up, feeling less perturbed though still confused. After we prayed I asked my mom if she understood my dreams; she said no, but I knew she wasn't being completely transparent. Maddened, I ask why she's holding back. Shrewdly she replies, "This is your journey. Why should I have the answers to *your* test?"

As if on autopilot, I walk out of the phone room back upstairs. When I get to my door I don't stop, I keep walking. I'm too tired; too scared to think straight, I just need a few hours of sleep. The curtains are drawn back, allowing light in from the street lamps and passing cars. It's harsh and un-natural but I'm thankful to not be in complete darkness. Aiden's sleeping, head cradled in his arms, covers thrown off the side of the bed. I smile, even in slumber there's easiness about him. I tiptoe to where Brice is asleep on his stomach, one arm thrown out, dangling over the side of the bed. I was hoping he was awake or that my appearance would wake him. I hesitate con-templating what to do. I should turn around and go back to my room, but I feel safe with Brice and he keeps the nightmares away more than anything right now, I need to feel safe.

I walk to the empty side of the bed, turn back the comforter and climb in. The springs squeak beneath the pressure of my knees digging into the mattress, I stop, waiting for a reaction out of either boy; neither budges. I continue my slow procession, halting at every noise, until I'm right next to him. Watching Brice's sleeping form, I feel the difference between now and all the other times we slept beside each other. Brice usually stays awake until I fall asleep; this time he's disconnected from me, far away in his own dreams.

I'm thinking I made a mistake when the springs creak where my hand presses into the bed supporting my body, this time the noise wakes him. Brice lifts his head off the pillow, turning side to side searching for the source. "It's me," I say, feeling I've disturbed him. The confusion on his face embarrasses me. "I'm sorry, so sorry, it was wrong of me to come . . . I had another bad dream, they don't come when you're around." Hot tears fall down my face, it's true the only peaceful sleep I get is when I'm with him, but I still shouldn't have imposed. No longer caring about being quiet, I move to leave. Brice catches my arm, with his husky, sleep-filled voice he says, "It's okay . . . stay."

Without any further conversation his head hits the pillow and his body eases into the mattress. I lay down as well, on the other side of the bed. Already I feel the pull of sleep, Brice's eyes are closed but he's awake. "Thank you for letting me stay." Without opening his eyes he says, "Tell me what guy would kick a beautiful girl out of his bed?" "The kind of guy that would sleep next to a beautiful woman multiple times and just sleep." He smiles into his pillow, "Yup, and I'm about to do it again. Good night."

I wake up later in the morning dazed and disoriented. Only after forcing myself to focus do I remember the previous night: the distress that led me to seek out Brice after I'd decided to distance myself from him. I'm alone. He and Aiden are gone. I should leave also but I'm glued to the bed with my brain in overdrive. Physically I'm refreshed, I haven't slept that well since even before the dreams started, mentally and spiritually I'm less so. My mind races with unanswered questions mostly about my nightmares and some about Brice.

Cashmere looks like my mom does when she's waiting up for me but pretending otherwise when I get back to my room. I haven't taken two steps before she's asking me where I was. "I woke up way too early, couldn't get back to sleep, so I caught up on some reading." I flop down on my bed, which I'm beginning to look at like a torture device. I'm not sleepy anymore but I am tired. "Where's the book?" Without missing a beat I say, "I left it downstairs in the phone room." While I was talking to my mom last night I saw Brice's copy of *The Odyssey* on the table. I meant to bring it upstairs with me to return to him. I forgot, seeing as how I was distraught. I'm happy I did, otherwise I would be caught in a lie.

"Okay, Leah, we'll pretend you don't have a super hot boyfriend and that most mornings I don't wake up to your empty bed." Cashmere pauses, waiting for me to acknowledge her insinuations. Frankly no one is happier about us becoming friends than me, but I'm not up for the third degree. Seeing I'm not going to respond, she continues on, "We'll just skip right over all that, we'll talk about Brice instead." Once upon a time Cashmere had a hand in trying to create strife between Trent and me by misrepresenting my friendship with Brice. Trent is not a subject I want to talk about with her; I'm thinking Brice isn't either.

Still it's important to me to maintain the friendliness. Being unclear on what exactly she's asking, I continue, cautiously, "What do you mean?" I hear the squeaking of the mattress, indicating Cashmere has gotten up from her bed. Seconds later she's sitting on mine. "I mean you two are close, you've gotten to know him the best of everyone here." I open my mouth to tell her she has the wrong idea about us, but she stops me. "I know you're just friends, you have . . . *Trent.*" I hear a tremor in her voice and remember her saying she would hate me forever because he loves me; I wonder if she still feels the same?

"What do you think of Brice . . . Specifically Brice and me?" She clarifies. Brice is the most phenomenal man I've ever known, any woman would be lucky to have him even if only as a friend. Cashmere's great too, hanging out yesterday she showed she's more than a beautiful face; when she's in her element, she's electrifying. Any man would want her, including Brice. I'm also fairly certain I saw a spark between them last night.

In the spirit of friendship, I offer an answer to her question, "Brice is . . . atypical. He's thoughtful and cares deeply about things most people forgot to value a long time ago." Once I start talking about him, I have a lot to say; belatedly, I question how wise it is to let on how much I do know about him. I switch the weight of the conversation back to her. "Well, what do you think of him?" Turning on my side, I prop myself up on my elbow to have this very uncomfortable conversation. "I picked up on some of what you were saying the day we were talking about our perfect mate," Cashmere says. "I kind of thought after I kissed him he would try to, you know . . ." her cheeks color in a flattering way, "get to know me better; but we've hardly spoken since then, until yesterday."

I fight the part of me that isn't happy about a possible "Bashmere" hookup and tell her the most important thing I know about him. "He isn't motivated by shallow and superficial things, Brice needs to be fed." She looks at me wonderingly. "He's not like Zack, Corey, or Aiden, is he? Especially not Corey, those guys have no standards. Women throw themselves at Brice but he hasn't noticed any one except for—" Cashmere stops short of her point.

Eyes cast down, looking shamefaced, she says, "Leah, I'm sorry for what we told Trent about you and Brice, I know it's not true. Beverly and I spent a lot of our time figuring out how to piss you off. Trent seemed to always be at the center of it, telling him about Brice was perfect because all we had to do was tell the truth. Except it wasn't the truth, I didn't know that then. I spoke with Brice last night. He told me you two are just friends with shared interests. Anyway, the point is that even if there was more, it wasn't my place to tell Trent, you don't deserve that. I'm not proud of myself, but I felt like you'd stolen from me, I wanted revenge. I get it now and I'm moving on, hopefully with . . . someone new. What I'm really trying to say is, sorry."

"Thank you for apologizing. As far as Brice goes, if you two are on the same page that's great." Cashmere reaches for my hand; when she squeezes it I feel the weight of her sincerity and am touched. When the moment passes she conspicuously clears her throat, covering or foreshadowing awkwardness, "Do you think he's into me?" I was hoping she wouldn't ask me that.

If I'm being completely honest the answer is I'm not sure. Brice is obviously not completely healed from what happened with Serayiah, their love still exists, just on two different planes. I don't think he's even looked at another woman since he fell in love with her.

On the other hand, I could be completely wrong and he is ready to date again. Why shouldn't it be Cashmere, he didn't exactly push her away when she kissed him. Not being sure either way, I say, "I think we'd be hard pressed to find a man who doesn't find you attractive. I know you're more than that and so does Brice; he isn't the type to play games. If you feel you guys have a connection then that's probably the case." She smiles, assuring me I said the right thing. "I'm not sure if it's anything," she says, "but I do want to find out."

I'm wearing a red floral-print floor-length wrap skirt with a white off-the-shoulder bodysuit, my cross at the hollow of my neck. I dressed for lunch meticulously; I plan on dropping in on Trent when we get back. I'm nervous about seeing him. I have to keep reminding myself we're engaged, twenty-four hours later and it still feels surreal. "You're beautiful," my stomach lurches at his voice. I kind of thought he was avoiding me, I haven't seen him all day, but here Brice is, standing half in, half out of the doorway.

"Why are you standing there like that, why don't you come in?" My tone is friendly but my stomach is in knots. "I'm being respectful, giving you the option to invite me inside or not to." I motion with my hand that he should enter. "How are you?" Brice asks. A simple question with a complex answer, he's referencing last night. My thoughts, however, are on this morning and all that Cashmere said. He's watching me closely, waiting for an answer; I look away, returning my focus back to the can of glitter I was spraying my braided hair with before he interrupted me. The truth is too messy, therefore I say, "I'm fine what about you?" He chuckles like it's a silly question, "I'm okay, I wasn't the one who couldn't sleep last night." In the mirror our eyes connect as he walks up behind me. Lightly I say, "Neither was I, I slept great, actually it was the most sleep I've had in days."

Easiness leaves the air between us, something I feel in the pit of my stomach and see in the shadow of his eyes replaces it. It's not an entirely unpleasant breathlessness but feeling it with Brice is disquieting. "You wear that cross a lot," he says. "Why is that?" Reflexively my hands fly to my neck, "It was a gift. I wear it in appreciation of the giver and acknowledgment of my faith." I shake my head at him imploringly, why is he asking about my jewelry. Brice looks back at me steadily with deepening intensity. "Don't you know that your faith is of greater worth than gold, which perishes even though refined by fire. It was not with perishable things such as silver or gold that you were redeemed from the empty way of life."

"It's a necklace, Brice, a necklace, not some representation of a greater spiritual battle waged within me. I really can't take anymore of your constant preaching, especially since you're far from perfect yourself. Before you point out the speck of dust in my eye remove the plank in yours." I remember that much from the Bible, "Judge not lest you be judged." Where does he get off constantly questioning everything about me, making me feel guilty when he's flawed just like the rest of us? I saw how he responded to Cashmere's advances, for all that spiritual talk at the end of the day he's as susceptible to sin as the rest of us.

On his way out the door, Brice stops abruptly; what I see in his expression quells my temper. "You're right, I'm not perfect, I never intended to make you believe I am. I see you, Leah, I see you and I've been where you are: doubting, confused, disappointed, and pretending, but here I stand. 'The godly may trip seven times, but they will get up again,' Leah, why haven't you?"

Lunch is a relatively subdued event, we share a few laughs, filling in the blanks for each other from yesterday's performances and last night's outing. Beverly and Corey, made up from the previous night, sit side by side. I sit between Zack and Aiden, about as far as I can get from Brice. He doesn't seem to mind. He spent most of his time on the ride here and now talking to Cashmere. I avoid speaking directly to or looking at him, but he is at the center of my thoughts—even now, as Zack and Aiden mercilessly tease me. "Why Leah, would you like to get into the groove?" Suppressing a laugh, I say, "Aiden I'm about five seconds away from hurting you." "Honestly Leah, I don't know why you're so upset, you said it yourself. 'Music can be such a revelation,'" Aiden laughs. Zack collapses in mirth over his penne. Motioning my fork back and forth between the two of them, I say, "I hate you both equally. I didn't hear either of you saying anything last night. In fact, if memory serves me correctly, you both sang along, every single word."

I engage in conversation, smile, and laugh when appropriate, but my heart isn't in it. Brice's words haunt me: "*I've been where you are: doubting, confused, disappointed, pretending.*" I might have been that a month ago, not anymore though; Trent changed all of that. I'm so much better than I was. I tune back in to Zack telling the story about the time he got invited to a party at a certain celebrity's house; it takes a weird although not unexpected turn; he loses me after feathers and acrobats. I'm arrested mid-laugh by Brice staring at me, I can't read his face and we're too far away from one another to communicate verbally. I hold his gaze until Cashmere, unaware she's interrupting, demands his attention with a flirtatious hand on his arm. More confused than before, I rejoin my conversation with the guys, being extra attentive and careful to not look in Brice's direction again.

"Leah, you feeling any better?" Zack is on a bathroom break when Aiden approaches the conversation I've been dreading. I'd devoted some of my morning to thought about what I'd say to him if he asked about my being in their room. I was unsuccessful in thinking of an excuse. Ultimately there was no need, Brice had me covered, as usual he has my back. He really has been a great friend to me, one day I'll have to be the same to him.

"Yeah mostly," I say, "thanks for asking." I hold onto the lifeline Brice threw me without having the slightest idea of exactly what illness I'm supposedly recovering from. "Imagine my surprise and jealousy when I woke up this morning and found you asleep in Brice's bed. I mean, yeah, he's got the whole tall, dark, and handsome thing going for him, but I'm Aiden." Initially I was apprehensive about having this conversation, but Aiden and his nonthreatening way makes even the most difficult conversations easy.

"Of course, if it were me, I would've actually been in the bed with you. Not Brice, though, he was draped in a blanket sitting in the chair watching you. He said he found you drunk in the living room last night, he didn't trust you to make it to bed and stay there, so he put you in his and took the chair. He also said you'd probably be embarrassed so to not mention it to you, but I wanted to make sure you were okay." Brice is impossible to figure out, I trust him implicitly; I know he would never try anything or even want to, what was the point of sleeping in the chair? Also for such a noble person he is an accomplished liar. Keeping my face impassive I say, "And you just completely disregarded sound advice, how very like you." He smiles his easy smile, "Of course I did, look at me. I'm not really the sound advice following kind of guy. If I were I would've listened to my dad and went to business school."

"I didn't hear you come in, L." Trent's sitting behind his desk in his office, he gets up when he sees me. "I've missed you, Mrs. Shaw," he says while picking me up and swinging me around in his arms. "Future Mrs. Shaw, and if you missed me why didn't you stick around last night? I saw you for all of two seconds before you were gone." Setting me down without letting me go, we sit on his desk. "I wanted to stay, I really did, but I had a dinner with the head of the distribution company I'm trying to broker a deal with, I couldn't keep him waiting. However, I did get to see you leave the competition in the dust, I'm proud of you babe."

I've never been the kind of girl that enjoys pet names, but for Trent I can learn to, "'Babe' is it? Now that we're engaged will I become pumpkin, sweetheart, and every other sort of desert?" He playfully bites my neck. "You were always those things, I just never called you pumpkin, sweetheart, or candy drop because then you'd know exactly how head over heels in love I am with you. Now that you're going to be my wife I want you to know, my little lemon tart." I smile at the irony of being called a tart, "Okay, my gummy bear, but do me a favor and keep the love bites to a minimum."

Trent holds me at arm's length, looking me over, "I see no love bites." I turn to my left while stretching my bruised neck into the light, I've covered it with foundation but it's visible to anyone who's looking, I explain to him. "So what, we're engaged, I can leave bites on you wherever I please." This is twice now he's shown me he has no idea what the word marriage means. I'm forced to give him a lesson in semantics. "Excuse me, I'm your fiancée not you're teething ring." His lips quiver with the restraint of suppressing his laugh, "That's what I love most about you. Your wittiness." I lean back into him, wrapping my arms around his torso, "That's what I love most about you, you're constant acknowledgment of how great I am." I feel rather than see his laughter. "Why are you chuckling, do you disagree?" He kisses the top of my head, "No, I'm just happy for the first time in my life, I'm whole-heartedly happy, it's intoxicating."

I'm happy too, at this exact moment life is perfect, but we don't live in a bubble, and even those pop. "By the way, I'm mad at you," my tone purposely contrasting with my words. "Why are you mad at me?" Moving out of his embrace, I sigh, "I dressed specifically for you, I look awesome too, but I haven't heard one word of appreciation from you. Now that we're engaged, are you going to stop noticing me, because that won't work?" Trent looks at me incredulously, "Are you kidding me, you're the only person I've noticed in six years. Are you going to stop noticing me?" I kiss him slowly and deeply, wanting Trent to know he's the one I love, the one I've agreed to spend the rest of my life with. I want no question in his mind or mine, "How's that for an answer?"

Between spending time with the roommates and Trent, our first weekend goes by in a blur. We are becoming a very tightknit group, it's surprising how close we've all gotten in such a short amount of time, especially Cashmere and me. We enjoy each other's company, actually seeking one another out. We spend a lot of time in our room trying to hide from the cameras, which is ineffectual because they find us anyway. I could be imagining it, but I get the feeling the cameras are spending extra time with us. Not that I could blame them, some of our conversations are very entertaining. With the cameras rolling, Cashmere reveals to me she and Beverly had a falling out, the old saying "the enemy of my enemy is my friend" comes to mind. I doubt they were ever friends, I think they were brought together by their mutual dislike of me; with that commonality gone their friendship fell apart.

"Honestly it's no great loss, Beverly was kind of boring." I lift my head off my mountain of pillows to look at her, "Not her biggest fan, but I wouldn't use boring to describe her." Cashmere blows on her drying nails,

"Not boring exactly, her obsession with you was, though. Anyway I'm over her, Brice too." I've been keeping my distance from Brice these last few days; though, where I'm distant from him, Cashmere is present. It looked to me that they were getting along well. That they aren't comes as a complete surprise.

"When did that happen?" She shrugs and continues adding a topcoat to her nails, but her stiff posture says she cares more than what she's letting on. "I like the man, he is just . . . I don't know that we have chemistry. Sometimes I think if I wasn't sure he wasn't involved with anyone I'd think he was involved with someone." If only she knew the truth, Brice is in love with a memory. She shrugs again, "My feelings aren't hurt or anything, in fact I'm better than ever. He and I hung out yesterday after Scrabble." I know they did, I saw them looking cozy on the couch when I came in from Trent's; Cashmere invited me to join them, I declined.

"He said something to me that really hit home, he said, 'Love yourself without the approval of fans, followers, retweets, likes, or a relationship.' I've been thinking he's right, I need to love me. I'm going to start by taking the time to get to know myself by myself." Brice has that effect on people, he makes you want to be better, makes you believe it's possible. I miss him. I'm happy being around him has been good for Cashmere the way it is for me. "You're an interesting person, I'm confident you'll find that you like yourself." Dubiously, she replies, "I hope I do."

I walk into the living room early Sunday morning and see Brice perched on his favorite windowsill reading. I can't see the title. I do see he's in deep thought though. I wonder if he spent the night there or if he woke up early to read in the dawning light. Trent's uncomfortable with my relationship with Brice; I have to respect his feelings, although it's difficult staying away from my best friend in the house, maybe in life. It's been over a month since I spoke to Amanda last; I miss her too a great deal, yet not half as much as I miss Brice.

I attempt to go back up the stairs undetected by him, but he catches sight of me. He calls out to me, putting an end to my escape. I face him, determined to keep our interaction brief and casual. Brice smiles at me one of his rare smiles: beautiful and endearing. He's genuinely happy to see me, which is why I turn back around and walk away. Every ounce of me wants to sit across from him on that windowsill making up for lost times. The problem is I want to do it as much as I know Trent wouldn't want me to. Every moment I spend with Brice is a betrayal to him, I've promised Trent to be his wife, to always choose him; I have to do that now no matter how tough.

As challenging as the days are avoiding Brice, the nights are even worse. My nightmares are unrelenting; I wake up from my dreams with fresh terror. Deep breaths and constant reminders that I do not have a spirit of fear calm me enough to drift back asleep, to more nightmares. In spite of the renewed panic at waking up to an almost pitch-black room, I don't go searching for Brice, I won't let him comfort me again. Instead I sit under the window in our room, huddling closely to the light, and write. I write everything that comes to mind, random words at first, contemplative ones eventually.

Relief comes with daybreak; I've made it through the night. I shower, dress, and drink lots of coffee. The ease of the weekend is gone. We're back to business, meeting Morgan in an hour. I leave the apartment early, needing the feel of fresh air against my face. In the stairwell on my way to the lobby, Brice, who must've followed me, corners me. With a finger to his lips he signals me to be quiet. His arms reach behind me, fidgeting with my mic pack, switching it off; once he's done with mine, he does his. Satisfied we're able to speak privately, he asks if I'm okay. I tell him I am.

"No, Leah, you're obviously not okay. You're still having nightmares, I see it in your face." I'm touched that he cares, but nothing's changed between us. I steel myself against my soft spot for him and try to walk away, he catches the tips of my fingers, between one second and the next we're holding hands. I look at him for the first time in days; he looks sad, more sad than usual. It's cruel to let him worry about me when he has his own burdens.

"Brice, I really appreciate your concern but I'm fine. Don't worry about me," I say with the most carefree smile I can manage. "I get that you're mad at me, that you're not talking to me, you might not even want to ever talk to me again. You don't have to but you do have to sleep. If you need rest, just crawl in with me, no questions asked." It's hard to say whether the surge of emotion I feel that leads me to hug him is the result of exhaustion or sadness at his inherent goodness.

Begrudgingly I release him, "I'm not mad at you, Brice, I have no rea- son to be." He searches my face wonderingly, "So why all this between us?" Distress chases confusion across his face. I didn't want to tell him like this, but I can't keep hurting him and letting him think it's his fault. "I'm en- gaged," I blurt it out without tact or finesse. My eyes are to the ground when he walks away. I don't see his face before he does. Brice leaves the stairwell dealing with the revelation that honesty has irrevocably changed our bond.

Chapter 18

Morgan begins with praising most of us on a job well done. "Those of you with less-than-stellar performances, you have an opportunity to redeem yourselves. For your challenge this week, you will partner up for a scene. The twist is your script will be a mashup of two famous scenes from different movies. The point of this is not to test your mastery of the script but the spirit of the words. Memorization doesn't make a scene, what matters is the chemistry between actors their ability to make you feel what they're feeling." Collective muttering ensues as we take in the enormity of the task. "There are seven of you, one group will have a third member. You are free to select your partners, but the scripts have already been decided upon. You will be given ten minutes to do so, starting now."

Without thinking, my eyes seek Brice. I look away instantly, but not before I see him shake his head at me and turn to Aiden and Corey. "Want to be partners, roomy?" Zack would've been my choice for scene partner, but saying no isn't an option with Cashmere looking vulnerable and expectant. Our friendship is too new, too fragile to survive a blow like that, "Yeah, I'd love to." That leaves Zack and Beverly. I'm surprised Zack's without a partner, not so much about Beverly. She had the weakest performance of us all last week, plus she is miserable to be around, especially lately. Not having a minion has made her more disagreeable than usual.

We are given our scripts and time to work with our partners under Morgan's supervision. Our scene is a mashup of *Dolores Claiborne*, with me playing Dolores, and *Georgia Rule*, with Cashmere as Rachel. I have a bit of a phobia of rehearsing for the cameras after what happened last time; I'm positive Beverly was given access to my rehearsal footage. Granted, she can't just take my scene this time around but I won't put it past her finding some other way to sabotage me. I don't trust Amy, either, weaving her way through us, filming us, plotting on me, but what choice do I have, the show must go on.

Very much aware of the cameramen, Cashmere and I do a cold read. "This is ridiculous, how are we supposed to be characters from two different scenes?" Cashmere is psyching herself out, the characters don't exist in the same film but they are telling a similar story. "I like it, you're just resistant to it because we know it's two different works. I know Eloise was hard on you, but that's because she didn't get to see how talented you are. This is your chance to show her."

She rolls her eyes at me halfheartedly, "Great, now you're becoming Morgan." Growing familiar with her defense mechanisms, I continue, "Seriously, it's not that bad. Both scenes, independent from one another, deal with a mother-daughter combination, the abuse of the daughters suffered at the hands of their fathers, and both parties trying to come to terms with that." Cashmere's expression changes from indifferent to guarded. "You don't have to explain abuse to me." I look at my hands, afraid to meet her eyes, to see confirmation of what I hear in her voice. "I think we're going to do a great job, I'm going to show Eloise exactly how shallow I am." Determination and an emotion I can't pin down mark her words, we couldn't have been assigned a better scene.

"Leah, what's going on with you, you've been out of it all week, and since elimination's in two days, I kind of need your head in the game." Cashmere and I have spent the last few days in constant rehearsals. She is doing a great job with our scene. I wish I could say the same of myself. "Sorry Cash, I'm just tired. You wouldn't know this because you can sleep through anything, but I haven't been. I'm beyond exhausted, I can't think, let alone get into character." I'm not sleeping, the nightmares are getting worse, and I can't turn to Brice for help. We haven't even spoken since I unceremoniously told him about my engagement. To top it all off, Trent insists on us meeting with an event planner because he doesn't want to wait to get married. Beyond everything else, I'm borderline delirious with fatigue.

Lying down on my bed, I exhale loudly at the momentary relief closing my eyes brings from the throbbing pain behind them. "This is what we're going to do," Cashmere says, "I'm going to run you a bath, make you some chamomile tea, and tuck you in. Once you've rested, you'll be good as new." Hard to believe this attentive friend was once my enemy, "Thanks Cash, I really appreciate it but I can't . . . I have plans tonight." We never talk about Trent, ever, Cashmere doesn't bring him up, neither do I. Not having him between us simplifies things, I sense that's about to change.

"It's okay you have plans with Trent, Leah, he's your boyfriend. If you're worried about my feelings, don't be, it doesn't bother me anymore." I'm not certain she's completely unaffected by Trent, or my being with him, though I do believe she's less so. What I know for certain is we're friends. "In that case, I have plans with Trent tonight. I actually need to start getting dressed, I don't want to be late," I say, while slowly sitting up. "Then go get beautified for that gorgeous man. I'll probably be asleep when you get in, but if you need anything wake me up."

"Babe, what time did you say the event planner was getting here?" Trent and I are meeting with Meredith Butler, owner of Just the Right Touch event planning. Trent contracted her to plan our engagement party. According to him, she's the best in the city; she is also twenty minutes late. I take a break from my spot on the couch, planting myself near the window instead. I'm just in time to see a stylish middle-aged woman I assume to be her walk into the building. "Trent, Meredith's on her way up," I shout.

He comes down the stairs in the blue suit—a cross between iridescent steel grey and periwinkle—he was wearing when I arrived. His shirt, crisp white; shoes and tie, black. Apparently his business meeting earlier called for posh attire. There was no need to change to meet with Meredith, Trent looks good and he knows it. Seeing him, I'm glad I decided to dress more elegantly than usual, too, in a fuchsia crepe tea length dress. Trent takes my hand—now donning my engagement ring, in his. If nothing else we look good together. "Shall we?"

Meredith turns out to be a friendly, enthusiastic woman. She congratulates me on marrying a man wealthy enough to buy me a ring that big and handsome enough to be my arm candy. She obviously enjoys her work; in her mind, motifs and decor are as vital to the functioning of society as nurses and doctors are. She has a lot of great ideas, although eager to hear mine. "So tell me, how do you envision your wedding? It's very important we discuss these things now, it's crucial for creating symmetry between all the wedding events." I like symmetry as much as the next bride, but I haven't thought that far ahead. My priority is getting through the next two days. If it were up to me this meeting wouldn't be happening for another few months; I suggested as much to Trent, which turned out to be a colossal mistake.

We fought; he was passive aggressive about not "forcing me to do anything I didn't want to do," and I was overly vocal about my desire to be with him. In the end I gave in because of how important it is to Trent. I'm trying to be better about considering his feelings. Although I have no real answer for Meredith's question, I don't want to come across as unconcerned; consequently, I say the first thing that pops into my head. "I've always envisioned the moment." She nods, "That would be the princess moment." Every bride wants that moment of hushed reverence before she walks down the aisle, but that's not the moment I mean.

"That should be a given. What I want is that moment of suspended time. Reality and fantasy collide, it doesn't make sense that you're living your best dream, *how* doesn't matter because the man whose eyes you're looking into holds your life's source." Lifting our interlocked hands to his lips, Trent places the gentlest expressive kiss in my palm. I smile at him more confidently than I feel. In my mind's eye, I'm walking down the aisle to meet my "Godsend," his face is still indistinguishable, but his eyes aren't and I don't think their Trent's. On the verge of panic, I remember every bride gets wedding jitters; this is the first time I've thought about what the actual wedding will be like, it makes sense I would panic. Feeling better, I refocus my attention on Meredith.

"So are the parents excited?" Trent's fingers, laced through mine, stiffen; his parents are a difficult topic for him. I wasn't exactly excited about Meredith's question either, but I have to take the lead on this. He shuts down at every mention of them. "Well, Trenton's parents are unfortunately no longer with us; and mine," I pause, realizing I didn't think this through. Addressing the issue of my father is easy, I haven't told him because he isn't in my life; but what possible reason could I have for not telling my mother about the biggest thing that's ever happened to me? Of course Trent is unaware of my mother's ignorance, although to be fair, he hasn't asked.

It's not that I don't plan on telling her, I just haven't yet. "I'm not sure if you know I'm currently filming a reality competition, communication is rather limited. Owing to that, my mother has not yet learned of the good news; but knowing her, she won't have sufficient words to express how she feels." It's not a lie, it's creative truth telling; communication is limited, though I haven't attempted to talk to my mom again since the night I called, frantic and unnerved. It's true she will not have sufficient words, to express her disapproval; she'll use looks too. "I completely understand; doubtless, you'll tell her as soon as you can." Meredith's smile never falters, but there is a subtle shift in her attitude. She is still engaging but a bit more reserved, maybe she's having jitters about our wedding too. We wrap up the meeting with a promise to be in touch soon with a tentative date for the engagement party, being two months away.

"Do you want to tell her now?" My heart races as Trent's arms cage me against the door, "What?" I put a hand on the throbbing vein at the base of his neck as I search his eyes, desperately seeking something. I love this beautiful man, of course I want a life with him, I just wish I could shake this feeling. He puts a hand over mine, "Your mom, do you want to call and tell her?" His voice is steady but his pulse is wild beneath my palm. "We can't just call her and say, 'Hey Mom, you haven't seen me in weeks but surprise, I'm engaged.' We have to wait to tell her together, in person." This isn't something I want to tell my mom over the phone, plus I need time to prepare for it. It's going to be an arduous exchange, but maybe if I'm in front of her I can convince her of the rightness of my decision.

"Tell me again. I need to hear it," Trent says, sounding the way I feel. He's having doubts too, knowing that makes me feel confident enough to say, "Yes, I will marry you." He brushes his lips against mine briefly. "I've been meaning to tell you, I love it when you wear your hair like that." Which isn't often, it reminds Brice of Seriyah, but tonight isn't about him, it's about Trent and me.

By the time I crawl into bed, the whole house is quiet. I pray for a dreamless night and succumb to my soul-deep fatigue. I wake up choking on the dirt that covered me as I was dragged underground. I half fall, half jump out of bed, landing on the floor with a thud. Shaking uncontrollably, I pray, "God, please make it stop, I can't take it anymore, please make it stop." In a full-on panic, I leave my room, walking blindly to the one person I feel safe with.

Aiden's bed is empty; I have no idea where he is and no presence of mind to care about anything except getting to Brice. We haven't spoken in almost a week, but I kneel on the floor, shaking him awake. "Seriyah?" Half asleep, in the dark, with my hair like this, he thinks I'm her. "No," I say with sadness because Seriyah's gone but some part of him still believes she's coming back. "It's Leah." His shoulders relax, then tense again when he notices the tears on my cheeks. He throws off the covers and gets out of bed. "Leah, what's wrong? Did he do something to you?"

I'm taken aback by his thinking Trent would harm me. If I were thinking more clearly I would tell him so; for now it's all I can to not fall into his arms. "I'm so tired, Brice," is all I'm able to manage, he doesn't need any further explanation. Brice pulls me up off the floor into a hug, whispering soothing words to me I can't hear. I fall asleep, unconcerned about dreaming, I'm with Brice, now everything will be okay.

Chapter 19

Brice is asleep on his stomach, arms folded beneath his pillow, facing me when I wake up. For the first time in a week I'm clear headed and at peace, though I wouldn't mind sleeping a little longer. It's unusual for me to wake up before Brice, I suppose I'm not the only one that's tired. The mattress protests beneath my elbow as I lift myself high enough to check if Aiden is in bed, fortunately he is not. It's unclear whether he came and went or if he hadn't come in at all, I hope for the latter. Either way I'm not going to stick around for him to catch me here again. I'm halfway out the door before my conscious stops me. Last night I was undeserving of Brice's comfort, which he gave me anyway, the least I can do is thank him.

Leaning over his still form, gently I stroke his exposed cheek, I expected a more relaxed version of him in slumber but his eyebrows furrow at my touch. All these times I've run to Brice fearful from nightmares it never occurred to me that maybe Brice had bad dreams too. Concerned over what he is experiencing behind his eyelids, I renew my efforts to wake him. "Brice," I call his name while rubbing his cheek more vigorously. To my surprise he brings his hand over mine and holds it there, "I'm sleeping." Pulling away I say, "If you were sleeping you wouldn't be responding to me."

With a dramatic sigh he turns on his back and opens his eyes, "I guess I'm awake then." I take a seat on the edge of his bed, feeling unsure of exactly what I want to say. While I'm thinking it through, Brice pokes me in my side. "What was that about?" I ask. "I was making sure I wasn't dreaming." Interesting, I don't know how I feel about Brice dreaming about me or if I should feel anything about it at all. It does remind me of something though, "Were you having a bad dream before I woke you?" I didn't think Brice had any nervous habits but I'm sure that's what his current game of air ball is. He seems to think about it for a while before saying, "I'm not sure. Why do you ask?" Seized by the instinct that Brice is in need of comfort, accompanied by the impulse to be that to him as he has been for me many times, I carefully lie back down, sharing his view of the ceiling.

"When I first tried to wake you I touched your face. You didn't swat my hand away like I expected, you grimaced." Brice turns to face me while I keep my gaze on the ceiling. "I wasn't having a nightmare but I was seeing something I couldn't understand." I'm struck by his description of his dream, maybe it's because I'm seeing things in my sleep I can't understand either, I want to know more.

"Most people think their dreams are random images of unconsciousness, that they have no real meaning. If they do have significance, it goes only as far as revealing truths you already subconsciously know," I say. Revealing to Brice every rationale I've used since my nightmares started, disguising them as the beliefs of others. "But you put a lot of stock in your dreams, don't you?" I question, turning on my side to face him. "I do as a believer, I'd think you would also." He hesitates to continue, probably remembering one of our last conversations when I said he was "too preachy."

With a little prodding on my end, he continues, "Some dreams are just that, but the ones that are signs, messages, warnings, they're different; they feel different. God will talk to you if you care to listen." Brice confirms what I already know, my dreams aren't ordinary and should not be dismissed. But what does it mean that I can't understand them? Am I not willing to listen, to hear God's voice?

"Anyway I really just wanted to say thank you for last night." I wait for him to accept my thanks or acknowledge it in someway. After a few minutes of complete silence I feel silly and embarrassed for expecting gratitude for my gratitude. Following my thoughts, Brice puts a hand across me, stopping me from getting up. "I don't want you to say thank you then ignore me again until you need me. I don't want to do this with you, either you want me in your life or you don't."

It hurts that he feels I only come to him when I need his help, which isn't true; if that were the case I'd never leave his side. "It's not that simple, Brice, if you're asking if I want you in my life the easy answer is yes; I enjoy talking to you, your friendship nourishes me. With that said you know I'm . . . my situation . . . Having a male friend, albeit platonic, that I get along with as well as I do you, can prove to be tricky at times." It would be easier to tell him our friendship is an issue for Trent but it feels like a betrayal to do that. "What part of our friendship is 'tricky' and for whom?"

We're approaching shaky ground. I'm not sure it's avoidable though. Brice is right, it's not fair of me to run to him when I need help then ignore him the rest of the time. He deserves an explanation. "Trent, our friendship makes him uncomfortable and for good reason. Before you protest, just imagine how you'd feel having to watch your . . . person form a bond with another guy, literally, watch it happen and not be able to tell the world that she belonged with you not him. He's my . . . person, I can't disregard his feelings, they have to matter to me most."

Brice sits up, pulling me along with him. He nods his head in the annoying way he does when he's about to deconstruct my thought process. "What about me, do I matter to you?" He doesn't look away from me and he won't let me look away either. He wants an answer. I'm stuck between a rock and a hard place, between Trent and Brice. No amount of resistance to the question will or can change the truth. "Yes," I concede, "you matter to me." What I don't say is, "*too much, you matter to me too much.*"

"And you know you matter to me, a lot," the look in his eyes conveys this is greater than a statement. It's an undeniable fact; one I don't completely understand the expanse of. "I get you've made your choice," he says, "but don't suffocate under the weight of it." I swallow at the memory of being dragged underground, covered with dirt. "I'll keep that in mind," I choke out. "Thanks again." I'm gone before he can protest. Being around Brice is too confusing for me, I can't afford to be confused right now.

I track Cashmere down in the kitchen making a sandwich. Looping my arm through hers I tell her I'm ready. Talking around the spoonful of peanut butter in her mouth, she asks, "For what?" No longer sleep deprived I'm prepared to tackle the script, "To make you look good." She thrusts her hips to the side, running her hands down the length of her body, "You can't perfect perfection, anything more perfect than this would be sinful." I want to be offended but that's Cashmere, therefore I play along.

"Well forgive me, sister, for I will sin, because I'm about to murder . . . this scene." I scrunch up my face as Cashmere sticks the spoon that was just in her mouth back into the communal peanut butter jar. "What can I say, I like peanut butter," she shrugs. "Also I'm pretty sure you can't ask for forgiveness before you commit the sin. I am all for winning though, so do as you must."

Being well rested makes all the difference. Cashmere and I have a fantastic rehearsal. "Girl, I have no idea what you did but thank you for doing it." I roll my eyes skyward, getting her hint, "What I did was get some sleep. It's amazing what a few uninterrupted hours can do for you." Cashmere smiles wickedly at me, "I noticed you weren't in bed in the middle of the night when I got up to use the bathroom, did you make it back home last night?" She's being completely obvious with her exaggerated winking and dramatic nodding, subtly is not a talent she possess.

Cashmere thinks I spent the night with Trent in more ways than one, she couldn't know I was home just not in our room. I don't know that I can explain to her the truth of the situation without arousing suspicion, ire, and hostility between us. It wasn't long ago she admitted her dislike of me was a result of Trent's disinterest in her. To explain my relationship with Brice, platonic as it is, would hurt her. "What an inquisitive nature you have. Interesting that your thoughts weren't that maybe I was reading, which I often do, or asleep in the living room, but that I was with a man." Shaking my head, I say, "I'm hurt." I don't negate nor confirm her assumptions; most importantly I don't lie, I talk around the question.

"Okay then, Leah, were you reading when I got up at two a.m. and you were nowhere to be found?" I turn toward the mirror, away from Cashmere, putting my cross back on. Seeing it on after not wearing it for a few days makes me feel traitorous on more fronts than one. After what Brice said to me about not needing a gold reminder of my faith I took it off. I feel my disloyalty to Trent more acutely in wearing it again, for removing it in the first place and for turning to Brice. Avoiding Cashmere's eyes, I swallow down the bile of treason, "Possibly, it's hard to say, and 'nowhere to be found' is a stretch. Anyways the point is we're definitely not going home this week."

Cashmere looks conflicted, for a minute I think maybe she's deciding on if she should call me out for not being perfectly honest or not, "Do you think I'm any good . . . do you think I have a chance?" Cashmere, like Zack, had success coming into the competition. She has a million social media followers, beauty endorsements, and unlimited earning potential. Why subject herself to this? Zack, I learned, needed to prove himself to the acting community again. I thought Cashmere signed on because of Trent, but there's more to it than that, I try not to ask personal question, but since she opened up the conversation, I do.

Amy couldn't have chosen a more inopportune time to walk in, without knocking I might add, accompanied by a cameraman no less. They were just in here with us not twenty minutes ago. I suppose there's nothing more interesting going on elsewhere in the house. Trying to kill with kindness, I ask Amy if she could come back. "This is a real moment, we are here to capture those. This is what the people want to see, your story," she gives me a pointed look then adds, "and your story too." She kneels in front of Cashmere, appealing to her directly, "This is a platform, one you haven't already conquered. Your followers are loyal because you give them the real, always, don't let them down now."

Cashmere is clearly affected by Amy's application, I am too, although not in the way she expected. She's compelling but wrong. Cashmere shouldn't have to share what she isn't willing to on her channel or elsewhere. I've never been a slave to followers . . . not until recently. I used to post what mattered to me, which was seldom a selfie. I changed for the sake of this show, success, and notoriety. Giving strangers intimate access to my life, and me all the while pandering to comments both positive and negative.

I'm rewarded with likes and follows by the hundreds and thousands, but Trent says that isn't enough, "More followers, you need more followers." Lost in my own head I miss the question I just inadvertently responded to. "Yes," she says. "I have to do this. Amy, it's okay, I'll talk." I whisper to Cashmere, "Only what you want to share, not a word more."

"I didn't always look like this, or maybe I did, it doesn't matter if I did or didn't, what matters is what I believed. I believed my mother when she told me 'you're ugly' and when she told me no one would ever want me. 'Don't judge me, you ugly trick; you think you're better than me? You're not better than me, you'll end up just like me, high and on your back.' That was a good day, on her bad days she'd pound the message into me with whatever was handy. In some ways I preferred the beatings, at least those were . . . they were on my body, I could get to them, treat them, but the words." Cashmere tugs so violently on the throw pillow in her hand feathers go flying. "Well you can't put a Band-Aid on a heart can you?

"No one ever asked me what I wanted to be when I grow up because no one ever cared about me and certainly not my hopes and dreams." Amy passes me a box of tissues off screen, which I hand to Cashmere, whose tears are falling freely. She thanks me while dabbing at her cheeks. "I don't blame my mom, she raised me the way she was raised; without care and without love. But just because I didn't blame her doesn't mean I didn't want to be rid of her. I ran away multiple times after the last time, the city took me away. Since I was almost legal I was placed in a group home, I won't even talk about what that was like . . ." She pauses, possibly remembering some long forgotten abuse.

"You know, I waited for my mom to come get me or even make contact with me but she never did; I was lonely and alone with no one to notice. It's ironic how I could be so desperate to be away from a loveless home but also be desperate to be back there." I look at her through blurred eyes, "It's not ironic, we're all victims of what we know." She smiles sadly accepting my rationalization, "I changed schools when I moved into the group home, it didn't bother me much, it wasn't like I was leaving behind any friends. My new school was pretty much like my last. Everybody ignored me, except for my drama teacher; she was the first person to ever take an interest in me. The funny thing is I didn't even want to take drama, but the administration didn't care about what I wanted. I was another poor dumb kid with no parents to challenge them. They could do whatever they wanted with me, but everything happens for a reason, because if I hadn't met Ms. Figero I don't know what would've become of me.

"I'd been going to my new school for two weeks when I was asked to hang back after class by Ms. Figero. From what I could tell she was really popular among the student and teachers. She wasn't exactly beautiful, what Ms. Figero had was more than skin deep; she was radiant and happy and it attracted everyone to her. Self-consciously I stood in front of her aware of her crisp shirt and skirt. I looked down at the jeans I'd been wearing all week, grimy and faded from constant wear; I was used to not having any-thing worth wearing, it was the moments of obviousness that were difficult. Eager to get away from Ms. Figero, I hoped she'd get to why she asked me to stay behind soon.

"I assumed it was school related; drama isn't exactly a class where you can get away with not participating. What I was not expecting was for Ms. Figero to smile at me like I was worth being seen. I couldn't remember a time before that when anyone had ever looked at me like that, maybe not a time after that either. 'Cashmere, I asked you to hang back because I wanted to talk to you.' She took a seat on the bleachers, they were part of the set for the class play, *Grease*, then waited for me to sit too before she continued.

"'Did you know you have an extremely expressive face?' I knew what she meant but I asked anyway, 'What do you mean?' She smiled at me again, 'I mean that your face is very good at showing a variety of emotion. Looking at you day in and day out I have gotten to know a lot about you.' 'What do you think you know about me?' Ms. Figero always emanated joy except for when she answered my question. 'I know that you're very sad, that you live with a lot of pain, and that you have no hope. I know most days you don't want to be here, by here I don't mean drama or school, I mean alive.'

"I broke down into pieces, I cried without holding back. I could barely breathe, but Ms. Figero held onto me tight. No one, not even my social workers, the people paid to make sure I was okay, had ever noticed me enough to see my sorrow. For the first time in my life I was allowed to grieve the childhood and mother I never had. I cried for every time I'd never cried before and for some of the times I did, I cried so much I thought my heart would stop. I tried to pull away, embarrassed at soaking her blouse, but Ms. Figero held me firmer, then buried my head in the crook of her neck. Crying in the safety of Ms. Figero's arms made the pain go away, it was like she took my burden into her own body because she knew I couldn't handle anymore.

"When I finally stopped crying, she whispered, 'Come to me all ye who are weary and carry heavy burdens, and I will give you rest. Take my yoke upon you. Let me teach you, because I am humble and gentle at heart, and you will find rest for your soul. For my yoke is easy to bear, and the burden I give you is light.' I'd never heard anything like that before, it was beautiful, poetic, and utterly foreign to me. I asked Ms. Figero if it was Shakespeare or something, she laughed, 'Nope, someone even better. Jesus.' I'd heard the name, knew people believed in him, but I didn't know about him, not really. My mom was too busy getting high and drunk to ever take me to church. The only prayers I ever heard were 'God, what was I thinking sleeping with you?' Or 'God, let me hit the numbers tonight.' 'God, I hate you with your ugly face.'

"I heard it said of Jesus that he could make your life better, worth living, but no one had ever cared enough to save my life before, so why should that change now. But thinking back on it, knowing what I know now, maybe that was God, except he used Ms. Figero, I don't know. I didn't even understand the verse, all I knew was after I heard it I felt better.

"Ms. Figero died two months after that, congenital heart disease. She told me she'd been sick since infancy, she knew death would come sooner rather than later, but knowing death was near didn't stop her from being alive." I hold a hand out to Cashmere but she shakes her head, "No tears, Ms. Figero made me promise not to mourn her life because she'd had a good one. Actually I flew into a rage when she said that me, 'How could you die and leave me when you're the only person who's ever cared about me?' She looked at me with sad eyes, 'That's not true, someone cared about you long before I did. Whenever you feel alone, uncared for, and unloved, remember there's someone who loves you so much that they died for you, so that you'd never be without them again.'

"I've had hard times and harder times in my life, Leah, even after I met Ms. Figaro, but I do believe Jesus is watching over me. I'm not Brice or anything, I don't have this whole spiritual thing figured out, but he reminded me of something Ms. Figaro taught me before she died: 'The possession of faith doesn't mean the absence of hardships, there will always be heartache, but faith makes you the beneficiary of a promise to always make it through. And if you allow yourself to be led, you'll come out better than you went in.' At least that's how Brice put it, he's good with words, have you noticed that?" I nod my head, "Yeah I've noticed."

Cashmere continues after a beat, "Ms. Figaro's the reason I started my YouTube channel. One of the last times I spoke to her, she told me to live as she couldn't.' I asked her what she would've done if she had more time. She said, 'Perform on a grand stage.' At the time I didn't have any dreams of my own except to be happy, to be loved. Ms. Figaro took the time in the midst of her death to save my life. I know what it feels like to be forgotten, I won't let her become forgotten too. She fulfilled my dreams, I owe her the same; her dreams have become mine, I want to live them for her."

I recognize Cashmere's hurt in myself. I won't dare compare my upbringing of struggle but undeniable love, with hers of self-preservation and apathy. But I understand the ache that starts in your mind and travels to every part of your being, every cell, every atom, when as a child you learn hard truths. When you're taught by some manner or another that you're not good enough and have to somehow find value within yourself when you're not sure it exists.

Cashmere shared with me her purpose in being here, in doing so she inadvertently taught me a lesson. It was what Brice said to me about my necklace; faith isn't identified by jewelry, it's your actions in moments of strife. Ms. Figero was at complete peace with God's plan. She trusted his grand design; in the face of death she did not falter, she greeted it fearlessly. Meanwhile, waiting on God has exposed all the cracks in mine, what's faith if it fails you when you need it most? "Sister Priscilla, the youth mentor at my church, would always say, 'Every saint has a past and every sinner has a future.' I haven't the slightest idea who'll win the competition, but maybe you came here to win something more precious than that."

We could have sat for hours in tearful reflection if Amy hadn't called "cut." She was pretending to care, again adopting a sweet singsong voice, rubbing Cashmere's back. She doesn't posses the ability to be sincere, but she put on a good show of it, "Cashmere, thank you for your bravery. If you're up to it, let's go film your one-on-one. Leah, I'll need you to do the same in a few." I don't miss the blandness in her voice when she addresses me, clearly the dislike is mutual.

With Amy, the crew, and Cashmere gone, I'm left alone with my thoughts. I succumb to the weight of them. I slide down the side of the mattress to the floor, my body bereft of strength, and cry. I'm undeniably affected by Cashmere's story, I am also exceptionally empathetic, but the ache I feel is personal. I don't know if souls cry; if they can, mine is weeping. With a tremendous effort I shut my tears down without doing anything about the cause, you can't fix a problem if you don't know what it is. I don't have time to fall apart; I have a date.

I stand in the doorway, mesmerized at the beauty before me. Calla lilies, lilies of the valley, roses, peonies, tulips, stephanotis, and so many more flowers I have no name for cover every inch of the first floor of Trent's apartment. I smile in recognition of the candles lighting the room as the same kind Trent and I purchased the night he took me to his brownstone. Taking off my shoes and leaving them by the door I move further into the floral wonderland.

Soft music floats down the steps, bouncing off the flower petals encircling me. Between the sharp floral fragrance and my cushioned steps, I'm floating on air. Following the music up the stairs to the end of the hall I arrive at the master bedroom where the hardwood floor is replaced by a plush red sea of roses. Trent, the most beautiful thing of the evening by far, stands in the middle of the room waiting for me. "It took you long enough."

Without fail, the sight of him causes a flutter deep in my stomach. "If I would've known you were waiting for me I would have taken my time admiring every single flower." Emphasizing my point, I walk scrupulously slow to the center of the room. Trent pulls me into his chest, our bodies colliding hard though neither of us minds. His hands wrap around my waist, pressing me close, my heart quickens at the pressure of his body against mine. "Good thing I'm a patient man," he says. "We have that in common, me and you, I believe in taking my time too."

His meaning isn't lost on me as he slowly trails a hand down the length of my torso. "All day I've been consumed with one thought." I gasp as he bites down on my neck, probably hard enough to draw blood. "I want you." Despite the reciprocal hunger of my body I'm afraid. I squirm as he bites down on my neck again, trying to pull away, but he holds me tight. "Nope, you're not getting away from me that easily." His already tight hold on me becomes painful.

"You have all of me, I want the same of you." There's a wildness about Trent tonight. Gone is his usual smoothness. In its place is a primitiveness, borderline savagery. "Feel this, feel it." He guides my hand to his chest, "Do you feel that?" Through his shirt I feel the slamming of his heart. "My heart beats for you, the first time I saw you I loved you. I know you don't love me the way I love you. I know you don't, but that hasn't stopped me from wanting to be with you. You don't think in six years I haven't tried to let you go? But I can't, every part of me willingly belongs to you."

My dress hits the floor before I realize I'm no longer wearing it. I'm hardly aware of Trent lifting me off my feet and laying me gently on the bed of roses. I can't think through his mind-numbing caresses. I'm only aware of us fitting together perfectly, and the sensations gripping my body. Taking his time, he languishes over my form, admiring its bareness. Physically I'm here with him, my body responding to his leading, but deep down inside of me I protest. I lost the fight of chastity a long time ago, but it was hard loss, accompanied by guilt, shame, confusion, and more guilt; holding onto the finer parts of faith is difficult, especially while in a relationship.

It's easy ignoring your principals while in the throes of elation, it's afterward that's hard. My mind screams stop, but without any conscious volition my nails dig deeper into his shoulder blades, urging him on. "You're slipping away from me every day you're here; it's hard to know, harder to watch. Even now I can feel you retreating from me into your mind. I won't lose you, Leah, I won't. I'm going to fill you with my love, I need for you to know how strong and deep it runs. There's no higher form of intimacy than that, after tonight you and I will be connected spiritually, emotionally, and physically forever. Now tell me why should that be wrong?" I don't know how he knows of the war raging inside me, "Will you let me love you?" The part of me that is deeply troubled watches in horror as I pull him down on top of me.

shocked send help
this poor girl
HE'S NOT THE ONE!

ewwww

grosssssss

Chapter 20

"STAND AT THE CROSSROADS and look; ask for the ancient paths, ask where the good way is, and walk in it, and you will find rest for your soul." After all this time I'm finally able to hear what my mom is saying to me, not that I care. The mob is on my heels, I don't have time to decipher cryptic messages, "Mom, help me please, they're going to get me." I hold onto the hem of her strikingly white dress pleading with her, she looks directly at me and I fall back with the force of her gaze.

I didn't notice how different this version of my mom was until fire blazed in her eyes, she's never worn that look in wakefulness. "Stand at the crossroads and look; ask for the ancient paths, ask where the good way is, and walk in it, and you will find rest for your soul." Looking past my mom I see the houses looming ahead, each on a diverging path, "Mom, we have to go, they're coming, let's go." I try to take hold of her hand but despite how close we are I can't reach her. Between the second it takes to look down at my hands wonderingly and to look back up she's gone, vanished, leaving me alone with danger. I push down the hysterical sobs bubbling up inside me. I need to get undercover. I look over my shoulder to glimpse the approaching mob, I know what lies behind me and to the left of me, I don't know what the right holds, I'll just have to take my chances.

For the first time since the dreams started, I take a step in the direction of the dilapidated house. Once upon a time the house might have been a cheerful shade of yellow but now it's the color of dirt. I take a deep breath, preparing to walk through the gate, afraid it's going to finish the job the house of horrors began, but with the mob behind me what other choice do I have. As soon as I walk through, stillness washes over me, I don't need to look back to know the mob isn't on my trail.

A light breeze carries the sound of a hammer at work somewhere on the property. Believing the source of the hammering to be an ally and myself to be safe, I take my time in the front yard. I was wrong, someone has been taking care of the property; all around the lawn is germinating grass. Vegetation sprouts where I believed the soil to be dead. Suddenly I'm no longer standing in a premature garden of seedlings and buds, all around me are vibrant-colored flowers with thick leaves, a lemon tree too.

Contentedly I sit cross-legged in the shade of a coniferous tree talking to someone I can't completely see. That someone, a tall male someone, comes out of the yellow house holding two glasses of lemonade. I shade my eyes against the brightly shining sun to see him; right as he comes into focus, he and the luscious garden disappear. I'm back in the front yard of the run-down house, but I now know it for what it will someday be.

Something heavy and wet hits my neck, then my shoulder, and my shoes with a splat. It's raining, picking up momentum and pouring down in sheets, but the sun above shines brightly, unaware of the paradox. I'm not sure what drives me to do it, I usually hate rain showers, especially warm ones, but I open my arms wide and lean my head back, inviting the rain. It's the kind of rain that nourishes life and leaves behind rainbows in the mud as a reminder that something beautiful can come from a storm.

Just as abruptly as it starts it ends, but it's done its work—impossibly the seeded lawn has sprouted into lively green pastures. "Unless the Lord builds the house its laborers build in vain." The rich voice belongs to the man I couldn't see before, I can now; he's tall, dark-skinned, handsome, and powerful. His white tee shirt cannot hide the power of his arms, but I sense strength in him beyond the physical. He reminds me of the mud rainbow, like he too was born of a storm.

"It's about time you showed up." It should be odd, him waiting on me, someone I don't know but I feel as if I do. He's strangely familiar to me. "What does that mean, what you said about the Lord building the house?" He smiles at me not without affection. "It means, Leah, that unless God is working on your behalf your efforts are in vain. I planted all sorts of plant life; it took me a few days of hard work to do it. Once I was done all I had was a hope that these seeds would grow. It wasn't until God did his part that anything came of my labor: 'He provides rain for the earth.'" Without him saying so I understand the beautiful sun shower was God doing his part.

"How'd you know my name?" I ask him. "I've been waiting for you, of course I know your name. For a minute there I was scared you wouldn't show." I'm beyond confused about everything but I also feel safe. I want to stay here with him, whoever he is, "I'm here now . . . to stay." A single tear rolls down his cheek, "I wish you could stay with me but you live over there now." He points to the house of horrors in the distance, I shake my head vigorously, "No, I don't, I belong here with you." He takes both my hands in his, "I can't fight this battle for you, Leah; if I could I would. You have to go back now but all hope is not lost."

A gust of wind that only affects me tears through the garden, picking me up with it. I reach out to him and he to me; eyes locked as hands do not. "Stand at the crossroads and look; ask for the ancient paths, ask where the good way is, and walk in it, and you will find rest for your soul." He yells it over the howling of the winds as I'm hurled to my worst nightmares.

I wake with a jolt, trapped against Trent, who is fast asleep. No wonder there, last night he did everything he promised to do and more. Afterward, I spent the moments between wakefulness and sleep tearfully replaying the night in my head. Other than sore, I wasn't sure how I felt, although my tears were definitely not happy. I temporarily cleared my mind of it, running lines until I drifted off to my usual nightmares. They weren't my usual nightmares though; I made it to the other house. The house that starts out as an ugly duckling then is transformed into a beautiful swan, and then I met *him*.

There were times, like standing in the sun shower and when he held my hands, when I felt warm and safe. I felt safe with my mom too, but also afraid of her. Now I know what she said to me was important, something about choosing the "good way." He told me to choose the good way also, like that's not a given. I mean, it's not like I want to go to the house of horrors, I just always end up there. How could I choose the good way if I have no choice about where I end up at all?

I hit the mattress in frustration. Trent groans, snuggling closer to me. I'm burning up and uncomfortable beside him, I need to get away. I try lifting his arm, but the more I move the tighter he holds on, I'm trapped. None of my attempts to remove his arm from around me wake him. My whimper does. Without opening his eyes, he shushes me, tells me to go back to sleep, and holds me tighter still. Fed up, I yank his arm away and stumble to the bathroom, slamming the door closed behind me.

I collapse against the sink, expecting Trent to follow behind me. I don't hear footsteps or the mattress creak, my outburst doesn't wake him. Running the cold water, I stick my head beneath the faucet. Sitting on the toilet with my head against the wall, I begin to feel better. The cold water on my face helped some, having room to breathe helps most. When I walk out the bathroom Trent is exactly as I left him. I tiptoe out of the room to the den where I stored all the books I bought; rummaging through the bags I find the one I'm looking for, *The Odyssey.*

By the time Trent strolls into the kitchen, bare chested in briefs, I'm showered, dressed in last night's dress, and ready to go back downstairs. "I was wondering when you'd make an appearance." Trent wraps me in a hug while I'm seated on a stool. "I would think after last night your attitude would have improved." He ducks, taking shelter, as I attempt to thrash him with my book. "Well maybe you didn't do as good of a job as you think you did."

An amused grin splits his face, "Oh, is that so, well my apologies. My motto is one hundred percent satisfaction, if not the next one's on me. Let me make it up to you." An hour later, I'm more tired than before but back at the loft. Before going up to my room I go to confessional. Interviews must be done before and after the performances. I want to get mine out of the way, maybe nap long enough to take the edge off my lethargy.

"Hey Cash." If looks could kill I would be dead. "Nice of you to finally show up, I can't believe you would just disappear on me like that with only six hours before curtain call." I lie back on my bed, instantly feeling the pull of sleep but fighting it, "Relax, like you said, we have six hours and we're in good shape. If it'll make you happy we can rehearse as long as you like after I take a quick nap." She eyes me warily but agrees; my hands go beneath my pillow as I turn on my stomach. They brush against something that rustles like paper.

The last time I found a note beneath my pillow it was from Trent, but we were together last night. Exercising great will power I don't immediately pull it out. "Cash, can you do me a big favor please?" She crosses her arms over her chest, "Depends on what the favor is." Cashmere is still playing at being upset; I don't let that deter me from my goal though, "Do you think you can get me a cup of coffee, black, two sugars, please?" I have no intention of drinking coffee, what I need is a few minutes alone to investigate.

Cashmere looks at me for the first time since I walked in, really looks at me from head to toe. As she takes in last night's outfit, her eyes widen in revelation. "Why are you so tired, and don't tell me you were up reading some book by some old guy who died a really long time ago." She raises an eyebrow, "And even if that's what you wanted to do, I know for a fact, it wasn't what you did." I roll my eyes, apparently that's answer enough for her, "I'll get you the coffee, but then you're giving me details, and don't even try giving me the condensed PG version either, I need rated R."

Before I hear the click of the door closing behind her I unfold the note. Immediately I'm able to confirm it isn't from Trent, but it is written by a familiar hand, the same script scribbled all over my "new" Bible, the one Brice gave me. I smooth out the note against my pillow, "*It's three twenty-seven in the morning and I'm freaking out. I woke up a few minutes ago with the most frightening sound resounding in my ears, your voice crying my name. I can't remember if I was having a nightmare or dreaming at all but I thought maybe you were. I must've tripped over myself ten times trying to get to you but you weren't in bed or our usual place, you're nowhere I can reach you. Maybe I'm going crazy, I don't know, Wherever you are, whomever you're with, I pray you're at peace."*

I reach the end of the unsigned note with one sentence bouncing around my head, "You're nowhere I can reach." Obviously he meant I wasn't home, but if that is in fact what he meant, why isn't that what he said? Try as I might to deny it, Brice and I share this unexplainable connection, but this is too much. I did have another dream last night, but I don't know what time I woke up from it, is it even possible for him to have known? Hurriedly I stuffed the note into my pillowcase as Cashmere comes back with a steaming cup of coffee.

"I didn't think you'd be back here." He reaches for the hem of his shirt, using it to wipe off the thin layer of sweat on his forehead. "I wasn't sure I'd be back either, I didn't know if I'd be able to come back." I'm surprised but not disappointed. He frowns, "Did you want to come back?" I throw my hands up exasperatedly, "It doesn't matter what I want, I don't have a choice of where I go in this place. If I did I wouldn't chose to ever go to that house. That doesn't matter though, because in seconds I'll be taken away." He looks at me fiercely, "You always have a choice. *You* stood at the road between two paths, but *you* said you would not walk through the good one." His voice breaks with sadness, "You're—Leah, Leah, Leah!"

Drowsily my eyes open on Cashmere, "Leah, get up. It's time to rehearse." I'm furious with her for waking me. True, I did ask her to, but she woke me in the middle of something important, now I'll never know what he was going to say. I get up, determined to put all dreams out of my mind, because in a few hours I may very well be on my way home.

At five, we're all in the van, ready to go to the theater. I sit next to Aiden, behind Brice. I saw him briefly earlier in the day, but this is my first opportunity to speak to him. Leaning forward, I whisper, "I found your note." He leans his head against the back of the seat, "I meant you to." I feel things taking a heavy turn, with eliminations hours away I can't go there with him. Acting completely on impulse, I lick my finger and stick it in his ear. Brice jerks away violently, "Why just—why would you do that?" I've never seen Brice so flustered; laughing at him, I don't see Aiden inserting his wet finger in my ear. "Aiden, are you crazy! That is the most disgusting thing ever."

Looking the picture of mischievousness, he smiles, "Come on, Leahz, you know better than to start this up." Then Zack, who's been sitting next to Beverly rehearsing, puts his wet finger in her ear. Corey grabs Cashmere, and the wet willy assault happens in quick succession. All the girls squeal in disgusted horror, while the guys double over in laughter. Beverly feeling particularly affronted, promises us all retribution for being "gross and lame," especially me, then she whacks Zack across his forearm. No one pays her any mind because for a few minutes we managed to forget tonight would be our first elimination, that someone isn't coming back and it could be any of us.

In the dressing room, we change into our costumes, preparing to take the stage. Minutes later we stand before the judges once again; Eloise the ice queen in the middle, to her left sits Acer, wearing a broad smile, and to her right, Lawrence, looking indifferent. Iliana goes over the prizes, then states the pairs and the order in which we'll be taking the stage. Brice, Aiden, and Corey are up first, then Cashmere and me. Zack and Beverly are to go last. We're then sent back to the dressing room to await further instructions from Amy.

"I think we should go over some of the rough parts." Cashmere's grown and built confidence in her talent during this past week, but one sight of the judges sends her back to square one. "Cash, if we don't have it by now we won't have it in ten or fifteen minutes from now. You've worked hard, you'll do well, you've got this." She gives me a weak smile, which I return. "I'll be right back, I need to use the bathroom." I quiet her protest before she begins, "I promise I'll be right back."

Alone in the bathroom I acknowledge the churning in my stomach, allowing myself a minute of panic. I had to be strong for Cashmere, it wouldn't do to have us both losing our cool, but alone, minutes before we take the stage, my heart is beating like a jackhammer. "Leah, calm down, you've done it before, you can do it again, leave it all on stage." I smooth down my homely grey skirt and cardigan before leaving the bathroom, it's not my most appealing ensemble, but the part calls for it.

"Leah, thank goodness you're back, you were in there forever. I thought I was going to have to go in and get you," Cashmere says hysterically. Smilingly I say, "I came out all on my own, crisis averted," Roger, the production assistant, steps into the small dressing room, looks around for all of ten seconds, before he spots us. "Leah, Cashmere, you're wanted on set." Cashmere, overcome by a fresh wave of nerves, neither moves nor responds. I have to pull her behind me all the way to set.

When we get there, Aiden, Brice, and Corey are still onstage receiving feedback, although I'm unable to hear anything the judges say over the buzzing in my ears. "It's just nerves, you've done this before," I whisper to myself. Cashmere, pacing back and forth, overhears me, "Huh, did you say something?" I clear my throat, hoping to also clear my anxiety. "Yeah, I said, it's just nerves, you've done this before." Cashmere stops short in front of me, "That's easy for you to say, you're not nervous."

I look at her like she's crazy, "That is a falsehood. I am a nervous wreck, I'm just a wreck on the inside like a winner." We share a brief smile before the boys are walking off set. Corey walks past me, shoulders hunched, head down, Aiden looks as he always does, optimistic and adorable. Brice follows them. As he passes me, he discreetly hooks his pinky with mine, "Go be great, I'm going to cheer you on from right here." Taken aback, I ask, "Why?" "Because I want to be here for you as long as we're both around, maybe even afterward." I don't get to respond before Cashmere's pulling me on set.

"Good evening, ladies, I understand the two of you have partnered up. Not exactly the pairing I would have expected, but this should be interesting. Cashmere, I see your choice of costume has not changed much, hopefully your level of skill has." Didn't think it was possible, but Eloise may be worse than Amy and Beverly. She is equally as obnoxious, but more effective in her insults. Whatever confidence Cashmere possessed coming into tonight is lost at a word from her.

Not so discreetly she tugs at the hem of her provocatively short skirt, attempting to elongate it. Her top is a size too small also, but reflective of Rachel, a seductive young lady who lives for making people uncomfortable with her sexuality. It's not fair of her to tear into Cashmere like this before the performance; whatever the repercussions, I'm not going to let her get away with it. "For our mashup, Cashmere was assigned the character Rachel of *Georgia Rule*, and I was assigned Dolores of *Dolores Claiborne*. We've worked hard, and as you put it, Ms. Gunner, it turned out very interesting." My words are respectful; however, my tone is reproachful and I strongly suspect Lawrence's cough is a ploy to cover his laughter. Looking a little red around her cheeks, Eloise instructs us to begin, "If you're ready, ladies."

I take a seat in one of the two chairs at the table, set specifically for our scene. Cashmere as Rachel stands a few feet away, "What do you want me to say?" Her line is delivered with suppressed rage. "I'm not the one that hurt ya," I say pleadingly to begin with, then more forcefully, "I'm not the one that hurt ya!" I bring my fist down on the table with a resounding thud. "He must have said it to you. Why drive ten hours to hear it again?" Cashmere says flippantly.

Grabbing the edge of the table with both hands, I slide my chair back, and stand face to face with her, shaking with rage. Cashmere stands her ground physically but there's a waffling in her stare. "You sit down right this minute," I scream, "And you can just stow that Vassar stuff. Now we're going to sit down at the table you and me and we're gonna have us a drink. And when we're through . . . When I'm through you can run on upstairs and take whichever one of those little pills that makes you feel best."

Not quite recovered from the emotional scene, we hold hands, standing before the judges. Eloise and Lawrence are unreadable, but Acer smiles from ear to ear. "Ladies, you've moved me to tears. Wonderful, absolutely wonderful, I have no other words, superb." Praise from Acer is appreciated but expected, he's the nice judge. Eloise is the bad guy, and Lawrence is the wild card. I suck in my breath, preparing for his critique, which might go either way.

"After last week, I thought I knew the depths of everyone's talents, where you all stood, boy was I wrong. Cashmere, I've underestimated you, what I saw here tonight . . ." He shakes his head appreciatively, "You did a very good job." Then he fixes his eyes on me, "And you, Leah, are full of surprises. I didn't think you'd be able to follow up last weeks explosive performance, but you were amazing. You, young lady, are more talented than we knew, you're the one to look out for; and, Cashmere, you might just be our dark horse."

I smile at him, the knot in my stomach loosening. Eloise remained stoic through Acer and Lawrence's assessment of our performance; now the moment of truth is upon us. "I was right earlier when I said it would be interesting. As I said, I would not have chose this pairing, but it worked. There were a few things that could've been better, but take a bow, ladies, you were fantastic." Cashmere pulls me into a hug. I can't believe my ears, I was convinced my quip earlier would've garnered retaliation from Eloise, but she's unbiased and fair in her judging, maybe she's not so bad after all.

Backstage, Brice is standing in the shadows as he said he would be, he hugs Cashmere and me both, congratulating us on our performance. "That's it, next time we have a group assignment I'm teaming up with you two." Cashmere loops her arms around his neck, "I'm all for you and me working closely together." I thought she was over her crush on Brice and I thought he wasn't interested, but apparently I missed something. I'm not sure if Cashmere is reacting to the adrenaline of a positive review or if she still wants him and if he's into her too. I turn away from them, momentarily distracted by footsteps; Amy accompanies Zack and Beverly on set. By the time I turn back around, Cashmere and Brice are disengaged and I've missed my window of discovery.

Zack and Beverly work from a script combining scenes from *About Last Night* and *All about Eve*. I haven't seen either of those two films. Their performance does nothing to make me want to change that. Their scene is missing something, many somethings. Despite the seamlessness of the combined script, it is like watching two different scenes playing simultaneously; there is no chemistry between them. Frankly, it's painful to watch, especially when Beverly blanks on her lines. Instead of improvising, she stops and waits for the line to come back to her.

Eloise stops them before they reach the end of their scene, ready to rip their performance apart. I was fine with Beverly being mercilessly critiqued last week, but today, unprovoked, I can't bring myself to rejoice at it, especially since Zack's on the line too. It's too hard to watch, so is the conversation between Brice and Cashmere. I have no idea what's going on between those two. I decide I don't want to know. Without saying a word to either of them I go back to holding.

Chapter 21

THE STAGE FEELS SMALL, much smaller than it was only a short while ago when Cashmere and I performed. Everyone's on set today: Stephanie, Jeremy, Matt, Morgan, all the producers, and cameras, everyone except Trent. He told me he'd try to be here; I hoped after I expressed to him how important it is to me that he is here he would be, but he isn't and I can't dwell on it. I turn slightly to get a better look at my castmates, the anxiety I feel inwardly reflected on all their faces except Beverly, who exudes confidence. I don't get it, her last performance landed her in the theoretical bottom two, and based off of what I saw of her performance today, she has no reason to be anything other than petrified. My personal feelings about her aside, she's whom I would axe.

Stephanie calls us to attention, "I know you're all anxious and ready to get this over with, but we need to get interviews before judging begins, it's for our social media. We've been posting teasers, today we want to stream a live group interview, get people invested." We leave the stage in single file, none of us uttering a word. Aiden coughs a few times, maybe wanting to break the tension but not knowing how. None of us are excited about eliminations, but having to wait for elimination results and interview isn't better.

In the dressing room we sit in the same order we lined up in. Roger acts as cameraman, using his phone. After flipping it around multiple times, he says to Amy, "They're too many of them, I can't fit them all in the frame." Amy snatches the phone out of his hand, "Give me that." She does the same exact thing he does before coming to the same conclusion as him.

"Okay, I'm going to need you all to squeeze in. You've been living with each other long enough to be okay with getting into each other's personal space." Amy waits for us to reposition ourselves but no one moves. "Okay, how about I get all the men to back up. Being the tallest, Corey and Brice, grab stools; Aiden and Zack, stand on either side of them." Zack stands beside Corey with his arm on his shoulder. "Much better, now you actually look like you know each other; ladies, get in here."

Beverly sashays to Corey, sitting on his lap. They look good, the three of them, Zack leaning over Corey and Beverly on Corey's lap. "Oh that looks great, how about we get Cashmere with . . ." The obvious choice is Brice, since he's already seated, but why the hesitation? Amy's eyes catch mine for a fraction of a second. "Brice, Cashmere get comfortable with Brice." I don't wait to be instructed to move. Aiden and I are very comfortable with each other, it's nothing to lean into him, allowing him to wrap a loose arm around my waist.

"I always knew you wanted me, it's not your fault you know, I'm irresistible." It isn't until after we stop laughing that we realize Amy is recording us, "That was adorable, exactly what I was looking for." Aiden, encouraged by Amy, lists all the reasons why I should love him. I'm indulgent of him while being suspicious of her, she's being weirder than usual, that can't be a good thing.

"When I cue you in, I want everyone to greet the viewers and introduce yourselves. I'll ask one question that you'll all answer, then we'll quickly move on. We'll start with Leah." It isn't anything I haven't done before, though usually better dressed. I wish I had time to change into something more appealing, I need followers; I won't get them dressed like this.

Amy counts down from five on her fingers, on cue we all shout different salutations before she signals me. "Hey world, I'm Leah, known as Leahz to this guy," I point to Aiden, "and L to some, thank you for following us." I finish with what I hope is not a cheesy smile. Off camera Amy asks, "In one word, describe how you're feeling." Shrugging, I say, "Uncertain." I am uncertain about more than just the elimination results. More than anything else, I feel uncertain—about everything.

Amy goes through our introductions one after the other, then poses a question to the entire group, to be answered by whomever. "Who do you think is going home tonight?" Almost in unison, we all say some version of "I don't know," except Beverly. She waits until we're quiet before saying, "I don't know who's going home, but I think it should be Leah." At the mention of my name my heart plummets to the pit of my stomach. Beverly and I haven't spoken a word to each other in a week, why attack me now?

"I'm really concerned about her. I battled about whether or not I should come forward with this but I think I have to." She pulls off looking contrite fairly well, which is surprising since she has zero acting abilities. "Leah suffers from an anxiety disorder, I know because I found her collapsed against a wall barely conscious. If I hadn't helped her through it I don't know what would've happened to her. I'm worried she doesn't have the emotional stability to handle the pressure of this competition."

My arms hang like dead weights at my sides as I fight to keep myself anchored to what's happening. The last thing I need is to have a panic attack during a live stream, validating Beverly's accusations. Conscious of the eyes on me, I fight against the ringing in my ears and the other familiar symptoms, even as panic courses through my body. Little good it does, I can't prevent it, I'm going to have a panic attack in front of everyone; I can't stop it. Amy is talking to me, asking me something, but neither my mouth nor my ears are working. Then Brice is there, forcing my eyes to his with a hand under my chin, mouthing, "Look at me."

I want to want to pull away, but the pressure of his strong hand on my back and the resoluteness in his eyes ground me. I take refuge in his chest as he brings his arms around me, I forget about the waiting cameras and faces. Without turning around or releasing me, he says, "We're leaving. We'll be on set for judging, but this interview is over." Brice leaves no room for argument. We exit the room, neither of us looks back.

We reach the end of the corridor before Brice turns my mic pack off, then his. "L, are you okay?" Anxiety still lies heavy on my chest, but the anxiety that never leaves me, I can handle that. What I can't handle is Brice calling me L. I shrug his hand off my shoulder, "I'm fine." I'm not mad at Brice, I'm grateful to him, just flustered and in shock. "Brice, I'm sorry, you don't deserve that, you were great back there, thank you for coming to my rescue, again. I'd be lost without you." The words are out of my mouth before I can stop them. I don't regret saying them, though, because they're true.

We look away from each other, I suspect both pondering the significance of my admission. "It's okay" Brice says, "I know you're not upset with me, you're upset with Beverly. I'm sorry too, I'm sorry this happened to you. If I could protect you from this I would." For a dizzying second I'm at the swan house with *him*, he says, "*If I could protect you from this I would.*" But I'm not in a yard with *him*; I'm standing in a corridor with Brice, who's looking at me worriedly.

The world is spinning, or maybe it's that my life has been turned upside down. I press the palm of my hand into the wall behind me, needing to be anchored to something that makes sense. Brice's concerned voice calls out to me, "Leah, are you alright?" I hardly know. I need to be, though; we have to get back on set. "Yeah, fine, a little dizzy that's all." He looks me over skeptically, knowing I'm being less than truthful, but he doesn't challenge me. Brice smiles, holding his hand out in invitation. I love his smile, it always makes me feel like everything's okay.

I don't take his hand. I do return the smile, though, "Come on, they'll be sending a search party out for us soon." He chuckles as I walk past him, "Good to see you're recovered." I mean to ask him to turn my mic back on. What I actually say is, "What's going on with you and Cashmere?" I look at his bewildered face defiantly, it's too late to backtrack. I asked the question, now I have to own it. "Of everyone in this house, *you'll* be the hardest to say bye to. Now let's go see if I'll be doing that tonight." I debate pointing out that his response isn't an answer to my question, but decide against it. We will have to say goodbye to someone tonight, maybe even each other. If that's the case, I don't want our last conversation to be about Cashmere or anyone else.

I'm right about the search party. Amy cancels it when Brice and I walk on set. "Where were you?" I cut her tirade short with a furious look. Amy is low down and conniving, I'll hold my tongue only if she refrains from speaking to me. The morning of my first confession, on my way back to my room, I did collapse against a wall. I thought it went unseen, obviously that wasn't the case. Based off what Trent's told me about the production, one of the many motion-activated cameras must've picked it all up. Of course Beverly could only know this if someone with access to the footage told her.

Amy looks at me and thinks better of whatever she was going to say, "It's fine, you guys are here, just take your places." Cashmere smiles at me as I take my place beside her, and Aiden squeezes my shoulder affectionately. While walking in I avoided looking at everyone, not wanting to see the judgment or curiosity in their eyes. I chance a glance now; the cast has picked sides, mine. There is a clear rift between Beverly and everyone else, no one deals with her. As expected, she appears nonplussed by her cold treatment, but it warms my heart. Sooner or later I'll have to give everyone an explanation; that's if I'm still here. I'm not sure if eliminations are based solely on performance or if other factors are taken into account. I'm confident in what I've left on the stage but it's possible that Beverly just took me out.

Iliana walks on set with red hair and a flame-colored dress to match, "This stage has seen some great performances, but tonight we will close the curtain on one person's show. You know the judges: Acer, Eloise, and Lawrence. They've gotten to know you through your work. They've deliberated and come to a decision. When you hear your name, step forward and receive your headshot. If your name is not called, you must return back to the house and pack your bags."

Eloise rises from behind the judge's table with the headshots of the contestants that are safe to the next round. The first name called is, "Cashmere." She doesn't move, shocked her name is called first. "You don't want your picture?" I shove her forward. "I didn't expect to be called first." While she's still expressing her disbelief, Lawrence cuts her off, "Don't sell yourself short, believe in your own abilities. This week your performance demonstrated leaps and bounds of improvement. Take yourself seriously, then everyone else will too. I'm proud of you." I'm happy for Cashmere, she worked incredibly hard this week, she deserves the praise.

Called next, Zack quickly walks to Eloise. "Zack, there is no doubt that you are a rare talent; however, today we were able to identify your weakness. While you were good, you were not able to make your partner good. You moved as two separate parts. Acting is about feeding off energies, chemistry, not just mastering your lines. Your challenge this week was to work with characters from different stories in a combined script; we wanted to know it intellectually not to see it. You did not think outside of your own personal delivery. You stand here because of your potential and last week's performance, not what you did today. Our challenge to you is to be selfless in your work, get to know every character, which will allow you to excel in yours." Acer's analysis of Zack is a departure from his usual disposition, though spot on. Because Zack performed well it didn't occur to me that he had any blame for his and Beverly's performance, but Acer is completely right. It didn't matter that he was good, the scene was still painful to watch. Somberly, Zack takes his photo then his place beside Cashmere.

"Brice, you will be continuing on in this competition." Standing before Eloise, she says, "Of everyone here, I feel we've gotten to know you the least. You have unlimited potential but you will not maximize it until you let down your guard. You need to allow yourself to feel every emotion deeply without inhibition, I don't know what you're fighting but stop it. Lose control, use that emotion to help you become the best actor you can be. You may take your place with the other contestants moving forward in this competition." I disagree with Eloise, they mistake Brice's being haunted for inhibition. If they cared to look they'd see the shadows of his heart on his face. Silently he takes his photo and place next to Zack. He looks over at the remaining four, searching for me. With a look I say I'm afraid, he replies you'll making it through.

"Only four of you remain, three are safe, one is going home. Aiden, you are the epitome of good vibes only, extremely likeable, not bad to look at it either. You have a real knack for comedy and you have great comedic timing, but if you're not careful you will get locked in that genre. If you want to be the next great comedic actor, that's great, but don't do it, because it's what comes most naturally to you. Get out of your comfort zone, Aiden, you're safe."

Coming into this competition I believed I had nothing to lose. I didn't consider there could be any other outcome for me besides loss. Failure was inevitable until I got here, then everything changed. I was inspired by Trent, motivated by Morgan, tested by Beverly, entertained by Aiden and Corey, befriended by Cashmere, challenged by Zack, and Brice, he's been my rock through it all. I look down at my feet, refusing to lift my head. I don't want to see the judges' shrewd eyes or Brice, who I know is now ignoring everything but me. I fight the tears threatening to spill from my eyes, hearing Eloise call Beverly forward, "Beverly we'll see you next week." How could it be that Beverly's safe and I'm in the bottom two?

"Of everyone here, Beverly, you have the farthest to go. You are not safe because you've outperformed the two people standing behind you. In fact, your performances thus far have been mediocre. You don't even show any real disposition for acting, but you do have a certain star quality that's hard to ignore. Step it up in a major way, now go, take your place." I would've enjoyed the judges critiquing Beverly if my own spot in the competition was secure. As it is, it only built my anxiety.

Waiting for Eloise to announce our fates, Corey and I link hands. Idly I wonder if my hands are as sweaty as his. "I think it's safe to say, no one imagined this bottom two. Neither of you were who we imagined we'd be sending home today, but one of you is. Corey, the judges have felt every word you've spoken and the ones you have not. You're unsure of yourself, when you forget a word or a line you panic, as the audience we feel your frustration and when you break character. You wear your heart on your sleeve, which has been your greatest asset and your fatal flaw."

Turning to me Eloise says, "Leah, your name should've been the first name called today, you have set the bar for this competition, but instead you stand before me with a fate undecided. It has come to our attention that you may not be emotionally well enough to handle this business. We cannot in good conscious place you in a position that will cause you harm." Eloise pauses, before she can continue I jump in, taking the opportunity to speak my peace before I'm sent home. Beverly cannot have the last word on my fate here.

"The legendary Stella Adler once said, 'The theater was created to tell the truth about life and the social situation.' The truth about my life is that I'm twenty-six and I don't know what I'm doing. Sometimes when I see the success and progress of my peers I think I'm doing something wrong, that maybe I suck at life. I had a plan, but life didn't get the memo. My situation is that sometimes it hits me exactly how without a plan I am, but do you know what I do in those moments? I remind myself that I'm wonderfully and fearfully made, then I keep on fighting. I won't try to convince you or anyone else here of my emotional stability. The truth is that I don't care to, I am beautiful, talented, gifted, and resilient. I don't need anyone's validation."

I no longer care that my personal struggles are now common knowledge. I feel free and at peace with whatever decision the judges make. I'm ready for whatever comes next, which happens to be Eloise handing me my headshot. I'm safe. I clutch it to my chest, holding on for dear life. "That speech is exactly why you're safe. Every time you speak, you inspire. Head over there with everyone else." I'd forgotten all about Corey until I catch sight of him as I walk away. That's when I get it; if I stay, Corey has to go. Suddenly I don't feel so relieved.

I squeeze in line between Brice and Aiden, unable to stomach standing next to Beverly. "Corey, I'm sorry, but tonight you'll be going home," Eloise says. "You have all the goods to make it. Keep trying. I expect we'll be seeing you on the big screen." Without waiting for permission, we swarm him; Zack and Aiden murmuring consoling words, Cashmere holding him tight, Brice shaking his hand, and Beverly standing off to the side. She's doing her best to look contrite and overwhelmed with emotion. It's not fair, it should be her, she should be going home, not Corey.

I watch as Beverly hugs him, pretending to wipe tears from her eyes. I hang back on the outskirts of the goodbye, feeling partially responsible for Corey leaving. I hated that my staying came at such a high cost. Corey sets Beverly down, locking eyes with me, "Were you really going to let me leave without saying goodbye?" His green eyes are wet with unshed tears, his voice hoarse with the strain of it. "I'm so sorry." He pulls me into a hug, "You have nothing to be sorry about. Be that girl you were ten minutes ago and when you confronted Cashmere in the kitchen, when you thought she stole from you. Be fierce, unafraid, and unapologetically confident, we all believed you when you said you would win, I believe you now. Win because you owe me for getting me eliminated."

He pulls away with the laughter of his last comment still on his face; he waves to us all one last time, then walks off set with Stephanie. With Corey gone, Iliana addresses us as the now group of six, "Tonight we said goodbye to Corey, but six of you still remain. By the end of this competition there will be only one of you left, the person with 'Star Quality,' see you soon."

I survived my first elimination by the skin of my teeth; it didn't feel like a win, though, all I feel is lost. I need air, but our night isn't over yet. Amy informs us we'll be doing post elimination interviews once we get in. We wrap and load the van in silence. I sit next to Brice, staring blindly out the window, his warm hand closes around mine. I lay my head on his shoulder, closing my eyes, "How is it that you always know exactly what to do even before I know I need you to do it?" His only response is pulling me closer; we stay that way for the short remainder of the ride.

"Don't bother getting settled in, we're interviewing you first, meet me in ten," Amy doesn't wait for my response before walking away. I understand why I'm the obvious first choice: Beverly's allegations, surviving the bottom two, and Brice coming to my rescue; but I have no intention of speaking to her. I notice Roger, the production assistant, hovering around the living room and have an idea. Beverly isn't the only one who can make friends with producers.

"Hey Roger, I have a proposition for you." He seems taken aback momentarily but recovers quickly, "I'm listening." I'm not sure I like him, but since he isn't actively working against me he"ll have to do. "About what Beverly said, I wish it was a lie but it isn't; well it's mostly true. I have had panic attacks in the past but I'm by no means emotionally unstable. We both know that revelation's going to dominate my interview, which I'm fine with, I don't want to run from addressing it, I just don't want to address it with Amy. I was hoping that you could interview me instead, stream it too."

I stop to give him a moment to process before continuing, "Amy will be upset, but this might take you from production assistant to producer." He pushes his dark hair off his forehead, "Let's do it, but no mention of tonight's elimination results and you'll still have to do a confessional." I nod in agreement, "Follow me, I know just the place to do this."

My favorite thing about the seasons going from cold to warm is the late sunsets. It is well into the evening when I follow Roger to the rooftop, where the sky is a beautiful shade of coral. The idea of the sun demanding more time from the moon always made me smile, even now in spite of everything. "You ready?" Right, I'm not here to admire the view, there is work to be done.

My stolen moment of peace is over now. "Remember this is streaming live so make it count." I sit on the floor of the roof Indian style, ready to get it all over with. Roger signals to me that I'm live, "Some people feel guilty about their anxieties and regard them as a defect of faith, but they are afflictions, not sins. Like all afflictions, they are, if we can so take them, our share in the passion of Christ. Without my being ready for it or my consent, my *anxieties* were made public knowledge. This was an attempt to shame me, and up until the time that this happened I was ashamed,. I'm not anymore. The truth is that being a grown-up sucks sometimes."

I laugh shakily, "Seriously, I don't miss homework, my awkward years, or curfews, but sometimes I do miss the infinite possibilities of youthfulness. I bet I'm not the only one either. Life hits you with reality when you least expect it; like when you've been hung up on by another small business owner for what feels like the millionth time, when all you were trying to do was your job. Or when you want to invite someone over to 'your place' but 'your place' is really your mom's. Or when you wake up one morning and wham, you realize where you prayed you'd be in life at that very moment isn't actually where you are. You question yourself, what you've always believed and known, everything you're doing. You lose yourself so easily that you wonder if you ever knew yourself at all.

"I might be completely biased, but I think that's worthy of at least a smidge of anxiety. Some of us develop vices, others of us confront it head on, quickly realizing life is a worthy opponent. Life has grabbed me by the throat, pinned me against a wall, demanded of me to tap out, but in that moment, when my breath catches, my vision blurs, and defeat is imminent, I say no. I remind myself of who I am, that my life has purpose. Being in this competition has reawakened the fighter in me. I'll keep doing my best until I win or I lose, but even then I'll keep going until I take possession of what's mine; I hope you do the same."

Roger puts his phone down, beaming at me, "That was awesome. I get why Beverly hates you." "Do you?" He lets out an exasperated breath, "You're not very perceptive are you? Every time you speak to an audience, you captivate; you don't demand attention, it follows you. Beverly cannot beat you; the only way you lose this competition is if you sabotage yourself. Anyway, I need to get back inside to deal with this." He holds his phone up, "Are you coming?" I shake my head no, I want to enjoy the scenery a little longer. At the door leading back into the building Roger calls out to me, "Be careful." I look to both my left and right searching for the danger. "No, I meant watch your back, no one's interested in a linear story, twists and turns, that's what we like."

"Leah, where have you been? You knew, we told you we needed you in the interview room." I ignore Amy, walking straight past her up the stairs to my room. If she's upset now wait till she finds out about my interview with Roger. I push the door open to find Brice and Cashmere in a hug, breaking apart at my noisy entrance. There's little time do anything but look from one to the other before Amy follows me in.

"Let's go, we need you right now. I'm going to stay with you the whole time, seeing as how I can't trust you to do what you have to do." I completely ignore Amy, focusing my attentions on Brice. He doesn't look caught, although I did just catch him doing what exactly, I don't know.

Amy catches on belatedly, that we'd walked in on something upsetting, "Wait, did we interrupt something?" I head out the door, not caring to hear anything any of them have to say. I call over my shoulder to Amy, "If you want the interview, let's do it now." The way I'm feeling right now the best thing I can do is to get away from Cashmere and Brice both.

"Leah, tell me about your anxiety attacks." I roll my eyes at the expected question. "No, I've already addressed it tonight twice, once on set, then on social media. I went live a little while ago. Roger helped me out." Amy flushes with anger, sputtering for minutes before she is able to form a coherent sentence. "You did what?" I stand, removing my mic; I'm done with this tonight. "What are you doing, we're not done yet," Amy cries.

"Yeah we are. I know you've been helping Beverly. Don't try to deny it, I don't know what you're endgame is, but I'm done being your willing victim. I'm over today, this interview, and you. If you care about your job, stay away from me." Amy leans back in her chair, watching me remove the mic from the waistband of my skirt. "Don't take it so personally, my job is to find the story, create it if I have to." Disgusted at how cavalierly she responds, I throw my mic on the floor and storm out.

Chapter 22

LATELY WHEN I'VE GOTTEN this worked up I've sought refuge in Trent or Brice; unfortunately, neither of them are available to me at the moment. Trent isn't home, I checked on my way back from the roof, and Brice is not an option. I'm in no hurry to get back to my room. I'm not ready to face him or Cashmere. Intellectually I know they did nothing wrong. Neither of them need my permission to date the other, but I'm still upset. I'm conscious of how unreasonable I'm being. I have my own relationship; I'm engaged, I love Trent I'm going to marry him, but Brice has gotten under my skin in ways I don't even fully understand. I guess in the end it doesn't matter, because I'm committed to my relationship and Brice is trying his hand at a new one.

With no place to be, I let my feet carry me to where they want to go. I knock then wait for a response. When none comes, I slowly push open the door. I wanted to give Zack a chance to decide whether or not he wanted company, but he isn't here, neither is Corey, not even a trace of him. His clothes and personal belongings are all gone, all that remains is his made bed. I sit on it with my head in my hands, "What am I doing here?" I ask myself out loud. "You took the words right out of my mouth."

Zack looks good dressed in dark slacks and blue button down, "I was making sure today was real and not some sick game my mind decided to play on me." He sits beside me on the bed, "Well if you think Corey was sent home today you're not imagining it. In seven days someone else will be, and so on so forth. Stop beating yourself up because you stayed and Corey went home, we all knew what we were getting into when we signed up for this. I miss him too but he's not dead or in some faraway land. You'll see him again at the reunion show. Now go get dressed, we're leaving in half an hour."

At my confusion, Zack explains, "You were off interviewing or something when we made plans for tonight. We're checking out a lounge in Tribeca, I figured Cashmere or Brice would have told you by now." I tense at their mention, "I haven't seen either of them yet, but you know what, go on without me. I'm not really in a partying mood."

After an overly long pause, Zack puts his arm around my shoulder, pulling me in closer. "When my show was cancelled I went on hundreds of auditions. I booked a few things here and there but never another breakout role. After eighteen consecutive months of not booking a thing, I set an appointment with my agent. On my way there I narrowly avoided being run over by a car. People ran up to me asking if I was okay. 'What happened, didn't you see the car coming?' I did see the car, I thought about moving, then I thought, what's the point when all my best days are behind me. I would've let myself get run over, but the driver swerved and here I am.

"I've never told anyone the truth about that day, I was too embarrassed to say it aloud; I wanted to die. Thank you for saying what you did at eliminations. You'll never know what it means to me." I was so worried about what effect Beverly telling everyone about my panic attacks would have on my standing in the competition, I didn't think about what effect it would have on the people around me. Exposing my struggles set Zack free of his. Unable to speak around the lump in my throat, I nod.

In the hallway outside of Zack's room I remember something I'm sure only Zack would appreciate. He's still sitting in the same spot when I poke my head inside, "Step with care and great tact, and remember that life is a great balancing act." His eyes light with recognition, "Quoting the great Dr. Seuss, are we?" I shrug, "What can I say, he's one of the finest literary minds ever. Have fun tonight, see you in the morning."

The roof is quickly becoming my favorite place. I wasn't expecting to share it or for Brice to be here, but I'm not surprised he is. "Not in the mood for celebrating?" I ask. The light from the crescent moon illuminates half his body, causing him to appear to be caught between two worlds; maybe that has nothing to do with the moon at all. "There's not much to celebrate, although in all objectivity I don't think they're celebrating, they're trying to forget." I join Brice at the edge of the roof, "Is that what you're doing up here, forgetting?" He glances at me out of the side of his eye, "No, I'm remembering."

Brice hands me a worn, wrinkled sheet of paper, "Love is never lost, it is recommitted to the universe." The poem I wrote for him about Seriyah. With his eyes trained on the sky, he says, "I was recommitting my love for Seriyah to the stars. I hope she knows that no matter what I'll always love her." I hate when he gets like this, he's unreachable. It's difficult to stand by and watch because he always knows what to do to make me feel better, but I'm never able to do the same. "You loved her the best way you could while she was here, that's what matters."

Brice looks at me with wet eyes. "I feel like I'm letting her down," he cries. "You are the most honorable man I know, how could you possibly be letting her down?" He focuses his gaze back to the night sky, retreating from me. "Whatever it is, you can tell me." I put a hand on his arm, wanting him to know I'm there for him but afraid to do anything more. "From the day I met Seriyah I've never wanted anyone else, but lately when I dream it's not of her. When my heart aches it's for someone else, when I say 'I love you,' I'm saying it to another woman. I didn't mean for this to happen but it has and I don't know how to stop it."

I was furious with Brice earlier when I caught him with Cashmere. Looking at him now, taut with guilt, I want to console him. He needs to know it's okay to love again. Neither Seriyah nor I would begrudge him that. I hug him tightly though he doesn't hug me back. "The heart is a funny thing, loving at its disposal then afflicting you with guilt for its choices. You can't spend the rest of your life drifting along because Seriyah died and you lived. It's okay to have feelings for someone else, it doesn't diminish what you felt for her, but Brice, you have to put her away. I'm not saying to stop loving her, I'm saying to cherish the memories, honor her life, but don't plan the rest of yours with her ghost."

I went to far, I hear it in the silence. I went to far. I pull away, bracing myself for the fallout, though it never comes. Seemingly more composed, Brice ask if I want to watch a movie with him, "Since we're both staying in we can have a night of movies and popcorn." I want to keep talking about it, make sure he's okay, he doesn't. The most I can do now is give him my company, "Sure, on one condition, I get to pick the movie." His smile is weak but it's a start. "I'm feeling like a musical, maybe *Sister Act*?" Brice puts an arm around my shoulders as we head back inside, "Veto, I need nonstop action, besides my collection doesn't include any musicals." "Coincidentally mine does, how do you feel about *Pitch Perfect*?"

"You think we're alone; I mean, no cameramen or producers?" I don't see any of the equipment or hear any of the usual noises indicative of an occupied house, but I can't be certain. I do know that even if we are alone, we're being filmed. Echoing my thoughts, Brice says, "The crew's probably with the guys, but guaranteed we're being recorded right now." I've had enough reminders to never forget we are always being filmed, fortunately the cameras down hear have no audio.

"I hate to bring it up, but how do you think Beverly found out about you?" If there is anyone I can trust with my suspicions besides Trent, it's Brice. "I'm fairly certain Amy told her. I didn't tell you this, but the monologue I did last week wasn't planned. I was going to do . . ." I pause, catching myself before I tell him I was going to perform a love letter Trent wrote me.

"I was going to do an original piece, but Beverly did it before I could. I think Amy showed her my rehearsal tapes. I don't know why, but they're working together. I even called Amy out on it tonight, she didn't deny it."

Brice puts his palm to the side of my face, warming me where we touch. "Why didn't you tell me about this last week?" The anger in his voice subtle but present. "Because it worked out well. I did a great job, and I don't know, what would you have done? You have no power over Beverly and definitely none over Amy." He takes his hand away from me as his eyes spark with hurt, "What about your fiancé? Did you tell him about what was going on?" He spits the word "fiancé" at me like curdled milk; I didn't mean to hurt his feelings; despite my best intentions I seem to always do so.

"That didn't come out right, you've been there for me from day one, you've helped me through a lot, but in that situation there was nothing you could do. And no, I haven't told him yet." I know my apology does nothing to get me back in his good graces before he responds, I read it on his face. "You're right, Trent is much more valuable to you. I'm going to get my movies, I'll be right back." I want to call after him, say something, but what can I say that wouldn't be disloyal to Trent?

"Are you alright?" I don't hear Brice return from getting his movies. "I was thinking about Corey." With his back turned to me, loading a movie he did not consult me on, Brice says, "I didn't want it to be Corey. I didn't think it would be him, but I'm happy it wasn't you." I'm happy it wasn't me too, but I hate sentimental moments. I purposely ruin it by launching a throw pillow at him. The pillow bounces off the side of his head, landing on the floor next to him. "I take it back, I wish Corey would have stayed, he knew better than to attack a man with his back turned."

"Stop that crazy talk, you don't know what you'd do without me." Done loading the movie, he drops on the couch beside me like a bowling ball, "I know exactly what I would do without you, sleep." I poke him hard, in the ribs, "First, you had trouble sleeping before me so don't even try to blame me for the bags under your eyes." Wide eyed he says, "What, I was a well-rested, good-looking man without bags under his eyes before I met you. If I'm aging prematurely I blame you." Folding my arms across my chest, I say, "I don't care what you say, you know you love me, the bags, and sleepless nights I've caused."

It's not until the smile slips off his face that I realize my error. Not half an hour ago did he confide to me the emotional turmoil he feels for liking Cashmere, then here I go throwing around the word "love." I'm supposed to be cheering him up, not adding salt to the wound. Luckily for me, Brice is as determined as myself to have a good time. He ignores my slip and starts the movie.

It's a relief to laugh, talking aimlessly about idle things. "Are you cold?" I roll my eyes at him, only half seriously, "Obviously, you're over there wrapped tight in that quilt while I'm left to face the elements." Brice shrugs the quilt off, rubs his hands together, blowing them intermittently in imitation of me. "Oh, I'm so cold, the big bad monster doesn't want to share the quilt with me, he's left me to face the elements." His imitation of me is so poor I wonder how he made it through to the next round, "You jerk, that's nothing like me."

I move closer to him on the couch while tugging the quilt toward me. He tugs back. "I asked you if you wanted to get in, you said no. Suddenly sharing a blanket with me is a problem for you? Did you forget we do this all the time, what's the issue tonight?" We were supposed to be joking, but the strong overcurrent of truth takes the laughter out of it. When Brice asked if I wanted to share his blanket I said no because I had a flashback to my dreams. I'm not sure, I think he might be the guy in my dreams; but if it is him, I don't know what to make of that.

I let go of the blanket, shrinking away from him, "Leah, don't be ridiculous. Come here." I shake my head while keeping my eyes trained on the screen. He pauses the movie, forcing me to look at him. "Do you know how I knew I wanted to spend the rest of my life with Serayiah?" I'm not sure what brought on this change in conversation, but I go along with it. "She was a challenge," Brice says. "I didn't want her because she was hard to get, I wanted her because she challenged me to be a better person, an accountable person. She was genuinely good, to date her I had to be good too, and chaste."

Brice pauses, waiting for the reaction I'm too stunned to give. "Yeah, that was about the same reaction I had when she told me." His smile is a nice departure from his usual reaction when he talks about Seriyah. "We were standing outside her house doing the awkward end of the night dance when I got a little handsy with her. Seriyah pushed me off so hard I stumbled backward, falling to the ground. I was confused because we'd been on a few dates, and in my juvenile mind that entitled me to an invite inside.

"'Who do you think you are? I don't care that you're probably going to a division one college, I don't even care that you have a chance at the pros. I'm not in need of likes and I'm not interested in your earning potential. Sleeping with you won't do anything for me but make it difficult to walk past you in the halls. You're an obnoxious pig, suffering from a narcissistic personality fueled by the vanity of this generation. You think a ten-dollar movie ticket entitles you to something?' She reached into her purse, took out her wallet, threw a twenty at me while I was still on the ground. 'Take it and keep the change, now you owe me, jerk.'

"I watched her walk inside, positive I would die if I couldn't see her again." I imagined Seriyah as meek, not once did I imagine she was a firecracker or that once upon a time Brice was a typical guy. "If she hated you, how did you end up engaged?" The blanket falls off his shoulders, pooling around him. Free of its constraints I'm able to commandeer it over to me. Brice raises an eyebrow but makes no move to retrieve it. "I stopped treating her like a fan. She was right, I had an inflated ego. I liked her and expected her to automatically like me back, without showing her I was worth her time.

"After months of groveling, she let me take her out again. Things between us were going well, the only way they could be better is if we took things to the next level; I told her as much when she got to my house one day after school. 'Brice, I need to say something without you interrupting me. I'm not going to sleep with you and that's not going to change because you want it to. I won't ask you to be okay with it, I also will not justify my decision, I don't feel it needs argument. I will, however, explain why—after all this time we've spent getting to know each other you deserve that much.

"'I know sex isn't a big deal anymore, but it is to me. There's an argument to be made about not sleeping with everyone, just the person you're in love with, but to me that's feeble. Humans are fickle and impatient, we fall in and out of love as often as we see an attractive face; it's always love, we never call it what it really is—lust. If we loved as much as we claim we do there'd be no hate. If it's real love we can have an intimate relationship with intimate touches without being sexual until marriage. I want a spiritual connection, I want to know my lover's soul, sex won't strengthen our bond, it'll convolute it.'"

That is exactly what I wanted to say to Trent, give me intimacy. Late night phone calls, talking until the sun comes up, eating off of one plate, being able to read my husband's heart because it's mine too. "What did you say?" Seeing him shiver, I throw one end of the blanket to Brice while moving closer so he can get in, "I told her sex is a natural part of life. She and people like her have allowed religion to make it into something bad, there is no greater connection than the physical union."

Trent and Brice are like night and day, they both shine in fundamentally different ways. How could these men so vastly different say the same things? "She laughed, I loved Seriyah's laugh; that was the only time I can remember I didn't. 'No, Brice, people like me have made sex special, people like you have made it a god. You worship at its feet, surrendering your insatiable temple, knowing not what you do. Yes, sex is a natural desire, but I'm waiting for you to explain to me why I should be captive to the every calling of my flesh. I'm not sexually active, but I'm not a virgin, once you open that

Pandora's box it's hard to close. I should've told you before, I'm sorry I didn't. I want you to know I don't expect you to walk my path, no hard feelings.'

"You know, of everything she said to me, what stuck out most in my mind was that she wasn't a virgin. I was upset because I didn't want anyone else to ever have that part of her but me. I wanted to claim her body right then and brand it as mine. I pulled her toward me, trying to kiss her like I didn't hear one word she'd said, but she turned her face away from me. 'Stop it, just stop. I tell you I don't want to sleep with you and what do you do, try harder. What is your motivations for all of this?' She pointed at the candles I lit before she got there, 'I don't care how many times you tell me you love me, love didn't set this up, lust did; it's unoriginal like that.'

"After she left, I sat in bewilderment, I liked her but I wasn't going to give up sex to satisfy her. Truthfully I wasn't sure that I could be celibate even if I wanted to. That thought lead me to another, I'd slept with a few girls, but then there were the girls I didn't sleep with but had a sexual encounter with. I tried to remember each girl, more than her name, I wanted to remember specific details. I could for some; for others, no. I couldn't remember specifics about these women or our time together because it wasn't significant. Of all the women I'd gotten to know, none of them made a lasting impression on me. The one woman that did, I let go because she didn't want to have a meaningless relationship.

"Maybe she's not crazy, but at almost eighteen years old I was no longer curious about sex, I liked it, and needed it, I could never go back. I wasn't like Seriyah, I didn't grow up religious, taught to believe all carnal desires were wrong." I stop him, because at this point in his story I understand something that he didn't. "She never said it was wrong, she said giving yourself away without thought and clear understanding of what you were doing was not something she could do." Brice nods, "That was part of what she was saying, but I would learn it was much more on my own journey."

Minutes pass before Brice continues, "I spent the rest of the weekend thinking things through. By Monday morning I came to the decision that I wasn't sure how long I could abstain, but I was willing to try for Seriyah." I looked at him, unconvinced that he went from being absolutely positive he could not abstain to willing to try abstinence in two days' time. "Don't look at me like that, I'm being honest, I'm not saying it wasn't difficult, but Seriyah helped me through it. I've learned a lot about self-discipline, I started my walk because of Seriyah, but she's been gone for four years, we dated for five, and I'm still walking this path. I've gotten to know myself, self assessed, healed, and grown, especially spiritually. When your spirit is right everything else is okay.

"I won't lie and say I don't sometimes get the urge, but it's fleeting, like my desire for all of those women I slept with in the past." Nine years, is the only thought I can process, "And you and Seriyah never slept with each other?" If it's awkward for him to have this conversation with me, he hides it well, "No, we never did. I kissed her with passion, because I was passionate about her, but we respected our boundaries, mind you we had to learn those boundaries, but Seriyah loved to remind me to 'resist the devil and he will flee.'"

Brice's laughter turns into a melancholy silence, "After Seriyah died I was angry, I questioned God, demanding to know why he would take her away from me. She was so young, so good, how could God allow this to happen? I cried out to him but he didn't answer me. I decided Seriyah was wrong, he doesn't exist. From that day forward I would live how I saw fit. Then one day, not long after, as clearly as I hear you I heard a voice say, 'Good people pass away; the godly often die before their time. But no one seems to care or wonder why. No one seems to understand that God is protecting them from evil to come. For those who follow godly paths will rest in peace when they die.'

"I knew it was God speaking to me, God had seen my tears, and he shared in my grief and sought to console me. I realized although Seriyah was the catalyst that brought me to him, his plan was always to bring me nearer." I believe God can speak to you in all sorts of ways, I'd like to say I'd be as willing as Brice was if I heard God's voice, but frankly I'm not sure I would be. "You and Seriyah were lucky to have that rare love." The screen is paused so long it goes black, the only light comes from the windows, but even in the relative dark I see his earnestness. "We weren't lucky, we were blessed. Are you, do you have a blessed romance?"

I'm completely blindsided. We weren't talking about Trent and me, we were talking about him and Seriyah. "What kind of question is that, why would you even ask that," I say angrily. "I asked because I honestly don't know." I shrug the quilt off, no longer needing its warmth. This conversation is doing a fine job of heating me up. "You don't need to know, Trent does. If my saying so is enough for him, it should be more than enough for you."

Brice must've been worked up himself, because he pushes what's left of the quilt onto the floor. "If you can say being with Trenton is the best thing for you, if Trenton has penetrated your spirit, possessing your heart, then I wish you two good fortune. If loving him has righted your wrongs, challenged you to be the best you; if his love has healed you, brought you peace and joy, then much marital bliss to you. Tell me, Leah, has his love touched your soul, liberating you from fear, has he saved you?"

I don't understand what Brice is doing asking me these questions. I get that he misses Seriyah, but this is wrong of him. Furiously and without consideration for his feelings, I shout, "I'm not her." "No, you're not . . . You're Leah, and that's just as amazing. I haven't known you for a long time, but I do know you. You're not doing well, your eyes are shadowed, which means you're still not sleeping. When you have a nightmare, it's me you run to, because he can't chase your nightmares away. You should be ecstatic, the happiest you've ever been, but you don't even wear an engagement ring." Reflexively I look at my ring finger, wishing my beautiful pink diamond were there to shut Brice up.

"What is it, three, four carats? Your dream ring, right from your dream guy; smooth talking, successful, powerful, but yet you haven't told anyone." I get to my feet, "How dare you? You don't know anything about us, there's nothing Trent would not do for me, including wait six years to meet me. What you and Seriyah had was special and rare, but so is what I have with Trent. It's unfair of you to diminish it. You've grown to be special to me, you're probably the best friend I have in and outside of the house, you matter to me, but if you speak another ill word about my fiancé or my engagement, I'll cut you off and never look back. I'll choose him every single time without fail."

In my hurry to get away from Brice, my feet tangle in the discarded quilt. I never hit the floor, Brice's quick hands catch me against him, "I understand why you're upset with me. I was out of line," he says softly. "It's not my place or my business, I wish you and Trenton Shaw all the happiness I wished for Seriyah and myself." The words are perfect, with just the right amount of contrition, but his eyes are sad. Making sure my feet are firmly planted on the ground, Brice lets me go. Almost instantly a chill creeps up into my bones. I wrap my arms around myself so I won't wrap them around him.

"Thanks for the movie, I'm going to go to bed, good night." The sight of his retreating back troubles me; it feels like everything is ending. Despite what I said earlier about cutting him off, I don't want to lose him. Swallowing down irrational tears, I call to him. Brice stops, one foot on the stairs, "I meant to tell you earlier that I'm happy your heart is still working." He looks at me with obvious confusion. Walking as quickly as I can without running, I fall into his arms, hugging him as tight as I can. I hope he feels how unwilling I am to lose his friendship, even if I do have to share him from now on.

"I'm happy for you and Cashmere." With difficulty he pulls me away from his chest, "Leah, you have—" I cut him off, "It's okay. Sorry I lost it earlier, it's just that it came as a surprise to me. I know you're not ready to talk about it yet. When you are, I'll be ready to listen." He looks to be on the verge of saying something but decides not to. Silently he pulls me back into his arms, returning the intensity of my hug. It does little to reassure me if anything, It troubles me further. I can't rid myself of the feeling that he's saying goodbye. "I'm going to sleep now, for real this time. See you around, Leah Shaw."

I haven't given thought to using Trent's last name. Hearing myself called Shaw now by Brice feels odd. "Albanese, I'm still Leah Albanese, and of course we'll see each other, we're roommates." I will be Leah Shaw soon, but even then I want to be Leah Albanese to Brice. Still climbing the steps, he shrugs, "Maybe." I watch him go, all the while fighting off the immense sense of loss.

"Hey," I'm happily surprised to see Trent. I didn't think he would be home, but with Brice asleep and everyone else partying, I figured if I had to be alone, I'd be alone surrounded by Trent's presence. "Where've you been all day?" He kisses me briefly on the cheek by way of greeting, "I've been knee deep in preproduction, but that doesn't mean I haven't been thinking about you." Trent pulls me down onto his lap, holding me tight, he bites my neck. I scream bloody murder, "Thank you for that, I'm sure I now need a tetanus shot. Anyway, how are things going so far?" He turns my hand over to kiss my palm, it's all very sweet but distracting. "Things are kind of up and down right now but that's to be expected.

"What about you, how'd you do tonight? Well obviously, you're still here," he says, holding onto me so tightly I can barely breathe or speak. I panic, pushing him away more forcefully than necessary. "Hey, what's wrong?" Needing my own space, I slide off his lap into the seat next to him, "Tonight was unexpected. Cashmere and I did an exceptional job, for all that I'm only here by the skin of my teeth," I say. "What do you mean?" he asks. "Well somehow Beverly found out." I don't know why I'm hesitating on the words. I spent most of the evening talking about it to perfect strangers online; after all this time, I still had trouble talking about it to Trent.

"Beverly found out about my panic attacks. Instead of blackmailing me like a good little villain, she told everyone during a live streamed interview." He shakes his head in disbelief, "Wow, I'm so sorry that happened, L. Are you okay?" I nod, watching him closely, "What I really want to know is how she found out." This would be the hard part, telling Trent I believe Amy was behind it all. "There is a slight possibility that she happened upon me mid attack on my second day here, but the more probable likelihood, considering her stunt last week, is that it was caught on camera, then shared with her by someone. The someone being that conniving, treacherous producer of yours, Amy."

Trent collapses into soft laughter, the very last reaction I expected. "I don't mean to laugh, especially considering the magnitude of your allegations, but your insults need work." I clamp my mouth shut tight, working extremely hard at not laughing. "Okay, so my insults suck, thank you for volunteering to be my sparring partner, you heathen." "L, that was a sorry attempt, you're better than that, I'll chalk it up to the stress of the day. Tomorrow I fully expect a better effort." I roll my eyes skyward, "Whatever, Trenton." I purposely call him Trenton, he hates it when I do. "What do you think though?" He's no longer laughing, "I think I have no idea what you mean when you say 'considering last week's stunt.'"

I fill Trent in on the truth behind my performance last week. With Beverly's power play this week I gather all bets are off. "I'm certain Amy isn't involved with whatever you and Beverly have going on. Beverly probably snuck on set during your rehearsals, which is how she knew about your monologue. As far as today goes, like you said, I think Beverly saw you, she's smart with a wicked streak. She waited for the best time to reveal what she thinks she knows with maximum impact."

I should've told Trent Amy basically admitted to trying to sabotage me, but his reaction is dismissive and flippant, I doubt there is anything I can say to make him take this seriously. "I think what's important is to look online and see what the fallout is." I'm not sure I want to do that, I feel good about my interview with Roger, but I'm not ready to read about how crazy people think I am. "I forgot to mention, I did an unapproved interview with Roger." Taking hold of his iPad, he asks, "Who's that?" I look at him disbelievingly, "The production assistant, don't you hire these people, I think knowing their names is critical."

Trent puts his arm around my torso, pulling me from my seat back onto his slap, "I didn't hire him. I sold a concept to a network; the network then put together the production crew. You've yet to meet anyone on my payroll. When you do, you'll like them, they'll love you too." I haven't thought about it before, but I don't know any of Trent's friends. Granted, I've met Lawrence, he's met Amanda, but both instances were pure coincidence. We've been living in this bubble, cut off from our friends and family. What happens when we get back to the real world?

Meredith wants a guest list I can't complete. I don't know one person Trent would want at our engagement party. "Whoa, combining both interviews you have a hundred thousand hits." While I've been deep in thought, Trent has pulled up Real TV's Facebook page. At the very top is my interview; the group interview is right below it. "You're probably remembering it worse than it was, we should watch it." I cover my face with my hands, unwilling to. "You can if you want to, but I can't relive it." I don't see Trent press play, but I hear an unfamiliar version of myself say, "Uncertain." I decide it's best to not only cover my eyes but to try to focus my thoughts elsewhere as well.

I'm thinking about the photos Meredith sent over when I feel Trent tense beneath me. I move my hands and see why. I watch Brice and me in what to the entire world must look like an intimate moment. The clip ends with Brice and me walking away hand in hand. This is not good. Trent is scary quiet, I've never seen him so upset. I brace myself for the fallout, ready to defend myself.

After a long time, he says, "That was a good play on Beverly's part, you looking stricken makes her accusations very believable. Luckily Brice came to your rescue. I imagine Stephanie's happy, it's the angle they've been working all along, every story needs romance, right." I want to explain, but Trent won't be receptive to it. He scrolls down to the comments section, "Let's see what the people have to say."

The comments are positive for the most part, a lot of suggestions on how I should have handled Beverly. @hellobella commented, "Girl you're better than me I would've had to see her outside." Most of the comments followed that line of thinking. Someone posted a meme of my clearly shocked face that read, "The face you make when it's almost noon and you still haven't received a good morning text." There are a few memes actually, some of which are funny enough to get a genuine laugh out of me. The most satisfying comments are those expressing their own struggles with anxiety, some even posted links for wellness sights.

Trent and I read through the comments without further hiccup until we come across the hash tag #lice. When I see #lice trending I think there's an outbreak I hadn't heard about. After reading the accompanying comments we realize it's a mashup of Brice and Leah. I try to swipe quickly past the comments with that hash tag, but there are too many, it's impossible. Trent's careful not to mention Brice, he's beyond angry though. When I can stand the tension between us no more, I speak up, "I know it looks bad . . ." Trent's mouth comes down on mine hard, cutting me off. He pulls and bites at my lips with no tenderness. With rough hands, Trent pulls at my blouse, at my skirt, until there are no barriers between us; he moves without words, fineness, or love. Later, I cry myself to sleep feeling hollow.   U m m m ... wha

"You're back," I nod, letting him take hold of my hand. We walk around the yard admiring the progress of the rose bushes and the lemon tree. I notice he isn't wearing his usual tee shirt, tonight he's dressed in a light pink button-up with well-fitting navy slacks. He looks to be going somewhere special, "Are you on your way out?" He laughs, "No, I was waiting for you, do you like it?" I do like it, he looks handsome. I wish I were in something other than jeans and a tee. As I have the thought, my ratty jeans and shirt transform into a beautiful hot pink cocktail dress. Without mirrors, my loveliness is reflected to me in his eyes, they light up as they take me in.

"May I have this dance?" We dance without music and without growing tired. "Why can I see only part of your face, why can't I see you completely?" He dips me with all the grace of a professional dancer, "That's a question for you to ask yourself." The reply dies on my lips as the wind howls like a hungry beast, "What's going on?" He points toward the road separating the houses, "And a highway will be there; it will be called the way of holiness; it will be for those who walk on that road. The unclean will not journey on it. Wicked fools will not go about on it." My head spins with more talk of roads, "I don't understand."

The sound of shutters rattling against the house of horrors carries on the wind, drowning out his voice; within seconds the wind howls all around me. I'm tossed to and fro while he holds his ground. I can't hear his shouts over the wind hissing my name; it catches me up, carrying me to the house of evil. At the front door, my left foot is chained and fettered to the ground, it rattles violently as I struggle against it. I fall, hitting the ground, opening up another tear in my now destroyed dress. I can't fight anymore, I just don't have it in me. I bring my knees to my chest waiting to be taken. I scream as darkness closes in on me. I make it to the bathroom just in time to retch. I have to figure out what these dreams mean before they kill me.

Chapter 23

THE DAYS FLEE AS quickly as they come, taking Aiden then Cashmere with them. "Cash, what am I'm going to do without you?" I hate seeing Cashmere go, without her the house won't feel the same. "Leah, it's okay, we both knew this day would eventually come, I was never going to win this. The best part about this experience was meeting everyone, especially you. We're friends for life, me not sharing a room with you won't change that. Now suck it up and win this, because you deserve it, and wipe the smirk off her face."

Something between a laugh and a sob escape me. "Oh yeah, take care of him," I track her eyes to Brice. He and I haven't spoken much since our movie night, other than polite conversation. It hurts that the person I need most right now won't even look at me. An awkwardness has settled between us. At first I thought maybe it was something I had said or done to push him away. I apologized to him, hoping it'd make things better between us. "So basically what I'm trying to say is, I'm sorry and I miss you, please be my friend again."

Brice sat on his favorite windowsill in the middle of the night, which could mean only one thing; he was thinking of Seriyah. He looked at me for what felt like the first time in days, I almost forgot how startling his eyes were in the moonlight and how easily they saw through me. "You'll always have my friendship, Leah, whenever you need it, but the dynamics of it had to change. I'm not mad at you, that would be a hard thing for me to be, but I also don't want to talk to you."

Brice reached into my chest, tore out my lungs, and asked me to go on breathing without them. Without another word I went back to my room, where I muffled my sobs with my pillow. I had another nightmare that night and every night since. *He* no longer shows up in my dreams, but sometimes I can hear him hammering away.

Now here I am, sleep deprived, saying goodbye to my last lifeline in the house, at a loss for how I'm going to get through this. "I'll try, but I don't know that he'll let me. In case it's escaped your notice, and I know that it hasn't, we aren't exactly friends anymore." Cashmere hugs me tight, "You're friends going through a difference of opinion. You'll get through it." She spends a long time saying goodbye to Brice. I'm too afraid of the answer to ever ask Cashmere exactly what the nature of her relationship with him is.

They've grown close during the time we drifted apart; she does a good job of splitting her time between us. I spend mine rehearsing, planning my engagement party with Meredith, and nursing a bruised heart. I haven't seen much of Trent lately, either; he's hardly ever at his loft. I guess he's spending his nights at the brownstone or working. Lately he's always working, last I heard they were in the middle of castings. I asked him if he needed me to audition for the part of Nia, he said it wasn't necessary because it was written for and about me. I've offered to help him with things so we could spend more time together, but he rejects my offers of help. As of late our only communications have been scribbled notes expressing disappointment left on his kitchen counter.

When we have seen each other it feels like a shadow of what we used to have, all we talk about is the engagement party and the wedding. Trent wants to be married in three months, relocate to LA, and begin filming. We've argued about the time frame, I just don't get why we're moving so quickly, but it's important to him so I've dropped it. I've thrown myself into my work; Morgan says I've grown leaps and bounds. He's even offered to introduce me to some people once this is all over. I mentioned it to Trent, he said, "You don't need to be introduced to anyone that I can't introduce you to. You have a leading role that we're going to start filming soon and a wedding to plan, you have enough on your plate."

In my dreams I remain fettered to the ground, waiting for the horror that'll inevitably come without knowing when it'll arrive. That's how I feel now, like I'm bound and waiting for something horrible but I'm not sure exactly what.

It's been almost a week since Cashmere left and the dreams are getting more intense. I turn in early, in dire need of rest before the next day's performance. Unfortunately I wake up from a nightmare only a few hours later. I've been having these dreams for weeks now, yet I still wake up heart pounding, adrenaline pumping, and frightened, while no closer to understanding why they came, why they haven't left.

I head downstairs for a drink of water to help calm me down. Standing in the middle of the living room is Brice. "I opened to my beloved but my beloved had withdrawn herself; and was gone: my soul failed when she spake; I sought her, but I could not find her: I called her, but she gave me no answer." No wonder he's still in the competition, he's good. I believe his longing for his gone lover; then again, he does have experience in that area. If he performs the exact same way for the judges tomorrow, I expect him to be first name called. Sadly, I have much less confidence in my own performance. Tomorrow's showpiece must be from a pre-twenty-first-century work. I chose a scene from *A Doll's House*. Morgan says I do a good job with Nora, but I'm missing something. Hopefully I get points for set design, which we were in charge of this week, because I'm not sure my Nora will be enough to keep me safe.

I watch silently as Brice starts over, this is the first time I've seen him perform. He's never wanted me to before so I respected his wishes; seeing this now, I wish I hadn't. Part of his performance piece is recognizable to me, although I'm not sure from where. The stair creaks beneath me, making Brice aware of my presence. Nervously I stand my ground, waiting for him to react. "You don't have to look like you got caught with your hand in the cookie jar. You do live here, this is a public space." I'd become used to Brice being distant, the friendliness in his voice confuses me, "I wanted to get water but I can go." Brice looks at me in a way he hasn't in two weeks, like my presence doesn't bother him. "Leah, really it's okay, get your water."

I descend the rest of the steps quickly, unsure of what to make of the shift in his attitude toward me. In the kitchen I fill a glass with water but don't drink it, running into Brice disorients me. "Enjoying your water?" The sound of his voice startles me, I didn't expect him to make conversation with me, and least of all I wasn't expecting a chance encounter with my friend Brice. "Yes, thank you for asking. I'll go back up to my room as soon as I'm done." I answer him as if he were a stranger, because that's what we'd become, I don't know how to talk to him anymore. "Why so formal?" After Cashmere left, I tried talking to him again but he brushed me off with some excuse about being busy. How could he now ask why I've taken on an attitude of formality with him?

"That's what you've reduced us to. I've tried to resume a normal friendship with you, but you've shut me down at every turn. Mind you, I have no idea why, now I don't know how to speak to you." He keeps a safe distance from me, standing on the opposite side of the island, "Speak to me like you, like you used to." I slam down my untouched cup of water, "Don't you think I've tried? You were my best friend, my rock, now you won't talk to me, you barely even look at me. Why should I keep banging my head against the wall?" I knew I was angry, I had no idea how angry until this very moment.

"I came to your room earlier, right before I came down here, I needed to talk to you but you were asleep." I'm not upset Brice came to my room, I'm upset I was asleep. "That's shocking, you haven't needed to speak to me in weeks." His face falls, seeing his reaction, I know I've gone too far. Brice is retreating back behind the wall he put up to block me out. If I want to get our friendship back, I'll have to let my anger go.

"What'd you want to talk to me about?" I say, significantly less angry. His hands knot atop the counter, "Did you recognize what I was rehearsing?" Upon first hearing it I was sure I knew it. I can't for the life of me place it, though, "Yes and no. It sounds like something I heard before, or maybe it's the writing style I recognize, I'm not sure." He smiles at me approvingly, my answer must've pleased him.

There's something different about Brice. He's more handsome, his eyes aren't haunted anymore, there's something else there. "It's from Song of Solomon," he says. That's why it's familiar to me, I have read it before. At thirteen it was the most romantic thing I'd ever read. Admittedly I was perplexed as to what it was doing in the Bible. Hearing it again more than a decade later, I understand love is beautiful, complex, and sometimes heartbreaking. I figured after what Brice told me on the roof that being with Cashmere is helping ease the pain of his loss. I guess some pains never leave you. "Missing Seriyah?" Brice walks around the island to my side, "This isn't about Seriyah, it's about you."

I'm sure I misheard him, there's no possible way I heard him correctly, "What did you say?" Walking slowly, but sure of his destination, he closes the gap between us. "I sought the Lord; he directed me to you. The first time I saw you, my heart that had long been a phantom organ beat again. I knew God wanted me here, I thought for my career but I was wrong, it was to meet you. Talking to you, spending time with you, holding you revived me. Loving Seriyah saved me, loving you healed me."

I watch him as he comes closer to me. I want to want to push him away as he brings his arms around me, holding me, hugging me. I don't. For the first time in weeks my body relaxes. If I were being completely honest with myself, I'd have to say it isn't so unbelievable, there have been moments when I thought Brice might like me, but I always thought better of it. However, I never imagined him being in love with me.

"Brice, I'm engaged, and what about Cashmere?" "There are no pretenses between Cashmere and me, we were never anything more than friends. You, you're the one I love." I make the mistake of looking in his eyes. What I see in them quiets every protest. "'Place me like a seal over your heart, a seal over your arm: for love is as strong as death, its jealousy as unyielding as the grave. It burns like blazing fire, like a mighty flame.' Leah, Trenton isn't for you, you are not equally yoked, but you know that already. I know the rhythm of your heart and the depth of your soul; loving you has taken my breath away. I would gladly fight for every breath for the rest of my life if you would keep taking it." Both my mind and my heart turn traitor;

I search them both for the truth of how I feel, neither will tell me. "Look at me and tell me you don't feel this connection between us." I can't, because I do, I always have. "Everything, that's what I'm asking of you. Let me love you, Leah, let me love you with the love of Christ. The maiden had a choice to make, King Solomon or her shepherd, as it was for her it is for you." He releases me but not before placing the most delicate of kisses on my cheek. He leaves as quietly as he came without as much as a backward glance.

I try to run my lines one last time in my head, but Brice's words keep coming back to me. "*I would gladly keep fighting for every breath for the rest of my life if you would keep taking it away.*" That's all I've been able to think of every second of the last twelve hours, but I'm no closer to understanding my thoughts or my feelings. It'll have to wait until after elimination, though; tonight determines top three. I need to focus on nailing the character of Nora and moving into the last phase of the competition. "Leah, they'll be ready for you on set in a minute," I thank Roger, then follow him.

I introduce my piece to the judges and call "scene." Before delivering my first line, I glance up at the balcony in the shallow hope Trent's there. It's empty, as I thought it would be. "You have never loved me. You only thought it would be pleasant to be in love with me." All week I struggled with my scene, disconnected to this woman, but sitting perched on this chaise, seeing the empty space Trent should be occupying, I could've been Nora. She has no identity because she let the men in her life manipulate her thoughts, her desires, her being. I go through the scene feeling heartbreakingly sad; ironically, being Nora helped me figure out something about Leah.

"I have existed to merely perform tricks for you, Torvald. But you would have it so. You and Papa have committed a great sin against me. It is your fault that I have made nothing of myself." A solitary tear slides down my face as I deliver my last line. Although through with my scene, I can't pick out which emotions belong to Leah and which are Nora's. Dazedly I receive my evaluation from the judges. I nod when I should, and thank them when I think it appropriate, but I don't take in one word spoken to me. The feedback is generally good but specifics escape me. While I was Nora I realized I need to talk to Trent. No matter how this judging goes, the first thing I need to do is find him.

We sit in the dressing room, waiting to be called back on set for judging. Beverly and Zack sit close together in the middle of the room, with her body curved into him, the way people in a relationship normally do. They've been honing in on a weird relationship for the last few weeks. I think she's the devil's cabana girl, but Zack doesn't seem to mind. He and I have managed to maintain our friendship despite the constant friction between Beverly and me. Just three days ago, at breakfast, Beverly handed me a list of what she called "qualified therapists to help me with my personality disorder." It was one of her lamer attempts at humiliation; I ignored her as I've been doing for the last few weeks.

I'm still baffled as to how she's made it this far when she should've been gone week one. Her acting hasn't gotten any better, if anything it's gotten worse, yet she's still here; and so is Brice, sitting in a corner across the room not looking at me. After twelve hours I'm still not sure how it is I feel about everything. I am sure that I miss him; I hate the distance between us. "Moment of truth, people, we need you all back on set for deliberation." If I got eliminated tonight, the bright side would be never having to see Amy again, it's getting harder and harder to stomach her every day.

Iliana walks back on set, reintroducing the judges and prizes, then turns judging over to Eloise, who speaks for the group. "It's been a very interesting ride. When I got the call to be part of this show I really had no idea what to expect, but I was excited to get the opportunity to meet fresh talent. Sending someone home, crushing someone's dreams, is never easy. It's difficult deciding who it is you're not going to move to the next round, but what we keep in mind while judging is that we're looking for the next star. That doesn't necessarily mean the most talented person. We're looking for the person with the most star potential. With that said, the first person to join the top three is the most consistent person. This person has been able to transform week after week, challenge after challenge, today we acknowledge your star power. Leah, step forward and take your place."

I'm pleased to move onto the final three. Not as happy as I thought I'd be, though; it's a hollow victory without knowing Brice is safe too. "The next person definitely moving forward to the top three is someone who is without question one of the most talented people I've met in my career. Zack, please come forward." My teeth begin chattering uncontrollably as I realize Brice is up against Beverly. She's been in the bottom two almost every week but safe every time.

I didn't watch him perform, I wasn't ready to face his feelings for me, but I know he had to outperform Beverly. I fear it won't matter. Beverly and Brice stand side by side as they await the judges' decision. I've thought a lot about Brice, but I've never thought about him not being here in the house with me. If he's eliminated, he has to leave immediately. I won't be able to talk to him and tell him, I don't know what exactly, but I won't be able to say it. "Brice, you're new to the bottom two, throughout your stay here you've always landed somewhere in the middle. You've never been the worst but the problem is you've never been the best either. Today you gave your best performance, full of feeling and powerful emotion, but the judges wonder why it took so long and will you be able to repeat it. Beverly, you're a resident of the bottom two. Your 'it' factor saves you every time. Brice outperformed you tonight. We knew he was talking to the woman outside his grasp, it was fantastic, but it came too late. Brice, tonight we send you home."

"Oh my gosh," without a doubt the cameras are on me. I reacted even before Brice did. I wish I hadn't, but I wasn't prepared for this version of events. Brice's eyes meet mine for the first time since last night. It's only for a second, but it's enough for me to see something I think I always knew. He graciously accepts Eloise's praise of his talents and best wishes for his future without a moment of discomposure. I reach him before either Zack or Beverly leaves their spots. Hot and uncomfortable as I am, we hold onto each other, uncaring of the cameras.

A million incomplete thoughts run through my mind. This will be my last chance to speak to him, yet I'm at a loss for words. Maybe for the last time, Brice saves me, "I left something for you in your top dresser drawer." These are the only words he speaks to me before releasing me to continue his goodbyes. Tearfully I watch him walk away, escorted by Amy.

The ride home is a somber affair. I sit in the last row sniffling, while Beverly and Zack sit quietly side by side up front. Back at the loft I pull myself together long enough to do my post elimination interview. Somehow every question comes back to Brice. I don't have enough in me to even be mad at Amy's insensitivity. I suck it up until I'm able to return to my room to sob. He's gone, he's really gone. "*I would gladly fight for every breath for the rest of my life if you keep taking it away.*" What does it mean that he's taken mine?

With the ebbing of my tears comes the recollection of his last words. On top of everything in my trinket drawer lies a neatly folded sheet of paper. With trembling hands I read, "*I've been dreaming about you, ever since the night I woke up hearing you scream my name, I've dreamt of you. These aren't romantic dreams, mostly I hear you whimpering in pain, I run around looking for you, every time I think I'm close I lose you, I never find you, except last night. I'm still far away from you, running through fields of high grass, but I see you. You're on the ground in front of an abandoned house, something's looming over you, threatening to attack. I call your name even though I know you can't hear me. I get to the house but I can't get through the gate, I rattle it, try to break it with my bare hands, but it won't budge, then I hear a voice say, 'This is not your place, neither is it hers. She must stop at the crossroads and look around. Ask for the old, godly way, and walk in it. Then I woke up, rattled and afraid for you. I don't think I'll be going back to sleep tonight, I can't bear to see you that way again. I've been thinking about it, I think I understand what the dream meant. It isn't my place to say though. Instead I'll keep you in prayer, asking the Lord to bless you with discernment. Don't be pressured by the constraints of time, God isn't; his timing is perfect. I meant every word I said before, I love you, Leah. If I never get the chance to say it again, I wanted you to know. Forever in my heart, Brice."*

Every ounce of strength I have leaves my body. How is it possible? Why were Brice's dreams mirroring mine? The time has come for me to be honest with myself, there's no point in trying to deny the feelings I have for or connection I have with Brice, even if I don't understand it. Is the path I must choose between Trent and Brice? I've already chosen. I'm engaged to Trent, how could that be the choice? I love Trent, I am in love with him, I have to talk to him.

Quickly I change into jeans and a sweatshirt. I wash my face, ridding it of the mascara streaks. There's little to be done about my puffy eyes. Hopefully Trent doesn't notice or doesn't ask. I don't want to explain my tears to him. I don't bother checking his loft, he hasn't been there in over a week. I head straight to the train station. Trent gave me the code to the lock box outside the first time we came to the brownstone. I punch it in now and let myself inside. He's gotten the electricity turned on since we were last here together. Some of the furniture we picked out has been delivered too; other than that it looks exactly as I remember.

I go from room to room hoping to find him to no avail. In our would-be bedroom, there's no evidence that Trent's here or that he has been recently. Before I can think about it too much, I hear the front door open. Hearing Trent's voice I hurry out the bedroom, only to stop dead in my tracks, realizing he isn't alone. Mind racing, I stand flat against the wall at the top of the stairs listening.

"We always had a good time together you and I, I can't understand why on earth you'd settle down with her?" I cover my mouth, preventing the scream building up inside of me from escaping. What is Beverly doing here with Trent? "Listen to me, are you listening? Don't ever say a word about her to me, she's not your business. If you bring her up again you'll regret it." I've never heard Trent speak so sinisterly before. It frightens me that he could threaten Beverly like that, even if it's in my defense. Beverly laughs seductively in response, goading him. "Don't believe me, try me, see if the part of Nia doesn't go to another actress."

He barely gets his words out before Beverly is calling his bluff, "No, that won't happen, because that's not our deal and if you try to screw me over I'll tell Leah . . . everything." She says my name in clear provocation. "How do you think she'll feel about you taking her journal, showing me her rehearsal tapes, telling me about her psychosis, giving me the lead in your movie, and first place in this competition?" If I weren't leaning against the wall, I would've collapsed under the light of truth. All this time I believed

Amy to be behind all of Beverly's attacks, but the betrayal was much closer to home.

I fight the compulsion to run downstairs. I have to hear the rest of it, the extent of his treachery. "Why don't I tell her how friendly you've been, how much time we've been spending together?" She kisses him in the middle of their power struggle, he kisses her back. "Maybe I'll even tell her about Brice. You should've seen her all distraught; for a second I actually felt horrible for separating them."

My hand slips, hitting the wall with a thud, Trent and Beverly both look up, searching for the source of the sound. Hiding is no longer an option. I step onto the landing that they would see me more clearly. A strange calm washes over me. I don't want to scream, and shout, or fight, I just want the no-holds-barred truth. First, I want Beverly gone. Without taking my eyes off Trent, I tell her to leave. "Get out now, and Beverly, if you have any sense of self preservation, don't be at the loft when I get there." She leaves without argument.

Without haste, I descend the steps, my hard eyes keeping Trent in place. He watches me too, jaw clenched, ready for battle. I stop on the last step, watching this beautiful stranger, and he is beautiful, even standing in his deception, but hollow. His demeanor is defiant, devoid of regret and love. "Unless the crew's around the corner waiting to tell me I've been punk'd, I'm going to need you to say something." For every step he takes toward me, I take one backward. He doesn't need to touch me to speak. Seeing my determination to not let him near me, his face finally breaks of its hard exterior.

"I don't think there's anything I can say that you'll understand, so I don't see the point in saying anything at all." I shake my head disbelievingly. The man that asked me to marry him would never give me up without a fight. This person doesn't even care enough to explain, "Answer me this, why?" He puts his hand on his chest, where his heart should be, "Because I love you." The edges of my calm begin to fray, how could he do everything he did but still claim to love me? "That's not love, what we had wore a mask of love covering deceit, scheming, betrayal."

As I stand in this beautiful empty house watching my world crash and burn around me I finally understand everything. Trent came along at my lowest point. At the time I didn't know it, but I stopped believing in God, in his might, in his love. I was lost, susceptible, no longer on guard against temptation. Trent seduced me with my heart's desires when I didn't trust God to carry out his promises. Trent is my house of horrors, his words, his promises were alluring until I got close enough to see the truth of him. But for all of that, Trent's just the most obvious way my life had veered off track. I can't blame him for how far I've fallen, that's on me.

The swan house was the good things God had in store for me if I had long-suffering, patience, and most importantly, willingness to put in the work on myself. That's what *he* meant about the laborer building in vain unless God builds it. All of this is my fault. I tried to make it without God, now I've learned the hard way, without him it's impossible. I whisper in horror-stricken discovery, "Underneath your charm and good looks you've been my personal nightmare all along."

Trent reacts to my every word like a knife to the gut. Maybe in his own sick way he does love me, but his love will ruin me, the man for me is waiting to help love me back to wholeness. "I loved you the first moment I saw you," Trent says falling to his knees. "You took my heart and walked out of my life for six years. With you I'm different, you've affected me in ways I was not prepared to handle. When I look at you I have an uncontrollable desire to touch you, hold you, kiss you, keep you right here, right by my side." I back away from him, as far as possible, I can't stomach more of his deception. "I wanted you in this competition because everything you want for yourself I want for you and I want to be the one to give it to you, but it's taking you away from me. I won't share you and I won't let you go; you promised you wouldn't leave me, you promised."

Trent has always been disarming, now being no exception; the first time we spoke at the club, I remember having a nagging feeling that he wasn't trustworthy, which followed for some time. I questioned him and his motives constantly until he convinced me of his love. I know he's lying, omitting, or flipping the script, but part of me wants to comfort him. My back against a wall, he wraps his arms around my waist in an impossible grip. I try to get him off me but he won't let go.

"When I woke up the morning of move-in day, I watched you sleep with this ache in my heart; I knew I would lose you. Worst of all, it'd be my fault for bringing you here. I wanted you more than I've ever wanted anything in my life, yet every day I watched you moving further and further away from me. If I didn't lose you to Brice, it would be to your career. I wasn't willing to lose you again. I did some things with Beverly's help, but I never meant to hurt you. I want *you*, two point five kids, a white picket fence. You are my happily ever after. So tell me what to do to fix this and I'll do it."

It physically hurts to say it, but it needs to be said, "There is no fixing this. If I put aside the fact that you were cheating on me with Beverly, it won't change the fact that we don't belong with each other. You know, I remember that day, the first time you saw me. I saw you too, I didn't remember until recently though. I asked myself why it is I didn't notice you then. I couldn't come up with an answer, but it finally makes sense.

"All these years, if you really wanted to find me you could've, we have enough mutual friends on social media that it wouldn't have been difficult. So why now and not then? You came into my life at my lowest point, my most vulnerable point, because I was most receptive. I had a few setbacks, I became impatient and disillusioned, while I was learning humility, going through the process, I lost track of who I am. The girl you saw six years ago was so sure of herself that she couldn't be seduced by promises of things she believed she already had coming. The girl you met a few weeks ago was weak, and you preyed on me. But the man I marry will pray for me. I made a lot of mistakes on my way to rock bottom, but I see the light at the end of the tunnel."

My words strike a chord with him. His grasp on me slackens. I dislodge myself from him and walk quickly to the front door. "L, please don't go." He sounds helpless and defeated. I feel for him, but I won't be led back. I reach up around my neck, unfasten the cross that belonged to his mother. I hold it loosely in my hand. "You know, the saddest part of all of this is I would've loved you, I did love you. I don't know that we wouldn't have ended up right here in this exact same spot anyway, but if we did it would have been because love ran its course, not because you forced my hand. Your love is dangerous with a nasty habit of trying to destroy to me. I want you to get your happy ending, I really do, but I won't be part of it. I've never been interested in pyrrhic victories." I hang the necklace on the doorknob and close the door behind me.

I half expect him to chase after me. I'm happy he doesn't. All the way back to the loft I pray about what I should do. The answer doesn't come as a surprise but it is a blow. I'm almost through packing when Amy walks into my room, "Where the hell do you think you're going?" I don't stop packing as I tell her I'm leaving, "I'm done with this show. I'll make it eventually and I won't have to compromise to do so." She rolls her eye in annoyance. Amy has never had an abundance of patience when it comes to me, "Don't give me any of that moral crap, I've had access to your every move for weeks, I know you want this.

"Look at you, you're twenty-six years old and everything you have fits into those bags. You know how hard it is to break into the industry after a certain age, but I could make it happen for you. You're good, the judges love you, and you're the fan favorite. You should see the comments they leave, we could do a spin-off, we'd chronicle your life as you begin your professional career. I've been doing this long enough to make great connections and I'd use them all on you. I can make you a star, that's what you want, isn't it? I could make it happen for you."

Even if Amy wasn't working with Beverly she is still no ally to me. "Get thee behind me, Satan." Her eyes gleam with anger, "Good riddance to you, you were boring and whiny. You will never have more than you can fit in those two bags." The lies of the enemy don't work on me anymore. "We both know that's not true, I'm good at this. I might even be great. My success doesn't depend on you. I will make it while you watch from the sidelines." She points a red nailed finger in my face, "Remember we have the rights to your likeness and footage in perpetuity. We own you. If you leave you will regret it."

"Do whatever you want, I don't care." I skirt around her, ignoring her threats, even as she shouts them to my back. Zack stands at the foot of the steps watching everything play out. He doesn't ask any questions, I don't of-fer any explanations. We hug briefly but meaningfully, then I'm walking out the door, out the building, away from it all. Jobless, boyfriend-less, without a plan, but confident. I have stood at the crossroads and asked for the ancient paths. I am determined to walk in the good way.

YES GORL!

you don't need them!

Epilogue

Before leaving, I go up to Trent's loft to get my phone. Even as I dial her number, I'm afraid she won't come through for me, but of course she does. I spend the car ride trying to apologize, but she won't hear it. She's just happy to have her friend back. I can't say I don't feel the same. Pulling up in front of my house, I'm reluctant to get out the car, fearful of how my mom will receive me. I haven't spoken to her since I called that night half frantic, but there is nowhere else to go or that I want to be. I watch Amanda pull off before ringing the doorbell. I could've used my key, but I'm unsure of my welcome.

My mom comes to the door and freezes when she sees me, tears of joy well in her eyes. Smiling brilliantly, she envelopes me in a hug. "Let's celebrate, because this daughter of mine was dead and is now alive again; she was lost and is now found." We hug and cry and hug some more, then we celebrate. My mom makes all my favorite dishes, Antonia comes over to help us eat them. We reminisce and laugh, I feel at peace and at home. I don't know what tomorrow will be like and I'm not concerned. "Tomorrow will worry about itself." Maybe it'll be a good day maybe it won't, but that won't change the things that matter: I'll still be "fearfully and wonderfully created." God's compassions will still be new every morning and the Lord will fulfill his purpose for me. Thank you for taking this journey with me and for all your support. Thank you for watching, liking, and sharing, until next time, "Above all else, guard your heart, for it is the wellspring of life."

Made in the USA
Middletown, DE
19 June 2022